A Killer of Influence

JD Kirk is the author of the multi-million bestselling DCI Logan series, set in the Highlands of Scotland. He also does not exist. Instead, JD is the pen name of former children's author and screenwriter, Barry Hutchison, who was born and raised in Fort William. He still lives in the Highlands with his wife and children. He has no idea what the JD stands for.

Also by JD Kirk

DCI Logan Crime Thrillers

JD KIRK

A KILLER OF INFLUENCE

First published in the United Kingdom in 2024 by Canelo Crime

This edition published in the United Kingdom in 2025 by

Canelo Crime, an imprint of
Canelo Digital Publishing Limited,
20 Vauxhall Bridge Road,
London SW1V 2SA
United Kingdom

A Penguin Random House Company
The authorised representative in the EEA is Dorling Kindersley Verlag GmbH. Arnulfstr. 124, 80636 Munich, Germany

A CIP catalogue record for this book is available from the British Library.

Hardback ISBN 978 1 80436 827 5
Paperback ISBN 978 1 80436 834 3

This book is a work of fiction. Names, characters, businesses, organizations, places and events are either the product of the author's imagination or are used fictitiously. Any resemblance to actual persons, living or dead, events or locales is entirely coincidental.

Cover design by Tom Sanderson

Cover images © Shutterstock

Printed and bound in Great Britain by Clays Ltd, Elcograf S.p.A.

Look for more great books at
www.canelo.co | www.dk.com

To all the Loganites, Hoonigans, and Filson Fanatics who have been with me from the very start.

This one's for you.

Chapter 1

Detective Chief Inspector Jack Logan had seen his fair share of corpses, but it had been a long time since he'd seen this many all in one place.

They were in varying states of decomposition and decay, the wet mulch and muck having taken their toll. It would take expertise far beyond anything he possessed to say just how long the poor bastards had been down there, but he knew it was months, not weeks. Years, possibly.

A stretch of the boggy, pock-marked landscape roughly the size of two tennis courts had been carved into a square by standing poles and fluttering lengths of cordon tape. Grasses that had grown tall in the recent-but-fleeting summer sunshine swayed anxiously on the breeze, as if sensing the coming of autumn in the air.

Or the odour of death.

Beaten tracks cut curved lines through the undergrowth, stretching up into the mountains beyond, their peaks already grey with a thin dusting of early season snow.

The site itself was a hotbed of activity, with two different Scene of Crime teams currently digging, brushing, and peering curiously into a growing number of holes in the Earth.

Geoff Palmer, head of the local unit, had tried several times to assert his authority over his female counterpart from Aberdeen, and make clear that he was the one in charge here, but her derisory laughter had soon set him straight on that one.

The look of defeat on Palmer's pudgy red face had been the one and only highlight of Logan's day so far.

The DCI watched as the flap of a white evidence tent parted. The pathologist, Shona Maguire, stepped out, pulled down her mask, and let out a breath she must've been holding for a while. She met his gaze, and the look in her eyes told him everything he needed to know.

Whatever she'd seen in there wasn't anything good.

But then, nothing about this situation was.

Palmer straightened suddenly like a meerkat, looked around, then started to stride in Shona's direction as if some internal targeting computer had sensed her presence and automatically locked on. Clocking him, she pulled her mask back up over her nose and mouth, and quickly ventured into the next tent along.

She'd rather face a decomposing corpse in a confined space than hold a conversation with the Scene of Crime man.

It was a testament to Palmer's ego and cast iron self-confidence that he hadn't yet taken the hint.

Over the din of the excavation, Logan heard the soft crunch of footsteps approaching confidently from the rear, followed by the sound of a grown man tripping over his own feet and ejecting a panicky, 'Ooh, shit!'

Detective Constable Tyler Neish stumbled to a stop beside the DCI, then shot an accusing look at an unremarkable patch of ground behind him as if it had tried to trip him on purpose.

'Alright, boss?' he asked, running a hand through his neatly coiffured hair. Despite the stiff breeze and the near-fall, not a strand of it was out of place.

Logan watched, teeth clenched, as another body was raised from the fetid mud. 'Had better days.'

'Aye. Bit grim,' Tyler said, in what was quite the understatement, even for him. 'I had a chat with the guy who called it in. The fella that found them.'

'Dog walker?' Logan guessed.

'Bingo,' Tyler confirmed. 'Bit of a weird old guy, but had plenty to say.'

'Weird in what way?' Logan asked.

2

'Just a bit odd, boss,' Tyler said. 'Harmless enough, though, I think. His dog ran away and when he eventually caught up with it, it was digging away. He spotted a hand in the hole and called it in.' Tyler hesitated. 'Aye, the guy, not the dog.'

Logan didn't even bother to tut. Many of the things Tyler said warranted some scathing response or other, but Logan quite frankly didn't have the energy this morning, so he chose to let it slide.

'You get all his details?'

'Got them, boss, aye.'

Both men stood in silence for a while, watching as a white paper suit standing by a hole gestured urgently to another a few feet away. Palmer and the Aberdonian woman both spotted this and immediately rushed to try and be the first on the scene, while a ripple of something that wasn't quite excitement but was close enough to stand in for it raced through the rest of the SOCOs.

Another body, then. How many was that now? Six? Seven?

'Jesus,' Tyler muttered, reading the same signs that Logan had. He pulled the zip of his jacket right up to his neck, like it might protect him from something he couldn't quite put a name to.

Shoving his hands in his pockets, he turned and looked at the house behind them. It was several hundred yards away, and under most other circumstances he wouldn't necessarily assume any sort of connection.

But not with this house.

This couldn't be a coincidence.

'You think it's anything to do with—?' he started to ask, turning back to the DCI.

'Aye,' Logan said, cutting him short. 'Got to be. I mean, I hope so.'

'You hope so, boss?' Tyler asked, unable to hide his surprise. 'How come?'

It was Logan's turn to look back at the house. It stuck up like a tumour from the windswept landscape.

'Because we've already stopped that bastard.' He buried his hands deep in the pockets of his coat. 'And I'd rather not consider the possibility that there might be another one of him out there.'

Chapter 2

'Here, what the hell's this?'

Detective Inspector Ben Forde stared at the woman with the blue rinse who stood across the counter, one of his fingers pointing quizzically at a handwritten sign on the wall behind her.

He'd seen the same words on a sheet of paper in the window, and had almost tripped on his way in the door. He'd tried very hard to dismiss the message as nothing more than a misunderstanding on his part.

It hadn't said *that*. It couldn't have. He'd misread it, that was all.

And yet, here were the same words again, inexpertly etched on the paper in thick black marker lines, staring him straight in the face.

'"Thank you to all our loyal customers,"' he read aloud, in case the woman standing directly beside the sign was somehow unaware of its content. '"We will be closing at the end of this month."'

Ben looked between the woman and the sign with big, deliberate head movements, the wrinkles on his face arranging themselves into an expression best described as 'puzzled horror'.

'What the hell does that mean?'

'What does what mean?'

'That! That sign!'

Ben gestured around them at the small, cramped cafe, with its plastic chairs and crumb-dotted tablecloths. Aside from him and Gladys, the woman on the other side of the counter, there wasn't a soul in the place.

'You can't be closing!' he insisted.

Gladys hacked a smoker's cough into a heavily creased handkerchief, then tucked it up her sleeve. 'I can, and I am,' she replied.

'But why?'

'I'm retiring.'

Ben's eyebrows shot up his forehead. 'Retiring? What do you mean? Retiring from what?'

'What do you think? From this place. From work.'

'Work?!' He spluttered, as he indicated an old telly on the wall with a wave of a hand. 'You're always sitting on your backside watching *CSI Wherever-it-is* when I come in. You've nothing to retire from! You're living the life of bloody Riley!'

'Here! I'm a grafter, I'll have you know! It's not easy running a business!' Gladys countered. 'And it's *NCIS*, not *CSI*. *CSI's* all arseholes.'

'But this is where we get the rolls!' Ben cried, and there was a note of genuine anguish to it. He gestured out through the film of grease that hazed the window. Beyond it, just across the car park, stood the backside of Burnett Road Police Station. 'Where are we meant to get the rolls if you shut?'

Gladys appeared unmoved by his plight. 'Dunno,' she admitted with a shrug. 'Though, Lorimer's is literally five minutes' walk away. Just saying.'

'Aye, across a bloody dual carriageway, and it's twice the price! And they don't do caramel wafers or teacakes! *And* they're always busy! You've never got a queue.'

'Well, maybe if I had, it'd be worth me carrying on!' Gladys shot back. 'But most days you're the only bugger in here!'

'I spend a fortune, though!'

'Oh aye! Fifteen quid a day. Wait and I'll buy myself a penthouse.'

Ben threw his hands towards the grease-yellowed ceiling in despair. 'Come on, Gladys, you can't be serious. You're winding me up here!'

But the woman with the blue rinse didn't answer. Something exciting had happened on *NCIS*, and her attention had switched to the telly.

Ben sighed and cast his gaze across the sad-looking assortment of breakfast meats that sat congealing in metal trays under a barely functioning heat lamp.

'Oh well, I'd better make the most of it, I suppose. Give me six full belly busters, white toast all round, and throw in half a dozen teacakes while you're at it.'

He placed his fingertips lightly on the counter and traced the scratches on the flimsy plastic, like he wanted to reassure himself that, at least for now, the place was still real.

The next few words came as a whisper, his voice cracking in the gaps between them.

'And may God have mercy on your soul.'

–

The breakfasts were cold by the time Ben made it back to the Incident Room. Though, to be fair, they hadn't been all that warm to start with. He dished them out in a sullen silence that did not go unnoticed by the others.

Detective Constable Sinead Bell was the first to pass comment as the DI dropped her polystyrene box on the desk in front of her.

'Eh, you alright, sir?' she asked, concern forming creases on her otherwise smooth skin.

'The hell's this?' Logan demanded. 'I thought I was getting a roll and square?'

'I got you the works,' Ben said, shuffling across to his desk with his own box of lukewarm food. 'All of you. It might be your last chance.'

'How come, boss?' Tyler asked. 'Are we dying, or something?'

Beside him, Detective Sergeant Hamza Khaled flipped open the lid of his box and winced. 'We might be if we eat that.'

Constable Dave Davidson, sitting in his wheelchair at his desk in the corner, didn't share the others' reservations. He was already half a rubbery sausage and a mouthful of baked beans into the breakfast, and was hungrily eyeing up the black pudding.

'You know Cathy's?' Ben asked, slumping down into his seat. 'The wee cafe out back?'

The others confirmed that they were familiar with the establishment, and had been for some time.

'It's shutting,' the DI announced.

'Shutting?' Logan asked.

'Aye.'

Tyler looked up from his breakfast. He'd been rearranging things so his sausage kept his beans away from his bacon like a little dam. Not because he had any issues with baked beans, it just felt like a fun way to pass the time.

'What do you mean, boss? *Shut* shutting?'

'Aye. *Shut* shutting,' Ben confirmed. 'The owner's retiring.'

'Cathy?' Hamza guessed.

Ben frowned. 'What?'

'Cathy,' the sergeant said again. 'I'm assuming she's the owner?'

'No. Her name's Gladys.'

'So, who's Cathy?'

Ben stared back at the sergeant as if he was speaking in tongues. 'What you on about? Cathy who?'

'The shop! The bloody shop!' Logan cried, pronging at a slice of bacon with a plastic fork. 'Why's it called Cathy's if the owner's name is Gladys?'

'How the hell should I know?' Ben asked. 'I don't know who Cathy is. Does it matter? That's not the point! The point is, it's shutting.'

Sinead was peering down at her breakfast like she thought it might start scurrying across her desk the moment she looked away. 'Shame we'll miss out on quality grub like this.'

'There's always—' Hamza began, but Ben raised a hand to silence him.

'Don't say Lorimer's,' he warned. 'I'm not racing across that dual carriageway at my age, and they don't do biscuits.'

Hamza hesitated. 'I was going to say the canteen downstairs.'

They all laughed at that, even Hamza himself.

'Good one, son. But come on, be serious,' Ben replied. 'The situation's desperate, but we're no' quite at that stage yet.'

'Speaking of desperate situations,' Sinead said, plucking a slice of toast from the box and quickly closing the lid, 'anything more from the scene?'

She offered the tray of food to Tyler. Her husband could usually be relied on to dispose of any leftovers. Even he shook his head, though.

Logan blew out his cheeks in a noncommittal way. 'They'll be at it for hours yet. But we're looking at at least seven bodies so far. They've got ground radar going over the surrounding area and looking at the house again.'

'Wasn't that done last time, boss?' Tyler asked through a mouthful of tattie scone.

'That's why I said "again,"' Logan snapped, then he sighed and shook his head. 'Sorry. Long day, and it's not even lunchtime.'

'No bother, boss,' Tyler said.

He knew exactly how the DCI felt. He'd been gripped by a sense of dread ever since they'd set off south along the A9 that morning, and it had only deepened as they'd approached the scene.

It had been months since Tyler and Hamza had first ventured into that house, with its rotten door and boarded-up windows.

And, of course, its dilapidated but fully functional freezer that stood alone in an otherwise empty room.

Tyler could still remember the look on the sergeant's face when he discovered what was being stored in there, and the feeling of gut-wrenching horror when he'd seen it for himself.

Fingers. Ten of them. All laid out side by side on a tray, like they were ready to be slung in the oven.

The sight of the fat, gristly sausage nestled in the polystyrene box made the detective constable shudder.

Across at his desk, Dave slapped at his stomach and leaned back in his wheelchair. 'Well, that was bloody delicious!' he announced, despite all evidence to the contrary.

Ben adjusted his glasses and regarded the constable in disbelief. 'You've no' finished, surely? You can't be finished already.'

Dave held up the polystyrene box he'd been eating from. Aside from some bright orange bean juice residue, it was completely empty.

'Jesus Christ!' Ben exclaimed. 'What did you do, inhale it? Just tip your head back and pour it straight in?'

'Pretty much,' Dave admitted, then his face lit up with glee when Sinead handed him her nearly full container.

'Go nuts,' she told him, and he immediately got to work.

'We'll head back down the road shortly,' Logan said, steering the conversation back onto work-related matters. 'Hopefully by then, Geoff Palmer will have pissed off back to his cave, or his wee Hobbit hole, or wherever the hell it is he goes.'

'I nearly went to see one of his comedy gigs last week,' Hamza announced, and a worried hush fell over the room.

'Oh,' Tyler said, flashing the sergeant a supportive smile. 'Mate.'

Hamza's separation from his wife had come as a shock to all of them. Not least of all Hamza himself, who'd come home early from work to find her in bed with another man.

He'd moved out, and Ben had immediately invited him to stay in his spare room until he was back on his feet. It wasn't ideal, but it had helped take some of the stress and pressure off.

Still, Hamza was only seeing his daughter a couple of times a week, and the whole thing had obviously been hard on him.

They just hadn't realised quite *how* hard, until now.

'You didn't, though?' Logan asked, with the slow, cautious air of a man trying to disarm a ticking nuclear warhead. 'You didn't actually go?'

'No. No, course not,' Hamza said, though even he looked troubled by how close to it he'd come.

Sighs of relief were breathed. Smiles broke out. The others went back to picking at their now stone cold breakfasts.

'What's he calling this one?' Tyler asked. 'Is he still "Just Geoff"?'

Hamza shook his head. 'It's called "Palmer's Perfect Package".'

Everyone in the room either scowled or shuddered.

'Jesus,' Ben muttered, then he quietly returned the sausage he'd just picked up back to the box.

'Package!' Sinead announced. She pointed to Logan with her unused plastic fork. 'Sorry, sir, forgot. You got a package.'

Tyler waggled his eyebrows. 'But is it "Palmer's *Perfect* Package"?'

Everyone, including his wife, ignored him.

'A parcel, you mean?' asked Logan, deliberately correcting the Americanism. He jammed a pinkie finger up between his gum and his teeth, dislodging a lump of fatty gristle. 'Who the hell's sending anything to me?'

Chapter 3

Logan hadn't been aware that he was holding his breath until he felt the burning at the top of his lungs.

He exhaled slowly through his nose, the air coming out unsteadily, with a suggestion of a tremble to it.

The square of card on his desk sat there. Unmoving. Unremarkable.

And yet, the moment he'd seen it, his stomach had flipped, like the whole damn world had been tilted off its axis.

He didn't touch it. He daren't. Touching it would make it real. Touching it was as good as an admission.

Instead, he turned away from it and studied the envelope it had been sent in. It was a small padded Jiffy bag—brown on the outside with bubble wrap innards. His name and the address of the station were printed on a label on the front. A single stamp was fixed to the top right corner.

There were no other markings. Nothing else inside. No obvious way of identifying the sender.

He'd bag it up. Run it for prints. See what, if anything, he could find out.

He'd have to keep it quiet, though. He couldn't have anyone asking too many questions. Not yet, anyway. Not until he had some clue as to what the hell this was about.

Unable to delay the inevitable any longer, he directed his attention back to the contents of the envelope. It was a beer mat, mostly square, but with rounded edges. A few creases and some fading of the print marked its age, but he'd recognised it right away.

It was a beer mat from a pub that had closed years ago.

A beer mat from a very different time.

Words he'd heard earlier that year now rang in his ears.

We all have our sins and our secrets, Jack Logan. You should know that better than most.

Someone knew.

Somehow, after all these years, someone knew.

Somebody out there knew what he had done.

'Alright, boss?'

Logan blinked and looked up to where Tyler was crossing the room towards him. He was suddenly dimly aware of having heard knocking, and of his lips muttering an instruction to come in.

'You OK?' asked the young detective constable, stopping on the other side of the desk. 'You look like someone's pissed on your chips.'

'I'm fine,' Logan said. He moved some paperwork around so it covered the beer mat. It was clear that Tyler noticed, but in a rare display of good judgement, he chose not to comment. 'What do you want?'

'Eh, just had something come in,' Tyler said. He produced a sheet of paper he'd been carrying down by his side, and passed it to the DCI. 'Some social media influencer has gone missing.'

Logan's total lack of reaction spoke volumes about his thoughts on the matter.

'CID's looking into it, but they think they might end up bumping it over to us, boss,' Tyler continued.

He indicated the printout with a glance, urging the DCI to take a look. Tutting sharply, Logan begrudgingly complied. He snatched the sheet of paper away and tried to force his still-whirring brain to make sense of the text.

'It's some guy from Hull,' Tyler told him.

'Hull?'

'Aye, but he was up here for some sort of convention thing at Eden Court. Some kind of meet and greet event. He didn't make his flight home. He hasn't posted anything in over thirty hours, which I know doesn't sound like a lot to… well, anyone normal, but he usually posts eight to ten times a day.'

'Jesus Christ. Saying what?'

'He does comedy stuff, apparently. But, from what I can tell, he basically just puts on wigs and says unfunny things in screechy voices.' Tyler shrugged. 'Although, *Mrs Brown's Boys* has done pretty well out of that, I suppose,' he added, with a troubled, slightly glassy-eyed stare into the middle distance.

'And people watch that, do they?'

'*Mrs Brown's Boys*? Aye, loads of folk, boss. God knows what they see in it, though.'

'Not *Mrs Brown's*…' Logan lowered his head for a moment, composing himself. He flapped the sheet of paper in the DC's direction. 'This guy, Tyler. The boy with the wigs.'

'Oh! Aye! Sorry. Yeah, three million subscribers, boss.'

Logan huffed out a sigh like he thought the world was doomed. He forced himself to look at the words on the paper, but he was still struggling to comprehend what they said. All he could think about was that beer mat on his desk.

And the terrible secret it implied.

He shook his head and handed the printout back.

'How old's he?'

'Twenty-six, boss.'

'And he was last seen…?'

'Day and a half ago.'

'Missing non-vulnerable adult.' Logan leaned back in his chair, folding his arms across his barrel of a chest. 'Given that we're currently neck deep in dealing with a mass burial site, why the hell would that be coming to the MIT?'

'Well, because, boss…' Tyler cleared his throat, turned the printout over, and handed it back. 'It looks like he's not the only one.'

Logan sat perched on the edge of a desk in the Incident Room, trying his best to focus on what Sinead was telling the team. But, his attention and his gaze kept being dragged over to the door of his office, drawn by the envelope and its contents that lay within.

A question from the detective constable pulled him back to the here and now.

'What do you think, sir?'

'What? Aye.' Logan turned to her and shook his head. 'Hang on. Sorry. What was that?'

Sinead missed a beat, like she was the one who'd been caught on the hop. 'Uh, I was just saying, we could bounce back to CID and get them to go through the full list of people who appeared at the convention and follow up with them all.'

'How many do we think are missing?' Logan asked.

This time, Sinead's pause was a longer one. She stole a fleeting glance at DI Forde before replying. 'Um, three, sir.' She pointed to the printout in Logan's hand. 'Those three. They were all due to be flying from here down to Gatwick on Saturday night, but none of them made the flight.'

'Makes sense to bounce it back,' Ben suggested. 'They seemed hell of a quick to pass it over to us. Let them do some of the bloody donkey work.'

Logan nodded. 'Aye. Do that. If they find out more and still want us to take over, we'll look at it again. For now, though, we've got enough on our plates.' He checked his watch. 'Any word from the scene?'

'Uh, aye. Aye, there was an update.' DS Khaled fumbled through his notebook, looking for whatever it was he'd jotted down.

Usually, the sergeant would have such information locked and loaded. Since the break-up, though, he'd been distracted and off his game.

His shirt was creased, and there was a little ink stain on the breast pocket, where a pen had presumably leaked. His hair was a little longer and untidier than usual, and though he was usually clean shaven, a few days' worth of stubble was darkening his jaw.

It was in his eyes that you could really see the damage, though. In the red bloodshot flecks, and in the deep bags below.

'They found an eighth body,' Tyler said, coming to the sergeant's rescue. 'They reckon that's them all, but they're still going over the place with the ground radar.'

'Eight?' Logan muttered, gazing thoughtfully out of the window. Outside, traffic trundled both ways along the dual carriageway, and an ambulance siren wailed in the distance.

He thought back to the tray of ten severed digits that had been found in the house a few months previously. They'd identified the owners of two of them. The rest, however, had remained a mystery.

'They checked the hands?'

'Yes!' Hamza jumped in, trying to redeem his failure from a few moments before. 'Some of them are quite badly decayed, but it's looking like at least a couple are missing a finger. Shona reckons they've been down there for at least—'he flicked frantically through his notebook, then gave up'—a while.'

'Is that her professional medical opinion, is it?' Logan asked. He immediately felt a pang of guilt when Hamza flashed him an apologetic smile.

'Sorry, sir,' the DS said.

'It's fine,' Logan replied, rising to his feet. 'I'm going to head down there, anyway. See what's what.'

'You want company, boss?' Tyler asked.

'No, you're alright,' Logan replied.

It was a pretty straight shot down the A9, but Tyler's travel sickness was a thing of legend. Granted, he hadn't spewed in Logan's car for a while now, but he'd looked a bit queasy on the way back up the road earlier, and it was only a matter of time. Logan couldn't handle another footwell full of vomit. Not today.

Besides, he needed time on his own. Time to think. Time to figure things out.

'Ben, keep an eye on it all until I get back,' he instructed. He turned and headed for the door at the back of the room. 'There's just something I need to get from my office before I go.'

Logan left the others behind, entered the office, and closed the door. He had just finished securing the envelope and beer mat in two separate evidence bags when knuckles rapped on the glass behind him, and DI Forde let himself in.

'What's that you've got?' Ben asked, as Logan whipped around with the evidence bags in his hand.

'None of your business,' the DCI replied, slipping the bags into the inside pocket of his coat. 'What do you want?'

Ben studied Logan's face for a few moments, his bushy grey eyebrows knotted in concern. 'You alright, Jack?'

'I'm fine.'

'You don't look fine. You look worried. You look… old.'

'Jesus Christ. Pot calling the kettle black there, Benjamin,' Logan replied.

Ben chuckled. 'Aye, well, I *am* old, that's the difference. I'm meant to look like this. You're not.'

Logan straightened his shoulders and ran a hand down his face, like he could wipe away the weariness and worry Ben had seen there. 'I'm OK. Honest. Nothing to stress about.'

He attempted a smile. This was a rare and unusual enough sight at the best of times, and bordered on terrifying when it suddenly appeared out of the blue.

'And you're not *that* old,' he assured the detective inspector. 'Not yet.'

'Aye, well. No' a kick in the arse off it,' Ben said. He looked down at his hands, and for a moment, he seemed to shrink. 'Eh, which is something I wanted to talk to you about, actually.'

He wasn't looking Logan in the eye, and was instead suddenly fascinated by a ragged piece of skin next to one of his thumbnails. He picked at it with a finger, like it was some fascinating new scientific discovery he'd just made.

Right away, Logan knew what was coming. He'd sensed it coming for a while, like a train hurtling down the tracks towards him. Even though, generally speaking, that sort of thing tended to happen more to DC Neish.

And now, here it was. Right before him, racing up, about to thunder right through him.

He shook his head. He couldn't deal with this right now. He wouldn't. He refused to.

'Aye, well, whatever it is, it's going to have to wait,' he said, brushing past the detective inspector and opening the door. He jerked his head to the side, indicating that Ben should leave. 'Come on. Out. Some of us have got work to do.'

Ben finally met his eye and held it for a moment. Then, with the slightest of smiles, he nodded.

'To be continued,' the DI declared.

Then, he walked out of the office past Logan, and failed to notice the way the senior officer's shoulders sagged behind him.

–

DING-DONG.

Fifteen-year-old Olivia Maximuke wriggled into her jeans as she stumbled along the hallway from the kitchen. She raised her voice to be heard above the frenzied yapping of the little dog that darted back and forth at the front door, the fur on the back of his neck raised into a mini-Mohican.

'Alright, alright, I'm coming!' the girl shouted to the silhouette on the other side of the frosted glass.

Hearing her voice, the dog stopped barking, just long enough to shoot her a look that seemed to say, 'Can you believe the nerve of this guy?' Then, he turned back to the door and let rip again.

Olivia caught sight of herself in the hall mirror and was momentarily shocked by the state of her hair, which made her look like an 80s popstar being blown backwards by a brisk wind. She ran a hand through the tangle in a futile attempt to do something with it, then shouted, 'Give me a minute! Jesus!' when the doorbell rang again.

Grabbing the barking Taggart, she searched for somewhere to stick him, then settled on the cupboard where the jackets and shoes were kept. The little dog looked utterly affronted when she gently tossed him inside with a quick, 'Sorry,' but then the door closed in his face, and all he could do was double down on the barking.

Finally, after thumbing some sleep from her eyes and making herself as close to presentable as she was going to get, Olivia unlocked and opened the door.

'Do you know what time it is?' she demanded of the hooded figure on the front step. He was an older man, she thought. Late fifties. Although, between the hood and the bushy beard, there wasn't a lot of facial real estate to base that on.

He carried a rectangular parcel that was roughly as long as a shoebox, but a little narrower.

'Uh, eleven-twenty-ish?' he replied, not bothering to check.

That knocked the wind from Olivia's sails a bit. 'Is it? Right,' she said. She stifled a yawn, then nodded at the package. 'That for us?'

The courier didn't need to consult the label. 'Mr Jack Logan?' He glanced past her into the hallway, which still rang with the sound of Taggart's barking, albeit now slightly muffled. 'He in?'

'No.'

The man's head tilted slowly back and forward inside his hood. 'Right. Anyone else in?'

Olivia opened her mouth to reply, but then hesitated. The doorbell had been a rude awakening, but the further she got from sleep, the sharper her instincts were becoming.

And her instincts did not approve of this stranger on the doorstep.

He smiled at her. There was nothing particularly troubling about it, but it made her skin itch.

'I just need an adult to sign for it, that's all.'

'My brother's in, but he was working most of the night, so he's sleeping. He'll go mental if I wake him up,' Olivia said, the lies coming effortlessly to her lips. She put a hand on the door, preparing to close it. 'He's a bouncer.'

The man on the doorstep held her gaze. 'Is he?'

'He's got a mental temper,' Olivia warned.

'Does he?'

She nodded and looked furtively back over her shoulder, like she was afraid her huge, angry brother—imaginary, though he was—might be storming along the corridor towards them.

'I mean, he'll definitely hear if I shout him, but it's best for both of us if I don't.'

The hooded man's gaze shifted to the cupboard door just a few feet into the house. 'Does the dog not wake him up?'

'You learn to tune him out,' Olivia quickly replied. She nodded at the box in the man's hands. 'So, you want to come all the way back with that, or do you want me just to sign for it?'

He looked down at the parcel, then around at the quiet residential street. A few cars were parked outside some of the neighbouring houses, but most people were at work. It was a school in-service day, but as far as Olivia had been able to tell, she was the only one under thirty living on this road.

When he turned, she couldn't see his face for the hood of his jacket. There was nothing unusual about having a hood up in the Highlands, of course, regardless of the time of year. Something about this one bothered her, though.

'Ah, what the hell?' the man muttered, turning back to her. He handed her the box, and she heard something sloshing around inside it. He put a finger to his lips and smiled through the thick, straggly beard. His teeth were burnished by yellows and browns. 'It'll be our little secret.'

Taggart's barking reached fever pitch. Olivia could hear him scratching at the cupboard door, desperately trying to claw his way through.

'Right. Aye. Very good,' she said, then she closed the door and hurriedly spun the lock.

The silhouette remained there on the other side of the glass for a few moments, then faded as the man turned and walked back up the path.

It was a few minutes later, when Taggart was mooching around her in the kitchen, laying the groundwork for a share of her breakfast, that it occurred to Olivia why the man's hood had bothered her.

It hadn't been raining.

She considered the parcel sitting on the kitchen worktop with its printed address label and its 'This Way Up,' instructions inked onto the cardboard.

It was alcohol, she reckoned. A bottle of booze of some sort. Weird. She'd been living with him and Shona for a few months now, ever since they'd signed up to be her foster carers, but Olivia didn't remember ever seeing the DCI drinking anything but tea, coffee, and the occasional can of Irn Bru.

Across the kitchen, the toaster popped with a loud, jarring *clack*. Olivia plucked the toast from the slots, slathered on some butter, and took a big, crunchy bite.

Then, with Taggart trotting hopefully along at her heels, she left the kitchen and its mystery package behind, and headed back up the stairs to bed.

Chapter 4

'If you're looking for your girlfriend, you're too late. She's gone.'

Logan didn't reply to Geoff Palmer until he'd picked his way across the uneven ground and met the Scene of Crime man at the swaying length of yellow cordon tape. Palmer's white suit still looked remarkably clean, given the amount of mud that was around. Either he'd recently changed, or he'd been avoiding doing any of the manual labour elements of the job.

Logan was pretty sure he knew which of those answers was the correct one.

He'd already known that Shona was no longer at the scene. She'd called from her car on the way up the road to fill him in on their findings so far, and they'd flashed their lights at one another as they'd passed in opposite directions.

The final tally seemed to be eight sets of human remains. At least five, from what she could tell, were missing a digit on one of their hands.

'I wasn't looking for her. I was looking for you,' the DCI said.

A thin veneer of panic painted itself across Palmer's face. His eyes twitched and his lips moved ever so slightly, like he was doing some sort of mental maths, trying to figure out what he could have done to warrant a special in-person visit from the hulking detective—particularly given that Logan usually seemed keen to get away from him as quickly as humanly possible.

Christ. Could Logan have snuck into Palmer's last stand-up gig and heard the thinly veiled rant about him? About how, even though his co-worker, 'Mac Rogan,' acted the big man, Palmer could categorically take him in a straight fight? And about how everyone knew that was true, including Mac's girlfriend, 'Fiona.'

Especially her, in fact.

He'd changed the names to avoid any workplace awkwardness, legal action, or a thoroughly good kicking, but what if Logan had been there and somehow seen through it? What if he'd managed to crack the code?

Palmer swallowed hard, almost choking on the possibility.

'Oh, you were looking for me, were you? You were looking for your old pal, Geoff?' He glanced around at the mass of SOCOs working away behind him, as if hoping they'd rush to provide back-up. Given that they'd been doing their best to ignore him all morning, though, he feared that this was unlikely. 'And why's that, then, eh, old buddy, old pal?'

Logan sniffed and chewed on his lip for a moment, like he wasn't quite ready to explain himself. Instead, he nodded at the various pits and tents beyond the cordon, and the stream of white suits marching around like ants at a picnic site.

'What's the latest?'

Palmer turned again, but this time he kept one eye on Logan, like he was fearing some sort of sneak attack. Not that the DCI would need the element of surprise on his side to turn Geoff into a lumpy paste on the landscape.

'Uh, eight bodies. Think that's the lot, but we'll expand the search a bit, just in case. They were all buried close to one another. The holes were all dug by hand, I'd say, no sign of machinery.'

'Someone was determined, then,' Logan reasoned.

'Ish. Most of them weren't that deep. Deepest we found was about four feet down. A guy. Most likely a jakey, I think, given how he was dressed and how he looked. Or how he would've looked before being murdered and put in a big wet hole in the ground, I mean.'

He swallowed and looked the detective up and down.

'Is, eh, is that why you wanted to see me? For an update? Because you could've just phoned, or waited on the report.'

'No. It's not that,' Logan said, and Palmer's face turned almost the same colour as his suit.

'Oh. Right. I see.' Geoff's shoulder rolled forward and his head lowered, instinct already starting to fold him into the foetal position. 'So, um, what was it you wanted, in that case?'

The mud squelched beneath Logan's boots as he shuffled awkwardly on the spot. Palmer's look of panic gradually morphed into one of curiosity.

And then, a moment later, into an expression of unbridled joy.

'I need a favour,' Logan told him.

'A favour?' Palmer's voice was such a high-pitched squeak that a woman working a metal detector nearby backtracked over the spot she'd just scanned, then frowned when the sound didn't come again. 'You're asking a favour *from me*?'

'Keep your bloody voice down,' Logan hissed. 'And yes. Much as it pains me to say it, I need a favour from you.'

'Well, well, well,' Palmer said. He tucked his thumbs into an imaginary pair of braces, then mimed stretching them out. The circle of his face that was visible inside his elasticated hood became two-thirds smug grin. 'And they said the day would never come. The great Detective Chief Inspector Jack Logan on his hands and knees, begging for my help.'

'I'm not on my hands and knees. And I'm certainly no' begging,' Logan corrected. 'I just need you to check something for me, but if you're going to be an arsehole about it...'

He started to turn away, drawing a yelp of, 'Wait!' from Palmer, who had sensed there was an opportunity here. Quite what that opportunity was, he didn't yet know, but he had sensed it all the same.

Palmer crossed his arms, but it made the one-piece suit ride up and give him a wedgie, so he immediately let them fall back to his side again.

'Alright, Jack. I'm listening,' he said. He brushed two gloved fingers against a cheek and nodded, like he was the Godfather dishing out favours on his daughter's wedding day. 'What is it that you need from me?'

Logan hesitated, as if having second thoughts about this whole endeavour. Then, before he could change his mind, he reached into his coat pocket and produced the two plastic evidence bags he'd taken from his office.

'What do we have here?' Palmer asked. He bent forward at the waist, studying the bags without yet taking them. 'An envelope and a beer mat? What's the big deal?'

'I want prints run on them,' Logan said. 'And anything else you can do that might shed some light on who sent it to me.'

Palmer brought up a finger and pointed at the beer mat like he was choosing a magician's card. 'That came in the envelope, did it?'

'Aye.'

'Addressed to you?'

Logan nodded. 'That's right.'

Palmer squinted up at him. 'Why?'

'I don't know,' Logan said.

'Why's it say "Malkie's Arms"?' Palmer asked, turning his attention back to the beer mat.

'It's the name of the pub.'

'Sounds a bit rough. I don't think I'd do a gig there.'

'Probably for the best.'

The Scene of Crime man straightened up again. The sun was poking its head through the clouds, and he had to shield his eyes with a hand while looking up at the detective.

'And why do you want me to look at it?'

Logan frowned. 'What?'

'Well, I mean, if it's just a beer mat, what's the problem?'

'I don't know who it's from,' Logan said, but even as he spoke the words he knew they weren't enough.

'So? What do you want to do, write them a thank you note? Hardly seems like a good use of police resources, does it? Could it be from Malkie?'

'He's dead.'

'Christ, what happened?'

'Old age.' Logan sighed. 'Look, Geoff, can you do it or not?'

'I *can* do it. Of course I *can* do it. Meaning, I'm capable of doing it,' Palmer said. 'But I still don't get why. Is it connected to a case?'

'Maybe,' Logan said.

'God Almighty. This is like pulling a bloody wisdom tooth. What's the big secret? Am I going to get into trouble for this?'

'No, Geoff, you're not going to get into trouble,' Logan assured him. He shifted his weight from foot to foot, making the mud squelch again. 'I just need you to keep it off the record for now. Just until I know more.'

'That sounds like I'm going to get in trouble.'

'You're not. I give you my word,' Logan said.

On the other side of the tape, Palmer drew a long, slow breath in through his nose, then let it out as a pained groan that resonated at the back of his throat.

'One condition,' he said.

'And what's that?'

Palmer smoothed down the front of his suit. 'You come out for a drink with me.'

Logan blinked. He hadn't been expecting that one.

'Aye, not like on a date, or anything,' Palmer was quick to add. 'Just a couple of guys hanging out. Couple of lads out for a few beers, getting the craic. Having a laugh.'

'I don't drink,' Logan told him.

Palmer tutted. 'For God's… Fine. Coffee, then. Or tea. I'm more of a tea man. I find coffee too bitter, personally. Bit claggy at the back of the throat. But I don't mind if you want to have some.'

'That's very generous of you,' Logan said. He swallowed down a sudden urge to vomit, then managed a, 'Fine,' through gritted teeth.

'Really?' Geoff stared up at the detective in disbelief and wonder. 'I mean, great. That's great! Good. It'll be fun. We'll have a laugh. Couple of lads out on the town, drinking tea and possibly coffee—although, the smell does bother me a bit— setting the world to rights.'

'Aye, whatever you say.' Logan tried to hand over the evidence bags, but Palmer wasn't quite ready to take them off his hands yet.

'When?' he asked.

Logan hesitated. 'Sorry?'

'When are we going to go out? I don't want you just agreeing and then not following through. I want a date.' Palmer held up his gloved hands. 'Again, I don't mean it's a date, I'm definitely not gay. Please, don't think that. I just want to know when we're going to go out.'

'Jesus, Geoff. I don't know. Next week.'

The evidence bags were presented again. Once again, Palmer didn't take them.

'What day? I can't do Mondays.'

'Thursday,' Logan said, picking a day at random.

'What time?'

Logan had to resist the urge to reach over the cordon tape and twist the other man's head off.

'Three o'clock,' he said.

Palmer nodded. 'A.M. or P.M.?'

'What the fu—? P.M., Geoff. Obviously not the middle of the bloody night.'

'Right. No, that makes sense,' Palmer conceded. 'Three o'clock. *P.M.* Next Thursday. Right?'

Logan huffed out another weary sigh. 'Aye. Now, are you going to take these, or not?'

He stole a cagey look around, then thrust the evidence bags forward again. Palmer regarded them with a sense of triumph, before plucking them from the detective's hands.

'Bros before bosses, eh?' he said, then he winked and made a loud *clack* sort of sound with his tongue and teeth. 'Leave it with me, good buddy. I'll find out what I can.'

Logan buried his hands in his pockets, partly to warm them up, and partly to stop himself from snatching back the evidence bags and calling the whole thing off.

'Right. Aye. Good,' he muttered, then he quickly turned away and set off back in the direction of his car.

'See you on Thursday, pal!' Palmer called after him. 'Looking forward to it!'

'Dear God,' Logan whispered to himself as he trudged through the damp undergrowth. 'What have I done?'

–

Logan's phone rang just before he reached the car. He fumbled the door open and slid into the seat, then waited for the mobile to connect to the BMW's Bluetooth speaker system before hitting the answer button.

Outside, a blanket of brooding dark cloud wrapped itself around the mountaintops, throttling them.

'Morning, Detective Superintendent,' he said, as the name flashed up on screen. 'What can I do for you?'

There was something different about Det Supt Mitchell's voice when her reply echoed around the car's cabin. Usually, her tone had a sort of robotic authority to it, like she was well aware that she was the one in charge, but had no real further opinion on the matter.

To be fair, she didn't sound entirely dissimilar today, but there was something else mixed in there. Some ingredient that wasn't normally present.

Something that sounded almost human.

'Jack. Where are you?'

'I'm down at the scene. Couple of miles off the A9,' Logan replied. Something about her tone made him uneasy. He thought back to the snarl of traffic he'd passed on his way south from Inverness. Shona would've had to drive through it on her way up north. 'Why? What's wrong? Has something happened?'

'I need you back up here right away,' Mitchell said, evading the question.

Logan started the engine. 'I'm on my way. What's happened? Is it Shona?'

'What?' Mitchell sounded almost irritated by the suggestion. 'No. No, there's been a development in the case.'

Logan breathed out some of the tension in his chest.

And yet, there was something about her voice.

'Just get here, Jack,' she told him. Pleaded, maybe? 'Just get here as quickly as you can.'

Chapter 5

His name was Adam Parfitt. He was twenty-six years old. And he was very, very afraid.

He lay on the floor of a dimly lit room, backed right up against the far wall. A shaky camera peered at him through thick wire mesh as he choked and sobbed and begged for his life.

The lighting and camerawork made it hard to be sure, but he looked unhurt. There were no obvious injuries to those parts of him visible in the footage, at least. Aside from a slick wash of snot and tears, his face was unmarked.

There was no ambient sound on the clip, only some upbeat music overlaid on top. It was clear, though, that he was pleading with the person holding the camera, or perhaps with those watching the footage at home.

Logan stood with his arms folded and his jaw clenched, watching the young man recoiling as a gloved hand slammed against the wire mesh, shaking it violently. Adam wrapped his arms around his head and curled his knees in as close to his chest as he could get them, like he was bracing himself for some sort of punishment.

His eyes stared out from beneath the shadowy hood of his elbows, wide, and wet, and desperate.

The footage jerked, like the camera had just started to lurch forward, then the screen cut to black and the music slowly faded into silence.

'Is that it?' Logan asked.

'Hang on,' Ben urged. He stood beside the DCI, a mug clutched between both hands. For the first time in living memory, his tea had remained untouched long enough to go stone cold. 'There's more.'

Just as he said it, a series of words flashed up on screen, one after the other. By the time the third word had appeared, Logan's heart was in his throat.

A New Player Has Entered the Game.

'Oh, Christ,' he hissed.

There was silence from the rest of the team. They'd already seen the video, so had known what to expect. Even so, their expressions were as grim as Logan felt.

That same message had been sent to a series of blackmail victims several months previously. There had been a connection between some of those people and the severed fingers found on the tray in the abandoned house.

The abandoned house right beside where the current crop of eight bodies had been uncovered.

There had been so much death, and so much pain. He'd thought they'd wrapped it all up, but the video he'd just watched told him he'd been wrong. Whatever that last case had been, it was just the beginning.

Someone else was behind it all. Someone had a bigger plan.

And Logan couldn't shake the feeling that he was somehow at the centre of it.

'It appeared on his Instagram feed just over half an hour ago,' Hamza said. 'He mostly uses TikTok, but there's nothing on there yet.'

'Can we get it taken down?' Logan asked.

'Maybe, but not quickly,' Hamza replied. 'There are already over a thousand comments on it. Most people seem to think it's a publicity stunt. Just one of his sketches. A few are starting to wonder if it's real, though.'

'And do we know if it is?' Logan looked around at the others. 'Could he just be pissing about to get more bloody followers, or subscribers, or whatever the hell it is?'

'I mean, it's not out of the question,' Hamza admitted. He looked to Ben for guidance, then turned back to the computer when the DI gave him a nod. 'Except there's this.'

Hamza flicked to another tab, showing another Instagram video. The set-up for this one was similar—same drab room, same wire mesh, same shaky camera—but the prisoner this time was a young woman with long blonde dreadlocks, colourful tattoos on her neck, and a smear of dried blood that ran from her nose to her chin.

She was wearing what looked like a wedding dress, all frilly neck and puffy shoulders. There were multiple piercings in her eyebrows and one in her bottom lip, and Logan wondered if the blood on her mouth could have been the result of a nose ring being forcibly removed at speed.

Unlike the last guy, she wasn't begging. Instead, she sat with her arms wrapped around her knees, staring blankly into space, her bottom lip jerking about like she was a fish on the end of a line. There was no sound except another loop of frenetic instrumental music, but Logan could practically hear the desperate, uneven rasping of her breath.

'Eliza Shuttleworth,' Hamza announced.

'El-eee-zee-a,' Sinead corrected, drawing out the middle syllables.

'Elizia, sorry,' the DS said. 'She's a spiritualist influencer from Essex. Astrology. Crystals. Tarot cards. Finding your inner spirit animal, all that guff. One-point-eight-million followers. She's just turned twenty-six.'

'Jesus,' Logan muttered. 'I don't recognise the name. Was she one of the three meant to be on that flight?'

Sinead shook her head. 'No, sir. Not one of the three. One of the eight.'

'Eight?'

'Aye, boss,' Tyler said, jumping in. 'I got onto the airline and they gave us the details of the passengers who didn't turn up for the flight to Gatwick. There were eleven all in all. Three were the same family. Had to pull out of their trip because the mum has the flu. Checked the other eight, though, and they were all appearing at the convention. None of them has posted since they left for the airport.'

He gestured at the screen with a look of revulsion. 'Well, not until now, anyway.'

'So, we have eight missing people?' Logan asked, making sure he had things clear.

'Looks like it, Jack,' Ben told him.

Eight missing people. Eight bodies.

A New Player Has Entered the Game.

It all had to be connected. It had to be.

'How many videos have been uploaded?'

'Four so far, sir,' Hamza told him. 'These two, a guy who does boot camp style fitness advice, and a lassie who lip syncs to stuff.'

Logan frowned. 'Lip syncs to stuff? What do you mean?'

Hamza shrugged. 'Just that, sir. Either songs, or just, like, clips from movies and TV shows. She lip syncs along to it.'

Logan rubbed at the knot of pressure he could feel building between his eyes. He made a sound that was part sigh, but mostly groan.

'And people watch that, do they? That's a thing that people sit down and actually watch?'

'Over six million subscribers, boss,' Tyler said.

Logan felt his jaw drop. 'My arse. Surely not?'

'She also dresses like a Japanese cartoon character,' Sinead said. 'And she's twenty-eight, but looks about twelve.'

'Right. So, six million weird pervy bastards, then?' Logan said, nodding his understanding. 'Got it. Are those videos the same as these?'

'Pretty much,' Hamza confirmed. 'Similar location, same handheld camera. The fitness guy looks more angry than afraid. The miming lassie's a mess, though.'

'What, hurt?'

'No. Just scared.'

Logan ran a hand down his face. 'Aye. I can imagine.' He looked back at the thumbnail of the video on screen. It showed a grimy, grainy looking close-up of Elizia's thousand-yard stare. 'Get onto the people at Instagram. See what you can find out. Are we keeping an eye on the other profiles?'

'We are, sir, aye,' Hamza confirmed. 'Nothing so far, but if anything pops up, we'll know.'

'We're also getting in touch with the families of the eight who didn't make that flight, boss,' Tyler added. 'To see if they've heard anything.'

'And I'm waiting for a call back from the convention organisers about the travel arrangements to the airport,' Sinead said. 'The woman I spoke to thought they all went together by minibus, but she's going to double check then call me back with details of the company.'

'Right. Good.' Logan nodded, pleased that the gears had already started to turn without him around to turn the handle. 'Has anyone talked to Mitchell?'

The question was mostly aimed at Ben. Being the most senior officer in Logan's absence, he'd be the one stuck dealing with the Detective Superintendent.

'Eh, aye. Briefly,' Ben replied. 'She seemed a bit weird, though. Bit off. Wants you to go through once you're up to speed.'

Logan looked around at the others. 'Am I up to speed?'

'About as much as the rest of us, aye,' Ben confirmed.

'Right, then.' Logan pulled off his coat and draped it across the back of his chair. He felt an urge to steel himself for what was coming next. 'I suppose I'd better go and see what she wants.'

—

Logan watched from the half-open doorway as Detective Superintendent Mitchell shoved a stack of ring binders into a storage box, and placed it down on the floor next to a couple of others. She had her head down, and was busy sorting and tidying. If it wasn't so absurd a thought, he'd guess she'd just been given ten minutes to clear out her desk before uniformed officers escorted her from the building.

'Well, don't just stand there, come in,' she instructed, not looking up from the stack of paperwork she was neatly squaring together.

Logan entered and closed the door behind him. 'Ma'am,' he ventured, not quite sure what else to say.

'Sit,' Mitchell instructed, gesturing to the chair across the desk from hers. She ran a hand through her short crop of dark hair, then tutted. Logan got the impression she was annoyed with herself, though, rather than him. 'Or don't. It doesn't matter. You can help me move these boxes.'

'Move them, ma'am? Move them where?'

'Another office on the first floor. Temporarily. Just until all this is dealt with.'

Logan watched as she gave up trying to neaten the stack of papers and just dumped them in another open box, instead. Normally, she was fastidiously tidy and organised. The haphazard stacking of the boxes' contents wasn't like her at all.

'Sorry, ma'am, I don't understand,' the DCI said. 'Until what's dealt with?'

Mitchell straightened and looked at him for the first time. Her dark skin looked paler than usual, like some of the pigment had been bled right out of it.

'The case, Jack. What do you think?'

'Oh. Right.' He watched her return to her packing. 'Why?'

She placed a hand flat on the desk, fingers splayed, and leaned on it like her legs no longer had the strength to hold her up on their own. With the other hand, she found her chair and rolled it beneath her. She fell into it, gripped the armrests, then closed her eyes for a moment and breathed deeply.

When she finally opened them again, she had mustered some of her usual air of authority.

'The Assistant Chief Constable thinks I'm too close. And, though it pains me, I have to agree with him. Detective Superintendent MacKenzie will be coming up from Glasgow to relieve me.'

'The Gozer?' Logan asked. He had nothing against his old boss, but bringing him all the way up here was a strange move. 'What do you mean, you're too close? Too close how? You a subscriber to one of them, or something?' he asked, trying to lighten the mood a little.

'Denzel Drummond,' she said, her voice flat, her face expressionless. '*DenzelDIYFit*. One of the missing. One of the ones in those videos.'

Logan didn't quite know what to make of this. 'Right. And… what, you're one of his followers?' he asked. It had been a joke a moment ago, but neither of them was laughing now.

Mitchell shook her head. She crossed her hands on the desk in front of her. A finger tapped on the back of her wrist.

'No, Jack,' she said, still in that same monotone. 'I'm his mother.'

Logan understood the words, of course. The words themselves were not the issue. He just hadn't ever expected to hear them coming out of the Detective Superintendent's mouth.

'You're his…?'

'I'm his mother.'

'So, he's your…?' Logan frowned, like he was trying to work out a particularly knotty maths problem. 'He's your son?'

'That's generally how it works, yes.'

'Right. OK. I see. Bloody hell.'

Logan continued to stand for a few seconds, then the lure of the chair became too great. He lowered himself into it, the whole thing creaking beneath his weight.

'It's just… I thought you were…'

'Oh, I am. I very much am,' Mitchell said. She glanced at the window, then met his eye again. 'But I wasn't always as honest with myself about that as I should have been. Even less so with others.'

36

Logan wanted to ask more, but decided it was better to keep his mouth shut and wait.

Sure enough, after a short spell of stilted silence, Mitchell started to talk again.

'I had a past relationship. A few, actually, but one of note. It was with a man. Not the best man, either, I have to say. But, we had a son. We *have* a son, I mean.' She stumbled over the next part. 'He… hasn't spoken to me since I came out. He was sixteen at the time. Very much like his father. Too much like his father.'

'I'm sorry,' Logan told her. 'I had no idea.'

'No. Well, it's not something I tend to crow about, how I turned my own child against me.'

'Here, been there, done that, bought the t-shirt,' Logan said.

Mitchell bit the tip of her thumbnail. 'Yes, well. You know the shame of it, then.'

And she was right. He did.

'I didn't even know he was in town. He didn't tell me. Why would he, I suppose?' Her voice cracked. She swallowed a few times, doing her best to repair it. 'And now this. This video. I feel…'

She clutched at the centre of her chest, her fingers curving into a claw like she wanted to pluck her heart out.

'I feel so helpless. I'm a Detective Superintendent of police, and I just… I don't know what to do. I don't know where to start. And they're taking me off it. They're making me step back.'

'It's probably for the best,' Logan told her.

She nodded like she was in agreement, but then asked, 'Would you, though? If it was your child? Would you back off if they asked you to?'

He wasted a second wondering if he could get away with lying to her. But she'd see through it. She already knew the real answer.

'No,' he admitted. 'I wouldn't.'

Tears formed on her lower eyelids, and she wasn't quite quick enough to blink them away before the DCI could spot them.

'I'll put together a statement. Everything I know about Denzel that could be relevant. You'll have it within the hour. And, you'll need to talk to his father, of course.' She scowled with distaste. 'Good luck with that. I don't envy you. Feel free to bounce him down a staircase if you need to. I'll take full responsibility.'

'I'm sure it won't come to that, ma'am,' Logan replied, but the way the Det Supt rolled her eyes made him wonder if it might.

'I need you to promise me something, Jack,' Mitchell said, in a voice that was no longer her own. All the pomp and authority had left it. She wasn't his boss anymore, she was just another helpless, frightened mum. One of the many he'd met. 'I want you to promise me that you'll do everything you can to find him. All of them, of course. I mean all of them. But him. You'll find him. You'll do what you have to. You'll call in everyone you can. And you'll find him.'

'Of course, ma'am. I'll do my best.'

'I don't want your best, Jack,' Mitchell snapped. 'I don't care about your best. I want your word. I want you to swear to me that you'll find him. And that you'll find who has done this. Promise me.'

It was a mistake, Logan knew. But then, she must have known it, too. There were no guarantees. Not in this job.

Despite that, he nodded.

Despite that, he agreed.

'I promise,' he told her, and the words acted like some sort of spell, wiping away all her grief, and rising her up onto her feet.

'Good. Thank you,' she said, her usual curtness returning. She pulled open a desk drawer, and lifted the lid of another packing box. 'Now, if you'll excuse me, I should really get back to it. MacKenzie will be here in a couple of hours, and this desk isn't going to clear itself.'

Chapter 6

A change had come over the Incident Room by the time Logan returned. It had felt in a state of shock when he'd left, but now everyone was on phones or computers, or—in Sinead's case—working at the Big Board. Or, more accurately, the Big Boards.

The detective constable had sourced images of all the missing influencers, and pinned them across two large freestanding cork boards that she'd placed side by side at the head of the room.

The pictures all looked like actor headshots, and each of the missing people seemed to be in their full influencer persona.

Logan almost didn't recognise the young man, Adam Parfitt, from the first video. He was laughing uproariously, and while it looked a little forced, he was undoubtedly happier than the last time Logan had seen him. Then again, it would be hard not to be.

His face was jolly and quite portly, like he might age into a fine Santa Claus in thirty or forty years. And yet, there was something in the expression that made Logan suspect he might be something of a diva when the cameras stopped rolling.

Adam's grinning photograph stood in stark contrast to the one beside it. There was no smile on the face of the second man, just a no-nonsense grimace and a dead-eyed stare. He was mixed-race, in his mid-twenties, and, going by what Logan could see of his muscular shoulders, wearing a military green vest.

Sinead hadn't got around to adding names below the photographs yet, but Logan knew this had to be Denzel Drummond. This was the face of Mitchell's son.

He was a good if not particularly pleasant-looking lad. Logan imagined him as one of those shouty army PT types, screaming at new recruits to drag their lardy, useless arses up steep muddy hills while carrying rocks in their rucksacks.

Logan had found it hard to believe that a son would completely disown his own mother on account of her sexuality, but one look at that face and suddenly it didn't seem quite so unlikely.

Of the other pictures, Logan only recognised the young woman with the blonde dreadlocks and tattoos. In the video, she'd been staring blankly ahead like she was in shock. In this picture she had her hands pressed together in front of her as if in prayer, but was also winking and biting down on her tongue which stuck out of the side of her mouth.

Her hair looked like it hadn't been washed in a decade, and she had so many piercing that, had he ever found himself standing behind her in the queue for an airport metal detector, he'd have picked up his bag and called the whole trip off.

Although, to be fair to her, she was the first one who looked genuinely happy at having her photo taken. Adam Parfitt's big laughing grin had been insincere, and Denzel Drummond looked like he wanted to strangle the photographer to death with his own camera strap. This lassie—Elizia something or other—at least looked like she was enjoying herself.

That thought made him recall how differently she'd looked in that video, and his fingers balled themselves into fists.

'Anything more on the other accounts yet?' he asked, turning away from the row of eight faces. 'Any other videos popped up?'

'Two more, sir,' Hamza replied from his desk. He pointed to one of the other photos on the board, a thirty-something, dowdy looking woman holding a little toy cat. 'Kelly Wynne.' He searched the row then indicated a sneering young lad wearing oversized headphones. 'And Matthew Broderick, not the actor. He's does gameplay livestreams on Twitch, and she does unboxing videos. The videos turned up on their profile a few minutes ago. Same sort of thing as the others. I've sent the links to the inbox.'

DI Forde popped his head above his computer. From the frown on his face, it was clear he had some questions. 'What the hell's an *un*boxing video? Does she dance around a ring deliberately not punching anyone?'

'Eh, no. Not that sort of boxing, sir,' Hamza told him. 'I mean boxes like the type that toys come in. She opens them on camera and shows off what she's got.'

'Toys?' Ben blinked several times, his look of confusion only deepening. 'She opens toys?'

Hamza nodded. 'Aye. Blind boxes and bags, mostly. As in these sort of mystery things kids can buy without knowing exactly what's inside. Dolls and figures, mainly. She sometimes does videos where she acts out wee stories with them and does different voices. Does this like, baby girl voice that creeps me out.'

The others looked at him with raised eyebrows.

'Aye, I'm not a fan myself, like. Kamila used to watch her when she was a bit younger,' he explained.

Ben looked from Hamza to the first photo he'd pointed at on the board. 'And how old is she?' he asked.

'She's thirty-two, boss,' Tyler said, joining the conversation.

'Thirty-two? Christ, she looks about forty-five. And she's opening toys?' Ben's expression had switched from confusion to disapproval. Although, confusion still wasn't off the table. 'Does she at least get her kids involved?'

'She doesn't have kids, boss. We checked. Mum's dead, no siblings, no dad listed on the birth certificate. It's just her and her cats.'

Ben sucked in his bottom lip, chewed on it for a moment, then spat it out again. 'Bloody hell,' was all he had left to say on the matter, then he sat back down again.

Logan got the impression that he still wanted to ask what 'gameplay livestreams on Twitch' meant, but he clearly needed time to process the toy thing first.

The DCI turned back to the boards, and the faces spread across them. Sinead was adding names now, as well as ages, social media handles, their follower numbers, and a brief description of what they did.

Cassandra Swain was a natural looking redhead wearing a big smile and holding a half-eaten apple. She was twenty years old and apparently a 'women's health and wellness expert.'

Logan wondered briefly how a twenty year old could be an expert on anything, much less a topic as wide-ranging and complicated as women's health, but three-point-eight million people clearly didn't share his reservations.

Bruce Kennedy's eight-hundred-thousand followers seemed paltry by comparison, but of all the faces in the bunch, Logan reckoned he'd get on with him best, despite some slightly pretentious facial hair. He was thirty-five, had a warm, friendly smile, and had apparently built his following by offering cooking tips and sharing budget-friendly recipes. It was a rare gem of an actual talent, Logan thought, in amongst all the other largely pointless nonsense.

The last photo on the line-up was Natalie Womack, who went by the name 'JunBuggy'. Her hair was a bubblegum pink, and her face was a mess of painted-on freckles and angled eyeshadow that gave her a vaguely Asian appearance, despite her being nothing of the sort.

She was winking, tilting her head to one side, and had raised two fingers in a peace sign. According to the note beneath the photo, she was twenty-eight, but, either through accident or design, she looked like she was half that age. Her skillset apparently extended to 'dancing and miming,' and more than six million people felt that was worthy of their collective attention.

'Jesus Christ,' Logan muttered, then he shook his head, annoyed at himself.

It would be very easy to dismiss them all as caricatures. That was, for the most part, what he was looking at. But this—these pictures—that wasn't real. That wasn't who they really were. Beneath the make-up and the flawless skin, these were actual people. Young people, mostly. Kids, some of them.

Some bastard had taken them all. Some bastard was hurting them.

And it was Logan's job to bring them safely back home.

'There's something you all need to know,' he said, in a tone that made it clear they should all pay very close attention to the next words out of his mouth. 'Detective Superintendent Mitchell is having to step back from this one. The Gozer—Gordon MacKenzie, my old super in Glasgow, is coming up to fill in. For those of you who haven't worked with him, he's decent enough. He won't get in the way.'

'Why's Mitchell stepping back?' Ben asked. Some DIs would've been annoyed at not being told such news ahead of more junior officers, but when Ben had been put together, they'd neglected to install an ego. 'Is she OK?'

'She's fine,' Logan said, then he grunted. 'Well, no, she's far from fine.' He tapped the photo of the scowling mixed-race man in military colours. 'Denzel Drummond. He's her son.'

Tyler almost choked on his own tongue in his rush to get out a response. 'Her son?! I didn't know she had kids! Is she not gay?'

'Gay people can have kids,' Sinead pointed out.

'I mean, aye. Of course. I know that. I just… I didn't think that she had any. I'm surprised, is all.'

Sinead shook her head slowly. 'I'm not. I mean, I didn't know, but when I was pregnant, she seemed to have an idea of what I was going through. Like an insight. She said she'd seen friends going through it, but…' Her voice trailed off and she looked over at Denzel's picture. 'It makes sense. God. She must be going through hell.'

'Did she talk to him recently, do we know?' Hamza asked. 'Did they meet up when he was here?'

'No. Don't think they're on the best of terms,' Logan replied. Mitchell hadn't asked him to keep anything back from the team, but he felt uncomfortable revealing the extent of her and her son's relationship issues.

Despite all they'd been through together over the years, he couldn't even bring himself to trust them with his own secrets, let alone someone else's.

'She's putting together a statement for us. Full report on him, and what she knows. I'd imagine it'll be thorough, but if there's any follow-up needed with her, it goes through me or Ben.'

'Got it, boss.'

'She's suggested we talk to his father, but warned he might not be particularly forthcoming. Mitchell'll give us an address and number for him, but if we find anything before then, let me know.'

He tugged on the knot of his tie, loosening it a little.

'And I know it goes without saying, but I'm going to say it anyway. We pull out all the stops on this one. We do whatever needs doing to get these people safely back home. That's our first priority. If we catch the bastard who took them, great. But keeping these people alive is our goal here.'

'Got it, sir,' Sinead said.

'Sounds good to me, boss,' Tyler agreed. He leaned back in his chair and tapped a pen on his knee. 'Is there a possibility that it's all just a set-up, though?'

'What do you mean?'

Tyler gestured to his computer. 'Well, these videos are already starting to go viral. They've all usually got big numbers of views on their normal posts, but these are skyrocketing. Your man, there, Denzel. He's got another quarter of a million subscribers in the last hour alone. You can't buy this sort of publicity.'

'Oh, God,' Sinead groaned. 'The media's going to be all over it. Not just UK, either. It'll be international.'

The thought of all that press attention immediately gave Logan a headache. Or, at least, made the one he'd had all morning significantly worsen. He ran a hand down his face, but couldn't wipe away the grimace that had formed there.

'Christ. The Gozer can deal with that. Our focus is on finding our missing crew here.' He looked across to Tyler before answering the detective constable's question. 'And, if it turns out they've faked the whole thing, you can rest assured that I'll personally murder the bastards myself.'

–

Olivia sat at the breakfast bar in the kitchen, sharing her lunch—a small pile of yet more toast—with the dog sitting patiently at her feet. A bite for her, a bite for Taggart. A bite for her, a bite for him.

Since moving in, she'd learned to always make double the amount of food she planned to eat herself, because she couldn't resist the little dog's big brown eyes, or the way they regarded every single morsel that she brought to her mouth like it was some sort of long-lost love.

She gave the dog the final piece, then held up the plate to show him that it was now empty.

'See? Done,' she announced.

It was important to present him with this evidence, other-wise he'd continue to mooch around, hoping there was more food coming his way. When he saw the plate had been cleared, he appeared momentarily dejected, then scampered over to the back door and stood there staring pointedly at the handle.

'Give me a minute!' Olivia told him. She took a moment to dump the plate in the dishwasher and to brush the crumbs off her hands over the sink, then she stretched over the dog and pulled the door open.

Usually, he'd trot out and wander around the grass for a while, taking his time to choose the best possible spot in which to relieve himself.

Today, though, was different. He shot out with a surprising turn of speed, then ran a quick loop around the garden, his head angled upwards, his nostrils flaring as he sniffed the air.

'What's up?' Olivia asked, then both she and the dog reached the same realisation at the very same moment.

The door to the garden shed stood open.

Olivia didn't think she'd seen the shed door open even once since her arrival a few months previously. Neither Shona nor Jack were big into gardening, and Olivia wasn't even sure what, if anything, they kept in there. It had never seemed interesting enough for her to pay it much heed.

The door was open now, though. Now, the shed had her attention.

'Taggart. Taggart, here,' she hissed, but the dog stood his ground, nose pointed at the open door, body crouched low, the fur on the back of his neck rising to a mohican-like point.

He was growling—a low sound somewhere far back in his throat that grew louder when the shed door gave an elongated *creeeeeak.*

Olivia held her breath, clenched her fists, getting ready for someone to come bursting out from within the little wooden structure.

Instead, the door settled back into its original half-open position, and a breeze swirled an empty crisp bag around the garden.

Taggart was hunched down now, like he was getting ready to pounce. He was standing ten feet from the shed, though, so it would have to be one hell of a jump for him to reach it.

Olivia tried calling him back one more time. Then, when he continued to ignore her, she darted back into the house, wriggled her feet into her trainers, and grabbed the biggest knife she could find from the wooden block in the kitchen.

It was the length of her forearm, and razor sharp. She didn't want to use it, of course, but the sight of it should be enough to give any opportunistic shed-robbers cause for concern.

And she would use it, if she had to.

The dog still hadn't moved by the time Olivia returned, although it now seemed like he was struggling not to get distracted by the shiny foil of the empty crisp bag. It was snagged on the grass over on his left, just at the edge of his line of sight, and his head twitched between it and the open shed door.

Olivia's arrival in the garden helped refocus him, though. He straightened up as she came marching across the grass, then stuck close beside her when she approached the shed, sensing strength in their number.

They both stopped a few feet from the half-open door. There were no windows, so the inside of the shed was cloaked in a dank, stuffy darkness that harboured cobwebs, and spiders, and God knew what else.

It was the 'what else' that worried her.

'You'd better come out!' Olivia shouted. 'I've got a knife!'

She waved the blade in front of her, just in case anyone was watching from the shadows.

'Come out, and you can go. If I have to come in there, I'm stabbing everything that moves in the face.'

Taggart gave a shrill, sharp bark, like he was lending his weight to the threat. It caught Olivia off-guard and made her hiss out a panicky, 'Shit!' The dog's stumpy tail flicked back and forth a few times, like he was pleased he'd been able to have such an effect.

The shed remained silent, the darkness unmoved.

'I'm warning you!' Olivia bellowed. 'You don't want me coming in there. I'll mess you up!'

Taggart offered another bark of back-up, but this time it didn't come as a surprise. Instead, Olivia felt emboldened by it, and took a couple of paces closer to the open shed door.

The dog took this as a cue to charge. He rocketed forward before she could stop him, barrelled in through the door, then vanished into the darkness.

'Shit, shit, shit!' Olivia raced after him, knife held low at her side, ready to thrust upwards into anyone who might even contemplate harming a rough, wiry hair on Taggart's body.

She shoved the door all the way open, let out a banshee scream, and then stopped when she realised that, aside from an electric lawnmower, a few other tools, and a slightly dejected looking dog, the shed was empty.

Taggart recovered quickly from his disappointment. He lowered his back end onto the floor and looked up at the girl, his tongue hanging out, like he was waiting to find out what their next game was going to be.

Olivia checked behind the door to make sure no one was lurking there, even though they'd have to have been some sort of circus contortionist to fit, then relaxed her grip on the knife.

'Well, looks like if someone was in here, they're gone,' she announced, and Taggart drooled happily in agreement. 'And just as well, for their sake,' the girl added.

Across the garden, out of their sight, the back door of the house stood open and exposed.

Chapter 7

Logan paced up and down a few feet in front of the boards, leaving room for Sinead to keep working at it. All the photos were now in place, and she'd started to compile additional information onto a stack of cards and Post-its.

'Four male, four female,' he noted, his gaze flitting across each of the influencer's photographs in turn. He tapped a hand lightly on the side of his leg as he gave this some consideration. 'We heard any more from Shona yet?'

'Not yet, sir, no,' Hamza replied.

Logan tapped a few more drumbeats on his leg, then stopped. 'Someone get onto her, will you? See if she can tell us anything about the sexes of those bodies that were dug up.'

Across at his desk in the corner, Constable Dave Davidson raised his hand. 'I can get onto that.'

'Thanks,' Logan said, turning back to the board.

He'd love to think there was no connection, but how could that be? That message at the end of those videos—'A New Player Has Entered the Game'—was no coincidence. Whoever was behind this was involved in the horror show of the team's previous case. They had to be.

And the thought of that chilled him to the bone.

All eight influencers had videos posted on their Instagram accounts now, each one showing them cowering in a makeshift cell. For the most part, they seemed to be unhurt, but afraid. Sickeningly, devastatingly afraid. If they were staging all this themselves, then they all had far more performing talent than Logan had been giving them credit for.

Matthew Broderick, the youngest of the bunch, had been particularly hard to watch. From what Logan had been told, he was quite an unpleasant little shit on his livestreams, which were full of rampant misogyny and casual racism.

Seeing him there in that cage, though, red eyed and struggling to breathe through his snot and tears, he could have been any one of the many terrified children Logan had seen in his career.

One of the far-too-many.

He thought of the three young missing boys he'd spent half his career obsessing over. Despite all his efforts, despite it costing him his marriage, his family, and a good chunk of his sanity, he'd failed to save a single one of them.

This time would be different. This time, no one died.

The DCI's train of thought was derailed by a sudden shout from across the room.

'OK! OK! We've got something! Just came in from the convention venue,' Ben announced. He stared in befuddlement at his computer screen, then poked at his keyboard. 'But I can't remember how to make it do the thing.'

'What thing?' Logan asked.

'The thing! The thing they do, when they show you the stuff.'

Everyone gazed glassily back at the detective inspector, clueless as to what he was on about. Picking up on his cue, the team's resident tech expert, Hamza, scooted his chair across to the DI's desk, and Ben leaned back to let him see the screen.

'It's a video,' the sergeant stated.

'Aye, I know it's a video. I'm no' *that* far gone. I know what a video is, son. It's from a security camera at the front of Eden Court. Apparently, it shows the internet people getting on a minibus,' Ben explained. 'But how do I make it play?'

'You just, eh, you just click the play button,' Hamza said.

Ben's gaze searched the screen. He made no move to reach for the mouse, and visibly relaxed when the sergeant took over.

'Gather round!' he instructed, as Hamza hovered the mouse pointer over a little triangle icon in the centre of the image.

He pulled himself in closer to the desk, making room for the rest of the team to gather around him and the sergeant. Even Dave rolled over, leaning sideways across an arm of his wheelchair to get a better look at the PC's monitor.

'Everyone ready?' Hamza asked, looking up.

The others nodded. Logan let out a little sigh, like this hardly seemed worth all the fanfare, but then waved his hand for Hamza to start the video playing.

The sergeant clicked to make the box fill the screen, then hit the triangle icon. A series of jerky black and white images began to play. It wasn't so much a video as a stop-motion slideshow, with just one or two frames passing every second. The resolution wasn't great—there was a blurry softness to the pictures, and the odd visual artefact that obscured some of the details—but they'd all seen worse quality CCTV footage over the years.

'Is that them?' Tyler asked, pointing to a group of people at the top right of the frame who were surrounded by bags and suitcases. Their faces were hard to make out at that distance, but Denzel Drummond and Kelly Wynne were both recognisable.

'Got to be,' Sinead confirmed. She glanced up at the boards, then back at the screen. 'That has to be Natalie Womack at the front there.'

'Which one?' Tyler asked, squinting at the low-res image.

'The one dressed like a Japanese schoolgirl.'

'Oh, aye. Got her now,' Tyler said, straightening again.

It was difficult to see much of the building behind them, other than part of a canopy and a bit of a sliding door. For those familiar with the place, though, it was enough to confirm that they were waiting at the front of Eden Court Theatre.

'Who's this now?' Ben asked, leaning in closer as a man approached the group.

They watched nine or ten images flicking by, and the newcomer was revealed to be just an autograph hunter, who gathered a couple of signatures before Denzel Drummond appeared to get angry and attempted to send him packing.

There was a bit of an altercation between them, then the autograph hunter turned and marched off, affording the camera a straight-on look at his face.

'I want to know who that is, and I want him brought in,' Logan intoned, and both detective constables jotted down a note of the timestamp on the screen.

The video continued to jerk by for thirty seconds or so, then the smallest member of the group—the gamer, Matthew Broderick, Logan guessed—pointed off camera. Everyone picked up their bags, then stuttered off screen like the skeletons from *Jason and the Argonauts*.

The video continued for a few more seconds, then stopped and returned to the first frame, ready to be played again.

'Is that it?' Logan asked. 'I thought you said it showed them getting on a minibus? Unless it was a *very* fucking mini bus indeed, I didn't see one.'

Ben shrugged. 'I don't know! It's just what they said in the email,' he protested. 'This is my first time looking at it, too.'

While the DI had been talking, Hamza had taken control of the computer again. He minimised the window, switched to the inbox, then skimmed the contents of the email from Eden Court.

Then, he scrolled to the bottom, double-clicked the second attachment, and sat back as footage from a different camera began to play.

'Here we go,' he announced, drawing everyone's attention back to the screen.

This camera showed a wider angle view of the front of the theatre, taking in part of the pick-up and drop-off area at the front. There were a few cars coming and going, but the low frame rate meant they popped into existence in one image, only to immediately disappear again in the next.

Way in the background, so out of focus and low-res that they looked like a single homogenous entity, the influencers were being approached by the man with the autograph book.

If they hadn't already seen a clearer version of events, the detectives would've sworn that the man was absorbed into the multi-headed monstrosity standing by the front door, before being spat out again like he'd been rejected by the hive-mind.

The theatre really did need to invest in better cameras.

'Oh ho! Here we go!' Ben announced, pointing to the screen with a finger of a *Kit-Kat* that he'd rustled up from somewhere without the others noticing.

Everyone leaned in for a better view as a dark coloured minibus staccatoed into shot. It stopped dead in one of the empty spaces, its nose facing the influencers, its arse end to the camera.

In the distance, over by the doors, the blob's many limbs gathered up its bags.

'This must be it,' Tyler said. He and Sinead both took a note of the timestamp to make it easier to find when they reviewed the footage again later.

The minibus was parked slap bang in the middle of the frame. It was impossible to see anything of the driver, but Logan kept watching, hoping that he'd hop out to help his passengers with their bags.

No such luck. Instead, a door in the back end of the bus unfolded itself upwards, and the influencers all lined up to put their bags in place. Now they were closer to the camera, they were no longer all one creature, and had returned to their individual forms. Denzel Drummond was first to put his bags in place, with the dreadlocked Elizia Shuttleworth going next.

The chef, Bruce Kennedy, was the last to load his bags in. By that point, there was very little room left, and he spent a frustrating thirty or forty frames trying to make room for it, while the others boarded the bus.

Finally, when he'd got his bag in, he stepped back.

The boot was shut in the next frame, and Bruce was ducking in through the minibus's side door.

For the next ten frames, nothing happened, aside from a couple of cars blinking in and out of existence as they passed by.

And then, as if some passing wizard had cast a spell, the minibus vanished, leaving only an empty parking space behind.

'That's it,' Hamza said, once the clip rolled back around to the beginning. 'That's all they've got.'

Logan had been so fixated on the people, that he realised he'd missed an important detail. 'I didn't notice, was the number plate visible?' he asked, sounding annoyed with himself. 'Did anyone get a note of it?'

Tyler looked down at his notebook like it was a bingo card, then looked disappointed when he didn't match a number.

'Forgot, boss. We can wind it back.'

Sinead shot her husband a teasing look, then recited the vehicle's registration out loud. 'SX22 YBL.'

Tyler pulled a face and stuck his tongue out at her like they were children in a playground, then frowned as what she'd said sunk in.

'Hang on. I know that number. I've seen that,' he declared. 'I know that, I'm sure I do.'

'You do,' Logan replied.

His eyebrows were angled steeply downwards, bunching together in a knot above his nose. At first, Tyler thought he was about to erupt, but then realised it wasn't a look of anger, but of confusion.

'Where do I know it from then, boss?' the detective constable ventured.

Logan looked back at the screen. He rubbed at his chin, his fingernails scraping across the salt-and-pepper stubble that shadowed his jaw.

'From my car,' he announced, and his voice was like the sound of boots on frosty gravel. 'That's my number plate.'

Chapter 8

DCI Jack Logan was pacing. This was rarely a good sign.

After the whole number plate thing, he'd barked out a few orders, then gone storming off to his office and slammed the door. The blinds were pulled, but the others could see his bulky shadow passing back and forth behind them, and hear the regular squeaking of the floorboards beneath his feet.

'Think the boss is going to be alright?' Tyler asked, his eyes slowly creeping left and right as he followed the shadow's movements.

'He'll be fine,' Ben said, though there was a note of caution in his reply. 'Whatever's going on, he can handle himself. It's all these other poor buggers we need to be worrying about.' He wheeled around in his chair to face Hamza. 'You heard what Jack said. You got the details yet?'

Hamza rose to his feet, pressing the button that shut down his computer monitor. 'Got the address of the minibus company, sir, aye,' he confirmed. 'It's on the Longman estate, so quicker to walk it than bother with the car. I'll go and see what the story is with that plate.'

'Take Tyler with you. You're no' going over there on your own. If things seem fishy, you call for back-up right away, no messing. That understood?'

Hamza nodded. 'Will do.'

'No worries, boss,' Tyler agreed, reaching for his jacket.

'Good lads. Dave, get the picture of that autograph hunter circulated internally, see if we can get a hit. Doubt he's involved, but he might have seen something.'

'No bother,' the constable confirmed. 'I've also been in touch with the CCTV guys to see if we can track where the minibus went after it left the theatre.'

Ben clapped his hands together then pointed across the room at the PC. Technically, Dave was just there to log any physical evidence that came in, but he'd long since proven himself to be a much more valuable member of the team.

'Christ, we'll make a detective of you yet, son,' the DI declared.

'I bloody hope not,' Dave replied. 'Far too much like hard work, and you have to go out when it's raining.'

He raised a can of Irn Bru in toast to the detective inspector, chugged a few big glugs of it, then turned his attention to his computer.

Ben waved Hamza and Tyler off as they left the Incident Room, then continued issuing instructions.

'Sinead, when you've got the board updated, I want you to get the dog walker brought in,' he said.

'The dog walker, sir? Who found those bodies?'

'Aye.'

The DC's gaze crept to the photos of the missing influencers. 'Should we not be focusing on…?'

Ben drummed his fingers on his desk, studying the pictures that had been laid out across the boards. 'Aye. Probably. But, if that lot are connected to those bodies in some way, then it's quite the coincidence that some fella walking his dog randomly stumbled upon them today of all days.'

Sinead blinked, as all the many implications of this hit her at once. 'You don't think he found them by accident.'

'I think it's statistically unlikely,' Ben told her. 'Could be nothing, of course, but it's no' sitting right down here.'

He patted his stomach, which rumbled in reply. Breakfast had been a long time ago, and it was looking like that *Kit-Kat* he'd snaffled earlier was going to have to last him until dinnertime.

A quick check of Logan's office confirmed that the DCI was still pacing back and forth. He knew Jack well enough to know that, for him to be as rattled as this, something else had to be going on besides the number plate.

Something else for him to worry about, then. It would have to wait its turn.

'Right, you two crack on with that, then,' he instructed.

With a grunt of effort, he got up out of his chair. He drew in a couple of breaths, like the effort of standing had taken it out of him.

'And I suppose I'd better go prepare for the coming of the Gozer.'

–

Logan's office felt small. Stiflingly, restrictively small. He wanted to pace, to burn off some of the adrenaline that had surged through his veins when he'd realised his car registration had been used on that minibus, but he could barely manage four steps in any direction before being forced to turn back on himself.

The number plate had been a message. It had to be. The driver had deliberately pulled into that space, right in the middle of the camera's field of view, the plate in plain sight for anyone watching the footage to see.

Someone was taunting him. The same someone, he suspected, who had sent him that beer mat.

It was too early to be sure, of course, but he knew it in his gut. This was about him. Somehow, this whole thing was all about him.

And eight innocent people were now in danger because of that.

He felt sick, like he'd been spun around in a rickety fair-ground ride.

It was too soon to check in with Geoff Palmer. He should've stressed the importance of it, but he could hardly bump it up the queue when they were dealing with the contents of a mass grave.

Forensic evidence would have to wait. But he was a detective. A damn good one, too, at least if the others were to be believed. He had ways and means other than fingerprints and fibre samples.

He'd have to put in a damn sight more legwork than four paces in each direction. But, right now, that suited him just fine.

Chapter 9

The minibus hire company was less than a ten minute walk from the front door of the Burnett Road station. On a good day, the car might have been quicker, but all the traffic lights on Harbour Road made most journeys a stop-start slog.

Besides, the rain was off, the breeze had a suggestion of late summer warmth to it, and it had been far too long since Tyler'd had a chance to chat freely with the detective sergeant.

'How's it going at Ben's?' he asked, once they were safely across the dual carriageway. They naturally fell into step with each other, and Tyler had to resist the instinct to tuck his hands behind his back as they ambled along.

'Aye, fine. Not bad,' Hamza replied, his gaze fixed on the pavement ahead. 'I think he likes having a bit of company. Although, he's had Moira over to visit a couple of times.'

An image of the sour-faced guardian of the Fort William Police Station's front desk forcibly imprinted itself upon Tyler's mind's eye. She had been a bitter old battle-axe when the detectives had first met her, and despite now being in a relationship with Ben—vague and undefined as that relationship was to the rest of them—she hadn't softened in the slightest. If anything, she appeared to hate them all with even more passion and drive than she used to.

'What, like, an overnight visit?' Tyler asked, some of the colour draining from his face.

Hamza nodded solemnly. 'I, eh, went and checked into a hotel on those nights. No idea if anything was going to happen, but better safe than sorry.'

'God, aye. Can you imagine being in the house if they were going at it?' Tyler asked.

They both tried very hard not to.

'I'd have checked into the hotel, then blinded and deafened myself, just to be doubly sure.'

Hamza laughed at that. It wasn't much—barely a chuckle—but it was more than Tyler had seen him manage in a while.

He took it as an opportunity to ask the big question.

'And, eh, how's it all going with Amira?' he ventured. 'You two managing to work anything out?'

They walked on in silence for several more paces. Tyler was just starting to think that the DS was going to ignore the question completely when Hamza finally shrugged and sighed.

'Nah. Think it's done,' he said, with a weariness that made clear how much he wished it wasn't. 'I mean, how can I trust her again, after…?'

Tyler nodded slowly. 'I get that, mate. It must be hard. What's she saying to it, though?'

'Not much.' Hamza shrugged. 'She was full of apologies to start with. It was a mistake. It should never have happened. All that. But now, she's just, like, I need to get over it. Like it's my fault for still being hurt by it, or whatever.'

'Sounds messed up.'

'Aye. Feels that way,' Hamza agreed. He inhaled deeply, then shook his head. 'But it is what it is. And, I don't know, even though I know it's over, part of me thinks maybe I *should* just forget what happened. Like, I still wish it could just go back to the way it was. Or, you know, better, even. Maybe we could still work it out.'

'Eh, aye. Aye, maybe,' Tyler said, though he sounded doubtful. 'You're still seeing Kamila and everything, though, aye?'

'Oh aye, course! I'm still seeing Kami. I have her a couple of nights a week. She loves it at Ben's. He's great with her. It's like she's got a new grandpa. I think he gets nearly as excited as I do when she's coming round.'

'Well, that's good,' Tyler said. He smiled. 'Mind you, I'd always have pegged him as being good with kids. It's Hoon who shocks me. You should see the twins with him. They go mental when they see him. He pretends he's got no real interest in them, but then you hear them giggling and catch him making faces, or whatever.'

'Who'd have thought it?' Hamza said.

'Aye. He's full of surprises,' Tyler said. A worry line creased his brow. 'Although, I'm pretty sure Cal tried to call me a fuckwit the other day, which wouldn't be an ideal first word.'

Hamza did laugh then. A proper, deep in the belly eruption that brought tears to his eyes. 'Oh! That would be amazing!' he cried.

'Here, come on! It's no' that funny,' Tyler protested, though he was grinning, too.

'No, it is,' Hamza insisted. 'It's definitely that funny. It's the best thing I've heard in weeks. Imagine the first day at nursery. "Who's this you've got with you, kids?" "That's Mummy and that's Fuckwit!"' He thumbed at his eyes, wiping away the tears. 'Oh, man, that's brilliant. Keep me posted on that, will you? The day he calls you a cockless jebend, I think I'm actually going to burst.'

He stopped suddenly, and put a hand on Tyler's shoulder. For the first time in months, despite the stubble and the unkempt look, Tyler fully recognised his friend smiling back at him.

'Cheers, mate. I needed that.' The sergeant gave the DC's shoulder a squeeze, then straightened his collar and fixed his tie. 'Now, game faces on,' he said, nodding ahead to where a row of vans and minibuses stood parked outside a squat office building. 'And let's go find out what the hell is going on here.'

–

'Benjamin Forde. Long time no see. How the devil are you?'

Ben smiled and nodded a welcome to the man with the white shirt and shiny coat buttons as he marched stiffly along the corridor.

'Had better days, I'll be honest,' Ben replied, then he and Detective Superintendent Gordon MacKenzie shook hands by the open door of what was going to be the Gozer's temporary base of operations in Inverness.

'I can well imagine,' MacKenzie said. 'You're looking well, though.'

Ben doubted that very much. It had been years since he'd last seen the Detective Superintendent, and he was only too aware of his many physical failings since then.

Before he could say as much, the Gozer jerked his head towards the door beside them. 'This me, is it?'

'Aye. Aye, this was—is—Detective Superintendent Mitchell's office. I'm not sure where she's set up, or what she's doing at the minute, but I'm sure she'll want to check in with you.'

'No doubt, no doubt. And Jack?' the Gozer looked past the DI along the corridor. 'He around?'

Ben nodded. 'Aye. He's around. Just tied up with something at the moment. Wanted me to roll out the welcome mat.'

'Right. Good.' MacKenzie sniffed and nodded, like he was pleased by how things were going so far. 'I'll go get settled in, then let's bring the team together and I'll introduce myself. I want everyone to know that I'm not here to get in anyone's way, or to make anyone's life more difficult. I'm here to shoulder some of the burden, not add to it. I want to reduce their workload as much as I possibly can.'

'I'm sure they'll all be pleased to hear that, sir.'

'Good stuff!' the Gozer declared. He started to head into the office, then stopped. 'Oh, and Ben?'

'Sir?'

'Before you do anything else, how about you do me a favour and fetch me a coffee? I'm gasping. And maybe a wee sandwich or something, if there's one going. Ham, or egg, or whatever. Nothing fancy.'

Ben managed to scrounge up a smile. So much for reducing his workload.

'Of course, sir,' he said. 'I'll see what I can do.'

Chapter 10

Michael Muggeridge, owner and manager of Muggeridge's Minibuses, was shiteing himself. He was shiteing himself over the intercom when the secretary buzzed through to tell him the detectives were here. He was shiteing himself when he emerged, cowed and blinking, from his office to beckon them in. And, he was still shiteing himself when Hamza and Tyler sat on the seats on the opposite side of the flimsy desk to his.

He was short—five foot two or three—but drastically over-weight, so he looked a bit compressed, like he was on a TV screen that was set to the wrong aspect ratio.

Upon seeing him Tyler's first thought had been, 'Holy shit, he's a Hobbit!' but he had drawn on all his years of police training and experience to stop himself from saying as much out loud.

Instead, he and Hamza had introduced themselves, politely declined the offer of tea, coffee, or 'something stronger,' then followed him into his office.

It was definitely a manager's office, rather than merely an owner's. It felt like the nerve centre of the whole operation, with multiple calendars pinned up on the walls, stacks of paper-work on every flat surface, and colourful sticky notes dotted around the room like a flutter of butterflies had all momentarily stopped for a breather.

A load of receipts were impaled on an old-style metal spike. A wall-mounted map of Inverness had been stuck with a rainbow of plastic-headed pins. There were so many old holes in the map that the centre of the city had almost been obliterated, and the airport was in bad shape, too.

He might be oddly proportioned and oozing a glossy film of flop sweat from every pore in his body, but it was clear that Michael Muggeridge was a grafter.

'You sure I can't get you anything?' he asked for the third time since the detectives had arrived. 'There's a machine. Does tea, coffee—few different kinds—hot chocolate...'

'We're OK, thanks,' Hamza said.

'Soup! It does tomato soup. It's not great, and it's sometimes a bit chocolatey, depending on who had what last, but I can get you one.'

He started to rise back out of his seat again, then looked disappointed when the detectives assured him they were fine on the soup front.

Michael forced a smile as he sat down again. He rubbed his sweaty hands so forcefully on his nylon trousers that there was a faint crackle of electrical discharge.

'So, um, how is it that I can help you, exactly?' he asked. He cleared his throat. 'Because, you know, whatever you need. Just say. Because... Because...'

He lunged sharply forwards, snatched up a business card from the holder on his desk, then grinned like a lunatic as he showed them the message printed beneath the minibus firm's logo.

We care.

'Uh?' he uttered, nodding to them both, the manic leer still fixed in place.

'Eh, aye. That's good. Glad to hear it,' Tyler said, and Hamza could tell immediately from his tone that the detective constable was struggling not to laugh.

'It's true. That's why it's on the card,' Michael told them. 'I came up with that myself. A company needs a motto.' He sat back again. 'Ideally, I wanted something rhyming, but there's not a lot rhymes with 'Muggeridge' except 'buggerage.' That's an actual word, too. I looked it up. Apparently it's the supplementary charge that prostitutes make for doing it up the bahookie.' His lips and gums made wet, sticky sounds. He swallowed noisily. 'Which isn't really the, you know… From a branding perspective, it's not…'

He dabbed at his shiny brow with his forearm, using the sleeve to mop up the slick of sweat.

'Sorry, I don't know why I said that. That's probably not really any concern of…' He smiled desperately. 'Anyway, how can I help?'

'We've got a query about the pick-up you made at Eden Court on Saturday afternoon,' Hamza told him, doing everyone a favour by glossing over the last few moments of the conversation.

Michael pressed both index fingers together in front of his mouth, interlocking the others. He looked upwards, like he was consulting a diary in his head. 'Eden Court. Saturday afternoon.' He nodded, just once. 'Eight people for the airport. Multiple bags. Pre-booked by a convention. They asked for a discount in return for an advert in the print programme, I think. But we don't do that sort of thing. We've got more than enough business to keep us busy.'

Muggeridge blinked, like he was emerging from some deep hypnotic trance, and immediately went back to rubbing his clammy hands on his thighs.

'Is that the booking you mean?' he asked, slightly breathlessly, like the effort of recalling the details had taken a physical toll.

'Sounds very much like it, aye,' Hamza confirmed. 'We were hoping you could tell us who was driving? Also, we're going to need to get a look at the vehicle.'

'Driving?' Michael frowned. 'No one was driving.'

Hamza and Tyler exchanged glances.

'How d'you mean?' Tyler asked. 'It's not one of them self-driving things, is it? They're not road legal.' He stole another look at the sergeant. 'Are they?'

'No, no, I don't mean that. Sorry,' Michael said, stumbling over his words in his rush to get them out. He tugged on his shirt, the pale blue material visibly darkening in patches as his sweat soaked through. 'I meant we didn't send a vehicle.'

'What do you mean?' Hamza asked.

'The booking. It was cancelled.'

Both detectives sat forward in their chairs. 'Cancelled?' Tyler echoed. 'When?'

Michael's eyes flitted upwards again, but it didn't take him long to retrieve the information this time. 'Saturday morning. We got a call to say it wasn't going to be needed. I told them they were within the twenty-four hour no refund period, and they said that was fine.'

Tyler opened his notebook. 'They? Who did you speak to?'

'Uh, I'm not sure. I didn't get a name.'

'Male? Female?'

'Male. A man.'

'Had you spoken to them before?' Hamza asked.

Michael squirmed in his chair and popped a button to loosen the collar of his shirt. 'Um, well, no. The booking was done through the website, so I hadn't actually spoken to anyone from the company. But he had the booking reference. He knew the date and time, the destination, all of it. I just assumed... Why would I think otherwise?' He swallowed. 'Why? What's the matter? What's this about, anyway?'

'It's just background for a case we're working on,' Hamza assured him. 'So, you didn't send a bus to Eden Court on Saturday night?'

'No.'

'And nobody else here could have just taken one? None of the drivers?'

Michael looked wounded by the suggestion. 'No! We're a family. No one would think of moonlighting! There's an unbreakable circle of trust here.' He sniffed. 'And besides, all the vehicles have hidden trackers on them. If they'd gone anywhere,

I'd know about it. But, please don't mention that to the drivers, though. They'll lose their shit.' He glanced warily at the door, before turning his attention back to the detectives. 'I can send you the route history of the vehicles, if you like?'

'That would be useful,' Hamza told him. 'Does your phone system keep a note of incoming numbers?'

'Uh, yes. Normally. It was withheld, though,' Michael said. He winced, like this was his fault. 'Sorry.'

'What about the call itself?' Tyler pressed. 'Anything else you can tell us about that? Anything about the voice, or…?'

Muggeridge looked upwards again, deferring the question to some other part of his brain that only his eyes seemed able to access.

'Not really. He sounded a bit older, maybe? Forties, fifties?'

'Accent?'

The manager wrinkled his nose. 'Scottish? Sort of generic Scottish, I suppose. Couldn't really place it, though I wasn't actively trying to. Maybe Glasgow? I was more worried about charging their credit card before they could put a block on the payment. You'd be amazed at the lengths some people will go to avoid paying a bill.'

Given his current levels of personal debt, Tyler chose not to pass comment on that, and instead steered them back onto the subject of the caller.

'Nothing else you can tell us? Speech impediments, background noise, any specific words he used that seemed unusual or out of place?'

'No. No, nothing like that,' Muggeridge said, then his brow creased. 'Although, there was one thing that struck me as a bit odd.' He shook his head, dismissing the thought. 'But it was nothing, really.'

'Please,' Hamza said, urging him to continue.

'Well, it might just have seemed strange to me, because I'm not really a fan of football, or rugby, or… well, any sport at all, really. If I was, I probably wouldn't even have noticed.'

'What was it?' Tyler asked. 'What did he say?'

'It was right before he hung up,' Michael replied. 'It was the last thing he said before he put the phone down.'

Tyler's pen sat poised above the paper. Hamza's chair gave the faintest of creaks as he shifted himself forward another half inch.

'He told me that he hoped I enjoyed the game, and that he'd been looking forward to it for a long time.' Michael shrugged. 'Like I say, it's probably nothing.' The nervous smile that had been plastered on his face since the detectives' arrival now fell away. 'But, I don't know. Something about the way he said it made me glad to be off the call.'

–

Logan sat hunched over his desk, notebook open, with the intention of making a list of names that might have sent him that beermat. Unfortunately, he'd only been able to come up with one.

It sat there like a scar on the paper. A festering wound across the page.

Shuggie Cowan.

Cowan was a figure from Logan's past, both recent and distant. Once, his name had been known and feared all across the central belt. Now, although he still had his hand in a few dodgy dealings, he was little more than a relic—an old-school Glasgow gangster in a world that had long since moved on.

Logan wasn't even sure if Cowan knew his secret. He'd know some of it, no doubt. He'd know what had happened. But did he know about Logan's involvement? Did he know what Jack had done?

Surely, if he did, he'd have done something about it before now? Why would he wait until he was in his dotage to act? Besides, he had a family now—a daughter and a grandchild. In as much as a man like Shuggie ever could, he was trying to do what was right by them. From what Logan had heard, Cowan was trying to be a better man.

If he had known the truth all along, it made no sense for him to target Logan now. Not if he'd been harbouring the grudge for thirty years.

No. It couldn't be Shuggie. They'd had plenty of run-ins when Logan was stationed in Glasgow, and if Cowan thought he had any leverage on the detective, he'd have used it long ago.

Besides, Cowan would never pull a stunt like this with the influencers. No doubt he was a killer—though they'd never been able to pin a conviction on him—but everything he'd done had been about building and securing his empire. It had been business to him, nothing more.

Kidnapping and murdering innocent people just wasn't his style, and Logan would've been surprised if he'd ever heard of Instagram, much less figured out how to use it.

It could be worth talking to the gangster to see if he could offer any insight, but that might just open up a whole other can of worms. For now, Logan scored a line through his name, reducing his list of one back down to zero.

There was one other possibility, but it was a stretch. More of a stretch than Cowan, even.

He had only told one other person what had happened that night—a uniformed sergeant working the front desk of the police station he'd randomly stumbled into. He'd been nine or ten years older than Logan himself—pushing thirty, maybe—and had seemed weary of the job, or of the world in general.

Whatever, he'd half-heartedly jotted down the statement, taken Logan's details, then promised to pass it all on to someone in CID.

Logan had shuffled out again in a daze, and had never heard anything more about it. No one had ever followed up.

Even after his confession.

A knock at his door made him flip the notebook closed. He looked up just as the door was opened a few inches and Ben stuck his head through the narrow gap.

'Sorry to barge in, Jack…' The DI stopped when he saw a stack of paperwork lying scattered on the floor in front of the desk. He raised a quizzical eyebrow. 'Everything OK?'

'Fine. Just knocked it over when I was looking for a pen. Meant to pick it up,' Logan said, his gruffness hiding a suggestion of embarrassment. 'What's up?'

Ben regarded the mess on the floor again, then continued. 'Eh, aye. Hamza and Tyler are on their way back, and the Gozer is keen to speak to everyone together.'

'Christ, is he here already?' Logan checked his watch. 'What did he do, teleport?'

'Helicopter, apparently,' Ben said. 'He told me all about it while he was drinking the coffee he had me go and make for him.' There was a slight note of caffeinated bitterness in the DI's tone. 'But don't worry, he tells me he's not going to add to our workload, or anything like that. God forbid.'

'Sorry,' Logan said. 'I should've been there. I'll keep him in check. He'll just be doing that thing where he tries to assert his authority. If he tries it again, tell him to get up off his arse and find the tea room.'

Ben let out a little snort of laughter. 'I think I'll maybe kick that one up the chain of command to you, if that's alright?'

'Aye, happy to do it,' Logan assured him. He tried very hard not to look down at the notebook that he realised he was pinning beneath the weight of a splayed hand. 'Is he through there now?'

'No, he's still making himself at home in Mitchell's office. I think he wants to make a grand entrance when we're all gathered waiting.'

Logan nodded. 'Sounds like him, right enough. Give me a shout when Hamza and Tyler are back, and I'll come through and join you.'

Ben's gaze locked on the notebook for a moment, and on the hand pressing down on it. From there, it shifted to the scattered paperwork on the floor.

When he met the DCI's eye again, there was a slightly puzzled look on his face, but whatever questions were troubling him, he decided not to ask them.

'Eh, aye. No bother, Jack. Will do,' he said.

Then, he slipped out of the room, closed the door behind him, and left Logan alone with his list of no names.

Chapter 11

Detective Superintendent MacKenzie stopped outside the Incident Room long enough to straighten his tie and huff a quick breath into his hand to make sure it didn't smell. There was a hint of egg in there from his sandwich, so he took a packet of Polos from his pocket, popped one in his mouth, then circulated it for a few seconds until it had a chance to work its minty magic.

That done, he crunched it, swallowed the debris, and marched straight on into the room like he was its rightful owner.

'Afternoon, lady and gentlemen,' he announced, before being silenced by a hissed *shhh* from DCI Logan.

Jack stood with the rest of his team, gathered in a semi-circle around one of the computers. The flickering lights of a moving image played across their stern, sombre faces.

Not one of them had so much as glanced in the Gozer's direction. He didn't care, though. All thoughts of grand entrances and big speeches had died away when he'd seen their faces.

He knew those looks. He'd seen them on hundreds of coppers' faces before, his own included.

'What is it? What's happened?' he asked, striding over to join them. 'What are we looking at?'

He took up a spot at the back of the group, where his height advantage let him see the screen over the top of DI Forde's head. There were four different browser windows open, each one taking up a quarter of the available monitor space.

A video played in each window. The footage was in colour, but it was grainy and muted, like something from an old VHS video nasty.

'Is this…?' He pointed to the screen. 'What is this? Is this to do with the case?'

'Aye,' Logan muttered, not taking his eyes off the monitor. 'That's four of the missing people.'

In each of the browser windows, different influencers were giving what could only be described as some sort of perform-ance. The Gozer checked the names against the photos on the Big Boards, familiarising himself with who was who.

Denzel Drummond, who he already knew to be Mitchell's son, was alternating between star jumps and push-ups. There was no sound on the footage, but subtitles appeared every time his mouth moved, urging the viewers to, 'Do five more,' or to 'Move that lardy ass!'

In the next window, Matthew Broderick, the seventeen-year-old, was sitting on the floor, his thumbs frantically tapping away at an imaginary video game controller he was pretending to clutch in both hands. Tears rolled down his cheeks as he stared directly ahead, presumably at where a TV screen would usually be.

Just as with the other clips, there was no soundtrack on his video, just an eerie, ringing silence.

'What the hell are they doing?' the Gozer asked.

Logan drew a breath in through his nose. 'The shite they usually do,' he said. 'The bastard's making them perform.'

'Started five minutes ago,' Hamza added. He was sitting in front of the computer in case of any technical issues. 'Just these four. The other four have scheduled livestreams set for just under an hour from now.'

MacKenzie looked down at the top of the sergeant's head. 'What are you saying? This is live? This is happening now?'

Hamza indicated the timestamps at the bottom of each video. 'Looks like it.'

The Gozer checked the time against his watch. 'Bloody hell.'

On the bottom half of the screen, a tearful Kelly Wynne was miming opening a small box. Her lips moved, and subtitles appeared one word at a time.

'Oh! Who do we have to pay?'

'What does that mean?' Ben asked.

'I think it's meant to be "Who do we have today?"' Hamza explained. 'Looks like automatic real time subtitles, so if she's not speaking clearly enough, it takes a guess.'

Hands shaking, Kelly pretended to pull an invisible toy from the make-believe box. Despite the sobs that were choking her, she made a valiant attempt to appear delighted by her imaginary haul.

'Look, it's a sparkly Rainbow Dash,' the text at the bottom of the screen declared. Kelly tried to look at the camera, but her eyes kept darting to whoever was holding it, then hurriedly looking away again. 'Isn't she pretty with her shiny hair?'

'The hell's a Rainbow Dash?' Logan asked.

'It a My Little Pony, boss,' Tyler told him without a moment's hesitation. He cleared his throat and grimaced. Everyone knew better than to pass comment now, but he had no doubt that his cartoon pony knowledge would come back to haunt him.

The Gozer pointed a spindly finger at the screen. 'What are those numbers in the corners of the videos there?'

Ben rolled his eyes, as if this should've been obvious. 'Those are the viewing figures. It's the number of people watching,' he said, repeating almost word for word what Hamza had patiently explained to him just a few moments before.

'Jesus Christ! Seriously?' the Gozer ran a hand backwards across his balding head—a muscle memory from when he used to have hair. 'That's hundreds of thousands of people. And they're all watching this? They're all watching this live?'

Logan nodded. 'It would seem so, aye.'

'We need to get it pulled! Why haven't we got this pulled yet?'

'We're trying. It's working its way through the Instagram corporation now, or whoever the hell it is.'

'Meta, sir,' Hamza told him. 'They own Facebook and Threads, too.'

Logan just shrugged at this information, then turned to the Detective Superintendent beside him. 'If you want to make yourself useful, sir, you could help that along.'

The Gozer shot him a warning look, but there was no real bite to it. Instead, he stole a quick glance at the bottom right browser window, where a pink-haired woman dressed like a Japanese schoolgirl was dancing on the spot while trying desperately to smile for the camera. He gave a quick shake of his head when he saw the number of people tuning in for the show, then locked eyes with Logan.

'Might as well do something to earn my keep,' he said. 'Leave it with me. I'll get this taken down before the next batch goes live.'

'You've got forty-eight minutes,' Logan told him, turning back to the screen. 'Good luck.'

–

The four livestreams ended without fanfare or ceremony. They all just cut off at the same time while the influencers were midway through whatever actions they had either chosen, or were being forced to perform.

At first, the detectives assumed that the Gozer had managed to get them pulled, but the accounts were still active, and the livestream could be rewatched from the start. A quick check in with the Detective Superintendent revealed he was on the phone, and his frustrated tone made clear that he wasn't any closer to achieving his aim.

At their peak, a couple of the influencers—the dancing Natalie Womack and the gamer, Matthew Broderick—had hit over half a million viewers. Likes, and loves, and laughing emojis had rained down on all four influencers as those watching had shared if not their opinions, then at least their enthusiasm.

Mercifully, commenting had been turned off. Just as well. Logan's thoughts on the human race were low enough at the best of times without the additional insight that several thousand rabid internet commentators would undoubtedly afford him.

'It could still all be a stunt,' Sinead ventured as she stood in front of the adjoining Big Boards. 'The publicity they're getting online is huge, and as soon as the press jumps on it, it's going to go through the roof. Some of them are up literally millions of followers in a matter of hours.'

'I hope you're right,' Logan replied. 'Then, I'll take great pleasure in live-streaming their arrest and incarceration. But, for now, we need to assume this isn't a set-up and work on the basis that it's real. That some bastard—or, more likely, some bastards—have got these people locked up.'

'Thirty minutes until the next streams go live,' Hamza announced. He was still sitting at his computer, flicking through browser windows, keeping an eye open for any new developments.

It was Tyler who asked the question that had been starting to niggle away at Logan, too.

'What happens then? What happens when all eight of them are done?'

Nobody answered, because nobody knew. There had been no explanation offered at the start of those first four broadcasts that clarified what was happening. They had just opened on the four influencers already acting out their various roles, the camera peering in at them through gaps in the metal meshes that caged them in, like some sort of sinister voyeur.

They were being made to perform, that much was clear. But why? Why abduct eight social media stars then stream them doing the very things that made them famous? What was the point?

Like it or not, the only thing that made sense right now was the publicity angle. And yet, Logan couldn't bring himself to believe it was that. Not because he didn't think anyone would sink so low—that part wouldn't surprise him—but because of the connections to the previous case.

Eight bodies.

Eight abductees.

A New Player Has Entered the Game.

He could buy the idea that the influencers had set up their kidnappings to gain more social media clout, but he didn't peg any of them as blackmailing serial killers. Not even the middle-aged looking woman who spent her days playing with toys.

And then, there was Denzel Drummond. Was it just coincidence that he was Det Supt Mitchell's son? With that beer mat and the number plate, someone was clearly trying to get at Logan. Were they targeting Mitchell, too? Was she more involved in all this than they currently suspected?

And if two of them were in the crosshairs, would the rest of the team be far behind?

The doors were thrown open before Jack could dwell too much more on it all. The Gozer stormed in, and from the look on his face it was clear things had not gone to plan.

'Right, they're a shower of useless arseholes,' he announced, his voice rolling around the room like a peal of thunder. 'Whole lot of them. It's like shouting into a bloody black hole. I'm passing it up the chain. We'll get the government involved, if needs be.'

Logan checked the clock on the wall. 'But not in the next twenty-six minutes.'

MacKenzie ran out of steam a bit. He sighed and slowly shook his head. 'No. Unlikely to be by then. But,' he said, in a way that suggested he had a consolation prize to offer, 'I spoke to CID, and they have a digital security expert they've consulted with before. Very useful, clued-up guy, with a lot of experience. I'm going to bring him in to consult.'

'We've got Hamza. He's our tech guy,' Logan said.

The Gozer smiled kindly, like he was appreciating the artistic efforts of a four-year-old child. 'That's great. And I'm sure

DS Khaled has a lot of useful knowledge. But this man is an accredited expert. Maybe, if he's willing, he'll let DS Khaled work closely alongside him. Two heads are better than one, after all.'

Logan opened his mouth to object, but Hamza got in first.

'That's great, sir. We could end up needing all the help we can get on this.'

The Gozer's smile widened. He pointed to the sergeant and nodded to Logan. 'See, Jack? He gets it. It's not about the individuals, it's about us all doing our bit for the team. That's how we're going to get these people home.'

Logan didn't enjoy being lectured to, but he voiced his agreement through gritted teeth. 'Of course, sir. That's all any of us wants.'

'Good! I'm glad we're on the same page. And speaking of doing our bit for the team…'

To Ben's surprise, the Detective Superintendent picked the DI's mug up off his desk, then reached for the one on Tyler's.

'I suppose it's my turn on the tea run.'

Chapter 12

Shona Maguire was ninety percent certain that this wasn't going to kill her.

Well, maybe eighty-five.

Sure, it was eight months out of date, and had been lurking at the back of the cupboard above her desk for almost two years, but when it came to Pot Noodles, she was made of stern stuff.

She remembered buying the special Christmas edition flavour from Asda, and being very excited at the thought of trying it. That had been back in the winter of 2022, and she'd almost immediately forgotten all about it.

While late summer didn't feel like the perfect time to be tucking into a novelty Christmas-themed flavour of anything, she had nothing else stashed away in the cupboard, and it was going to be a long time before she was able to pack up for the day.

The first of the bodies had been brought in half an hour earlier. It was a tranche of three, with a promise of five more still to come. She wouldn't get through them all today, of course. Each one would take her two or three hours, and longer still to write up her preliminary reports. The lab work would take days, if she was lucky, months if she wasn't.

Of course, the condition of the bodies she was dealing with meant everything could drag on much longer. With eight of them to get through, she was looking at four or five days at a minimum, and long days, at that.

It all would've been quicker, of course, had she still had Neville around to assist. She'd been resistant to being given an assistant to begin with, but had come around to the idea when he'd proven himself to be a capable and useful right hand man.

Unfortunately, one of the things he'd got up to with that right hand had got him both sacked and arrested. And, thanks to Olivia posting a video of the incident online, had briefly turned him into a viral internet meme.

So, once again, Shona was flying solo.

She peeled the lid off the Pot Noodle and gave it an experimental sniff. It smelled fine. Not great—but then, they never smelled *great*—but perfectly acceptable, and certainly not poisonous.

Or not *too* poisonous, anyway.

In fact, now that she'd got a good whiff of it, she was quite excited by the prospect of getting stuck in. She filled the kettle, slotted it into its base, then clicked it on to boil.

While she waited, she took out her phone and tapped out a text message to Olivia, asking how she was getting on. It was after lunchtime now, so even fifteen-year-olds would generally be up and out of bed by this time.

Still, Olivia tended to take her time replying, so Shona returned her mobile to her desk, and waited impatiently for the kettle to boil.

A moment later, the phone rang, and the pathologist was surprised to see Olivia's name appear on screen. The girl rarely, if ever, chose to call. The thought of using a telephone for its principal purpose always seemed to disgust and horrify her. Why talk when you could text?

And so, Shona felt a note of trepidation when she tapped the icon to answer.

'Hey! You OK? What's up?' she asked, the words coming out so quickly they formed one short but continuous sentence. 'Everything alright?'

There was silence from the other end.

No, not silence. Not quite. Shona could hear what sounded like wind blowing—the faint whistling and low howling of distant gale force gusts.

'Olivia?' she said. Beside her, the water in the kettle rolled towards the boil. 'Hello? Can you hear me?'

There was a click from down the line. For a second, maybe more, Shona thought the call had been disconnected, but then Olivia's voice came on, and the shrill echo of Taggart barking in the background.

'Alright, yes, shut up!' the girl was saying.

'Hello? Olivia! Is everything OK?'

'Sorry, phone was still connected to my earphones,' Olivia explained. 'Had to switch it in the settings.'

Shona looked down at her hand and realised she had been clutching a fork like a weapon, ready to stab some imagined enemy. She dropped it onto her desk, and the colour returned to her knuckles.

'Are you OK? What's wrong?'

'Nothing,' Olivia said. 'Well, nothing really.'

Shona lowered herself onto her chair. 'The 'really' bit has me worried. What's happened? Is it Taggart? Why was he barking?'

'Don't know. He's being weird,' Olivia replied. 'He went mental at a guy delivering a parcel earlier.'

'He always goes mental at guys delivering parcels, to be fair,' Shona said.

'That's true. But the shed door was open earlier. We went and looked—'

'You went and looked?' Shona cried. 'You shouldn't have! There could have been someone in there!'

Olivia tutted. 'I had a knife.'

'Oh, you had a knife! Great! So, if there was someone in there, at least you could have stabbed them to death!'

Olivia either missed the sarcasm or, more likely, chose to ignore it. 'Yeah, exactly. But it was fine, there wasn't anyone there. But, it seems to have put Tag on edge, though. He keeps sniffing about, running to the doors, going up on the couch to check the windows and stuff like that.'

'Have you locked the doors?'

'Yeah. And there's no one about, or anything. Like, no one I can see. I just really wanted to know if there's anything I should do to calm him down?'

The kettle clicked off. Shona picked it up and sloshed some of the boiling water into the plastic pot beside her. 'Have you tried feeding him?'

'Yeah, he scoffed it all,' Olivia replied. 'Then went right back to pacing around. He keeps barking at the door, then goes to the window and growls.'

Shona returned the kettle to the base. Such behaviour from Taggart wasn't entirely unusual. He spent most of his days in close proximity to detectives and murder suspects, and he went through occasional spells of being a bit highly strung. It usually passed in a day or two.

'Norma down the road just got that wee terrier from a rescue centre. She's probably just on heat,' Shona said. 'Aye, the dog I mean, not Norma. That'll have sent him all wrong.'

'Yeah. Yeah, that's probably it,' Olivia agreed, though she didn't sound all the way convinced. It wasn't like the girl to panic, and even less like her to show it. She was putting a front on now, but the fact she had called meant she was worried.

'But, listen, I'm going to have Jack send someone round,' Shona assured her. 'They'll probably be in uniform, or they'll be someone you know. If it's anyone else, don't answer the door, and call Jack right away. You've got his number?'

'Yeah. I've got it,' Olivia confirmed.

'Good. It'll be fine. If you want to calm Taggart down, you could try putting on *Paw Patrol*.'

She could almost hear the confusion on Olivia's face. '*Paw Patrol*? Like, the cartoon?'

'The cartoon, yeah. It has a weirdly calming effect on him. He likes Chase, the police dog. There's a load recorded on the Sky box.'

'I wondered why they were on there,' Olivia said. 'Thought maybe Jack was dead into it.'

Shona smiled. 'He is, but don't tell him I said that or he'll kill me.'

Olivia laughed, and Shona heard some of her nervous tension melt away. '*Paw Patrol*, doors locked, phone the big man if any weirdoes turn up. Got it.'

'Good. You sure you're OK, though?'

'I'm fine. I've got Tag to protect me,' Olivia said. Her smirk was audible, even over the airwaves. 'And, if it comes to it, I've still got that big knife…'

Chapter 13

Logan stood in the middle of the Incident Room with his phone to his ear. He had a finger raised to silence Tyler, despite the fact that the detective constable hadn't been about to say anything. Past experience told Logan that it was better to be safe than sorry.

'And you're sure she's OK?' he asked. 'It's tricky for me to get away, but if she needs...'

He listened to the response from the other end, then nodded.

'Aye. No bother. I'll get Uniform to check it out. Like you say, it's probably nothing. Weird about the shed, though.' He shook his head. 'No, it wouldn't have been locked. Never bothered. Nothing worth nicking, so if someone broke in it'd cost more to fix the door than to replace anything. The bolt should've been shut, though, so doubt it was the wind.'

'Everything alright, boss?' Tyler whispered, forcing Logan to hold his finger up higher, and closer to the DC's face.

'Aye. No, I'll send someone now, and I'll swing by if I can,' he said into the phone. 'You got an idea when you'll have done the...?' He listened to the reply, then nodded. 'Aye. Well, once you've got anything, let me know. If I don't see you before then, I'll see you at home.'

He looked over to the Big Boards, and to the row of faces plastered across them.

'Eventually,' he added. Then, after saying his goodbyes, he ended the call.

'Everything alright, boss?' Tyler repeated, before the DCI even had a chance to return the mobile to his pocket.

'Aye. Think so,' Logan said. 'Shona thinks Olivia's a bit freaked out. Some guy was at the house, and the shed was open.'

'Jesus. What guy?'

'It was just a delivery by the sounds of it,' Logan said, then he blinked at the force of the thought that hit him.

Shona had mentioned a parcel had been dropped off, but hadn't told him who it had been for.

He became dimly aware that Tyler was talking to him, and forced himself to pay attention.

'Sorry, what?'

The DC hesitated. 'Uh, I was just asking if you wanted me to go round?' Tyler asked. 'Check it all out, sort of thing?'

Logan shook his head. 'I need you here. But get Uniform to go past and check in on her, will you?'

He looked around the room. The Gozer had returned to his borrowed office, and the rest of the team was tied up with various tasks. Nobody appeared to be listening, but Logan still felt the need to lower his voice and lean a little closer to the detective constable.

'The parcel that arrived. Get them to ask who it's for. If it's for me, tell them to bag it up and bring it here. Straight here.'

'Bag it up? How come, boss?'

'Doesn't matter. Just have them do it. Understood?'

Despite his obvious confusion, Tyler nodded. 'Got it, boss.'

'Right. Good.' He caught Tyler's arm before the DC could leave to carry out his orders. 'And, Tyler?'

'Boss?'

'This stays between us for now.'

Tyler was used to being on the receiving end of warning looks from the DCI, but this one screamed at him like an air raid siren.

'Sure, boss,' he said. 'No problem. Leave it with me.'

He hurried out of the room to make the call. Sinead glanced over from the boards as he left, but, otherwise, nobody paid the slightest bit of attention.

Logan checked the time. Less than fifteen minutes until the other four livestreams were due to start. Despite the Gozer having bumped it up the chain of command, there had been no word yet on getting the accounts shut down.

He checked in with Hamza to make sure the situation hadn't changed.

'Not yet, sir, no. Still up and scheduled,' the sergeant replied. He adjusted himself in his seat. 'But, actually, I was thinking... Should we be shutting them down?'

'How do you mean?'

'Well, it's just... They're all we've got, aren't they? They're the only window we have into what's actually happening to those people. Aye, it's bloody horrible, and whoever's using them to put on a show is sick, obviously, but...'

His eyes darted to the screen, and the four browser windows open on it, with four different timers counting down towards zero.

'What if the show's what it's all about?' Hamza wondered aloud. 'What if, if there's no audience, he's got no more use for them?'

Logan ran a hand up and down his face a few times like he was trying to wipe off a cobweb.

That done, he stared at Hamza for a few moments, regarded the four browser windows on the screen, and muttered an exasperated, 'Fuck.'

'Sorry, sir,' the sergeant offered. 'Just thought I should throw that out there.'

'Aye. Good. Thanks,' Logan said, though he sounded quite a long way away from being grateful.

He studied the screen again. His mind was racing, the cogs whirring around, but not a lot seemed to be happening. Normally, he was quick to make decisions, for better or worse.

Now, though, he had no idea what the best course of action was. Should he keep trying to get these accounts shut down, or do whatever was necessary to ensure they stayed up? Which

87

move was the right one? Which choice would save the most lives?

He realised, to his horror, that he had absolutely no idea.

'OK! Two things!'

The shout from Dave Donaldson's desk provided a welcome distraction. The constable had a hand raised above his head, two fingers extended in a peace sign, which he dropped, one at a time, as he made his announcements.

'First up, I spoke to the organisers of the convention thing. They don't know anything about cancelling the minibus. Wasn't them, they say. The boss is on her way over here now. Says she has some information that she didn't want to tell us over the phone.'

Sinead's eyebrows shot up. Logan pointed to her, indicating she could deal with the interview.

'Second, and saving the bigger news for last, I got bored while on hold and started scrolling back through old videos on some of the victims,' Dave said. He realised his arm was still held aloft, and brought it back down to where his computer mouse sat waiting. 'And this one is worth a watch.'

Everyone made their way over to his desk, Ben grumbling and limping slightly on a stiff hip.

'We need a big bloody telly to show all this stuff, so we're not all gathering around a wee screen every time something happens.'

'That's actually a great idea, sir,' Hamza said.

Ben looked surprised. 'Is it? Can we do that?' He jiggled a finger vaguely in the direction of Dave's screen. 'Can we get that stuff on a TV?'

'We could cast it,' Hamza said.

Ben's raised eyebrows crashed back down again. 'Is that a yes or a no, son?'

'It's a yes, sir. Sorry. It's possible.'

'Get it sorted,' Logan instructed. He shuffled into position behind Dave's seat. 'But let's watch this one here, first.'

'It's Matthew Broderick,' Dave told them. 'Goes by the name Matty B on Twitch.'

'Which is…?' Ben asked.

'It's a streaming site for gamers.'

'Which is…?' Ben asked again.

'Basically, it's a video streaming site where people play games and talk a load of old bollocks at the same time. It shows the game footage, and the person playing,' Dave explained. He answered Ben's question before the DI could ask it. 'And yes, people do watch that shite.'

Ben's puckered expression did not look happy about that fact, but he chose not to say anything more. Instead, he crossed his arms and watched the screen as Dave hovered the mouse pointed over the play button.

'Right, he's playing Fortnite, which is your standard Battle Royale shooting game, obviously.'

Sinead tutted. 'God, not Fortnite. Harris was obsessed with this for about two years.'

'He's not the only one,' Dave said, indicating where a counter on screen revealed that over two million viewers had watched the video, either during the original livestream, or in the six months since it went live.

'Good God,' the detective constable remarked.

'I'll be honest, he's an unpleasant little fucker,' Dave said. 'Makes a lot of jokes about immigrants, some pretty rapey stuff about female streamers, and he seems to think anything that isn't actively celebrating straight white blokes is 'woke A.F.' '

'A.F?' Ben asked.

'As fuck,' Dave clarified. 'But he only ever uses the initials.'

'Maybe his mum'll give him a row if he actually swears,' Sinead suggested, and Dave laughed at the thought.

'Aye, maybe.'

'What is it we're meant to be looking at?' Logan's tone was even more gruff and impatient than usual. It silenced the rest of the team, and prompted Dave to turn back to his screen.

'Right, aye. Here we go. I've cued it up to about thirty seconds before. Watch this.'

He clicked the mouse button and the footage on screen began to play.

Most of the video window was taken up by the game Matthew was playing. An irritatingly colourful character was running through a field with a cartoonishly large sniper rifle nestled in its arms.

Matthew himself could be seen in a much smaller box tucked away in the bottom right corner. He sat in a low gaming chair, giant blue headphones over his ears, and a microphone hanging down into the shot from somewhere above.

The bedroom wall behind him displayed posters of semi-naked women, sports cars, and semi-naked women lying on top of sports cars.

Every so often, the character on the main screen would stop running and zoom in with the sniper rifle's sights, then pick off some unsuspecting other player who had been minding their own business in the middle distance. This was accompanied by an ejection of, 'Booyah!' or 'Eat bullet, bitch!' or '*Dayum*, son!' said in a clumsy parody of an American accent. And quite a racist sounding parody, at that.

'I hate the wee bastard already,' Logan remarked, and nobody voiced their disagreement.

'Here we go,' Dave said, tapping his keyboard and ratcheting the video's volume up a few notches.

'So, guys, I was thinking about how to get more subs, and you know what'd be funny A.F.?' Matthew asked, his eyes not shifting their focus from the game he was playing. 'If, like, I arranged a Swatting on my own house, or something. Like, imagine me just sitting here, and a load of armed feds just burst in and tore the place up behind me. Just, like—'he forced air through his teeth, approximating the sound of machine-gun fire'—and I'm just, like, WTF, guys? Chill!'

He cackled, like this was the funniest thing that anyone had ever said, then took a big slug from a can of an energy drink

Logan had never heard of, being very careful to show the label to the camera.

'Here. Listen to this,' Dave urged, bumping the volume up again.

'Or, what would be even funnier, is if I, like, staged my own kidnapping. Like, pretend I've been taken by the Cartel, or something, and I'm being held hostage.' He put on a Mexican accent. If the American one had been racially dubious, this one could've started a full scale land war. 'Hey, muchacho! We going to *keednap* you, and cut you up, and sell your *keednees* on the black market, si?'

He cackled again. It was a hyena-like bray that only made Logan dislike the lad even more.

'The Cartel?' Logan muttered. 'Where's he actually from?'

'Ipswich, sir,' Sinead said.

Logan tutted. 'Oh aye, that Ipswich Mafia's fucking renowned. I hear the whole of Suffolk's heaving with Triads these days.' He shook his head at the lad still laughing away on screen. 'What a gobby wee arsehole.'

Dave clicked the button to pause the video again, then turned to look up at the assembled detectives.

'What do you reckon, then? Think it's anything?'

Ben folded his arms and shook his head. 'I think I'm glad I never had kids. Imagine knowing you'd spawned that annoying wee bastard,' he said. 'I couldn't live with myself knowing I'd inflicted that on the world.'

'Eh, aye. I meant specifically about the kidnapping thing,' Dave said. 'But I get your point.'

'Seems a big coincidence,' Sinead ventured. 'I mean, I doubt he could've pulled something off like this himself, but if they're all in on it…?'

Hamza looked back over his shoulder at his own computer, to make sure nothing had changed. The streams were still scheduled, though the countdowns were now down to single digits.

'I mean, if this is fake, or even if it isn't, and they all survive, they're going to make millions from this. They'll get book deals,

TV interviews, their brands are going to go through the roof,' the sergeant said. 'They already are, in fact.'

The door to the Incident Room opened before anyone could add anything else. Tyler appeared, caught Logan's eye, then nodded to say he'd carried out his mission. He then stepped aside, holding the door open to let the Gozer come marching through.

The Detective Superintendent clapped his hands a couple of times to draw their attention, despite the fact they'd all already been looking his way.

'Right, everyone, quick update! The Chief Constable is dealing with the social media stuff. He's going to apply pressure and get all those accounts shut down.'

Hamza shot Logan a sideways look. The DCI ignored it for as long as he could, but then buckled.

'We're, eh, we're not so sure that's the best idea, sir.'

MacKenzie's expression had been fairly neutral, but now it tipped over into something a little darker.

'I'm sorry, Jack, what was that?'

'We had some thoughts on it all,' Logan said, stepping away from the rest of the team so the Gozer's anger would be aimed at him and him alone. 'We're concerned that, if it gets shut down—if the kidnapper doesn't have an audience watching—'

The detective superintendent filled the rest in for himself. 'Jesus Christ, Jack!' he snapped. 'So, why the hell have I been phoning all round the bloody place trying to get…?'

He closed his eyes and pinched the bridge of his nose, composing himself. When he spoke again, his tone was more measured.

'The wheels are already in motion. I don't know if I can stop them, but if I'm going to try, then I need to know now, Jack. I need to know what you want me to do.'

Logan could feel all the eyes in the room on him. The Gozer was the senior officer and could've elected to make the decision, but he was kicking the ball back to the DCI rather than taking responsibility for all the many ways this could go wrong.

It was down to Logan to make the call, then. On any other day, this wouldn't be a problem, but that beermat, and all the memories it had brought back, had knocked him off his game.

And that was before he'd seen his own number plate in the CCTV footage.

How could he choose? He had no idea what the right thing to do was. He had no idea which decision would cause the least amount of harm.

Then again, when did he ever have the luxury of knowing that?

'Keep it up,' he said. 'Keep it all running.'

The Gozer almost laughed, but the moment of mirth quickly fell away again. 'You are joking, yes?'

'It's the only insight we've got into what's happening. We can message those accounts, meaning we've got a line of communication.' Logan turned to Hamza. 'Right?'

'Right, sir. Yes. If they get pulled, we'll lose that. We'll be in the dark.'

'Get on that, will you?' Logan said. 'Get a message through to whoever's behind this. Send it on all eight accounts. Tell them we want to talk.'

'Will do, sir.'

'Oh, for...' MacKenzie threw his arms into the air and sighed. 'So we're keeping it up now? God Almighty, Jack. Fine. I'll go and try undo it all. I'll apologise to the Chief Constable for pulling him out of his meeting, and we can all keep our fingers crossed that he doesn't hand me my bollocks in an evidence bag.'

He turned to head back into the corridor, then reacted in surprise when he spotted something out there.

'Bugger it. Sorry. Come in, come in.'

He gestured to the person waiting beyond the door, and footsteps scuffed across the corridor floor, growing louder.

'Our IT consultant is here,' the Gozer announced. 'He's fully vetted and cleared, so I want you to give him full access to anything he needs. Sergeant, you'll be working closely with him, as previously discussed.'

Hamza nodded. 'Right you are, sir.'

'I'll let you all do your own introductions, but while I go off and throw myself at the mercy of the Chief Constable, I'll leave you with Mr Thomas Arden.'

Sinead heard the breath that caught in the back of Hamza's throat as a smiling man in his thirties entered, one hand raised in a slightly self-conscious wave.

Thomas's face fell when he spotted Hamza gawping back at him. He quickly looked around at the others, desperately trying to stick a smile back on like he was blindly pinning a tail on a donkey.

'What is it?' Sinead whispered to the detective sergeant beside her. 'What's wrong?'

'That's him,' Hamza choked. Down by his sides, his fingers balled into the fists. 'That's the bastard I caught shagging my wife.'

'No time for introductions now,' said Ben, oblivious to this revelation. He pointed to Hamza's computer, where the minutes had ticked down into seconds. 'Looks like we're getting ready to roll.'

Chapter 14

'Hi there!'

The uniformed constable on the doorstep was smiling so patronisingly he might as well have ruffled Olivia's hair and handed the girl a lollipop.

'I was asked to nip round and make sure everything's OK. I'm Constable Grigor. If you prefer, you can call me Alan. Can I call you Olivia?'

The girl in the doorway sniffed. 'I'd rather we kept it professional and you used Miss Maximuke, if it's all the same with you, Alan?'

The constable's smile took a dunt, but rallied again. 'Of course, Miss Maximuke it is.' He nodded past her into the hall. The sound of Taggart's barking echoed through the house. 'Is that a dog I hear?'

'I mean, I hope so,' Olivia replied. 'Either that, or there's something seriously wrong with the cat.'

'Right. Yes. Haha. Very good.' Alan nodded past her again. 'Can I come in?'

Olivia blew out her cheeks, but then stepped aside. 'If you must, aye. But Taggart might go mental.'

'I'm sure I'll cope!' the constable said. He stepped into the house, and his face fell when he clocked the chef's knife that Olivia had been holding out of sight behind the door.

'Oh, don't worry. It's not for you,' the girl assured him, then she shut and locked the door behind him. 'What do you want to see?'

The constable was still fixated on the knife, but eventually managed to drag his gaze away.

'Uh, I mean, I don't know. I was just told I should swing by and make sure everything was OK. There was something about a shed? Oh! And a parcel. I'm meant to ask who it's for.'

Olivia regarded him with suspicion for a moment, then shrugged. 'It's for Jack.'

'Jack?'

'Your boss. The big head honcho,' Olivia said. Then, when this didn't prove to be enough information, she tutted and rolled her eyes. 'DCI Logan.'

'Ah! Yes! Right. In that case, I've to take it to him.'

Olivia snorted. 'What are you, a delivery driver, or something?'

'I'm whatever I'm needed to be,' Alan replied, and there was a curtness to the response that made clear his patience was starting to wear thin.

'And you're happy with that, are you?' Olivia pressed. 'With that being your job? Just a general dogsbody?'

'Alright. OK. That's quite enough of the cheek, thanks,' the constable said.

'It's not cheek!' Olivia told him, looking hurt by the accusation. 'It's a genuine question about whether you ever feel like you've wasted your life, that's all.'

Alan's smile was gone now, replaced by a sharp downturning at the sides of his mouth. 'Alright, cut it out. I know who you are,' he told her. 'I know you might think you're big and clever, because of who your dad is, but cut the shit, alright? I'm here doing a favour. I'm here to help. I don't need your shite banter. That clear?'

He held out a hand and eyeballed her.

'And give me that knife before I have to take it off you.'

'Oh, and what are you going to do? Break my arm?'

He spat the reply at her. 'If I have to, aye.'

She stared back at him, feet planted, face to face in a battle of wills. Through in the kitchen, Taggart's barking reached all new heights.

Finally, with a sigh, she turned the knife around and presented him with the handle. The constable took it from her and turned it so the blade was pointing away from both of them.

'There. Thank you,' he said, his mood lightening a little. 'I think, if we put our minds to it, we're going to get along just fine.'

The girl grunted. 'Whatever.'

'Now, where is it? This parcel I'm meant to pick up?'

Olivia crossed her arms and shifted her weight from one foot to the other. 'I'll give you it in a minute.' She pointed along the hallway in the direction of the kitchen door. 'But first, the shed's out the back. Through that way,' she told him. 'You might as well take a look at it and, you know, do your actual job while you're here.'

Chapter 15

Cassandra Swain was getting the most attention from the general public. Then again, she was an attractive twenty-year-old lassie with blonde hair doing Yoga in tight leggings, and the general public was nothing if not predictable.

The expression on her face was impressively serene as she bent and stretched herself in all manner of ways. Occasionally, though, midway through a move, when she thought the camera couldn't see her, her features would contort, crumpling up in grief, fighting back the tears that were threatening to come.

Logan found himself wondering if that was deliberate. She always *just about* hid her distress, but not quite all the way. Was she painting herself as a brave little soldier, battling through her pain and distress? Could any of them be that manipulative?

It depended, he supposed, on what sort of reward was up for grabs. Experience told him that people would do a lot for wealth and fame. Most of them would do even more to save their lives.

The team were all gathered around Hamza's monitor, with the Gozer and Thomas Arden lurking at the back. The Gozer was stretching to see past the rest of them, but Thomas had his phone out, and was following events on that, instead.

In the next window along, Adam Parfitt had donned a long brown wig and was ranting at the camera while waggling a finger. Though all four videos were in silence, Logan could practically hear the shrill screeching of the young man's voice.

Going by the subtitles that hurriedly tried to keep up with his outburst, he was performing some sort of comedy skit about how British mothers and American mothers would cope with being locked in a windowless prison cell. The British version was comparing it favourably to a recent stay in a Blackpool caravan park, while the American one was remarking on how 'quaint and adorable' the facilities were.

Reading it, none of it was remotely funny, and Logan was fairly confident that listening to it would be even worse.

Still, the viewers seemed to like it. He had lots of little laughing face emojis popping up.

There was, the DCI thought, no accounting for taste.

The bottom two windows showed far less activity. On the left, Elizia Shuttleworth sat with her legs crossed on the floor, her hands just above her knees with the middle fingers and thumbs forming two loops. Her eyes were closed, and though the subtitle software wasn't picking anything up, she looked to be humming or *ohhhming* below her breath.

'What's she up to?' Ben asked.

'Meditating, boss,' Tyler said. 'She does loads of videos like this. Usually out by a pool or somewhere, though, not sitting in a dungeon.'

Ben couldn't quite get his head around the idea of people tuning in to see someone doing literally bugger all while sitting on their arse, but then the whole thing had been an eye-opening experience when it came to the shite that people wasted their time with online.

'I notice she's flashing a bit more cleavage than she was earlier,' Sinead remarked. 'Probably a clever move if you're trying to win people's attention.'

There had been no real discussion among the team about the reasons for the eight performative livestreams, but Logan realised that Sinead had at least contemplated one of the possibilities that he had.

It felt like a contest. A test of popularity. Of these four, Cassandra Swain was comfortably winning. But who would prove most popular overall?

And, more importantly, what happened to the loser?

'Have we tried contacting the abductor through these accounts?' Logan asked.

'We did, sir,' Hamza confirmed. 'We reached out through all of them, asking them to make contact. Nothing back, though.'

'Bold move by that guy,' Dave remarked, indicating the browser window in the lower right.

Bruce Kennedy, the chef, sat with his back against the wall, his knees raised in front of him in a position that wasn't a million miles away from being a more relaxed version of the meditating Elizia's.

Not dissimilarly to her, his hands were resting on his knees. Unlike Cassandra, though, he had the middle fingers of both raised in the direction of the camera, and was staring right down the lens.

He was, it seemed, refusing to take part in the whole spectacle. The watching viewers didn't seem happy about this, and were bombarding his stream with an onslaught of angry faces.

As he watched all the irritated responses flood in, Logan's already rock-bottom opinion of the general public quietly reached for a pick-axe and shovel.

They had all been mid-action—or mid-inaction, in Bruce's case—when the streams went live, like they'd already been performing for several minutes before the cameras had been turned on.

'Do we know where they are?' Thomas asked.

Had Logan not been so glued to the screen, he'd have stunned the man with the sheer ferocity of his withering look.

'If we knew where they were, do you think we'd be standing here watching?'

'Oh. Yeah. I mean, no. Daft question,' the consultant mumbled. 'Sorry.'

Hamza almost choked on a snort. He shook his head and continued watching the screen, trying to focus on it, and not on the home wrecker standing just a few feet away from his chair.

His presence was making the detective sergeant's skin prickle, like he was allergic to the man.

'What are we expecting to happen here?' asked the Gozer. He sounded impatient, like he had better things to be doing with his time than watching four random people doing very little of interest.

And, to be fair to him, he almost certainly did.

'We're waiting,' Logan said. 'The last time they went on for ten minutes, bang on the dot. We're at…'

'Eight minutes twenty,' Hamza said.

'Shouldn't be long now, then,' Thomas chipped in, but his contribution was met with silence.

Only Sinead had heard Hamza explaining who the consultant was, but they'd all picked up on the sergeant's dislike of the newcomer, and had automatically gone into cold-shoulder mode until they knew more.

'Where are we with everything?' Det Supt MacKenzie asked. 'We spoken to the families yet?'

'Most of them,' DI Forde replied. 'CID got them on the phone. Got a couple we still need to track down. Both down south. We've got the names of a couple of DCIs down there who we're going to contact. DCI Harry Grimm and DCI Robbie Kett.'

'You know them?'

'Very vaguely,' Logan replied. 'Good reputations. They'll handle it.'

The Gozer nodded, satisfied by that.

'Dave found something interesting, too,' Logan continued. 'Matthew Broderick—'

The Gozer frowned. 'The actor?'

'No, the kidnap victim.'

The detective superintendent glanced over at the board, had the decency to look embarrassed, then nodded. 'Right, aye. What about him?'

'He spoke about doing something like this on his... I don't know. Feed, or channel, or whatever the hell it's called. In a video, anyway. He spoke about faking an abduction.'

The Gozer rocked back on his heels. 'Did he now?' He looked back at the photo again, like he was suddenly seeing it in a new light. 'But he's just, what? Seventeen? No way he could organise all this by himself.'

'He seems like a... driven young man,' Logan said, choosing his words with care. 'And if he was involved, there's no saying he'd have done it on his own. The whole lot of them could be in on it.'

'That Australian chef guy doesn't look like he's in on it, boss,' Tyler pointed out. 'He looks furious.'

'Aye, furious,' Logan agreed. 'Not exactly scared, though. It's more like he's just pissed off at the inconvenience of it.'

'Maybe he was promised a bigger cell,' Ben said, only half-joking.

The Gozer rubbed at his chin. 'So, what are you saying? You think it's all fake? You think they staged this?'

'I'm not saying that, no,' Logan replied. The truth was, he didn't know what to think. That was a relatively new experience for him, and he was having some difficulty adjusting to it. 'I'm saying it's a possibility.'

'Here we go,' Sinead announced, as a timer she'd set on her watch at the start of the broadcast ticked down. 'Five, four, three—'

The livestreams all ended just before she could conclude the countdown. All four figures froze for a second, then the pages refreshed and the feed became available to watch again from the start.

The Gozer groaned and ran both hands backwards over his balding head. 'God. Right. So, what was the point in all that? What was that meant to bloody prove?'

'Christ knows,' Logan said. 'A demonstration of the kidnapper's power, maybe? Showing his control over them.'

'Didn't seem to have a lot of control over Bruce Kennedy, boss,' Tyler pointed out. 'He was basically telling them to go fuck themselves.'

'But we don't know what the consequences of his actions will be yet,' Thomas said.

Everyone, with the exception of Hamza, who steadfastly refused to look at him, turned to face the Gozer's consultant.

Thomas smiled awkwardly under the weight of their attention, and slipped his phone back into his pocket. 'I'm just thinking out loud, really. But, what if this wasn't a demo of his power? What if it was an audition of some kind? To see who pleased him best, or whatever. If it was something like that, then I don't much fancy Mr Kennedy's chances.'

When no one replied, he shrugged self-consciously. 'Or, you know, it might all be fake, like you said, in which case it probably doesn't matter.'

Still facing his screen, Hamza sat up straight and clicked his fingers to draw the team's attention. 'There's something happening.'

On screen, all four feeds had started up again. This time, though, Bruce, Elizia, Cassandra and Adam were all upright in their cages, as if standing to attention.

Hamza glanced at Sinead and pointed to the neighbouring computer. 'Check that. Check the others.'

Dropping into the seat, Sinead opened up a browser window and called up the account of Matthew Broderick. Sure enough, another livestream had begun to broadcast on his page, and showed him standing in a similar position to the others.

'Looks like they're all on,' she said, adjusting and opening up browser windows so that, between both screens, all eight feeds were visible.

'What the hell are they doing?' Logan muttered, his eyes flitting from each video to the next.

They all stood rigid and straight backed, eyes forward, hands by their sides, like dolls trapped in their original packaging. The shadows and metal mesh made it difficult to see their faces in much detail, but the pink-haired Natalie Womack and Adam Parfitt, still in his wig, looked to be crying.

The answer to Logan's question came a moment later, when all eight of them, presumably on some sort of cue, all bowed, low and deep, to the camera.

'Is that it? Is that the show over?' Ben asked. 'Is that it all——?'

A roar of gunfire erupted from the speakers of the computer Sinead was sitting at. Three shots in quick succession, all the more shocking as they were the first sounds on any of the feeds.

The toy collector, Kelly Wynne, was thrown back in a spray of crimson. Part of her skull was missing by the time she hit the back wall of the cell. She managed to get a hand to her chest, but couldn't stop the blood that surged and foamed between her fingers.

Despite the gaping hole in it, her face managed to register something like shock, but then her features went slack, her legs gave out, and a hot smear of red followed her as she slid slowly down the wall.

'Fucking hell!' Tyler cried, voicing a sentiment that was very much shared by the rest of the team.

On the other feeds, the remaining influencers were shouting, or screaming, or cowering as far back in their cells as they could, but the sound had been cut off again, so they did it all in eerie silence.

The livestreams for all seven of them ended abruptly. The footage of Kelly Wynne's dead body continued to roll, though, the camera sticking with her as her slide down the wall became a sideways topple that left her lifeless body folded unnaturally.

'Boss?' Tyler whispered, like he was afraid he might somehow make things worse if he spoke too loud. 'What do we do, boss?'

Logan stared at the screen. At the dead woman. At the blood.

His eyes were drawn against their will to a movement in the lower left corner. A digital thumb appeared. A *like*.

Another followed. Then a few shocked faces, followed by some more thumbs.

It was the laughing face emoji that sent the wave of disgust surging through him. He stabbed a finger at the screen, and hissed through gritted teeth. 'We get this shite taken down. All of it. Now. We stop these broadcasts.'

The Gozer's, 'Seriously?!' was practically a shriek.

At the back of the group, Thomas voiced an objection. 'I know it's an emotional moment, but I think it would be better if we still had access to—'

'An 'emotional moment'? A woman was just shot dead, and now there are bastards sat at home cheering for it.'

'No, I get that. I do. It's horrible. But, I just think—'

Sensing that his consultant may be about to be beaten to death, the Gozer stepped in. 'DCI Logan is right. We can't leave this up,' he said, though there was a note of resentment to it. 'I'll go get on it. *Again*. Given what's happened, I'd hope the company is already taking action, but if not, I'll make bloody sure they do.'

He locked eyed with Logan for a moment, and the graveness of the situation was reflected in that look.

Then, with a nod, the Detective Superintendent about-turned and left the room.

For a moment, the only sound in the place was the squeaking of the door, and the sound of the Gozer's fading footsteps.

Then, rising to his feet, Hamza broke the silence.

'Eh, excuse me, sir,' he said to Logan, pointedly not looking in Thomas's direction. 'You mind if I have a quick word in private?'

—

When they entered the office, Logan took a second to cross to the window and look out through the blinds. The office looked out over the car park of the Burnett Road station, and Logan was dismayed—if not remotely surprised—to see that a circus of media vans was already assembled.

BBC, ITV, Sky News—they were all there, and others, too. There had to be a dozen of the vans down there, with more pulling in. Presenters and camera operators were either getting themselves organised, or already up and running, and Logan suspected that if he turned on one of the news channels, he'd see at least a couple of them were broadcasting live.

'Damn it,' he hissed. 'The press is here.'

'Was only a matter of time, I suppose,' Hamza said.

Logan let the blinds snap back into place, then turned to the detective sergeant. 'Right, what's up? Make it quick,' he instructed, not wasting time on taking or offering a seat. 'We need to get back out there and get on top of this.'

Hamza looked down at his hands, realised he was fiddling with them, then tucked them behind his back. 'Right, sir. Aye. I'll be quick. It's this consultant.'

'What about him?'

Hamza straightened further, until he was practically standing to attention.

'I can't work with him, sir.'

Logan's frown moved at a glacial pace down his face. 'You can't work with him?'

'No, sir.'

'And why's that?'

Hamza swallowed. 'It's personal, sir.'

'*Personal*?!' For a moment, it looked like Logan was about to reach across the desk and rip the sergeant's head off, but then he exhaled and deflated a little. 'Look, Hamza, we're off the record here. What's the problem, son?'

Hamza chewed on his bottom lip, considering his response before eventually blurting it out.

'He slept with my wife, sir.'

Logan had not been expecting that one. The window blinds rattled metallically as he stepped backwards into them, like the weight of this revelation had momentarily knocked him off balance.

'Jesus Christ. You're not serious?'

'Of course, sir. I wouldn't joke about that. Especially not right now. It was him that I caught with Amira a few months back.'

'Bloody hell!' Logan grimaced and ran a hand down his face, his fingers compressing his cheeks like they were made of soft, spongey putty. 'I mean… Jesus Christ.'

'Sorry, sir,' Hamza said.

'Not exactly your fault, son,' Logan said, but from his silence, it wasn't clear if the sergeant was in agreement.

The DCI looked out at the gathering press again, and could've sworn there were twice as many vehicles out there as there had been a few moments ago.

'Right. Send him in,' Logan instructed.

'Sir?'

Logan indicated the door at Hamza's back. 'Go out there, and bring yourself to speak to him for long enough to tell him I want to see him.'

'Are you going to take him off the case, sir?'

'I'm going to talk to him, Sergeant. Beyond that, I don't know.'

Hamza straightened his shoulders. 'It's him or me, sir.'

Logan took a step away from the window. Hamza wasn't a short man, but the DCI loomed above him like a vengeful god.

'A woman is dead, son. Seven others might be about to go the same way,' he intoned. 'I get that you're not happy with the situation. I get that you're upset. But, if I think this man can help us save lives, then your personal feelings on the matter *do not* matter. Is that understood?'

'Sir, you've got to—'

'We're trying to save lives here, Hamza. Not make friends,' Logan said, cutting the objection short. 'I get that it won't be pleasant. I do. I understand that you'll probably hate every minute of it, but I don't care. I can't afford to give a damn about that. Not right now.'

He pointed past him to the door, and to the computer screens they'd just been watching.

'When we get those people home, you can do what you like. You can knock him out. You can forcibly evict the bastard from the building. I'll hold the door open for you and leave the roller-skate at the top of the stairs,' the DCI continued. 'But, if, after I talk to him, I think he can help us save these people, then he stays. He stays until this is over. And, if you can't handle that, then you are free to leave, in the knowledge that you're not nearly the man that I thought you were.'

Hamza's hands were still behind his back, but they were clenched into tight, shaking fists as he fought to keep his emotions under control.

'Are we clear on this, Detective Sergeant?' Logan demanded.

Hamza stared straight ahead, out past the other detective and towards some distant invisible horizon.

Finally, after what felt like an eternity, he nodded.

'We're clear, sir,' he said, though the words almost choked him. 'I'll do what we have to to get these people home.'

Logan placed a slab of a hand on Hamza's shoulder. 'Thank you, Sergeant. I appreciate that,' he said. 'Now, go and send him in.'

He stepped back, and a grim smile played across his lips.

'And, if it helps any, I'm going to make the next few minutes of the bastard's life *deeply* uncomfortable…'

Chapter 16

Shona had been just about to get started on the first body when the call had come through from Olivia. The victim—a man of currently indeterminate age—lay prepped and exposed on the table, the pathologist's tools all neatly laid out beside him.

Yanking a glove off with her teeth, Shona tapped the button that answered and then recoiled at the sound of Taggart barking.

'Hello? Liv? What's wrong?'

'Shut up! Jesus! It's literally just a woman pushing a pram, no need to have a paddy about—Hello? Shona? You there?'

'Yes! Yes, I'm here! What's wrong?'

'Nothing,' Olivia replied. 'Taggart's just going mental at that woman from along the street with the baby.'

Shona's heart, which had skipped several beats, settled back into a more regular rhythm. 'Oh. Yeah. He really doesn't like her. She wore a hat once. Really put him off her.'

'What kind of hat?'

'Big floppy thing. Made her look like an Eighties pimp.'

'Fair enough, then,' Olivia decided. 'Anyway, that cop came round. He was a bit of a knob, but he checked the place over. Didn't find anything. He took the parcel for Jack, so that's all done.'

'OK! Good. And you're fine? Nothing else weird, or anything?'

'Nope,' Olivia said. She started to speak faster, like the next part was the important bit. 'Did you see the video, though? Of that woman getting shot? It was mental.'

'No. And I don't think you should be watching stuff like that. What woman?'

'Kelly Wynne, the *Toy of the Day* woman. She's one of the social media people that went missing.'

Shona switched the phone from one ear to the other, matching the change of direction the conversation had taken.

'And, what? They shot her?'

'Live on Insta! It was *mental*,' Olivia stressed again. 'It was like an execution, or an assassination, or something, one in the head, two in the chest, *peow-peow-peow*! That's what they do, isn't it? Professionals? I mean, it was horrible, obviously. Really shit for the poor woman, and I can't imagine what her family must be going through. Although, from what everyone's saying on TikTok, she doesn't have any family so...'

She kept talking, but Shona was now only half-listening, so the girl's voice faded until it became little more than background noise.

Instead, the pathologist's focus turned to the body of the man on the table.

She hadn't yet started the post mortem, but a quick glance as he'd been unwrapped had pointed towards a likely cause of death.

There was a bullet hole in his forehead. She leaned closer to the body. The general decay made it hard to be sure, but she thought there were another two gunshot entry wounds near the centre of his chest.

'Eh, right. You sure you're OK?' Shona asked, cutting Olivia off in what she now realised had been mid-sentence.

'What? Yeah. I'm fine. Why?'

'I just... I need to go check something,' Shona told her. 'Sorry. It's urgent.'

Olivia tried her best not to sound put-out. To her credit, she almost pulled it off.

'It's fine. Don't worry about it. Go and do what you have to do.'

'Right. Yes. Sorry again,' Shona replied. 'And, that stuff. The videos. You shouldn't be watching stuff like that.'

'Everyone is, though! It's all over the internet. It's even on TV!' Olivia protested.

Shona knew that laying down the law didn't work when it came to getting Olivia to do things. She tried, instead, to appeal to her better nature.

'Just remember they're not characters. They're real people. That woman was a real person, just like you or me. Would you want people watching your death like that?'

'Are you kidding? That would be an amazing way to go!' Olivia cried. 'I'd be famous!'

'Yeah, but for being shot in the face!'

'Still famous,' Olivia countered. She sighed, and Shona thought she could hear the much younger, less battle-hardened girl that she had once been struggling to get out. 'But, I suppose you're right. I'll try not to watch it, even though it's literally everywhere.'

'Good. Thank you. It's the right call,' Shona told her. 'Now, sorry again, but I'm really going to have to go!'

–

Thomas Arden practically lunged across the room, arm extended, a wide and friendly smile taking up most of the real estate on his face.

'I didn't get to properly say hello before it all kicked off out there. It's Thomas. You can call me Tom, though.'

He tried to hide his grimace when Logan accepted the offered hand and squeezed it with fingers that felt as if they could crush coal into diamonds.

'Detective Chief Inspector Logan,' Jack said, and he stopped short of offering any friendlier alternatives.

He released his grip, motioned to the empty chair on the other side of his desk, then waited for Thomas to take a seat before continuing.

'Are you going to be a pain in my arse, Mr Arden?'

Thomas started to laugh, like the DCI had made a joke, then swallowed it back down and shook his head. 'No. No, of course not.'

'Well, that's funny, because you're already proving to be,' Logan told him. He pinned the man down with an icy cold stare. 'I believe you're acquainted with one of my officers?'

The consultant fiddled nervously with a rolled-up shirt sleeve that had started to slip down, pushing is back up above his elbow. 'Oh. Right. Yes. You mean Hamza?'

Logan shook his head. 'No.'

Thomas blinked. 'What?'

'Try again.'

'Um… I don't… I only know Hamza, and it's—'

Logan raised an index finger to silence him. When he spoke, his voice was like a distant brewing storm. 'You only know *who*?'

Thomas finished adjusting his sleeve and let both hands fall into his lap. He squeezed them between his knees, like a schoolboy bracing himself for a telling off from the headmaster.

'Um… Detective Sergeant Khaled?'

Logan lowered the finger and nodded. 'Better. See, your presence here, given what has gone on between you and Detective Sergeant Khaled… Well, it makes me deeply uncomfortable. He's a good man—'

'No, I know, I do, and I'm not—'

Logan's face darkened, making it very clear how he felt about the interruption. '*And* he's a valuable and proven member of this team. You, as of this moment, are some random guy I don't know. If I have to choose, I'm going to choose him. But, I don't want to choose. I want us all to work together to get these people safely home, and to find out who's behind this. And that won't happen if you two are making things difficult.'

'I won't. I swear. There'll be no trouble from me,' Thomas insisted. 'I just want to help, that's all. I get why Ham… Why *DS Khaled* hates me. I do. And I wish I could do something to undo all the harm I caused. But, right now, like you say, this isn't about us. It's about those people.'

He shimmied forward in his seat a little, so his arse was hanging half-off it. Logan watched as the consultant took out his mobile and turned the screen towards him.

'And, on that, I think I've got something.'

Logan continued to eyeball him for a few more seconds, then surrendered to his curiosity and took the phone.

'What am I looking at?'

'That's the video from Elizia Shuttleworth. The… What do you call her? Spiritualist guru, or whatever. From just before the shooting.'

Logan watched the tattooed, dreadlocked young woman in the footage. She was standing upright, getting ready to bow.

'And?'

'Well, two things, really. First, all the other cameras are locked down.'

Logan raised his eyes from the screen. 'Meaning?'

'They were on a mount, or tripod, or something. Something to hold them steady.' Thomas stood up and pointed to the phone in the DCI's hand. 'See the shake in that footage? Handheld. It's the only one that wasn't locked down. Someone was holding the phone or camera.'

'Right.' Logan's gaze flitted back to the screen to confirm this, then returned to the consultant. 'So, what does that mean?'

'I don't know,' Thomas admitted. 'But there's something else. Something more interesting.' He indicated the computer on Logan's desk. 'May I?'

Logan wasn't happy about it, but if the guy had something useful to share that might save those people's lives, then it trumped any other issues anyone might have with him.

For now, at least.

'Fine,' the DCI said, then he stepped aside to let Thomas loose on the keyboard.

'I didn't notice it at first,' the consultant said, as his fingers flew across the keys. 'Wasn't until the third watch through that it jumped out.'

'What did?'

Thomas hit the spacebar with a flourish, then leaned back and swivelled lightly in the chair. 'See for yourself,' he invited.

Logan scowled down at him as he sat there, semi-reclining in the detective's chair.

After a moment, some self-preservation instinct kicked in, and the consultant hurriedly scrambled back to his feet and out of the way.

'S-sorry!' he stammered, making room for Logan to sit. 'Just… In fact, I'll just…'

Thomas leaned awkwardly over the detective and prodded a couple of keys on the keyboard. On screen, four of the livestream recordings began to play—Kelly Wynne's in the top left corner, Elizia Shuttleworth's in the top right, and the Japanese schoolgirl and Mitchell's son, Denzel, side-by-side down at the bottom.

Seeing them together like this, the handheld nature of Elizia's footage became more obvious. While the other three were completely static, her footage wobbled and swayed as all four of them bowed at the same time.

'Don't watch Kelly. Watch Elizia and the others,' Thomas said in a low whisper, like he was trying not to ruin the moment.

The gun was fired, all three shots running out in quick succession. Logan's instinct was to watch Kelly Wynne dying again—he felt he owed her that, somehow—but he managed to keep his focus fixed on Elizia and the other two influencers.

It took him only a second to realise what the issue was.

'Jesus,' he muttered. 'Can you play that again?'

Thomas didn't say anything, but grinned triumphantly as he restarted the feeds.

Logan leaned in a little closer. This time, he knew what he was looking for, and wanted to be ready.

All four of them bowed.

All four of them straightened.

Three of them reacted as soon as the gun went off, Kelly by slamming against the back wall, Denzel Drummond and Natalie Womack by stumbling back and screaming in horror.

And then, a second later, Cassandra Swain covered her head with her tattooed arms and threw herself to the floor.

'She was late in reacting,' Logan said.

'Exactly.'

'But that's just the internet, isn't it? You get delays. Slow connections. It happens.' He looked up at the consultant standing beside his chair. 'Doesn't it?'

'Maybe,' Thomas conceded. 'It's not impossible. But everyone else was in sync. Between that and the fact her video's handheld, it just seems... I don't know. Odd. Worth a mention. It also implies there's more than one kidnapper.'

Logan drew a breath in through his nose, considering this, then nodded. 'Whoever was holding the camera didn't fire the gun. There'd be far more shake.'

'Just what I was thinking,' Thomas said. 'Great minds...'

Logan did not return the consultant's smile. Quite the opposite.

But, like it or not, Thomas was already proving his worth. Much as he hated to do it to Hamza, Logan had no choice but to keep the consultant around.

His mobile buzzed loudly, vibrating across his desk, Shona's name flashing up on screen.

'Interesting findings, Mr Arden, but none of it helps us until we know what it means,' he said, reaching for the phone. 'So, I suggest you get back out there and get to work. But, if I hear you've done anything to anger or upset any of my officers...'

He left the warning hanging there. The look on his face left no doubt as to how severe the consequences would be.

'Got it. Of course,' Thomas said, holding his hands up at the sides of his head. He reminded Logan of a dog exposing its belly. 'I promise, I won't cause any trouble.'

'Good. Now, piss off out of my office and get to work,' Logan told him. 'I need to take this call.'

The consultant scraped and bowed as he backed out of the room, like a peasant whose life had just been spared by some terrible, vengeful king.

Once he was gone, Logan answered the call. 'Shona. Hello. What's up? Is Olivia OK?'

'Uh, yeah. She seems fine. That constable you sent went round. Think he's bringing you a package that arrived. Did you ask him to do that?'

'Eh, aye. Sort of,' Logan said, evading the question as best he could. 'What's wrong? You found something?'

'Well, yes,' Shona replied, though there was a note of uncertainty to it. 'I think maybe I have.'

Chapter 17

Logan entered the Incident Room like the first big gust of a tropical storm, his voice booming and echoing off the walls.

'Right, new information! Sinead, get this written up and stuck on the...'

He stopped when he failed to spot Sinead. Or, for that matter, her husband.

'Where are they?' he demanded, his tone expressing his annoyance.

'I sent them out,' Ben replied. 'They're away to meet that convention organiser woman.'

'I thought she was coming here?'

Ben nodded and took a sip from a big mug of tea. 'She was, and then she saw two hundred journalists out front, and she changed her mind. Sinead and Tyler are going to meet her at her house.'

Logan's face paled as he thought about Tyler surrounded by a sea of cameras and microphones. The lad talked a lot of shite at the best of times, let alone when the eyes of the world were on him.

'Don't worry, I sent them out the back way,' Ben said, as if reading the DCI's mind. 'And under strict instructions not to say a word to anyone.'

Logan allowed himself to relax a little. Of course, Ben was already on top of things. He knew Tyler better than almost anyone. He knew everyone on the team—and all their many strengths and weaknesses—better than almost anyone, in fact.

What would they do without him?

Logan's moment of relief quickly passed when he saw both Hamza and Thomas hurrying towards him. They both started to speak, but Hamza practically elbowed his way to the front, cutting the consultant off before he could get more than two words out.

'The feeds are down, sir,' the detective sergeant announced.

Thomas stopped behind him and nodded, as if his confirmation was somehow required.

'What?' Logan asked. 'All of them?'

'The accounts have been removed,' Thomas interjected. 'They're gone.'

'They're shut down completely, all eight of them,' Hamza said, speaking over the other man. 'Not sure if it was us or Meta themselves. I doubt they'd want that on their platform, and they can't exactly have missed it, the videos are everywhere.'

'Aye. Understandable,' Logan said, though he still didn't know if the footage being removed was a good thing or not. The attempt at communicating through the hijacked accounts had been met with silence, but who was to say a reply wouldn't have arrived five minutes from now?

'We also ran the numbers, sir,' Hamza said. 'Kelly Wynne got the lowest number of likes out of all of them.'

It took Logan a moment to comprehend the significance of this. When he did, his tightening stomach ejected a low grunt up through his throat.

'So, you're saying what, exactly?' he asked, making sure he was clear on the matter. 'She got voted out?'

'Basically, yes,' Thomas confirmed. 'Although, DS Khaled is simplifying it a bit there. It wasn't just about likes, but overall engagement, so laughing faces, hearts, angry reactions all counted alongside the actual likes, and it was this total—'

'You don't need to show your working, son,' Logan said, cutting him off. He kept staring at the man, but pointed to Hamza. 'The simplified version suits me fine.'

Ben took a slurp of his tea. 'Tell him about the dancing.'

Logan frowned. He already didn't like where this was going. 'Dancing?'

'On TikTok,' Thomas said, beating Hamza to the punch. 'The original videos—the trailers, let's call them—they had music. People are stitching and duetting with them on TikTok.'

'I don't know what the hell that even means,' Logan said, turning his attention to his DS. 'But am I right in thinking that I'm going to hate it?'

'You are, sir,' Hamza confirmed. 'Basically, lots of people are making videos where they dance to the tune that was playing in the original clips.'

'The trailers,' Thomas said, but Hamza just gritted his teeth with contempt.

Logan stood there in silence for a few moments, taking this in. His nostrils flared. He was suddenly gripped by an urge to just go ahead and let everyone die. Not just the influencers currently being held prisoner, but everyone. The whole damn world. By the sounds of things, it would be for the best.

'Dancing,' he said again, and it sounded like the most offensively foul word that had ever been uttered. The sort of word that would make even Bob Hoon blush.

'What was it you were going to say, Jack?' Ben prompted.

Logan still hadn't recovered from Hamza and the consultant's news, but gave his head a shake to clear it.

'Shona's looked at three of the bodies so far,' he announced. 'All three were shot. One in the head, two in the chest. Same as Kelly Wynne.'

'Oh, good grief!' Ben set down his tea, and broke the foil on a brand new Kit-Kat. 'So, I take it we're pursuing the angle that this is all connected?'

'Aye. So, someone get me that dog walker. I want to talk to him. Either he's very unlucky with his timing, or he's a person of interest. Either way, I want him in here, pronto.'

'Sinead already asked Uniform to bring him in,' Ben said. 'But I haven't heard anything.'

'I can chase them up on that, if you like?' Dave suggested, reaching for his phone without waiting for an answer. 'There's heehaw in the way of exhibits come in so far, so it'll keep me out of mischief.'

Logan nodded his thanks then turned to the side-by-side Big Boards. 'We got anything else on any of them? The influencers? Anything more from the families?'

'Nothing of note yet,' Ben replied. 'We're in touch with stations in England and Wales, who're doing a lot of the legwork. One thing that might be of interest, though.'

Logan turned and raised his eyebrows. 'Aye?'

'Kelly Wynne. The lassie who was shot.'

'What about her?'

'No one has been able to track down family for her.'

Logan's eyebrows dropped back down again. This wasn't the big surprise reveal he'd been quietly hoping for. 'Right. I'm sure we'll find someone.'

'Hold your horses. I'm not finished,' Ben told him. 'There's some bits and pieces about her in the press, and floating around online. Rumours that her old man was in the polis.'

One eyebrow crept tentatively upwards again. A connection. If it was true, then both she and Denzel Drummond had police officers for parents. That was something, wasn't it? That had to be.

'What about the rest of them?' Logan asked, gesturing to the photos on the board. 'Any of them got relations on the force?'

'Not as far as we've been able to find out, no,' Ben said, and he looked as disappointed as Logan felt. 'And we're still trying to find out if it's true. If it's a connection, then it's weak.'

'Better than nothing,' Logan said, which was true, even if only barely.

Before the DCI could say anything else on the matter, the Gozer's voice rang out from the Incident Room doorway.

'Jack. You free?'

Logan allowed himself a momentary sigh before turning to face the Detective Superintendent. 'Not really,' he said, hoping to deflect whatever it was that MacKenzie wanted to dump on him.

No such luck.

'Tough. Press conference, downstairs, fifteen minutes.'

'Fuck off!' Logan ejected. He hadn't intended to say that out loud, but nor could he bring himself to regret it.

'Excuse me?' the Gozer asked, fixing the DCI with a cold, slightly manic-looking stare.

'Fifteen minutes?' Logan fired back. 'To say what, exactly? We've got nothing to tell the bastards. Some of the families haven't even been spoken to yet!'

'Then you'd better get your finger out of your arse!' the Gozer told him. 'This has come from on high. I'm not happy about it, either, but the Chief Constable feels this story is in danger of spiralling out of control.' He stabbed a finger towards the window, and his voice took on a shrill note. 'The New York bloody Times is out there! We've had Russia Today and Al Jazeera on the phone! We need to get ahead of this, Jack. We need to give them something!'

Logan knew exactly what he'd like to give them—a God Almighty kick in their collective bollocks.

He also knew that the Gozer was right. A press conference, however vague, would give them something to fill the schedules with for a while. Without that, they'd have nothing to do but to endlessly speculate, and harass the families of the missing victims.

'Jesus. Fine. Fifteen minutes,' he said. 'I'll do what I can here, in the meantime.'

'Good. Right. Yes.' The Gozer smoothed down his shirt, then pointed a warning finger at the DCI. 'But, do not even *think* about turning up late and leaving me sitting there looking like an arsehole!'

'I'll be there,' Logan promised. 'The looking like an arsehole bit? That, I'm afraid I can't help with.'

Chapter 18

Tyler had never seen a cat this large outside of a TV nature documentary, and most of those had been knocking about in sub Saharan Africa.

This one lay on the coffee table in front of him, looking like a big ball of grey fluff with yellow eyes. He assumed it was lying down, at least, but he supposed it could have just been sitting. Or, it might not have any limbs, and could just be a hairy cat torso with a tail. The bouffant nature of its long, thick fur made it impossible to know for sure.

What the detective constable was more certain of was that it didn't like him. He was no expert on feline body language, but the way its ears were folded back, its eyes were wide and staring, and its tail thudded menacingly back and forth made its feelings about him pretty clear.

The way it kept hissing at him was also a clue.

'Do you like my pussy?'

Tyler and Sinead both looked up at the woman who entered the room with a large glass of red wine in hand, a matching colour of lipstick marking the rim. She was the cat's owner, in as much as anyone could ever make that claim.

She grinned at them, enjoying some imagined sense of discomfort at her choice of words.

'Don't mind Poof. He's harmless, honest.'

'Poof?' Tyler asked. He glanced at the cat, and its beady gaze seemed to be daring him to pass comment. Daring him to say a fucking word.

'Yes! Because he's, you know, poofy!'

The cat's tail thumped on the table again. Its ears tilted backwards another degree or two.

Just you try it, pal, its expression seemed to say. *Just you fucking start.*

'Nice name,' Tyler said, and he left it there.

Gemma Murray, organiser of the recent 'Social Stars' convention at Eden Court Theatre, took a seat on the leather recliner across from the couch. She was in her forties, and dressed like she was wearing a 'sexy librarian' Halloween costume—short pencil skirt, open-necked blouse straining across the bust, and half-moon glasses hanging around her neck on a length of sparkly cord.

Her hair was 'messily' tied back in such a way that Sinead reckoned must've taken a good forty-five minutes to get just right. Whenever she looked at Tyler, she pinched one leg of her glasses between her white teeth and ruby red lips, and shifted it around suggestively with her tongue.

Tyler was yet to notice this, being far too concerned with what the cat might do to him if he ventured any further into its bad books.

'Thank you for contacting us, Mrs Murray,' Sinead began, but the organiser was quick to correct her.

'It's Miss. Never married,' she said, tearing her eyes from Tyler for barely a second. Her tongue manoeuvred the end of her glasses-leg from one side of her mouth to the other, as she swirled her wine around in the goblet. 'Never found anyone who could keep up, if you know what I mean? Except Poof, of course.'

Tyler looked again at the cat. Right now, it looked like a semi-deflated football wrapped in a fluffy towel. He couldn't imagine it having a particularly impressive turn of speed.

Unless the woman was talking about something else, of course.

He blinked.

What was she saying? Was she shagging her cat?

Tyler shook the thought away, then tried to ignore the hissing animal and to focus more fully on what Gemma was going on about.

'I had to talk to you. As soon as I heard what happened, I knew I had to tell you everything.'

Despite the lustful looks the woman was shooting at Sinead's husband, the detective constable smiled as she opened her notebook. 'We really appreciate that. Anything you can tell us would be helpful at this stage. We're particularly interested in the minibus...'

Gemma dismissed this with a wave of her glasses, like it didn't matter. 'I already told that man on the phone, I have no idea about any cancellation. That wasn't me, or anyone else on the team.'

'You have a team?' Sinead asked.

Gemma's expression of carnal desire was momentarily blunted by embarrassment. 'Well, there's me and Kate. She does the invoicing and payments. I do the rest. I've spoken to Kate, and she didn't cancel the bus, either. In fact, she's said they've charged us, so I don't know what's going on there.'

'It was within their no refund cancellation window,' Tyler explained, helpfully.

'*Was* it?' Gemma asked, like this was the most fascinating thing she'd ever heard. 'Right. That *is* interesting.'

She shuffled forward on her chair and leaned in a little closer. Her perfume snagged at the back of Sinead's throat, forcing her to lightly cough a few times to clear it away.

'Here's a juicy piece of gossip for you to repay the favour,' she said, all her attention fixed solely on Tyler now, to the point that Sinead may as well have stayed back in the office.

Although, given how the convention organiser was flashing her ample cleavage, she was glad that she hadn't.

'Saturday morning, before the convention kicked off, I did my rounds, checking in on everyone, making sure they were all happy. You know? We had fourteen guests in total. Quite a mixed bunch. YouTubers, TikTokers, Twitch streamers, you name it, we had it. Big names, too. I mean, you know some of them, obviously, but you've heard of PewDiePie? World famous. Global name. Broke all sorts of YouTube subscriber records.'

Even Sinead had to admit that she'd heard of him, although she couldn't really say what it was he was famous for.

'Well, we had a guy who once appeared in a video with him!' Gemma crowed.

It wasn't quite where Sinead had thought that story was going, but she just smiled, nodded, and tried to look impressed.

'Nice one. That's… good. Anyway… You said you had a juicy piece of gossip?'

'Ooh! Yes!' That was all Sinead got out of the other woman before her attention snapped back to Tyler.

Tyler's focus, however, was back on the cat. It had just twitched like it was about to move, and he was bracing himself for it to come leaping at his face, finally revealing its razor sharp claws as it unsheathed them for battle.

Instead, it just let out another hiss, and went back to doing nothing.

With the danger passed, Tyler looked up, saw that Gemma was staring at him with a similar intensity to Poof's, and realised she'd just said something to him.

'Sorry, what?' he asked.

Had he not become attuned to it, he might have missed Sinead's little sigh. He had no time to react to it, though, before Gemma repeated the words he'd just missed.

'Wild. Frantic. Animal. Sex.' She practically purred it at him, an eyebrow raised suggestively, her hands delicately balanced on the bare knee of a crossed leg.

It occurred to Tyler that he must have missed more than he'd realised. He shot a quick sideways look to his wife, then coughed his way through a reply.

'Um, sorry? I must've…' He pointed to Poof on the table. 'I was distracted by the cat.'

This just seemed to delight Gemma further. She fed the tip of her glasses-leg into her mouth and practically tongued the rubber coating off.

'All four of them. Denzel, Cassandra, Matty and Kelly. Half-dressed. Hammering away at each other. Proper, good old-fashioned foursome.'

'Matty? As in Matthew Broderick?' Tyler said. 'Is he not a kid?'

'Certainly not from where I was standing,' Gemma said, and this time even Poof heard Sinead's sigh. 'He's seventeen. All perfectly legal fun between consenting adults.'

She sat back, still chewing on her spectacles, and waved a hand in front of her face like she was trying to cool herself down.

'I mean, Denzel and Cassandra, they were really going at it. Can you blame them? Two young, fit, attractive people like that? The way they looked, the way their bodies moved together—'a shudder ran through her'—you could've framed that and hung it in a gallery. I'd buy a print for my bedroom wall.' A smile tugged at one corner of her red-painted lips. 'Or ceiling.'

'Jesus Christ,' Sinead mumbled below her breath, tiring of the woman's schtick. 'So, you're saying that all four of them were in the same room having sex? Denzel and Cassandra were together, and...what? Matthew and Kelly?'

'I got the feeling there was crossover involved. It wasn't a big room, and the clothes they'd removed were sort of scattered together, if you know what I mean? I imagine they may have swapped around. Mixed and matched.'

'I'm sure you do,' Sinead remarked. 'But when you saw them, it was those two couples?'

'Correct.'

'And did they stop when you came in?' Sinead pressed.

'Matty and Kelly—bless her, poor Kelly—they did. They got a fright when they saw me. The other two, no. They carried on.'

'And what did you say to them?' Sinead asked.

Gemma shrugged and continued to waft air across her face with a hand. She was reddening a little, but Sinead doubted embarrassment had anything to do with it.

'I said, 'Don't mind me, guys. Sound check in twenty minutes,' and then I left them to it.'

'You left them having sex?'

'Yes.'

'All of them? Together?' Sinead pressed. 'You left them all having sex?'

'Yes. I'm not their mum, am I? Why was it any of my business, who was fucking who?'

She stressed the obscenity, almost like she was taunting Sinead with it. If she thought that would fluster the detective constable, though—a woman who had not only worked dozens of Saturday night beats, but had spent time in the company of Bob and Berta Hoon—she had another thing coming.

Tyler quietly cleared his throat. 'Health and safety, maybe?' he suggested weakly.

Both women turned to look at him. The cat, who had already been staring at him, stared harder.

'Sorry?' Gemma asked.

'Just… I don't know.' Tyler scratched at the back of his head. 'I just thought maybe there might be some health and safety issues having four people in one wee room. Fire precautions, or…' He shook his head. 'It's fine. Probably not a problem.' He swallowed as he felt the weight of their stares on him. 'And it's most likely more of a council issue, anyway. Carry on.'

Gemma smirked, enjoying the way that Tyler squirmed. 'Yes. Well, I left them to it, like I say. But there's the funny thing. After it—during the actual convention—there was real tension between them all. Well, towards Kelly, mostly. She kept trying to talk to them, all smiles and whatever, but they either ignored or, or flat out told her to fuck off.' She held up her hands as if making an admission of guilt. 'I'm paraphrasing there. I didn't actually hear the words they said to her, but I got the meaning loud and clear from facial reactions and body language.'

'Did you talk to any of them about it?' Sinead asked. 'About what you'd seen?'

'No! Again, not my business, is it?' Gemma said. 'But, I did see Kelly a bit later in the toilets. She looked upset. Like she'd been crying.'

'Did she say anything?' Tyler asked.

The cat hissed again. Clearly, as well as disliking his face, it wasn't keen on his voice, either.

'She did. She thanked me for inviting her, but said she wished she hadn't come,' Gemma replied, in a tone that suggested she was building to a punchline.

Which, to Sinead's disgust, she was.

'So I said, 'At least you did, love! You never know with these young lads, do you? Lot of energy, but fuck all experience!' Gemma's smile thinned in disappointment. 'She didn't laugh. Don't think she really got it, poor cow. And, now, of course…'

She put two fingers to the side of her head and mimed shooting herself through the skull.

'*Ptchow*. Gone. Isn't she? Bless her. I can hardly believe it.'

She pulled a stricken face, but her sadness was a panto dame, grotesquely exaggerated and over the top to the point of being laughable.

Neither detective was in a laughing mood.

'During the convention, did you see anyone acting suspiciously?' Sinead asked.

'Suspiciously?'

'Anyone that struck you as unusual, or odd?'

Gemma snorted a laugh. 'It was a social media influencer convention. Everyone there was odd, guests and punters alike. I mean, no. That's unfair. There were a few parents who'd brought kids along, and who were clearly hating every minute, but everyone who was there and into the whole thing? Weirdoes, generally speaking.'

'That's not a very nice way to talk about people who've paid to support your event,' Sinead pointed out.

Gemma shrugged. 'They're paying punters, that's all. I've got no real interest in the *Who's Who?* of it all. I didn't know any of these people before we booked them. I'm a businesswoman, and the first rule of business is?'

She pointed to Tyler like a teacher calling for a pupil to answer.

Tyler straightened up in surprise. Poof didn't like that, and his tail rose rigidly towards the sky.

'Buy low, sell high?' Tyler guessed.

Gemma lowered her finger and smiled patronisingly. 'Know your customer,' she corrected. 'Know who you're selling to. I do. I know exactly who I'm selling to. I'm selling to a bunch of grown men and women who are obsessed enough with a group of strangers on the internet that they'll pay thirty-five quid a time to come and spend fifteen seconds in their company. Sixty-five if they want a photo. So, you ask if there were any oddballs there? Yes. About three-hundred and seventy of them.'

She angled her gaze to Tyler again, then uncrossed her legs before crossing them again the other way. Slowly. 'If you like, I can get you a list of their names?'

'What?' Tyler stopped eyeballing the cat. 'Oh. Aye. That'd be good. Cheers.'

'Great!' Gemma took a swig of her wine. 'It might take me a little while. Maybe you can hang back for it while your colleague here goes and gets on with things? I'm sure she's very busy.'

'Wife,' Sinead said.

Gemma's frown moved slowly down her face. 'Sorry?'

'I'm not just his colleague. I'm his wife.'

'His…?' Gemma looked from one DC to the other, her ruby red smile fading away. 'Oh. Balls,' she muttered, then she yanked her phone from her pocket, tapped sullenly at the screen, and glowered at both detectives. 'In that case, just give me an email address, and I'll send the bloody thing over.'

Chapter 19

There was just time to make a couple of quick calls and do a progress check with the rest of the team before Logan headed for his traditional pre-press conference pee.

The next-of-kin of all the kidnap victims had been contacted, and were being supported. They were scattered all across the UK, and it had involved co-ordinating with several different forces in England and Wales.

The dog walker had been collected and was being brought in. He'd asked if he should bring the dog, too, and the constable sent to pick him up had phoned the station looking for clarity on the matter.

When it had been pointed out that the dog was unlikely to have anything significant to add on the matter, he'd mumbled some embarrassed apologies and hung up.

Tyler and Sinead were on their way back, though Logan didn't yet know if they had got anything useful from the convention organiser. He hoped so, as they could really do with a win right about now, particularly given the news that the consultant, Thomas Arden, had shared as Logan was heading out the door.

Apparently, thousands of 'internet sleuths' were co-ordinating online, poring over every clue, and every frame of video which they'd all downloaded and shared around. There were already dozens of conspiracy theories floating around on social media. Many of them were about the whole thing being fake, which Logan couldn't really blame them for.

Others were much wilder, though. It was all a government experiment; the influencers had never actually existed, and had all been actors from the start; The Illuminati; Bill Gates; Trump; Biden; flat Earth; *Aliens*!

Dozens of the bastards—hundreds, maybe—were making plans to descend on Inverness so they could carry out their 'investigations' and make their awful videos to spew out into the world.

And still people were dancing to the music on those first clips.

And hundreds of thousands of others were laughing, and liking, and commenting on every scrap of content.

Logan had made a mental note to address this during the press conference. Then, after acknowledging the, 'Good luck,' from Hamza and the, 'Rather you than me, Jack,' from Ben, he had left the Incident Room, paused in the corridor to text an update request to Geoff Palmer, then headed for the toilets.

He used the time it had taken for his bladder to drain to workshop what he was going to say to the assembled bastards of the media, and had just finished washing and drying his hands when the door opened and Detective Superintendent Mitchell came striding in.

Logan met her eye in the mirror as he finished drying his hands on the paper towel. He almost made a light-hearted remark about missing the memo on mixed-sex bathrooms, but the look on her face knocked that idea right out of him.

Instead, he just nodded, offered a, 'Ma'am,' then binned the paper towel and turned to face her. 'How are you holding up?'

It was a daft question. Usually, Mitchell's expression was pretty much unreadable. She was a master at masking her emotions behind a look of stern disapproval that occasionally tipped over into contempt.

Now, though, there was something distant and detached about her, like she wasn't fully there. Not really. Not all the way.

Logan had seen that look countless times before. He'd seen it on the faces of people pulled alive from fatal car accidents. On people who'd witnessed a suicide, or found a murder victim. On people who'd stared back at him as he'd told them the person they loved most in the world would never be coming home.

On people whose lives had forever and catastrophically been changed by one awful, devastating moment.

'I'm holding up about as well as a mother whose son is being held captive by a murderer,' Mitchell replied.

Jack nodded. Like he'd thought, daft question.

'I'm not meant to be talking to you about this, but… Tell me we have something, Jack.' It didn't sound like an order. She wasn't talking to him as a senior officer. 'Please, just tell me we have something.'

Logan wished, more than anything, that they had. That he had something tangible to give her. Or even just something that might offer her a sliver of hope.

Although, he knew, it was often the hope that killed you.

'We're working on a number of leads, ma'am,' Logan told her, which wasn't, strictly speaking, untrue.

Mitchell saw through it right away, of course. She looked down at her feet, composing herself.

'They killed that woman,' she said. 'They executed her live for the whole world to see.'

Logan nodded. 'Aye,' he said, and his pain at his helplessness was all packed into that one syllable.

'And people cheered it on, Jack,' Mitchell said in a whisper. Her eyes darted left and right, like she was watching it all happening again. 'I mean, Jesus Christ, what state is the world in when they're sitting there in their millions, cheering it on?'

'I know. And that was my initial reaction, too,' Logan told her. 'But the world's always been full of arseholes. They're just more visible now. That's what I'm trying to tell myself, anyway.'

The bathroom door opened and a fresh-faced young constable strolled in.

'Get out!' Mitchell barked.

The constable let out a wobbly yelp of fear as he leaped back and shot a panicked look at the sign on the door. There was barely time for his confusion to register that he was, in fact, in the right place, before the door swung closed on him again.

That moment of authority restored something in the Detective Superintendent. Her expression became sterner, the vagueness of her features sharpening into focus.

'I've written up my statement about Denzel, and sent it to the inbox. I've spoken to his father, too. He blames me for it all, because of course he does. He insists it's someone trying to get at me through Denzel.'

'I don't agree with that,' Logan said.

'No, nor do I,' Mitchell replied. 'If it was about me—if someone was doing this specifically to hurt me—I'd have heard something.'

Logan tried not to think about that beer mat in that envelope. It was difficult, given that it had been flitting between the back and forefront of his mind all day.

'I'm sure you would,' Logan confirmed.

'And why involve the others?' Mitchell asked. 'The co-ordination it all must've taken. The effort. I don't know those people. If you wanted to get at me, why target the rest of them? It doesn't make any sense.'

She was right. It didn't. Mitchell only knew one member of the group, and Logan knew one fewer than that.

Maybe this wasn't a message to either of them, then. Maybe, it was just yet another terrible thing that had happened in the world, and any connection to them was entirely coincidental.

He'd like it if that were the case.

Given time, maybe he could even make himself believe it.

'There's some rumour flying around that Kelly Wynne—the woman who was shot—was the daughter of a police officer, too.'

Mitchell's eyes widened until the pupils were islands in seas of white. 'Have you been able to substantiate that?'

'Not yet,' Logan admitted. 'We've got Uniform calling around, and I'm sure the press are digging into it, too. If it's true…'

'Then someone could be targeting the police in general, not me specifically.' She put her hands on her hips and sighed. 'I don't know whether that's better or worse.'

'Nor me,' Logan admitted. 'But, anyway, I better run, ma'am. The Gozer's going to be waiting.'

'The press conference,' Mitchell said. 'I heard.'

'Waste of time, if you ask me.'

Mitchell shrugged, like she couldn't quite bring herself to care. 'It's all politics. The higher up you go in this job, the more you have to juggle operational secrecy with what *the people* think they ought to know. Something this size, you can bet the government's already stuck its oar in.' She sighed, and it was the weariest sound in the world. 'It's all becoming quite the circus, isn't it?'

'Unfortunately, aye.' Logan grimaced in distaste. 'Bloody vultures. And now, it looks like we're going to have a swarm of internet detectives headed our way, too.'

'That was inevitable, once it all spread online. You're going to need more resources allocated. I know other forces have had problems with similar situations before. They clog information phone lines, invade crime scenes, pester witnesses, you name it,' Mitchell said. 'If there's a way to make a nuisance of themselves, they won't just find it, they'll revel in it, and they'll tell others how to do it, too. And then, they'll find whole new ways to interfere, and repeat, and repeat, and repeat.'

Logan could've guessed all that, of course, but hearing it spoken out loud only hammered home the potential impact of it. 'Christ.'

'I can put in a request for more Uniform support, and give you direct authority over CID,' Mitchell began, then that look of uncertainty crept back onto her face again. 'I mean, I can talk to Detective Superintendent MacKenzie and suggest he take a similar approach.'

'It's fine. I'll talk to him myself.'

'It's not a problem, honestly,' Mitchell insisted.

'I know. But, I'm about to see him, anyway, and I'm sure if I explain—'

'Please, Jack.' The Det Supt's voice cracked in a way that Logan had never heard before. The sound of it resonated around the acoustics of the bathroom. 'Please, I can't just sit around. I have to do something. Let me help with this, at least.'

Logan nodded. 'Of course, ma'am.'

She inhaled slowly through her nose. Which, given the room they were currently standing in, struck Logan as a bold move.

'Right. Yes. Good,' she said. 'Well, I'll go make a full list of recommendations and have them ready for him for after the conference.'

'Good idea,' Logan said.

There was a squeaky sounding *parp* from one of the toilet cubicles, and they both realised for the first time that there was someone else in there with them.

An embarrassed voice rose up from behind the stall door. 'Um, sorry.'

Logan sighed. 'And, on that note,' he said, 'I think it's time we left.'

Chapter 20

Hamza could feel Thomas hovering a couple of feet behind him. Even over the sound of his own typing, and DI Forde's complaining about how his phone wasn't working properly, Hamza heard the shuffling of feet and the quiet clearing of a throat.

Though he was tempted to spin in his chair and rip the bastard's throat out with his teeth, the detective sergeant decided that such a quick death would be too good for him.

Instead, he pretended he hadn't noticed the consultant's approach, forcing Thomas to make the first move.

'I, uh, um, sorry...Hamza? You busy?'

'It's Detective Sergeant Khaled.' Hamza's fingers slammed at the computer's keys, making them clack loudly. 'And, what do you think? Yes. Of course I'm busy.'

'No, um, of course. Yes. Bound to be,' Thomas mumbled. 'It's just, something's come up. It's important.'

Hamza stopped typing, flexed his fingers a few times like he was warming them up for a strangling, then turned a one-eighty in his seat until he was facing the other man.

'What is it?' he demanded, in a tone that made clear he already knew it was going to be a complete waste of his time.

It wasn't.

'They've posted a link,' Thomas said. 'On Kelly Wynne's TikTok account.'

Hamza was on his feet before his response could tumble out of his mouth. 'What? When? What sort of link?'

Thomas held up his phone. A video showing Kelly taking her bow before she was shot played with a boomerang effect, running forwards and backwards so she appeared to bow over and over again.

Flickering animated text superimposed on the footage pointed viewers towards a gibberish domain with a .ru extension, and whoever had uploaded it had, for reasons not really clear, chosen to use *Africa* by Toto as the soundtrack to the clip.

'Went live a few minutes ago,' Thomas said. 'Nothing on the others yet.'

'Have you checked the site?' Hamza asked, his animosity towards the man sliding unbidden into the back seat for the moment.

'I did. There's nothing really on it yet, just a holding page with this video playing on loop.' He pointed a thumb back over his shoulder to where his police-assigned laptop sat on a desk. 'I can show you.'

Hamza followed him to the desk. Sure enough, the page was mostly blank, aside from a constantly looping version of the same video Hamza had just watched.

Although, it wasn't *exactly* the same.

'That's not a TikTok embed,' the sergeant said. 'There's no logo.'

'No,' Thomas confirmed. 'It's streaming from another I.P.—not the same as the site host—but it's well masked.'

'Can we trace it?' Hamza asked.

Thomas put his hands on his hips and puffed out his cheeks. 'Not sure. The site's hosted on Russian servers, and they're not generally known for being forthcoming on stuff like this. The stream…? Maybe, if they don't know what they're doing. But, like I say, they've made a decent stab at covering their tracks, so it could take time. It might well be Russian, too, of course. I don't know what authority you guys have, but I'm guessing accessing the home addresses of people using Russian VPNs and servers is somewhere above it?'

It was a genuine enough question, but Hamza couldn't shake the feeling the bastard was mocking them.

The annoying thing was, he was right. 'No. I doubt we can get that sort of information. Not easily, anyway.'

Thomas winced. 'Damn. Don't suppose you've got any pals in the secret service, do you? MI5 or 6 could probably find out the details.'

'No. Funnily enough, I'm not friends with many spies,' Hamza snapped, his anger returning.

There was a loud *thack* from behind him as Ben gave up trying to get his phone working and slammed the receiver back into the cradle.

'No, me neither,' said the detective inspector, who had been lugging in on the conversation. He sat back in his chair and reached for his mug of tea. 'But we know a man who is...'

—

Former detective superintendent, Robert Hoon, was irritable. This was not unusual. 'Irritable' was pretty much Bob's base level mood and, while it was theoretically possible for it to fluctuate either way, it generally trended downwards.

'Aye, hold your horses, sweetheart,' he said, shooting the woman on the other side of the counter a scathing look.

When she tried to speak again, he held up an index finger for silence, then pressed his phone to his ear.

'Benjamin. Aye. What do you want? I'm in a queue at JFK here.' He listened for a moment, then tutted sharply. 'No, I mean the fucking dead president of the United States. Aye, the airport. Of course the fucking airport. What do you want?' He shot a look at the uniformed woman who was currently glowering back at him. 'And make it fucking quick before this lassie starts whinging at me.'

'Sir, I'm going to have to ask you to step out of line,' the airport worker said. She was at the younger end of her thirties, with carefully arranged hair and a heavy dusting of make-up.

The painted rosy cheeks clashed with her current scowl. 'You can't just take personal calls in line, you're holding people up.'

'That's hunky-fucking-dory then, hen, because it's no' a personal call. It's police business.'

The woman looked him up and down, her face registering her disbelief and horror. Hoon had been wearing the same clothes for the last few days, hadn't shaved in the past week, and had just endured an overnight cross country flight in a middle seat, with two babies screaming their heads off a couple of rows away.

He did not look like a man with a police career. Or any career.

Or, for that matter, a permanent address.

'You're in the police?' she asked.

'Too fucking right I am,' Hoon shot back. He grimaced as Ben's voice rang out from the phone. 'She doesn't need to fucking know that, does she? She's no' after a fucking history lesson. Just tell me what the fuck it is you want.'

'Hey, can you hurry it up there, buddy?' a man in the queue said, taking his life in his hands.

'I'm no' your fucking buddy, pal,' Hoon said. He gestured back to the line of people snaking behind him. 'I fucking earned this place in the queue. I lined up like a good little fucking soldier. I did my time. It's no' my fault this old bastard's ringing me up, is it? That's on him, no' me.'

'You didn't have to take the call,' the woman on the other side of the counter pointed out.

Hoon turned to her, visibly appalled. 'Jesus Christ, you soulless kettle o' shite. There could be someone fucking dying here, for all we know. He's no' just rung me up for a fucking chat!' Bob side-eyed the phone he held pressed to his ear. 'You haven't, have you?'

Ben assured him that he had not, then there was some background noise before Hamza's voice replaced the Detective Inspector's.

Hamza started to explain exactly why they were calling, and why they needed his help, but Hoon cut him off one-and-a-half sentences in.

'Fuck me, son, that's the most boring collection of words I've ever heard spoken together in the same fucking sentence,' he retorted. 'I think I got about three percent of it before my brain started shutting itself down out of self-fucking-preservation. I'm no' going to remember a word of it. In fact, I'm actively trying not to. So, how about you thumb-tap me out a wee email on your fucking Blackberry, or whatever you geeky bastards use, and I'll forward it on to whoever the fuck can help with it when I'm on the plane?'

'Your cellphone will have to go in flight mode when you're on board,' the staff member interjected.

Hoon snorted. 'Oh aye. *Flight mode.*' He winked at her and grinned, like they were sharing a secret. 'Whatever you say, sweetheart.'

Turning his attention back to his phone, he listened to the detective sergeant's reply, rolled his eyes around at the rest of the queue as if they were all rooting for him, then he snapped out his goodbyes and hung up.

'Fuck's sake. People, eh? Inconsiderate bastards, some of them. Anyway—'he tossed something long and foil-wrapped onto the counter'—I'll just have the Twix. And, you'd better get a shifty on with ringing it up, because I was meant to be at the boarding gate forty-five fucking minutes ago.'

Chapter 21

There were dozens of them. A round hundred, maybe. Perhaps, even more.

Definitely even more.

Logan knew the faces of a few of the local reporters, and recognised a couple of the TV journos from the central belt, but most of them were new to him.

He hated them, all the same. He'd always found it quicker and easier to just go ahead and blanket-despise the whole lot of them. Then, if one of them surprised him by somehow proving themselves to be a decent human being, he could always make an exception for them.

Over the course of his career, he had granted precisely two exceptions. And one of those had technically been a weatherman.

The journalists were crammed into the briefing room, filling all the available seats and squeezing up side-by-side along the walls. There was the sense of a swarm about them, or a plague. Cockroaches, maybe. Or rats. Nothing pleasant, anyway.

Logan hadn't yet been able to count how many cameras and microphones were currently pointing in his and the Gozer's direction. Just when he thought he'd got an idea of their number, the door at the back of the room would open and a few more would be added to the mix.

The crowd was restless, too, the sheer number of them assembled in one place buoying them all with a sense of confidence and entitlement. Even more so than usual, if such a thing could be believed.

A few of them called on him and the Gozer by name, trying to get them to turn towards the cameras so they could get a good front-facing shot.

He ignored them all, denying them the footage they were after. The only time he did react was when someone shouted from the back of the room asking him to smile. He instinctively glowered in the direction the voice had come from, but whoever had made the suggestion had the good sense not to own up to it.

He gave up trying to count all the bits and pieces of sound and camera equipment, settled on, 'too bloody many,' then sat back with his arms folded as Detective Superintendent MacKenzie kicked the whole thing off.

Often, senior officers would stand when addressing the media. Logan respected the fact that the Gozer didn't bother his arse. He knew, just as well as Jack did that they didn't deserve the respect that standing would imply.

Logan always stayed seated for these things. If he thought he could get away with it, he'd even consider lying down.

He had sat by the Gozer's side for many press conferences over the years. Often, for major investigations, too. None of them, though, not even the more headline grabbing serial killer cases, had been as busy or as buzzing as this one. Despite all his experience, MacKenzie's voice had a bit of a nervous wobble to it as he addressed the room.

'Thank you all for coming. Apologies for the slightly cramped conditions. Had we known there would be this many of you, we'd…' He had no idea what they'd have done. This was the biggest space available in the building. 'Well, we'd have worked something out.'

There was a ripple of polite laughter, like the Gozer had just made a joke. He seemed momentarily surprised by it, but then continued.

'I'm Detective Superintendent Gordon MacKenzie, and this is Detective Chief Inspector Jack Logan. Obviously, we're still in the first few hours of a major investigation, so we don't have a huge amount to share at the moment, but given the intense interest in the case, we felt it appropriate to hold this conference.'

Logan didn't agree with the usage of the word 'we,' but he kept his mouth shut and said nothing.

Pulling on his glasses, the Gozer looked down at his notes, and at the statement he'd hastily written out by hand a few minutes before taking the stage.

'At around 6 P.M. on Saturday, eight guests of the 'Social Stars' convention held at Eden Court Theatre are believed to have been taken by an as-yet-unknown abductor. Their names and details are already in the public domain, and I won't be going over them again here.'

Logan watched the faces of the journalists crowded into the room before him. Most of them were listening to the Gozer's statement, but a few of the more experienced ones were watching Logan himself, trying to work out the story behind the story from his body language and facial expressions alone.

He hoped they could read the contempt that he was actively projecting in their direction as he sat there, stony-faced and motionless. Beside him, the Detective Superintendent used a large number of words to say very little of consequence.

It wasn't the Gozer's fault, of course. This thing hadn't been his idea. And, right now, the press in the room—anyone with an internet connection, in fact—was about as up-to-date on what was happening to the influencers as the police were.

The journalists had started to get a sense of that, too. Those who'd been listening intently to the Detective Superintendent were now starting to fidget and shuffle as it became clear that no big bombshells were about to be dropped.

Many of them sat up straighter, glancing around at their awful, awful peers, desperate to be the first to ask a question as soon as the opportunity presented itself. There was time set aside at the end for this, but there were always one or two of the bastards who couldn't bring themselves to wait until then.

Sure enough, while the Gozer was making assurances that the MIT was pursuing several avenues of investigation and that it was only a matter of time before they had a major breakthrough, some baritone voiced American piped up from near the front of the room.

'Darryl Kerner, NBC. Do you anticipate any more deaths, Detective Superintendent?'

The question caught the Gozer off guard. He removed his glasses and looked around the audience until he found the tanned, silver-haired Kerner with a hand lazily raised to just above the level of his eyes.

'We're not currently anticipating anything,' the Gozer replied.

Logan tried to keep his wince from registering on his face. It was an uncharacteristically weak response from the Det Supt. Anticipating what a killer might do next was generally considered to be quite an important part of the job.

Fortunately, MacKenzie realised this, and hurriedly tried to course correct. 'By which I mean, we're investigating a number of possible scenarios. Obviously, for operational reasons, I can't share any more detail on that at the present time.'

Operational reasons. A classic, catch-all excuse for not fully answering a question, although Logan much preferred the more direct, 'None of your fucking business,' which had seen him reprimanded by a number of more senior officers over the years.

'What I would say,' the Gozer continued, 'is, if the person or persons responsible for this are watching, then please get in touch. Let's talk. No one else needs to get hurt. It's in everyone's best interests if you get in contact.'

Another male voice rang out from the back of the room. 'Is it true that this has a personal connection to an officer here?'

Logan peered into the crowd. His mind raced back to a beer mat in an envelope. To a warning by a roadside a few months before.

A New Player has Entered the Game.

'Is it true that Denzel Drummond is the son of a—'the questioner consulted his notes'—Detective Superintendent Suki Mitchell? Is that a coincidence, or is someone either targeting her or the police more generally with this?'

The Gozer frowned, too busy trying to figure out how that information could be out in the wild to respond to the question.

Logan knew that the answer to that question was deceptively simple: the parasitic, dirt-digging bastards always found a way.

He leaned in closer to the microphone in front of him, coming to the detective superintendent's rescue. 'We are of the belief that's just a coincidence.'

'That's not what the lad's father says,' one of the other parasites chipped in. 'He says it's all Denzel's mother's fault. That this is on her.'

That explained how they'd found out, at least. By this point, they'd probably spoken to not just every parent and partner of the abductees, but their friends, colleagues, neighbours, exes, old teachers, and the baristas of any coffee shops they were regular visitors to.

Not only were the poor buggers being held prisoner, but soon, every secret they ever had would be raked up and pored over to help bring in a few more newspaper sales and advertising clicks.

'Mr Drummond can say what he likes,' Logan replied. 'It doesn't mean it's true. Like I say, we're of the belief that it's a coincidence, nothing more.'

'What about Adam Parfitt, though?' It was the Yank from NBC again.

This time, it was Logan's turn to hesitate. He pictured the wig-wearing, screechy-voiced 'comedian' currently locked in a cell somewhere.

'What about him?'

'Hang on.' The silver caterpillars of the American's eyebrows wriggled up his Botox-smooth forehead. 'Are you saying you don't know?'

Logan splayed his hands flat on the table in front of him and counted to five in his head.

'Don't know what?' he asked, managing to keep his voice flat and level. 'If you have information to share, I encourage you to do so. Otherwise—'

'Well, I mean, he's Owen Petrie's nephew, isn't he?'

The name hit the DCI like a kick to the sternum. He felt all the breath leaving his body, all at once. His lungs made no attempt to draw in any more.

Owen Petrie. *Mister Whisper.* The child-killer who had haunted Logan for the best part of his career. Who had ended his marriage, destroyed his relationship with his daughter, and driven him, shuffling and broken, into the welcoming arms of alcoholism.

The room was suddenly hot. Suddenly spinning. Suddenly silent. Logan felt all eyes on him. Watching him. Waiting for him.

He tried to clear his throat, but there wasn't enough air left in him to quite manage, and all he could do was wheeze.

'You did know that, didn't you?' he heard the journalist ask. 'Don't tell us you hadn't made the connection? How can the families of these victims possibly trust you to bring them home safely if you haven't even done basic background research?'

It was the Gozer's time to throw himself into the firing line. 'There are many different strands to the investigation, with Major Investigations, CID, and uniformed officers all working together, not just here, but in other forces across the United Kingdom. If what you're saying is correct—'

'It is,' the journalist insisted.

The detective superintendent closed his eyes for a moment, making his irritation clear. '*If* what you are saying is correct, then that will have been flagged up and will be examined in due course.'

'In due course?' a woman down the front asked. She was in her forties, with a dress sense best described as 'Tory chic' and skin that was unsettlingly shiny. She looked as if someone had sculpted Lorraine Kelly out of butter, and sat it under hot studio lights. 'A woman was murdered live on the internet. I'd say 'due course' has already passed, hasn't it?'

Mention of the dead woman triggered another question. 'Is it true about Kelly Wynne and her relationship to another former officer of Police Scotland?'

Still reeling from the Mister Whisper reveal, Logan found himself once again on the back foot. 'Who?' he asked.

The Gozer quickly chimed in. 'We're aware of speculation regarding Ms Wynne's family, and are investigating that thoroughly. We're looking into a number of possibilities, but if you've heard a particular name, please tell us, so we can check it against our own list.'

It was a load of old bollocks, of course—their own investigations had turned up nothing on the dead woman's family—but it was delivered so confidently and eloquently that he just about got away with it.

It certainly robbed the journalist of some of their smugness. 'Can you share that list with us?' he asked, which suggested he'd just been fishing for information, hoping to substantiate the rumours flying around.

'No. I'm afraid I can't share that information, for very obvious reasons,' the Gozer said.

It fell on deaf ears, though. Halfway through the detective superintendent's reply, everyone's phones started to bleep, and ping, and buzz, as messages came whooshing through the ether.

'Holy shit! It's coming back on!' cried a voice from up the back.

'The feeds are up and running!' squealed another, her excitement sickeningly shrill and high-pitched.

'New broadcast starting in two minutes. Quick, go live, go live!'

Chairs scraped on the floor. Footsteps raced. Bodies jostled. The room moved as one, surging towards the exit. The eyes of the reporters were glued to their phone screens. Nobody cared what Logan and the Gozer had to say now. There was new content coming. The game had begun again.

Logan caught his breath and grabbed for his mobile. He paused with his thumbs hovering over the screen, realised that he had no idea how to find the footage the reporters were so excited about, then he swore loudly at their backs as they continued to rush for the exit.

'Where the hell is Hamza?' he began, rising from his chair, only to find the detective sergeant marching through the doorway behind him.

'Sir, it's—'

'Aye! I know!' Logan barked. He thrust his phone into the other man's hands. 'Get it on there for me so I can see it.'

'There's nothing live yet. Just seven video windows with countdowns.' Hamza looked from Logan to the Gozer, then tilted his head towards the door he'd just come through. 'So, if we're quick, we can go and watch it all properly.'

Chapter 22

All seven video windows were laid out on a large screen that was mounted on a wheeled frame and positioned just to the right of the Big Boards. Four videos ran along the top of the screen, three along the bottom.

Unlike on Instagram, where the videos had been taller than they were wide, these were in a more TV-like horizontal aspect ratio, with the downward-counting numbers taking up the full width of each one.

Also unlike on Instagram, all seven feeds were embedded in a single webpage, making it easier for those watching at home to follow along with each of the remaining hostages.

The countdowns had showed just over a minute remaining when Hamza had led Logan and the Gozer back into the Incident Room. By the time they had taken up positions beside the rest of the team—and Thomas—there were just a few seconds left.

'Here we go,' Sinead said on an inwards breath, inhaling each word like she didn't want them out there in the world.

Logan said nothing. He just stood there in silence, his arms across his chest, one hand gripping his jaw, fingertips toying with his stubble.

'Are we able to record this?' Ben asked.

Thomas opened his mouth to reply, but then deferred to Hamza, who confirmed that they already were.

The countdowns reached zero. The Gozer whispered a tense, throaty, 'Christ,' then all seven timers were replaced by video feeds of the surviving influencers. As before, the streaming images had no accompanying audio, which somehow made the pictures all the more harrowing to look at.

They each sat on the floor of their individual cages, most of them crying or rocking back and forth. Elizia Shuttleworth, the spiritual guru who had appeared quite serene while meditating in her previous video, was now a haunted, wide-eyed mess of snot and sorrow.

The rest of them weren't faring much better. A couple of them—the gamer, Matthew, and the wig-wearing comedian, Adam—significantly worse.

Logan studied Adam, paying close attention to the lad for the first time since all this had started. Was it true? Was this portly, jocular clown really a blood relative of one of the most twisted, evil killers the DCI had ever encountered?

Logan had spent countless hours staring at that sick bastard's face over the years, both in print and in person. In his nightmares, too. He knew it better than he knew his own. Better than his ex-wife's. Better than his daughter's.

There was nothing of Owen Petrie's haunting hollow stare in Adam Parfitt's eyes. Nothing of the murderer's malice oozing from the pores of his skin.

And yet, there was something. Some similarity that Logan couldn't quite pin down. Across the mouth, maybe, or the shape of the nose. He'd never have spotted it, had the journalist not mentioned the connection. Even then, it was entirely possible that he was imagining it.

If it was true, then was that why he'd ended up here? Had his connection to Mister Whisper brought him to the abductor's attention?

Or his connection to Logan himself?

There'd be no answering that yet, so Logan turned his attention to Denzel Drummond. Mitchell's son knelt on the floor, hands on his thighs, like a karate master ready to spring up and roundhouse kick the head off some unseen opponent. It would be handy if he did, Logan thought. Right now, saving themselves was these poor bastards' best chance of survival.

'Elizia's camera is stationary this time,' Thomas remarked.

'They all are,' Hamza added. 'There's a couple of frames delay in her timecode, though.'

'What? Oh. Shit. Good spot,' Thomas told him, but Hamza didn't look pleased by the compliment. Then again, he didn't look furious about it, either, so that was an improvement.

'What does that mean?' Logan asked.

Thomas stretched a finger past him, pointing to the numbers birling around at the bottom of Elizia's video feed. 'You see those numbers there…?'

'I know what a timecode is, son,' Logan growled. 'I meant, what's the significance of hers being out of step with the rest of them?'

Thomas lowered his arm back to his side. 'I, uh, I don't know. But it's interesting.'

'She's talking,' Tyler pointed out. His eyes flitted across the other screens, then settled back on Elizia's. Of them all, she was the only one whose lips were moving. 'She's saying something to someone in the room.'

Logan squinted, trying to see the image more clearly. The resolution of the camera wasn't great in the low light of the cells, and though he'd seen the dreadlocked woman's lips moving, he'd assumed she was just babbling away to herself in terror.

But, Tyler was right. She still looked afraid, but she wasn't babbling incoherently, she was talking, her gaze regularly lifting in the same direction, as if addressing someone a foot or so to the left of the camera. The poor camera quality made lip-reading impossible, but Logan got the impression that she was pleading.

As he watched her, he couldn't help but feel there was something else in her expression beyond fear. Confusion, maybe, or something not too far away from it.

'Holy shit!' Dave ejected. 'Is that a knife?'

'Where?' the Gozer snapped.

'Top right. The chef guy.'

All eyes went to Bruce Kennedy's feed. The Australian sat against the back wall of his cell, looking down at something in his hand, which was currently below the edge of the frame.

'I don't see anything,' Sinead whispered.

'Wait for it,' Dave urged.

They all stared intently at the same spot on the screen like they were trying to warp the liquid crystal display with the power of their minds.

And then, they saw it. A turn of Bruce's wrist. A flash of a sharp silver blade.

'There!' Dave cried. 'I knew I'd seen it. That's definitely a knife. Big bugger of a thing, too.'

A whirlwind of jigsaw pieces spun in Logan's mind, trying to find a place where this new piece of information could be slotted in.

Bruce Kennedy had a weapon. A knife.

But it was a *chef's* knife, in the hands of a man who had found fame displaying his cooking skills.

So, what the hell did that mean? Had he had the blade with him the whole time, or had his abductor given it to him? Was he tooled up to do battle, or to show off his talent for chopping onions?

'What's her name? Dreadlock lassie's got one too,' Tyler announced, and all eyes shifted again.

No one had seen where Elizia had got the knife from, but now she gestured with it to whoever stood off camera, her hand trembling as she waved it vaguely in the unseen camera operator's direction.

It looked more or less identical to the knife Bruce was holding.

And, Logan realised a moment later, to the one in Cassandra Swain's hands.

'Hang on, have they all got them?' Ben asked, searching the other video windows. 'Why the hell have they all got them?'

'Are they going to fight?' the Gozer wondered aloud. He grimaced at the thought of it. 'Christ, they're not going to all kill each other, are they?'

'No.'

The rest of the team turned to Logan. He didn't take his eyes off the screen, but acknowledged them with a curt shake of his head.

'I don't think so, anyway.'

'Well...' The Gozer ran a hand back and forth across his bald head, as if polishing it like he'd buffed up his buttons. 'What, then?'

Logan thought of the bodies pulled from the bogs that morning.

He thought of the house. And the freezer. And the tray placed inside it.

He thought that he'd quite like to be wrong on this one.

He wasn't.

Tyler jumped as a robotic voice came blasting from the TV's speakers. It was a flat, synthetic monotone, and all the more sinister for it.

'Cut off a finger,' it announced. 'Fastest wins.'

The Gozer's face paled. His whispered, 'Oh, God,' was the only sound in the Incident Room.

On screen, a few of the hostages began to freak out, shaking their heads and recoiling, their terror almost tangible in the pixelated air around them.

Adam Parfitt blew a big panicky snot bubble. Elizia Shuttleworth clasped her hands in front of her and pleaded desperately with the person behind the camera. Matthew Broderick and the bubblegum-haired Natalie Womack both hugged their knees and wept. Cassandra Swain stared at her knife in disbelief. Bruce Kennedy tossed his into the corner of his cell.

'Fuuuuck!' Tyler grimaced and wrapped his arms around his head, as he clocked Denzel Drummond splaying his left hand on the floor.

Mitchell's son drew in several breaths, each one deeper than the one before, each one puffing out his muscular chest and pumping up his adrenaline levels.

And then, teeth gritted, forehead furrowed, eyes staring straight into the lens of the camera, he brought the knife down on his pinkie finger in one short, sharp slice.

For a moment, his expression arranged itself into a picture of regret, but then the lines of his face hardened again, his teeth bared, and he thumped himself in the chest with the hand that had, until a moment ago, been wielding the knife.

He held the other hand up to the camera, showing the spurting stump of his little finger. His mouth opened, but those watching could only imagine the roar of triumph, or of desperation, or of whatever the hell it was that had driven his rush to self-mutilate.

'Bloody hell,' Dave muttered. 'Hardy.'

'This is insane,' Sinead said. She stepped in a little closer to Tyler, taking comfort from her husband's presence. 'This is… I mean, Jesus. This is horrible.'

'He's looking at the camera,' Thomas said. 'He hasn't looked anywhere else.'

'There's nobody else in the room,' Hamza reasoned.

Thomas nodded slowly, but then shrugged. 'Or, he knows it's the people watching that he needs to impress.'

None of the others had made a move to follow Denzel's lead yet. Although, none of them had reacted to his bellowing, either, Logan noted. With the exception of Elizia, they'd all reacted immediately to the gunshots that had killed Kelly Wynne. Logan had assumed they were all in the same place, but if that was the case, then why did nobody bat an eyelid at one of their number hacking off his own pinkie?

'How do we find this?' the Gozer asked, gesturing to the screen. 'The website. How do we find the host?'

'It's Russian,' Thomas told him.

This information only served to infuriate the Detective Superintendent. 'But *they're* not in bloody Russia, though, are they?'

'No,' Thomas admitted, then he frowned. 'I mean, not as far as we know. They were missing for over thirty hours, though.'

'Christ Almighty! So we don't even know that?!'

'We're working on it,' Ben assured him. 'We've got a secret service connection trying to find the P.I. address.'

'I.P. address,' Hamza corrected, but Ben just shrugged, like this detail was unimportant. He had, after all, got the letters right, which was a better result than he or anyone else had been expecting.

Logan shot a look of confusion down at the Detective Inspector. 'That's news to me,' he said. 'Who the hell's our secret service connection?'

Ben glanced up at him. His expression told the DCI everything he needed to know.

'Oh, for fuck's sake,' Logan muttered, turning his attention back to the telly.

'Who?' the Gozer demanded. 'Who is it?'

'Best if you don't know, sir,' Logan told him. 'Plausible deniability, and all that.'

The detective superintendent's eyebrows shot halfway up his forehead. 'Wait, it's not...?' He grimaced like some phantom pain had suddenly struck him. Somewhere sensitive, too. 'No, you're right. I don't want to know.'

'Oof. Here we go,' Dave said, nodding to the screen. 'Yoga lassie, bottom left.'

They all looked in time to see Cassandra Swain raising the knife and staring at the blade. Her expression was hard. Determined. Like she was giving herself a talking to via her reflection in the steel.

'God. She's not, is she?' Tyler asked. 'She's not actually going to do it?'

'I don't think she has a choice,' Sinead whispered. She glanced up at Logan, as if seeking some words of wisdom from him, or at least of comfort.

The DCI said nothing. He had nothing left to offer.

Tyler clutched his head tighter and half-turned away as Cassandra raised the knife, point facing down to where her hand was splayed on the floor.

'Fuck!' Tyler cried. He shut one eye, his face contorting in horror. 'Don't do it like that! She's going to stab it off! Don't stab it off, love! Slice, if anything!'

The others braced themselves. Cassandra's hand shook, so the tip of the blade wobbled unsteadily from side to side.

'I don't know what she's thinking here,' Ben said. 'She's going to have her whole bloody hand off, if she's not careful.'

'Ooh, fuck!' Dave ejected. 'The lad! The game lad!'

They all shifted their gazes and saw Matthew Broderick silently screaming as he hacked frantically at the pinkie finger on his left hand. Tears, and drool, and sweat, and thick, mucusy snot exploded from every orifice of his face as his arm sawed back and forth, the blade cutting through sinew, flesh, and bone.

He fell backwards, clutching his hand, and the finger stayed where it was. He stared at it, eyes wide, cheeks puffing up and deflating like some sort of Amazonian tree frog trying to scare off a predator.

'Christ,' the Gozer muttered just as, down at the bottom left of the screen, Cassandra Swain stabbed herself through the back of the hand.

The blade pierced the flesh right at the base of her ring finger, just above the knuckle.

For a long, agonising moment, she didn't react. She just looked down at the handle of the knife sticking up in the air, wobbling from side to side in a way that would've paired nicely with a cartoon *ba-boing*.

'Oh, shit! She did it!' Tyler ejected. He clamped a hand over his mouth like he was fighting the urge to be sick.

And then, Cassandra's screaming started. Like the others, it was somehow made all the more harrowing by its silence. The Yoga instructor clutched her wrist and jerked her hand up. The finger remained attached, albeit dangling at a less than desirable angle. The knife, too, stayed fixed in place, and as she raised the hand, the detectives saw the tip of the blade, and a shiny slick of blood coating her palm.

'Oof. She's fucked that,' Dave winced.

Sinead turned away. 'I can't watch this. I can't. Sorry, sir,' she said.

'Don't be. No one has to,' Logan told her. 'Anyone who wants to step away, you have my full blessing.'

'Aw, nice one, boss,' Tyler said, and he quickly moved to join his wife by the Big Boards. He put an arm around her shoulder, pulled her in for a quick hug, then announced that he'd go and make some tea.

'I think I'll join you, son,' Ben told him. He gave Logan a fatherly pat on the back. Then, with a final glance at the screen, shuffled off to help Tyler.

The Gozer leaned in closer to Logan, his voice lowered to a whisper, but still clear enough in the silence for everyone to hear it.

'What are you doing, Jack? We need eyes on this.'

'No, we don't. Not everyone's.'

'And what if we miss things? Those of us left watching? What if we miss something important?'

'Then we'll watch it again,' Logan told him.

'Yes, but different perspectives could be vital in—'

Logan turned and stared at him. It was one of those moments where the Detective Superintendent was reminded of just how large and imposing the DCI was.

'Is this still my case, sir?'

The Gozer blinked. 'What? I mean, yes. Yes.'

'You sure you wouldn't like to take over and be directly responsible for trying to save these people?'

MacKenzie saw where this was going. He shrunk a little and shook his head. 'No. No, I'm happy for you to be SIO.'

'Good. Glad that's sorted.' Logan shoved his hands in his pockets and turned back to the TV. 'Coffee please, Tyler. Biggest mug we've got.'

'On it, boss,' the DC replied.

And then, without so much as another glance at the telly, he and DI Forde went hurrying out of the room.

The swinging of the door almost knocked a uniformed sergeant off his feet. He stumbled clear just in time to avoid the collision, then waved off the apology from Tyler, who had been leading the charge for the exit.

'It's fine. It's fine. No harm done,' he declared. He was one of the longer serving Inverness bobbies, and both detectives recognised him from around the station. 'I was just coming to let you know that Harold Foster is here.'

'Right. OK. Good,' Ben said. He looked across at Tyler. 'Who's Harold Foster?'

'Dog walker, boss,' Tyler told him. 'The guy who found the bodies this morning.'

'Right! Aye! Do we know anything about him?'

Tyler shrugged. 'A bit, boss. Sinead and I did a bit of digging. He's got no previous, or anything, but there's a couple of things of interest.'

'Great!' Ben turned back to the Uniform. 'Where is he?'

'Interview room three, sir.'

Ben nodded. 'Right. Good. Thank you very much, Sergeant.' He rubbed his hands together. 'I hope you've brought a pen and notebook, Tyler,' he said. 'Because it looks like the teas and coffees are going to have to wait.'

Chapter 23

Ben had a change of heart on the way to talk to Harold Foster, deciding that there was, in fact, enough time to make tea, albeit only for him and Tyler.

They stopped by the door of the interview room, and before Tyler could open it, Ben put a hand on the younger man's arm.

'Do you know, my throat's helluva sore, all of a sudden.'

Tyler frowned. 'What? You alright, boss?'

'Aye. Och, aye. Fine.' Ben took a slurp of his tea, and eyed the detective constable over the rim of his mug. 'But I'm going to let you do all the talking.'

'Me? Do all the talking, boss?' Tyler shot a worried look at the door. 'In there?'

'Aye. He's just a witness, that's all. You'll skoosh it.'

'I don't know about this, boss.'

'You've spoken to him before,' Ben pointed out. 'This morning.'

'Aye, but that was before we knew about—'he gestured with his mug of tea at the world in general'—everything else going on.'

'So? He's the same, you're the same. All you're doing is finding out why he happened to be where he was on this particular morning. That's all.'

'Exactly. Earlier, he was just some bloke whose dog found a body. Now, we think he might be hiding something.'

Ben nodded. 'And if he is, you'll find out.'

'Well, I mean, maybe, but…' Tyler glanced at the door again, more warily this time. 'It's a major case this. What if I mess it up?'

'What if *I* mess it up?'

Tyler snorted. 'You won't, though. You've got way more experience than me. Like, way, way, way more.'

'Easy on the number of 'ways' you're using there, son,' Ben told him. 'I'm no' bloody Methuselah.'

Tyler frowned. 'Who's that, boss?'

The DI smiled. 'Doesn't matter. You'll be fine. I have full faith in your abilities.'

Tyler squirmed inside his shirt. 'Right. Well, I'm glad one of us does,' he said. 'Maybe we should get Hamza, or…?'

Ben leaned past him and opened the door. 'Get your arse in there, Detective Constable,' he said. 'I want to see you shine before I…'

He aborted the sentence before it could reach its conclusion, covering up the missing words with a big, beaming smile of encouragement.

'Before you what, boss?' Tyler asked.

The detective inspector shook his head. 'Nothing. Forget it. Now, through you go, son. Your big moment awaits.'

–

Logan stood alone by the TV, his hands buried deep in his pockets, his stomach twitching like it wanted to throw up. To eject the memories of everything he'd just witnessed.

They had all done it in the end, all but Bruce Kennedy, who had once again refused to take part in proceedings, and had instead sat at the back of his makeshift cell, sneering disdainfully at the camera. It was a bold play, and while he still had all his fingers, he may not have the use of them, or any other part of his body, for much longer.

The Gozer had been the first to leave, just as Natalie Womack had sliced the tip of her right pinkie finger off. It wasn't the full thing—the cut was barely below the fingernail—but she looked so scared, and so hurt, and so young, and the Gozer had slunk off to prepare another statement for the press, rather than watch any more.

As the bloodshed continued, Dave had wheeled himself away to see if there was any follow-up from the CCTV team on the route the minibus had taken after the convention, Hamza had gone to check the shared inbox for any updates, and Thomas had rushed to the bathroom looking decidedly green around the gills.

Logan had watched it all. Every silent scream. Every anguished tear. Every slice of every blade. He'd taken it all in, committed it to memory. Months from then, in the wee small hours, he wouldn't thank himself for it.

It had been what happened next, though, that almost turned his stomach. Almost sent him racing to the bathroom after the consultant. Almost brought him to his knees.

The video feeds had all shut off at the same time. A moment later, screen grabs of the most harrowing or otherwise significant moments from each feed had appeared one-by-one to replace them—Denzel Drummond thumping his chest while holding up his mutilated hand; Cassandra Swain's bloodied palm; Matthew Broderick's puffed up, snot-slicked cheeks; Natalie Womack, eyes screwed shut as she hacked at her flesh.

The image captured from Elizia Shuttleworth's footage was the second-last to appear. She'd been the last one to give in to the abductor, and had moved like she was in a trance as she'd sliced off about fifty percent of her left thumb. Her eyes had remained fixed on the digit as she'd cut through it, her face blank and slack with shock.

The thumb had been a strange choice. That, Logan had assumed, would be the last one anyone would willingly choose to lose—not just from a practical, everyday use standpoint, but because it was thicker than the other fingers, and would've taken more effort.

Had she been specifically ordered to sever that one? That had to be it, surely? Otherwise, it seemed like a bad decision all round.

The last image to appear on screen was Bruce Kennedy, frozen in the act of tossing the knife away.

Logan had watched, eyes narrowed, as the images had appeared, then felt a fiery, prickly heat creeping up his neck as the page refreshed and buttons appeared below each image.

Seven buttons. Same shape, same colour, same two words written in the same red typeface.

'Save Me'.

And DCI Jack Logan, a man who had stood his ground and stared evil in the face more times than he could remember, had watched on in mute, helpless horror as the voting began.

—

There was something animal-like about Harold Foster. Not one of the better animals—not one of the ones you might want to find yourself compared to—but something small and scurrying. Mouse-like. Rodenty.

He sat perched as far forward on the interview room's hard plastic chair as it was possible to get without sliding right off the front, and fidgeted anxiously when the detectives entered.

His round wire-frame glasses threatened to slip down his nose as Tyler reintroduced himself and introduced DI Forde, and he slowed their descent by twitching his nose, before prodding them back up to eye level with a short, stubby finger.

Wisps of grey hair stuck out from the sides of his head, and every wrinkling of his nose exposed thicker, wirier hairs that hung clustered together from each nostril. Had Eden Court Theatre ever put on a stripped-back stage adaptation of *The Wind in the Willows*, Tyler could think of nobody better to play the mole.

'Um, hello there,' Harold said. He sounded like he was choked with the cold. 'It's, uh, it's a pleasure to be here.'

His wild white eyebrows dipped, expressing their disappointment in him. No one was buying that. It wasn't a pleasure to be there, of course. Nobody *actively enjoyed* being brought to a police station for questioning, especially when it involved running the gauntlet of reporters who'd set up camp out front.

He'd probably be all over the papers by tomorrow. They'd have him pegged as a murderer, even though he'd never hurt anyone in his life.

Not really.

'Eh, that's good,' Tyler said, as he and Ben took their seats. He stole a worried look at Ben, like he was already having second thoughts about agreeing to all this, but the DI deflected his concern with a nod and a wink.

Tyler took a breath, steadying his nerves. This wasn't the first interview he'd ever conducted, of course. It wasn't even the first time he'd spoken to this very man.

But the last time had just been chatting to a witness. Now, he was interrogating what might turn out to be a suspect, or at the very least, someone instrumental in solving this case. If he screwed this up…

He pushed the thought away, persistent though it was. He couldn't allow himself to think like that. He could do this. He could bloody do it!

And besides, DI Forde was sitting right behind him, should the shit hit the fan.

Still, he couldn't quite disguise the shake in his voice as he got down to business.

'We won't keep you, Mr Foster. I'm sure you're a busy man.'

'Ha! Yes! Oh, yes! Busy. Very busy. Always busy!' Harold chirped. 'Busy, busy, busy.'

Tyler smiled at him. It was a charming, friendly sort of smile. Disarmingly so.

'Oh?' the DC said. 'Doing what?'

Across the table, Foster's face became quite, quite still. 'Sorry?' he squeaked.

'You said you're busy,' Tyler reminded him. 'Busy, busy, busy.' The smile remained unchanged. The tone light and conversational. 'Busy doing what, exactly?'

Beside him, the detective constable felt DI Forde relaxing into his seat.

'Just, you know… stuff. Dog stuff. Life. Just busy in general.'

'Right. Fair enough,' Tyler said. 'You said you were retired, though, right? When I spoke to you this morning. You mentioned that you'd retired.'

'Yes. Oh, yes. Retired. I'm retired. Living the, you know, retired life.'

'But it's busy?' Tyler asked.

Harold swallowed and smiled at the same time. From the outside, both looked rather uncomfortable.

'Yes,' he confirmed.

'Uh-*huh*,' Tyler said. It wasn't a question, but it sounded very much like one. He drummed his fingers on the tabletop like he was giving all this some thought.

DI Forde hadn't said a word since the initial introductions, which Tyler was taking to be a good sign. It meant that he hadn't screwed the whole thing up yet.

Though, he still felt that 'yet' was the operative word in that sentence.

'It was the hotel trade you were in, wasn't it?'

Harold blinked, taken a little aback by the question. 'Um, yes. Did I mention that, too?'

Tyler shook his head. 'No,' he said. 'I looked it up. Manager of the Cairngorm View in Newtonmore.'

There was a moment of hesitation in which Harold's gaze flitted between Tyler and Ben. DI Forde just nodded, encouraging him to answer the question.

'Um, yes. That's right.'

'For nearly fifteen years. That's some innings.'

Harold straightened his glasses, even though they hadn't been skew-whiff to start with.

'Yes. I suppose it is.'

'Fifteen years. Until last year.'

'Yes.' Harold shuffled back in his seat a little. His fingers scratched lightly at his chin. 'Anyway, what, uh, what was it you wanted to talk to me about? I've already told you all I know this morning, and I have to get back to Muffin.'

'Muffin?' Ben asked, the mention of the sweet, cakey treat making him temporarily forego his vow of silence.

'My dog,' Foster said. He brightened just at the thought of her. 'My little Muffity-Muff. She'll be missing me. She's quite highly strung. She can sense things. Like when I'm upset.'

Ben's interest was already waning. 'Oh. Right. I see,' he said, and, with a sideways glance at Tyler, he settled back into saying nothing.

'She psychic, do you think?' Tyler asked. 'Because you hear about that sometimes, don't you? With animals, and that. They can, like, read minds, or whatever. I think I read somewhere about a duck that could tell the future.' He frowned, his voice losing some of its earlier certainty. 'Not sure how they knew that, mind you…'

Ben raised a quizzical eyebrow, but Tyler was already rallying.

'Did Muffin sense those bodies were there, do you think?' he asked. 'Was that how she found them?'

Harold let out a snuffling little laugh. He blinked rapidly, like sand was being blown in his eyes. 'Ha! Maybe. Maybe that was exactly it! I've always said she's special.'

Tyler nodded. 'A psychic dog. That's pretty unique, right enough.'

Prompted by Tyler's big, goofy grin, they all shared a laugh at that. Just three guys chuckling away about a magic wee canine pal.

'You said earlier that you don't usually walk that route,' Tyler said, still all smiles and good humour. 'When I spoke to you this morning, I mean. You said you just went that way today because you fancied a change.'

Harold's laughter faltered and died. He pulled a face like this was news to him. 'Did I say that?'

'You did, aye. I even wrote it down.' Tyler reached into his pocket for his notebook. 'I can read it back to you, if you like?'

Foster shook his head. The movement was small and furtive, like the rest of him. 'No, it's fine. That's right. I don't. Go there, I mean. Not regularly. I mean, I do sometimes, just not often. Not very often. Sometimes. Occasionally. I'd say occasionally.'

'Right. So, why today?' Tyler asked. The bottom half of his face was still smiling. The eyes had other ideas. 'Why choose this particular day to go on that particular walk? Did your psychic dog suggest it?'

Harold Foster's apprehension practically crackled in the air between them like static electricity. Tyler could sense how nervous the other man was, and realised, quite suddenly, that he wasn't.

Despite the reservations he'd expressed to Ben outside the door, and the way his heart had raced when he'd started the interview, he now felt relaxed. Confident. Completely in charge.

God. Was this how DCI Logan felt all the time? Was this how Bob Hoon felt?

OK, 'relaxed' probably wasn't in Hoon's emotional vocabulary. But still, if this was what it felt like to be either of those guys, then Tyler liked it!

'I, uh, I don't know, exactly,' Harold said.

Tyler leaned closer. He prodded a finger onto the tabletop between them, like he was pushing a button.

'See, I think you do, Mr Foster,' he insisted, and he could've sworn he felt Ben chuckling silently beside him. 'I think there's a particular reason why you went to that particular spot today. And you'll make this much easier on all of us, yourself included—yourself *especially*—if you just tell us what that reason was.'

Harold's lips formed a few different shapes, testing out a range of responses. He decided not to chance any of them.

'Come on, Mr Foster. You want to get back to Muffin, don't you?' Tyler said. 'She gets stressed. You don't want that, do you?'

'N–no.'

'Well, then. Why don't you tell us everything, and we can get you back to her before all her fur falls out?' Tyler suggested. He nodded, wide-eyed and earnestly. 'Because that can happen, I'm told. Dogs. If they get stressed like that, they can go bald.'

'I've heard that right enough,' Ben chimed in, mostly because he was really starting to enjoy himself. 'Nasty business. Who wants a bald dug?'

Harold squirmed. He wasn't a mole now, he was a rat in a trap.

'I just…' He swallowed. Tried to remember how to breathe. 'I just fancied a change. That's all. Honest, there was no real reason.'

Tyler looked disappointed by this answer. His smile thinned until his lips were barely visible. He raised his eyebrows, and tutted his tongue against the back of his teeth.

'Fair enough,' he said. 'Why did you leave, by the way?'

The slightly magnifying effect of Harold's glasses made his eyes look too big as he blinked. 'What? Um, that policeman said I could. In the uniform. After I'd spoken to you, I asked him if I could go, and he said—'

'Your job, I meant,' Tyler said, cutting him off. 'The hotel. Fifteen years, near enough. Why did you leave?'

'Uh, again, I just fancied a change, I suppose.'

'A change? Right.' Tyler tapped his index fingers on the edge of the table like he was playing the drums. 'Funny that. That's not what the owners said. Of the hotel, I mean. We called them up, just to check. They gave us a different story, Mr Foster. One that paints you in a bit of a different light. Do you want to know what they said?'

Across the table, Harold's head twitched from side to side. The movements were small, yet quite emphatic.

'Well, I'm intrigued, Detective Constable,' Ben said. 'Even if Mr Foster doesn't want to hear it, I do.'

Tyler folded his arms, mirroring the detective inspector's body language. 'Let's just say, sir, that it involved hidden cameras and holes in bathroom ceilings. I'm sure that gives you a pretty good picture.'

'Oh, aye. Aye, it does,' Ben confirmed. 'No' as good a picture as Mr Foster probably had, mind you.'

Harold was still shaking his head, his wisps of white hair flapping in the breeze like dog ears.

'No. No, they're not... That's not...' he began to mumble, then he sat bolt upright, spine straight, shoulders back, gaze locked on something far beyond the interview room wall.

His body trembled.

His bottom lip shook.

And then, with a sound like a balloon having all the air slowly farted from it, his face screwed up, and he collapsed into a flood of tears.

'OK! OK, please, I'll tell you! I'll tell you everything!'

As the howling Harold buried his head in his hands, Ben turned to Tyler, winked, and gave the young DC a surreptitious thumbs up.

'*Mess it up* my arse,' he whispered, then he raised his mug in a toast, and enjoyed a big satisfying slurp of his tea.

Chapter 24

Tyler returned triumphantly to the Incident Room, with DI Forde providing an accompanying fanfare of clapping and *bloody well done son*s to spur him on.

'Well done?' Sinead turned from the Big Boards. 'You were meant to be back with that tea half an hour ago.'

'Forget the tea!' Ben said.

'Easy for you to say,' Logan remarked, his gaze darting deliberately to the mug in the detective inspector's hand.

Behind him, the still images of the influencers remained on screen. Thousands of tiny thumbs floated up from the bottom of each one, indicating that people were still voting on who lived and died.

Although 'people,' Logan thought, was a generous description, and not the one that he would use.

A countdown timer had appeared shortly after the voting had started, informing those watching that they had just under twenty-hours to cast their votes. It was a weirdly arbitrary number, but Logan hoped that meant there would be no more deaths before then.

There was no saying, of course, if that would turn out to be true.

Ben gave Tyler a nudge with an elbow, ushering him forward. 'Tell them, son. Tell them what you did.'

Logan grimaced. 'Oh, Christ, what now? Is something on fire?'

'Aye, *he* is!' Ben shot back. 'Go on, son. Tell him.'

Tyler grinned, but simultaneously scratched at his head, like he was embarrassed to suddenly find himself in the spotlight. 'I, eh, I mean, me and DI Forde, we interviewed Harold Foster, boss. The dog walker.'

'*He* interviewed him. No' me,' Ben stressed. 'Him on his own. I just sat there and enjoyed the show.'

'Eh, well, aye,' Tyler conceded. 'Anyway, you know how we all thought it was a bit of a coincidence that his dog found those bodies today?'

'Hell of a coincidence,' Logan confirmed. 'Meaning, I don't believe it for a second.'

Tyler nodded. 'Exactly, boss! And, well, that's the thing. You're right. It isn't. A coincidence, I mean. He went there on purpose. Deliberately, like. To find the bodies.'

Chairs creaked as those members of the team who hadn't yet been looking in Tyler's direction now turned to do so.

'Eh... what?' Hamza asked. 'He told you this?'

'He wrestled it out of him,' Ben said, and he gave Tyler a big proud slap on the back.

The lines on Logan's forehead deepened. 'He knew those bodies were down there?'

'Um, well, no. Not exactly, boss,' Tyler said, wriggling his shoulders to take the sting out of the spot that Ben had slapped him.

'Jesus.' Logan grimaced. 'Well, *what* then, Tyler? Spit it out!'

'Tell him, son,' Ben encouraged.

Tyler took a breath. 'He was sent a card. Same as happened to some of the victims in that last case. He was being blackmailed. Someone called him up and said that if he didn't take his dog to that exact spot this morning, everyone would find out why he'd lost his job.'

'Why *did* he lose his job?' Hamza asked.

'Spying on lassies in the bath,' Ben said. 'And, you know, doing their business on the toilet.' He gave a reproachful shake of his head. 'The dirty old bastard.'

'Hang on, hang on,' Logan said. 'Someone called him? When? Recently?'

'Yesterday morning, boss,' Tyler said.

Logan felt the floor shifting beneath his feet as the walls went lurching around him. That settled it, then. There was no escaping it. There had been someone else behind the events of that case a few months back, pulling all the strings. Someone bigger.

Someone worse.

It was all connected. It was all a tangled web.

And the feeling was only growing that he was at the centre of it.

'Jesus,' he muttered. He pinched the bridge of his nose, forcing the room to stop spinning. 'The call, was it the same as the last lot? Robot voice?'

Tyler's body practically thrummed with excitement. Beside him, Ben gave him another encouraging elbow nudge.

'No, boss. Not this time. It was a guy.'

Logan's eyebrows crept higher. 'A guy?'

'Aye, boss. A guy.'

'What do you mean, "a guy"? What sort of guy?' Logan demanded. 'Can he describe him? Can he describe what the voice sounded like, I mean?'

'Better, boss. See, turns out he really leans into the whole secret voyeur thing.' The detective constable's grin spread out until there was barely any room for the rest of his features. He held up a mobile phone like he'd returned with fire from the gods. 'He recorded the whole conversation!'

—

The voice was gruff. Glasgow. It could've been Logan's own, had he not quit smoking twenty years previously. It was maybe a touch older and rougher around the edges, but the similarities were unmistakable.

The call had started with a stammered, 'H-hello?' from Harold Foster, which had been met by a long, pregnant pause. It had been clear that there was someone on the other end of the line—their breathing, faint though it was, could be heard on the recording—and though Harold had tried to hold his nerve, he'd eventually squeaked out a, 'Are you there?'

It wasn't the first time he'd spoken to the caller, then. That wasn't how anyone reacted to a silent call from an unknown number. Not unless they'd been expecting it.

Add in the fact that Harold had gone to the effort of recording the conversation, and it was clear the phone call had not caught him off guard.

'I'm here. I'm always here, Harry. You should know that by now.'

Menace oozed from every word. The shortening of Harold's name had not been done through familiarity, but as a deliberate show of strength. A reminder of just who was in charge here.

'Is that him?' Tyler whispered. He glanced around at the others, who stood in a circle around his desk, where the phone now sat blasting out its audio. 'That's got to be him, right? That's got to be our guy.'

Logan shut down the DC's wittering with a glare, and an abrupt, 'Shut up.' After loosening his tie and shirt collar, he directed his attention back to the phone.

'I, uh, I'm having second thoughts,' Harold's voice continued. 'About doing… whatever this is. I'm really concerned about it. I worry that Muffin's going to—'

'Stop talking, Harry,' the other man said, and his tone was eerily similar to the one that Logan had just used on Tyler. This didn't go unnoticed by the detective constable, who scratched at the back of his head like he'd just been told off twice.

'Trust me, you're getting off very lightly here. I could be making you do a lot more. A *lot* more,' the Logan-a-like continued. 'I could be making you eat that fucking oversized rat of a thing you call a dog. Just you remember that, Harry.

I'm doing you a favour here. I'm doing you a kindness. With what I know—with the dirt I've got on you—I could ruin you. I could destroy your life. Do you want me to do that, Harry?'

'N-no.'

'Do you want me to share it everywhere? To the papers? To your sisters? You want them finding out what a sordid, grubby little fucker of a brother they've got?'

'No.'

'Sorry? I didn't catch that.'

'No!' Harold said again, pushing the word out through the tight tunnel of his throat. 'Please…please, don't do that.'

'No, thought not,' the other man continued. 'So since, all things considered, I could make you give me anything I want, I think what I'm asking for is pretty fucking generous on my part. All I want you to do is to take wee Muffin for a walk. That's it. That's not a lot to ask now, is it, Harry?'

They all heard Harold swallowing then, just like they'd all heard him whimpering at the suggestion of him eating his own dog.

'I suppose… When you put it like that… Fine. OK. I'll do it.'

'Good boy. Knew you'd see sense,' the other man replied.

Logan closed his eyes, concentrating on the voice. Did he know it? Had he heard it before? The likeness to his own voice was hard to miss, but then the same could be said for half the men his age living in and around greater Glasgow.

And yet, there was something more there. Something just out of reach. A familiarity, maybe. A hint of recognition that went beyond the surface similarity.

An itch in his brain that he couldn't yet scratch.

From the first word the voice had spoken, Logan had felt the room growing hotter. Smaller. The walls felt like they were closing in, narrowing the space and squeezing the air out of the room, and from his lungs.

Did he know this man? *Had* he known him? Did that explain the primal, visceral reaction to his voice, and the way the DCI's blood was now surging through his veins, and the fast, rhythmic *whump-whump-whump* in his ears?

Was this *him*, Logan wondered? Was this the voice of the monster responsible for the fingers in the freezer, and the bodies in the holes, and the seven terrified people now performing for their lives?

Was this the man who had sent him that beer mat? The man who knew his deepest, darkest secret?

He wiped the sweat from his brow, and focused on the call again.

The voice hadn't sounded angry at any point during the conversation so far. If anything, there was a note of amusement to it, as if the caller knew that, despite the protestations, Harold was always going to do what he was told. As if his rodent-like victim was always going to lose in the end.

As if it was all just some twisted game he was playing, where the winner had already been decided.

'But I want you to thank me,' the man instructed, and while his tone was quite matter-of-fact, Logan couldn't fail to notice the cruelty underlying it.

'S-sorry?'

'Thank me, Harry. Thank me for letting you off so lightly.'

There was silence. Harold stood his ground. Retained his dignity.

But not for long.

'Thank you.'

'For?'

'For letting me off so lightly.'

'You're welcome,' the voice on the phone told him. 'Now, I'm going to ping you a time and a map reference. And I'm warning you, Harry, if you fuck this up, if you don't go, or you say the wrong thing to the polis, or you do anything at all that arouses suspicion, your sisters get that footage of you tugging your old lad to them wee lassies playing in the bath together. Is that clear?'

'P-please, I don't—'

'Is. That. Clear?'

Harold confirmed that it was. Crystal clear. He'd do what he'd been told. The other man told him he was a good boy again, then ended the call with no further fanfare or ceremony. The recording stopped at the same time, and a hush fell over the Incident Room.

'Bloody hell,' Tyler muttered, when the weight of the silence became too much for him. It broke the spell, and stirred the others back to life.

'Any ideas?' Ben asked. He looked around, but mostly in Jack's direction. 'Recognise the voice?'

Sinead was the first to point out that the man on the call with Harold Foster had sounded very similar to Logan.

'He did!' Tyler practically cheered. 'I thought that, too. Sounded just like you, boss. But, you know, like an evil version,' he hastily added. 'Not you, I know it's not you, but it sounds like a, you know, a worse you.'

Logan grunted non-commitally. They were right, of course. The similarity was undeniable.

But that rushing of blood hadn't stopped yet. The itch in his brain, and the sweat on his back were still there. The room was still too small. Too airless. His every instinct was telling him to run. To get out of there.

He railed against them all.

'I want a copy of that audio circulated down the road,' he instructed. 'Get it to Heather. Have her look into it. Maybe someone will recognise the bastard's voice and be able to identify him.'

'What about the press?' Ben asked. 'Are we sharing it with them yet?'

'Are we hell,' Logan said, his gut-reaction to working with the media kicking in before his brain had a chance to consider it.

He chewed on his bottom lip for a moment, second-guessing himself for the umpteenth time that day. Why was it so hot? Where was all the air?

'Not yet,' he said, his voice faltering just a little. 'Let's see if Heather can get us anything first.'

The consultant, Thomas, raised a hand but didn't wait to be asked before speaking. 'Sorry, who's Heather?'

'None of your business,' Logan said, absent-mindedly. 'Sinead, she likes you. She won't give you her usual shite. Get it over to her, quick as you can. She'll know about the case, but bring her up to speed. I want to know who that voice belongs to.'

'Will do, sir.' She gestured to the phone and raised a questioning eyebrow towards Hamza. 'Can you...?'

'I can do that, if you want?' Thomas volunteered. 'I can get the audio off.'

Hamza picked up the phone. 'It's fine. I've got it,' he said.

Logan shook his head and pointed to the consultant. 'Give it to him. There's plenty of polis work for you to be getting on with.'

Thomas flashed him a grateful smile and took the phone that Hamza reluctantly handed over. 'Thank you!'

Logan rounded on him so suddenly that he flinched back in fright. 'No thanks necessary, son. I'm not doing you a favour. Comparatively speaking, you're a useless bastard. You have one skill, and one skill alone, to bring to this investigation. DS Khaled has dozens. I'm not having him wasting his valuable time with stuff you could be doing.' Logan leaned over him, his chest puffed up, his eyes like two burning coals. A monster from a nightmare. 'Is that understood, *Thomas*?' he asked, spitting the man's name out like it was soaked in a jakey's piss. 'Is that clear enough for you?'

'Steady, Jack,' Ben said. 'He's just here to help.'

'Good. Well, he can bloody get on with it, then,' Logan instructed, then he turned his back on the consultant, dismissing him.

For one terrible, awful moment, it looked like Thomas was going to say something to escalate the whole thing further, but he caught the warning looks on the faces of the others—even Hamza—and scuttled off to the desk he'd set up as his own.

'Bit hard on the lad there, Jack,' Ben muttered.

The DI didn't know yet, of course. He had no idea who the man was, or what he'd done.

But, though Logan hated to admit it, he was right. He shouldn't have spoken to the consultant like that. He should own up to that. He should apologise.

Another handful of *shoulds* to add to a lifetime-long list of them.

'I'm guessing Harold didn't get a number?' he asked, ignoring the detective inspector's remarks.

'No, boss. Number was withheld,' Tyler said.

'Course it was,' Logan muttered. He loosened his tie further, and flapped the collar of his shirt. The fabric peeled away from the sweat of his chest. That voice wormed away in the shadows of his subconscious.

'What about the text?' Hamza asked. Curiosity got the better of his contempt, and he turned to where Thomas was now plugging the phone into a laptop. 'Can you see the text he mentioned?'

'He deleted it,' Tyler said, before the tech expert had a chance to check. 'He had to write down the details and then delete the message. Said it didn't come from a normal number, though. It just said 'messaging service' at the top.'

A look passed between the detective sergeant and the consultant. 'Might be possible to retrieve it,' Hamza posited. 'With the right software.'

'I might have the right software,' Thomas said. He tapped the top of his laptop screen. 'Right here. Want me to dig around?'

Hamza looked to Logan for guidance. The DCI nodded. 'If you can get it, get it. But I want that audio done and off to Heather first.'

'No problem,' Thomas said.

Reluctantly, begrudgingly, Logan gave him a nod. 'Thanks,' he said, then he raised his voice and turned away again. 'Dave, what's the score with the CCTV? Why don't I know where that minibus went yet?'

'I emailed it over. Sorry, thought everyone had seen it,' Dave Davidson replied. A few furtive looks from the others said they had, but they didn't want to put themselves in Logan's firing line by admitting it.

'Well?' the DCI demanded. 'Where did it go?'

'Down the A9. We've got it as far as Moy, but then lose it after that.'

Logan rubbed his eyes and sighed. That was no distance. Barely a handful of miles.

'So, we've got a vague direction, but nothing else,' he said. 'Great.'

'There's a team working on it,' Dave assured him. 'That ping was based on an ANPR camera after running a search for the number plate.'

'My bloody number plate,' Logan said, and the temperature in the room rose another degree.

'It's possible they changed it,' the constable continued. 'So we've got guys manually looking through footage from other cameras in the area to see if anything comes up.'

Logan shrugged, like he had no opinion on this. It was all part of the big machine that was a police investigation, of course, but at times that machine could be a slow, lumbering bugger of a thing.

'Your car reg, your voice,' Tyler said. 'You sure it's not you behind this, boss? Because if you want to own up, it'll save us a lot of bother.'

It was a joke. It was very obviously a joke. Tyler was laughing as he said it.

But the dark shadow that nestled in the nooks and crannies of Logan's face soon brought an end to that.

'Is this funny to you, Detective Constable?' he asked. His voice was quiet, but held the menace of an air raid siren. It was a warning sign. *Quicksand ahead. Sharks in the water.*

Abort. Flee. Run for your life.

Tyler's laughter had stopped, but he tried to rally a smile, like he was hanging onto the hope that the ground wasn't about to fall away from beneath him.

'Boss?'

'I asked if this was funny to you, Tyler?' Logan repeated.

'Jack. Come on now. We're all stressed here,' Ben said, but Logan raised a hand, ordering him to stay back and shut up.

'When I want your input, I'll ask for it, Detective Inspector,' he said, not looking at him. 'Tell me how this is funny, Tyler. Tell me why we should be laughing at a time like this.'

Tyler squirmed like a fly pinned by one leg. The rest of the team were looking between him and Logan, but nobody quite seemed to understand what was happening, so had no idea how to intervene.

'Well, I mean, just... Because that's what we do, boss, isn't it?' Tyler said. 'You know, when things are at their roughest, we have, like, a laugh about it.' He glanced around at the others, hoping for back-up. 'That's how we get through it, isn't it? That's what we've always done. We all take the piss out of each other. Well, mostly me, I suppose!'

He grinned, like he hoped this might get a more positive reaction from the looming DCI.

It did not.

'And, you know, that's fine, isn't it? We're allowed to do that. We're, like, a family.'

'A family?!' Logan did laugh then. It was a harsh, cruel-sounding thing. 'Is that what you think, is it?'

Tyler blinked rapidly, like he'd just taken a slap to the face. 'Um, I mean, like, I suppose, maybe...'

He floundered for a response, but then something solidified in him. Something that stood him up straighter and taller. Something that grew to fill the room.

'Yes, boss. That is what I think.'

'So do I, sir,' Sinead said, stepping up to join her husband in the DCI's firing line.

'And me, sir,' Hamza agreed, taking up a position on Tyler's other side.

'They're not wrong, Jack,' Ben said. He stood in front of them all, his arms folded, a shield for whatever might be about to come their way. 'Family. Always.'

Over at his desk in the corner, Dave Davidson raised a hand. 'I'm in. If it's going, I'll be the drunk cousin that turns up at weddings and Christenings with women half his age.'

Thomas, wisely, kept his mouth shut and got quietly on with his assigned tasks.

Logan felt his hands twitching. He looked down at them, and watched like a detached onlooker as the fingers curled themselves into tight, shaking fists.

'Something's not right, Jack. You're no' yourself,' Ben said, but Logan barely heard it. The DI sounded far off, far away. Another problem for another time.

This was it, then. This was the moment.

Finally, after all these years, there were going to see him as he really was. They were all going to see the man he'd been smothering, pushing down, keeping locked away out of sight for so very, very long.

The man he'd spent almost three decades pretending not to be.

You're no' yourself.

If only the DI knew how wrong he was.

'You OK, sir?' Sinead's voice was soft, her face a picture of concern. She stepped around Ben, so she was directly in Logan's line of sight. 'I think you should sit down.'

He couldn't, even if he'd wanted to. His feet wouldn't move. His body was no longer his own. His head was filled with blood, and doubt, and noise. His stomach churned. His heart was stone.

'Go home, boss,' Tyler told him.

It sounded like an order, not a suggestion, and Logan felt a wave of relief, like someone else—someone better—had stepped in, put a hand on his shoulder, and absolved him of all responsibility. Set him free.

'He's right, Detective Chief Inspector.'

The voice came from behind him. Logan forced his body to comply, and turned to see the Gozer standing there, buttons shining like beacons, eyebrows furrowed into a single line that could've gone either way between anger and concern.

'It's been a long day,' the Det Supt told him. 'We could all do with some rest.'

Logan managed to regain enough control of his head to shake it. 'Can't. Those people—'

'I'm not asking, Jack. I'll man the fort. I can get some kip in the office, if I need to,' the Gozer said. 'You, go. Get home. Have a shower, have some food, and get some rest.' He looked pointedly to the screen, where the voting countdown was still showing sixteen hours remaining. 'I've a horrible feeling that we're all going to need it.'

–

Logan hadn't argued. That was how sure he was that something was wrong. They'd know it too, of course. They'd have expected him to stand his ground, stick around, work through the night until the weak, watery Highland sun rose again on a brand new day.

But he hadn't. He'd just nodded, muttered a, 'Fine,' then gathered up his coat and gone marching out through the Incident Room door.

He should have apologised. He should have explained.

Two more regrets for the pile.

The lift was too small tonight, so he took the stairs, picking up speed at the bottom like he was going to break into a run and give chase to someone.

Or be chased, maybe.

He didn't acknowledge the nods and waves of greeting as he crossed the station foyer. It was only when he reached the door that he realised someone was clattering up behind him.

Logan spun, fist clenched and held low, ready to swing. A slightly breathless-looking uniformed constable clocked this, and slowed to a jog, then a walk, then stopped just beyond thumping reach.

'Eh, sorry, Detective Chief Inspector, I was shouting after you on the stairs.'

Logan grunted and forced his fingers to relax. 'Oh. Sorry. Miles away,' he replied.

The constable nodded. 'Aye. I can imagine. You've a lot on.'

'Aye,' Logan said. He glanced impatiently at the door beside them. 'Was there something you wanted?'

'What? Oh, yes! Tyler—DC Neish—asked me to go check in on your house earlier. I'm Alan. Alan Grigor.'

There was a questioning tone to it, like he was hoping the DCI might confirm he'd heard of him. It would be nice to know he was on the MIT's radar—beyond having once shared a room with Tyler at Tulliallan, at least.

Logan just looked blankly back at him, though, and all thoughts of moving up in the world were relegated to the back seat.

'Right. Thanks,' Logan said. Now that he knew who the man was, he paid more attention to the carrier bag he carried down at his side. 'Is that…?'

When the DCI didn't finish the sentence, Alan raised the bag up to eye level. 'Yes, sir. It's the parcel that was left for you.'

Logan didn't move to take it. Not yet. 'Took your bloody time.'

Alan swallowed. 'Uh, yes, sir. Sorry. Got called to an RTA. Nasty business. Little girl badly injured. Her and her dad in the car, it's not looking like he's going to pull through, so it was a rough—'

The snatching of the bag stopped him mid-flow.

'Right. Thanks, Alec. I appreciate this,' the DCI said. Then, without looking in the bag, he turned and marched out of the station.

'Oh, it's not bother, sir, but—'

The door closed in the constable's face. He raised a hand to wave, but only his reflection in the glass waved back.

'It's Alan, by the way,' he mumbled.

Then, with a quick glance around to make sure that nobody was watching and cringing on his behalf, he self-consciously fiddled with all the straps and buckles of his stab proof vest, and went back to work.

Chapter 25

Berta Hoon was going to fucking strangle someone. Specific-ally, the person she was going to fucking strangle was whoever was on the other end of the telephone that was currently ringing shrilly in the front hall.

It had taken her the better part of two hours to wrestle the twins to sleep. Lauren had been fine, and had nodded off during her night time bottle, lying on Berta's lap. She'd stayed sleeping even when she'd been placed in her cot, the blankets wrapped around her making her look like a taco, or an enchilada, or whatever that fucking Mexican dish was that Bob kept comparing the swaddled infants to.

They were all the same, anyway—spicy foreign muck, just folded in different ways. They were very clearly all the same dish, just arranged differently on the plate, yet no one but her could apparently see that.

Probably because everyone but her was a bloody idiot, she reasoned.

Cal had been the problem, like he always was. Lauren was a sensible, level-headed girl, like her mother. Cal, on the other hand, had too much of his father in him. She didn't like the idea of pigeon-holing a one-year-old, but Berta could say with absolute confidence that Cal was a shiftless, gormless, feckless wee cretin, who'd go teetering gleefully into traffic if not kept under round the clock supervision.

He was a thrawn wee bugger, too, wriggling and wrest-ling with her while she'd tried to feed him. Unlike Lauren, he had very little interest in a bedtime bottle these days, and would constantly try to sit up while pointing at random parts of the room that he was determined to find ways of accidentally hurting himself in.

He was a right clumsy bastard, too.

Definitely his father's son.

She'd finally managed to subdue him long enough for him to nod off. The moment Berta had lowered the bugger into the cot alongside his sister's, though, his eyes had opened. He'd let out such a forceful giggle then that Berta had started to suspect he'd been faking sleep the whole time for the sole purpose of winding her up.

It was the laugh, and definitely not Berta's hissed, 'For fuck's sake,' that had woken up Lauren. She hadn't been happy about having her sleep interrupted, and had immediately burst into tears.

Although undoubtedly an arsehole, Cal was always empathetic to his sister's upset. Either that, or he was just very easily led. Whichever, he then started screaming the place down, too, and Berta was back to square one on the getting them to sleep front.

That had been over an hour ago. She'd only just settled them back down, and now the phone was threatening to undo all that hard work.

She thundered down the stairs two at a time, despite the painful and audible protesting of both hips. At the bottom, she glared at the ringing handset like her sheer rage might compel it into silence.

No such luck.

The plastic casing of the handset cracked noisily in her grip as she snatched it from the base, stabbed at the answer button, and hissed a, 'What the fuck do you want?' down the line with the venom of a king cobra.

She knew who it was, of course. Only one person had such a knack for bad timing.

'Um, hi, Berta?' Tyler asked, as if he wasn't sure he'd come through to the right person.

'Naw, it's the Queen of fucking Sheba,' Berta spat. 'I've just got them bloody bairns to sleep! What the hell are you phoning for?'

She realised she was shouting, thereby compounding the risk of the twins waking up. She lowered her voice to a low, threatening whisper. 'If I could reach down this phone and put my thumbs through your fucking eyes right now, I would. I want you to know that.'

Down the line, Tyler swallowed. 'Um, OK. Thanks,' he said, and the questioning tone was apparent once again.

'Well?' Berta demanded. 'Why are you phoning me?'

There was a hesitation, like Tyler didn't want to say the next part. If she strained her ears, Berta may well have heard some whispered words of encouragement from Sinead.

'Eh, so, it's just… It's looking like we might have a bit of a late one here,' Tyler ventured. 'So, I was going to ask—and I know it's a lot—if you could maybe keep the kids tonight and put them to bed? But, um, well, it sounds like you already have, so…'

'So *what*, boy?' Berta snapped.

Tyler drew in a breath. 'So, um, thank you. Are you sure it's not a problem?'

'Oh, it's a big fucking problem. It's a complete fucking liberty, is what it is,' Berta shot back. She sniffed. 'And if they weren't so adorable in the morning, I'd be telling you to ram it sideways up your arsehole. But, luckily for you, they are.'

'Uh, great. Cheers!'

'And besides,' Berta continued. A smile crept from one side of her face to the other. 'It'll give us more time to work on their 'Daddy is a fuckwit,' flash cards.'

Chapter 26

Getting through the cordon of reporters and cameras had been tough. Ignoring their shouted questions and shrieked demands for interviews hadn't bothered him, but the urge to pan some of their faces in had proven harder to resist.

Fortunately, he'd held back, though had there been another call to smile like at the press conference earlier in the evening, he doubted he could've held so firm.

A couple of them had jogged towards their cars, making as if to follow him as he'd headed for his BMW. He'd taken a few moments to express to them precisely how much they would regret going through with that plan, then had gone speeding out of the car park with a notable lack of pursuers.

He was halfway home before he realised how badly his hands were shaking.

Before the Gozer had sent him packing, he had been going to get a copy of the audio recording from Harold Foster's phone made so he could listen to it again. He hadn't had a chance, but it didn't matter. The voice was playing in his head, over and over.

It had done something to him, that voice. It had poured into his ears like a witch's brew of potions and poisons, turning his own body against him, and stirring the muck in the deeper, darker pools of his subconscious.

There was a world, he thought, where what he was experiencing could be likened to a panic attack. But, it wasn't this world, and if anyone suggested as much, they'd find themselves on the wrong side of a size 13 boot.

He was passing the hospital when the replaying voice in his head became too much for him, and he made an awful, desperate decision. The sort of decision that, under any other circumstances, he would never have made.

He called Geoff Palmer's mobile.

The burring of a ringing tone filled the car's cabin for a second or two, before Palmer's voice slithered from the speakers.

'Congratulations. You're through to Geoff Palmer. Sorry, I can't take your call right now. If you're calling about police business, please use the landline during office hours, as I've previously instructed several times, both verbally and in writing. If you're calling to book me for a stand-up slot, then please leave a message after the tone.'

Logan waited for the tone, then barked an instruction for the Scene of Crime man to call him back.

He thumped his hands on the steering wheel a few times and hissed a frustrated, 'Fuck!' through his teeth.

And the bag containing the parcel he'd been sent lurked silently on the passenger seat beside him.

He arrived home just a few minutes later. The streets of Inverness, particularly away from the city centre, were near-deserted at this time of night. A few taxis criss-crossed each other's paths, like hungry predators all seeking out the same prey.

They were either new to the game, or stupidly optimistic. Most of the more experienced drivers would be comfortably tucked up in bed at half-eleven on a Monday night, ready for the school runs in the morning.

Logan pulled the BMW up a little way along the street from the house, shut off the engine, and snapped off the lights.

He sat there in the silence, his hands gripping the wheel, his chest rising and falling.

He wasn't sure how long he sat there for. The first he even knew of time passing was when he noticed how his breath had fogged the inside of the windscreen and side windows, blurring his view of the darkened world beyond.

His gaze crept to the white plastic carrier bag beside him, but he made no move to reach for it.

It could be anything. It was probably nothing. A free sample from some over-enthusiastic local business. An Amazon order he'd forgotten he made. A gift from a friend, even.

Except it was far too heavy for a freebie giveaway, he never shopped online, and the few friends he had were dwindling in number by the moment.

There was one way to be sure, of course. All he had to do was reach over, open the bag, and look inside. That was it. That simple.

And yet, his hands were stuck to the wheel like it was coated in superglue.

'Open it.'

He said the words out loud, like hearing them might force him to comply.

'Just open the bloody thing and look, you cowardly bastard. Just look.' He raised his voice, practically shouting at himself now. 'Just open the bag and look at it!'

His body fought him, his head turning away and staring along the road to where his house was just visible through the swirling haze on the glass. The lights were on downstairs. Shona's car was parked right out front. She'd be in there, waiting up for him, even though there was always the risk of him pulling an all-nighter. She'd wait up, all the same, dozing under a blanket on the couch with Taggart either curled up on the floor beside her, or down at the bottom of the sofa by her feet.

Logan rarely said so out loud—he rarely even consciously thought it, in fact—but he understood on some deep molecular level just how lucky he was to have her. He knew just how fortunate he'd been to meet her, and to have her in his life.

And how painful it was going to be when that ended.

Because it would. Once she knew the truth. Once she knew who he really was, there'd be no waiting up for him to come home. There'd be no neck rubs, or movie nights, or late-night chippies eaten on bridges above the river. No more bad jokes, board games, or stolen moments in the rain.

She thought she loved him. She thought she knew him.

But soon, she'd find out just how wrong she was.

One by one, he prised his fingers from the wheel, then flexed them in and out, asserting his authority over them.

He was about to finally reach for the bag when, through the mist of the window, he saw a shape detaching itself from the outside of his house. A wipe of the glass only smeared the moisture, but for a moment he was sure he saw a figure there, heading down the alleyway between his house and the one next door.

The car's headlights automatically illuminated when he opened the door. A shadow, head-down and hunched over, was projected onto the roughcasting of the house's wall, and then it was gone, swallowed by the darkness at the rear of the building.

Someone was there. Someone had been waiting there. Someone was waiting *at his home*.

The car door slammed. The lights snapped off.

Blood surging, heart thumping, rage burning in the furnace of his gut, DCI Logan launched himself along the pavement, and ran.

–

'You sure you're alright, son?'

Concern was drawn in the lines of Ben's face, and hummed in the gaps between his words. He looked tired, not helped by the way he stifled a yawn while waiting for Hamza's reply.

The detective sergeant tilted his head back over the top of his chair, so he was looking at the DI upside down. This afforded him a clearer view of the inside of Ben's nostrils than he would have liked, but what was done was done.

'I'm fine, sir. Honest. I'll keep going.'

'You can head home, if you like? Tyler and Sinead are getting a couple of hours' kip in the bunks downstairs. I was going to grab forty winks in Jack's office, but you can head home and get a proper sleep.'

Hamza smiled gratefully, but shook his head. What did he have to go home to? A single bed in a spare room in a house that wasn't his own. At least here, he had a purpose.

'I'm fine, sir, honest. If I get tired I'll put my head on the desk and shut my eyes for a bit.'

Ben gave up trying to hold back his yawn, and nodded as he covered his mouth with his hand.

'Fine,' he said, once he could speak again. 'If you need me, you know where I am.'

'Aye. Get some rest, sir,' Hamza said, then he brought his head forward again and fought hard against a yawn of his own.

Dave had gone home for the night, and the only sound in the room was the high-speed tapping of keys on a keyboard a couple of desks over on Hamza's right.

Normally, he wouldn't be bothered by the sound. Usually, he was the one making it, and so he rarely even noticed it. Tonight, though, each keystroke was like the thud of a jackhammer.

The problem wasn't the keys themselves, of course. It was whose fingers were using them.

'You should go,' Hamza said.

He didn't turn to look at the consultant, even as the hammering of the keys faltered into silence.

'Eh, sorry?' Thomas asked. 'Did you say something? I was, you know, *in the zone.*'

There were a few zones Hamza would like to send the home wrecking bastard to— 'danger' and 'twilight' being two of the main ones, but also any active war ones.

'Right, well, unless you've got something ground-breaking…' Hamza said, keen for the other man to leave.

'I'm looking through the hashtags on the socials. There are, like, millions of people trying to solve this. Coming up with all these mad theories, combing through the hostages' accounts on other platforms—'

'Captives,' Hamza corrected.

Thomas's chair gave a squeak as he turned towards the detective sergeant. 'Sorry?'

Hamza sighed. 'They're not hostages. There's no ransom demand. They're not being used as bargaining chips, or for any coercive purposes that we know of. They're captives.'

'Right. OK.' Thomas's expression suggested this probably wasn't all that important a distinction, given the situation, but he nodded. 'Good to know. Thanks. Anyway, some of the theories are wild. Lots of people still think it's fake, of course. Some think it's the 'woke deep state' worried that social media is destabilising their grip on the media. Because, you know, if anything's going to overthrow the Illuminati, it's a middle-aged woman doing baby voices for all the Sylvanian Families on YouTube.'

He laughed at the suggestion. The detective sergeant did not.

'Uh, yeah, so anyway, some people reckon it's all a promo for some new horror film that's going to be announced,' the consultant continued. 'And loads are trying to find connections between the influencers explaining why those eight in particular were chosen. Apparently, if you go far back enough, Natalie Womack and Bruce Kennedy are related. But, like, third cousins twice removed, or something. I think I'm probably more related to them both than that.'

Hamza shrugged. 'The internet's full of crazies. That's hardly news. It'll get worse before it gets better. If you want to go down the rabbit hole of it all, then fine, but I'd rather you did it somewhere else.'

He turned back to his screen, indicating that the conversation was over. He could still see Thomas right at the edge of his peripheral vision, though, still looking at him.

'Listen, Hamza, I get it. I do. When I walked in here...' Thomas glanced up at the ceiling, like he might find the right words written up there. When he didn't, he sighed. 'I didn't want to hurt anyone. Neither of us did, me or Amira.'

Hamza's jaw tightened. Danger blazed behind his eyes. 'Don't you dare say her name,' he warned, and the rumble of his voice would've given Jack Logan's a run for its money.

Thomas immediately held both hands up in surrender. 'Sorry, no, you're right. That was a mistake. I can't speak for her, only myself. I was in a bad place. I was... Christ. Believe me, the last thing I wanted to do was to hurt anyone.'

'I don't care,' Hamza told him.

'I'm really sorry.'

'I don't accept it,' the DS barked back.

'No. No, I know, I'm not asking you to accept it, I'm just—'

'You're just *what*, Thomas? What are you trying to do, exactly?'

Hamza didn't remember getting to his feet, but now, there he was, standing fully upright. He hadn't moved from beside his desk yet, but it felt very much like a possibility if the consultant said one more wrong word.

Which, given Hamza's current feelings on the bastard, would be more or less any word in the English language.

The consultant must've seen this in the detective sergeant's eyes. He raised the hands he'd only just lowered, though it was less like he was surrendering this time, and more like he was trying to calm an advancing wild animal.

And then, he was saved by the bell.

Hamza continued to stare him down for a second or two, then took out his mobile and turned away when he saw the name that flashed up there. Just like most of the caller's vocabulary, it was a four letter word.

'Hoon,' Hamza said into the mobile, then he winced, his head partly retracting into his shoulders. 'Um, Bob, I mean. Mr Hoon. Hello.'

'Aye, you stick with the fucking 'mister,' son, if you know what's good for you,' Hoon barked down the line. 'I'm still in fucking London, by the way. Fucking *easyJet's* stitched me right up. And here I thought Trump was the most useless of all the fucking orange-hued things out there, but compared to this hat full of tangerine arseholes, he's bordering on the fucking competent.'

Hamza had no idea how to respond to that beyond a quiet, hesitant, 'OK.'

'Anyway, you get that email from that guy?' Hoon asked.

'Email?' Hamza looked at his computer desktop like it might be sitting there waiting for him. 'What email?'

Hoon's tut could be heard on the other side of the Incident Room. Possibly on the other side of the airport, too. 'The fucking email. From the guy. The fucking guy you wanted me to… The fucking email!'

Hamza cradled his phone in between his shoulder and his ear, then bent over his computer and tabbed through to the shared inbox. 'I'm not seeing…'

There was a *ping* and the correspondence in the inbox all shuffled down to make room for a new addition.

'Wait. Something's come in.'

'Is it the thing from the guy?'

'It's from a Sebastian Muller,' Hamza said, already clicking to expand the mail to full screen.

'I don't fucking know what his name is, he's just some fucking secret service drone stashed away in an office somewhere. Probably in a fucking basement,' Hoon said. 'Is it what you were after? Because I couldn't make fucking head nor tail of what you were even asking.'

Hamza read the message. As he did, he lowered himself into his seat. His eyes scanned the page. His lips moved silently.

For the first time that day, he felt a surge of emotion that wasn't wholly negative.

'Uh, yeah,' he said, in a slightly breathless whisper. 'Yeah, this is exactly what we were after.'

He heard the distinctive whirr of a laptop shutting down. Thomas closed the lid, but before he had a chance to fully stand up, the sergeant stabbed a finger at him, his gaze still scanning the email on his screen.

'Wait! Change of plan,' Hamza said. He hung up the phone without so much as a 'goodbye' to Hoon, which would almost certainly come back to haunt him at a later date. 'Get your arse back in that chair.'

He turned his monitor so the consultant could see the email.

'Time to find out if you're as good at this stuff as you say you are.'

Chapter 27

Logan's coat was slowing him down. He shrugged it off and tossed it into the front garden as he passed, freeing him to pick up the pace and go barreling down the alleyway at the side of the house.

He could already feel his heart straining against the inside of his chest, like a prisoner trying to batter down the door of its cell. He wasn't *that* out of shape, so he knew that something else was driving the racing pulse. Anger. Panic. Fear. Some noxious cocktail of all three.

There was no sign of the figure he'd seen in the alley now. No sound of running footsteps, or suggestions of a shape lurking in any of the shadows. Logan ran along the path until he hit the T-junction with the passageway formed between the fences of his row of houses and those of the homes backing onto them.

The new path stretched away to the left and right, with branches running between all the other detached and semi-detached properties on either side.

A maze. That's what it was. A dark, twisting labyrinth with nothing to indicate where the person he'd seen had gone.

He had to have run. That was the only way he could have vanished. Logan had set off sprinting right behind him, and adrenaline had granted him a burst of speed that had only been heightened by the shedding of his heavy coat.

Had the guy just kept walking, the detective would've caught up with him. He'd have his hands round his throat right now, demanding an explanation for why he was there, for what he was doing, for why he was *at Logan's home*.

The fact he was gone meant he had run. The fact he had run meant he was up to something.

But what?

It was then, as his heart began to slow, and his breathing steadied, that Logan heard the barking. It was shrill and high-pitched.

It was coming from his house.

Taggart!

Logan lumbered down the alleyway, feeling his way along the shadowy fence until he reached the back gate. It stood half open, and he almost fell through it in the near darkness.

From inside the house, right by the back door just a few feet ahead of him, he heard Shona's voice.

'Alright, alright, calm yourself, for God's sake. Do you want out? Is that it?'

Logan felt a wave of relief crashing over him. She was alive, and apparently unhurt.

He wasn't sure why this came as such a surprise, or why he had to choke down a sob of relief as he clattered to a stop on the back path.

'Oh, thank God,' he whispered.

The door opened. Shona recoiled in fright and let out a, 'Wueeargh!' that rose and fell like the *wooo* of a cartoon ghost.

'Jesus Christ!' she cried, when the light from the kitchen spilled across his face. 'Are you trying to give me a fecking heart attack, or something?'

As she spoke, Taggart shot between her legs. At first, Logan thought he was racing out to meet him. But then, the barking ball of fur stopped a few feet from the shed, hackles rising, tail straight out behind him.

The shed door wasn't closed. Not all the way. The bolt had been slid open, and there was a half-inch of darkness between the door and the frame.

Logan caught Shona's eye, then pointed to the dog. It took her a second to understand, but then she crept out of the house in her Ghostbusters slippers, caught Taggart by the collar, and guided him back into the kitchen.

Taking his phone from his pocket, Logan pressed the camera flash against a palm, then activated the torch, trapping the light in his hand until he was ready to release it.

He crossed the garden in three big paces, brought up a leg, and kicked the door so hard that one of the hinges tore free of the wooden frame with an agonised screech.

The light from the torch illuminated the startled face of the man he'd glimpsed in the alleyway, blinding him. Logan bellowed, 'Down! Down! Down! On the floor! Now!' going for the full shock-and-awe effect.

It worked, too. The man immediately dropped to his knees, hands behind his head, ejecting a series of breathless, panicky yelps.

'Wait! Don't shoot! Don't shoot!'

It wasn't a man, after all, Logan realised. Not fully. Not yet. The voice gave it away.

'Jesus, calm down, he's not got a gun! He's not going to shoot us!'

The torchlight shifted until it settled on Olivia leaning against the shed's back wall. She was dressed as if for a night out, complete with a face full of less than expertly applied make-up.

'The hell are you doing?' Logan demanded.

Down on the floor, and trying to sink straight through it, a teenage boy frantically wiped traces of lipstick off his mouth with the sleeve of his jacket.

And not just any teenage boy, either. Logan recognised him now. He looked scared. Almost as scared as he'd looked both times he'd been held at knifepoint by child killers.

'Harris? Is that you?' he said, and the bark of his voice made Sinead's younger brother redouble his efforts to be swallowed up by the floor.

'Um, um, hi, Jack,' he squeaked.

Olivia kicked the back of his foot and he half-bowed, like he was scrabbling and fawning before some terrible dictator.

'Mr Logan, I mean. Mr Logan. Hi. Yes! It's me! It's, eh, it's Harris, we were just—'

'Stop talking,' Logan intoned.

Harris bowed again, like he was grateful to have been silenced.

The torchlight swung between the boy on the floor, and the girl at the back of the shed, dazzling them both in turn.

'Oh, God,' Logan groaned. He lowered the light and ran a shaky hand down his face. 'Please tell me this isn't what it looks like.'

—

'Watch where you're sticking that ginger, Moira!'

The cry was shrill and panicked. It echoed off the walls of Logan's office, and DI Forde looked around in surprise as his own voice came bouncing back to him. He twisted in the chair, looking behind him like he was afraid someone was lurking back there. Then, when the coast was clear, he spun clumsily to face front again.

Hamza hesitated, the door half open, one knuckle still raised from where he'd been knocking.

'Uh, sorry, sir. Didn't mean to give you a fright like that.'

'What?'

One of Ben's eyes was stuck shut, and the other swam in a full circle as it tried to figure out where he was. He ran a calloused hand down his face, but the eye remained closed, and the confused expression wasn't in a rush to be going anywhere, either.

He inhaled sharply, like his lower extremities had been plunged into an ice bath, yawned until Hamza could see all his fillings and one of his tonsils, then finally accepted the fact that, despite what that one eye was still insisting, he was awake.

'Sorry, son. Must've nodded off.' He yawned again, and this one seemed to pull him more into focus. He reached for his mug, was disappointed to find it empty, then set it back down again. 'Everything OK? Has something happened?'

'Yes, sir. To both. Everything's OK, no change on the influencers, the voting's still going on. But something has happened,' Hamza said. He hesitated, like he couldn't quite believe the news himself. 'Hoon came through for us, sir. We've got the details of the I.P. addresses for those streams.'

From the way the sergeant said it, this was an exciting and positive development. Unfortunately, Ben had no idea what the hell he was on about.

'And in English that means…?'

'Well, it's early days, sir. Thomas is still working on it now.'

Ben, who had eventually been brought up to speed on the whole Thomas/Hamza situation, was surprised by the apparent lack of animosity when the DS said the consultant's name. He chose not to mention it.

'But, if he's able to do what he says he can do, and if they're running, it's possible we can use these details to access the feeds directly.'

Ben rose slowly to his feet. Whatever it was that Hamza was on about, it sounded promising. And 'promising' was already the best news he'd heard all day.

'Meaning…?'

'Meaning, with a bit of luck, sir, we'll be able to access the cameras directly, without the kidnapper knowing,' Hamza explained. 'We'll be able to tune in and find out exactly what's going on.'

Finally, that was something that Ben understood. 'Bloody Nora!' he ejected. 'How long until we know?'

'Not sure, sir. Depends on network configuration, firewalls, what the VPN set-up's like, if he has one—'

'*At-at-at-at-at!*' Ben chastised, flapping a hand like he was shooing a fly. 'I don't need the mumbo-jumbo, son, just the numbers.'

'Sorry, sir,' Hamza said. 'Not sure. Three or four hours, maybe. Possibly a bit more, but hopefully a bit less.' His eyebrows dipped in uncertainty. 'Didn't know if we wanted to give DCI Logan a shout and keep him informed?'

Ben shook his head and sat down again. 'Let's make sure we've got something first. Maybe if he rests up he'll come back as less of an arsehole.'

Hamza chuckled at the back of his throat. 'Good point. Anyway, sorry again for waking you, sir. I'll, eh, I'll let you get back to your… ginger.'

Ben looked confused for a moment, then the colour drained out of his face and he wriggled uncomfortably in the seat.

'Eh, aye. Actually, son,' he said, reaching for his mug. 'I think maybe I'll just go and make myself a coffee.'

Chapter 28

It had been almost a year since Logan had last seen Sinead's younger brother. He'd grown in that time, as teenagers were wont to do. And yet, sitting there now down at one end of the three-seater couch, with Logan and Shona standing over him, he seemed smaller.

In the shed, Logan had thought that the boy looked nearly as terrified as he had while being held at knifepoint all those years ago. He realised now that this was incorrect.

He looked even more so.

Olivia sat at the other end of the couch, both of them making a show of keeping their distance. Taggart had initially jumped up to fill the space between them, but had jumped down and slunk off again when he'd picked up on the general vibe of the room.

'What the hell were you thinking?' Logan demanded.

'What were you doing in there?' Shona asked.

'I could've killed you!'

'How long has this been going on for?'

'Does Tyler know? I bet Tyler bloody knows!'

'Tell me you've at least been using protection.'

Both teens recoiled at that last one. Despite being at opposite ends of the couch, they somehow found a way to force themselves even further apart.

'Ew! No!' Olivia cried.

Shona's eyes became two big saucers filled with horror. 'No?!'

'I mean, we're not… Jesus. We were just, you know…' Olivia crossed her arms and shifted around, understandably uncomfortable at the line of questioning. 'It was nothing like that.'

Harris, who had been shaking his head emphatically for the last several seconds, rushed to confirm this. 'No, it was nothing like that. Honest! We weren't… There was nothing, you know, *going on.*'

'And yet, you were hiding in my bloody shed!' Logan shot back. 'And I've seen plenty of guilty bastards in my time, son, but none of them looked it half as much as you did!'

'We were just kissing, alright?' Olivia cried, then her cheeks burned red beneath her make-up and she pulled the knot of her arms tighter around herself.

'Is that why the shed was wide open earlier, is it?' the DCI demanded. 'You two been sneaking in there every night?'

'No! I didn't even know it was unlocked until then.'

'Oh, so you called the boyfriend over so you could have it away in there?'

Olivia snorted. '*Have it away?* What are you, eighty? Nobody says that.'

Logan's response was a roar that shook the walls and scared both teenagers into a stock-still silence. 'I don't care *what* they fucking say!' He saw a vision of the shed door tearing from a hinge, and felt the impact juddering up through his foot again. 'Someone could've got seriously bloody hurt!'

He felt Shona's hand on his arm, and heard her voice murmuring softly behind him. 'It's fine, Jack. It's OK, there was no harm done.'

'Tell that to the fucking shed,' Logan shot back.

Tell that to his nerves.

He screwed up his face and covered his eyes with a giant hand, the thumb and middle finger kneading at his temples. There was nothing they could do to fend off his growing headache, though. That one was a lost cause.

'Fine. You talk to them, then,' he said. It came out with more venom than intended, but he didn't have the energy to course

203

correct. Instead, he turned away from them all and marched towards the door that led to the hall. 'I'm going to get my coat from the garden then go get changed.'

'Why's your coat in the garden?' Shona asked.

'Because I threw it in there when I was chasing this wee bastard,' Logan snapped back.

As explanations went, it wasn't much of one, but it was the only one being offered, and nobody felt like digging any further.

Without another word, Logan left the room, slammed the door behind him, then continued out to the front garden where he retrieved his coat from the bush it had landed on. He gave it a wipe down, clearing off some of the broken bits of foliage, then he walked back to the car, opened the passenger door, and retrieved the carrier bag the Uniform had given him.

In hindsight, of course, he'd have been as well having the constable leave the package here, given how long it had taken for him to get his hands on it. But, in terms of things he regretted about how the day had gone so far, it was way down near the bottom of the list, below even the artery-clogging breakfast from that cafe.

He didn't look in the bag on the way back to the house, or when he was climbing the stairs in silence, or when he was walking along the upstairs landing with his teeth gritted.

It wasn't until he was in the bedroom, with the door closed behind him, that he set the bag down on a dressing table, took a breath, and peered inside.

It was a bottle. Had to be. It was still in the box, but he recognised the dimensions. The weight felt right, too. A litre of spirits, if he had to guess, but maybe a bottle of Champagne.

Leaving the bag where it was, Logan went to his coat and took a sealed packet of disposable nitrile gloves from the pocket.

He regarded the bag as he pulled the gloves on with a *snap-snap*, like he was worried it might make a break for the window the moment he looked away.

'Right, then,' he announced to the room at large. He flexed his fingers, really testing the limits of the one–size–fits–all gloves, then he carefully took hold of the top of the box, and removed it from the bag like it was filled with nitro glycerine.

Which, as far as he knew, it might be.

There was no address on the package other than his own. No stamps or postal labels, either. Both ends were secured by a strip of parcel tape, keeping the contents concealed.

The gloves made it impossible to peel the tape away, so Logan searched the top of the dressing table until he found a small pair of nail scissors, and used them to slice a slit in the tape, where the top of the box met the side.

The cardboard pinged up like a trapdoor being thrown open. Logan instinctively leaned back, turning his face away in case something corrosive came springing out at him.

When he looked back, he could see the cord handles of a gift bag and, nestled inside, the gold–coloured screw top of a green glass bottle.

Slowly, carefully, using the handles, he pulled the bag out of the box and sat it upright on the dressing table. He checked inside the box, but besides a little wad of bubble wrap, it contained nothing of obvious interest.

Just the bottle, then.

The gift bag was a shiny golden number, with the word 'Surprise!' emblazoned down the side in shades of silver glitter. There was a gift tag attached, but nothing had been written on it. No sender's name had been signed.

Pity. That would've certainly made things easier.

He rummaged around on the dressing table until he found one of the various make-up powders that Shona never got around to using. He unclipped the brush from the tray, dabbed it into the fine powder to load it up, then brushed it gently across the bottle's gold top.

No prints.

Holding it by the screw cap, he eased the bottle out of the bag and held it at arm's length, like it was some dead thing he'd just pulled from the ground.

Buckfast tonic wine.

A 75cl bottle of Buckie.

Christ. That brought back memories. Few of them good.

One of them awful.

He felt the same rising tide of panic that he'd felt when he'd heard that voice on the phone. Tiny spiders with hot, stabbing feet crept up the back of his neck and across his scalp. His reflection, warped by the curve of the green glass, looked ready to throw up.

Hands shaking, he returned the bottle to the bag, and stuffed the bag back in the box.

If only the memories that had been dredged up were so easily packed away.

Logan sat on the bed, elbows resting on his thighs, hands clasped in front of his mouth, like he was praying. And he was, in a way, though to whom or to what he couldn't say.

He stared at the box on the dressing table as if, even from this distance, it might offer some clue. Some explanation as to what was going on, and who was behind it.

He thought back to the list of people who might feasibly know what he had done. Shuggie Cowan and the nameless desk sergeant remained the only real contenders.

Maybe it was time to talk to Shuggie. Maybe that was all that was left for him to do.

He checked the time on the bedside clock. Midnight. If he left now, he could be in Glasgow in a few hours. Shuggie likely wouldn't appreciate the half-three-in-the-morning wake-up, but Logan was beyond the point of caring.

If he was right, and Shuggie was at the centre of all this, then the lives of the people trapped in those cages might hinge on...

Something niggled at him, derailing his train of thought. He looked back at the clock again, sensing it was something there on his bedside table that his subconscious had picked up on. Something there that shouldn't be.

The clock looked fine. His phone charging cable hung over the top of it as usual. The mug he'd sat there a few days ago, and which Shona was refusing to move as a matter of principle, was still right where he left it.

Except…

It was no longer sitting on the furniture's wooden surface. It was on a coaster now.

No, not a coaster.

A beer mat.

Logan swallowed and held that breath. He sat perfectly still, as if trying to avoid detection by some violent, deadly predator.

Several seconds passed. The murmur of voices rumbled away in the room below, as Shona continued to lecture the kids on the birds and the bees.

Finally, glove creaking under the strain of his fingers, Logan reached over, picked up the mug, and moved it aside.

It was the same mat. Same design. Same pub.

Same message, letting him know that someone knew.

His panic began to rise again, but then spluttered out, replaced by something rawer and more primal. Something he was far more familiar with.

Rage.

The bastard had been here. The bastard had been in his house, right here in the bedroom he shared with the woman he loved.

The beer mat was a message, yes, but it wasn't just telling Jack that the person who left it knew his secret. It was telling him that he could get to him anytime he wanted.

'Is that how you want to play it, is it?' Logan growled, rising to his feet. He looked around the room, searching for a microphone or camera left in plain sight. Though he didn't find one, he continued on the assumption there was one there. 'You just made a big fucking mistake, pal. If I was you, I'd get your affairs in order, quick bloody smart. Because, I am coming for you, and I will find you, and God himself won't be able to help you when I do.'

He left the words to ring out in the silence of the room, then snatched up his coat, the beer mat, and the box containing the Buckfast bottle, and went charging down the stairs.

Shona had an unpeeled banana in her hand and two beetroot-coloured teenagers sitting on the couch in front of her when Logan barged back into the living room. Taggart raised a head from where he'd been cringing under the coffee table, and his stubby tail thumped once on the floor in greeting.

'You need to get out,' Logan said to Shona. He pointed to Olivia and Harris, still sitting at opposite ends of the couch. 'Take them. Get a hotel somewhere. Book it under a fake name.' He shook his head. 'In fact, no. Go to the station. Burnett Road. I'll call ahead to let them know you're coming.'

Shona lowered the banana. 'Why? What's happened?' she asked. 'What's wrong?'

'No time to explain.' Logan looked very deliberately up at the ceiling, then around the room, then put a finger to his lips. 'Just get your jackets and go,' he whispered.

Shona opened her mouth to ask another question, but the pleading look in Logan's eyes made her think again. She trusted him. If he said they needed to go, they needed to go.

'Right, you pair,' she said, pointing at them both with the banana. 'On your feet. Chop chop.'

To their credit, both teenagers immediately did as they were told, jumping up and awaiting further orders. Both had suffered their fair share of trauma over the years, and neither was in a hurry to go through anything similar again.

'What about Taggart?' Olivia asked. At mention of his name, the dog sat up, head raised in full *good boy* mode, no doubt hoping that some sort of treat was about to be forthcoming.

'Take him with you,' Logan said, and he waited for the girl to pick the dog up before leading them out into the hall.

He raised a hand, warning them to wait, then opened the front door and looked out into the darkness. The pools of orange from the street lamps were all clear, but there was no way of knowing if anyone lurked in the shadows between them.

It was a chance they'd have to take.

And God help them, if they were.

'Right, go. Get in your car,' Logan urged, ushering them all along the path. He hung back long enough to lock the door, then rushed past them at the gate, a terrible thought occurring to him. 'Wait!'

Dropping onto his belly, he looked under Shona's car, using the torchlight from his phone to check the underside for anything unusual or untoward. Besides some light rusting of her exhaust, though, everything looked fine.

'Clear,' he said, lumbering back to his feet.

The look of horror in Shona's eyes almost knocked him back down again. 'Jesus. Seriously?' she whispered.

Logan shook his head. 'I don't know.'

'What the hell's going on, Jack?'

Logan ignored the question and turned to the teens. 'In the car. Get in the back. Belts on.'

They complied without complaint. Shona was still staring at him, though, her question still hanging in the air between them.

'What is this, Jack? What's happening?'

Logan could feel his body starting to betray him again. The prickling heat. The racing heart. The sense of the world closing in around him.

And then, she took his hand in hers and stepped in closer, and suddenly there was no more world to close in, there was only them.

'You're scaring me, Jack,' she told him, though her voice was a comfort blanket draping across his shoulders. 'What's happening? What's going on?'

He had to tell her. She deserved to know.

She, more than anyone, deserved to know who he truly was.

'Someone's coming after me,' he said, and each word took more effort than the last. 'I don't know who. Not yet. I think...'

He shook his head. There was no more time for lies or ambiguity. There could only be the truth now. It was all he had left to give her.

'I *know* that they've been in the house. Some point today.'

Shona's eyes grew wider, as fear crept in to fill them. 'Today? In the house? But Olivia was—'

'I know. I know,' Logan said. 'That's why I need to get you all safe, until I can find out who it is, and stop them. Someone's coming after me, and I won't have any of you in harm's way. I can't.'

Shona tried to smile, but it was a faltering and hesitant thing. 'I mean, this happens, doesn't it? You're in the police. Police make enemies all the time. It's probably just some angry ex-con with a grudge.'

'This is different,' Logan insisted.

'How?'

She squeezed his hand again, and the warmth of her touch almost brought him to his knees. He wasn't looking at her. He couldn't. She shifted her head until he was forced to meet her eye.

'How is it different, Jack?'

'Because this... what's happening, it's nothing to do with anyone I've arrested or put away.'

He felt it then, rising up from the pit it had lain dormant in for over two decades. The cave it had carved for itself deep down in his soul.

The truth.

The awful, terrible, horrifying truth.

'It's about the man I murdered.'

Chapter 29

Tyler was the cat who'd got the cream. The early bird who'd caught the worm. The surrogate older brother who'd just discovered that his younger sibling had a secret love life.

'Wait, you two are…?' His grin was dazzling. His eyes were like little bubbles of joy. His finger swayed from Harris to Olivia and back again. 'The two of you are…? Oh, God. This is the greatest thing I've ever heard.'

It wasn't that he was particularly happy with the coupling. He wasn't sure that Olivia Maximuke, daughter of a feared Russian gangster and borderline psychopath, was a suitable partner, any more than he was sure that Harris Bell, who could go days without changing his pants and couldn't work a dishwasher, was.

No, it was their awkwardness that he was enjoying. Their sheer ear-reddening embarrassment at having been caught. That's what Tyler was delighting in.

It was probably quite mean of him, he knew, but on a day like today, you had to get your kicks from somewhere.

'How long's this been going on for?' asked Sinead. She stood beside Tyler with her arms crossed and her face fixed in one of her more serious scowls.

Since their parents had died, Sinead had been the closest Harris had to a mother, and she was fully in that mode now. Tyler knew it was an act, though. He could tell she was as amused by the whole thing as he was. She was just a lot better at hiding it.

'Nothing's going on,' Harris muttered. 'Shut up.'

'Are you having sex?' Sinead asked, and Tyler made a sort of internal squeaking noise, like he was hiding a mouse in his mouth.

'Jesus. Ew! No! What are you even…? Ugh! Shut up!'

Olivia scoffed, like this was the most outrageous suggestion she'd ever heard. 'Pfft. As if.'

'Good. Because you're both far too young for that sort of thing,' Sinead said. She switched her crossed arms pose to full hands on hips mode for added effect. 'But, for God's sake, if you're going to do it—'

'We're not,' both teenagers insisted at the same time.

'Good! But if you are, then you need to use—'

'Jesus, don't say it!' Harris pleaded.

'Come on, buddy, you need to hear this,' Tyler said. He folded his arms and fought to keep his grin from spreading even further.

God, he was loving every minute.

'Protection!' Shona said, coming over to join them. 'That's what I said. I had a banana.'

Tyler turned a full one-eighty so he was looking the other way. Though he could hide his face this way, he couldn't disguise the shaking of his shoulders.

'Tell him to shut up!' Harris squeaked, which only made the DC's shaking even worse.

'You two go and grab a seat,' Shona said, pointing over to the couch in the corner of the break room, then ushering the teenagers towards it. 'I need to talk to Sinead and Tyler.'

Sullenly, and without so much as looking at one another, Harris and Olivia plodded over to the sofa and sat, once again, at opposite ends. They both took out their phones, and were instantly absorbed by the screens.

'What are they doing here?' Sinead asked. 'You didn't bring them in just to tell us they were snogging, did you? I mean, I'm glad I know, but…'

Shona shook her head, and glanced furtively over at the couch. 'No, not that. It's, eh, it's something else,' she said.

Tyler had composed himself enough now to join the conversation. The serious edge to Shona's voice had helped immensely.

'What's up?' he asked.

'Um…' The pathologist put her hands in the pockets of her jeans and shrugged. 'I think maybe Jack should be the one to explain. I convinced him to come in.'

Sinead's brow creased with concern. 'I thought the plan was he was going to go home and get some rest?'

'Oh, he came home, but it's safe to say that things didn't quite work out as planned.' Shona's face was tight with worry. Her eyes darted to the door of the break room. 'But I really think this is something he'll want to tell you himself.'

Chapter 30

Something was different about DCI Logan. Something had changed. Tyler spotted it as soon as they entered the Incident Room. Sinead did, too, going by the little intake of breath she gave when she saw him standing by the Big Boards.

Usually, he was a bit like gas, in that he expanded to fill whatever space he was in. If he stepped into a room, it immediately became *his* room, his very essence reaching into every corner of it and marking it as his territory.

It wasn't a conscious thing, Tyler had eventually come to conclude. The DCI was never deliberately trying to come across as the big man. He just *was* the big man, in every sense. Physically, he was tall. When it came to presence, though, he was a giant.

But not tonight.

It looked like him—same coat, same face, same hair—but everything that made him Jack Logan seemed to have been squeezed out of him.

Though he couldn't explain why, something about the boss, and how he stood, and how he looked, made Tyler suddenly feel very, very afraid.

Ben and Hamza were both standing up, but half-leaning on the desks nearest the boards. Thomas was nowhere to be seen, presumably having been told to make himself scarce while Logan shared whatever his update was. The Gozer was getting a couple of hours' sleep in Mitchell's office. Ben had offered to wake him, but Logan had quickly shut that idea down.

The DS and the DI both turned and acknowledged Tyler and Sinead with quick, short nods, but Logan himself was looking at the floor by his feet, and didn't raise his head even when Sinead greeted him with a, 'Back so soon, sir? Could you just not bring yourself to stay away?'

The questions sounded jokey and light, but Tyler knew her well enough to hear all the cracks in all the wrong places.

The Incident Room door opened and closed again behind them as Shona came sidling in. She didn't come any further, and just stood there, her back against the wall, saying nothing. Waiting.

Dreading, if her face was anything to go by.

'What's all this about then, Jack?' Ben asked. 'The Gozer said you should go home and get some sleep.'

'Aye,' Logan admitted. He ran a hand down his face, then scratched at the stubble on his jaw, his fingers pressing so hard they left red and white lines on his skin. 'He did say that.'

When nothing else seemed to be forthcoming, Sinead shot a worried look around at the others, then took a faltering step closer to him. 'Is everything alright, sir?'

Logan's whole upper body twitched and he huffed out a one-note laugh. 'Is everything alright?' He considered the question for a few moments, then shook his head. 'No.'

'Jesus, Jack, you're no' hosting the bloody X-Factor. You don't need to drag out the tension for the viewers at home,' Ben told him. 'We're no' going to cut to an ad break. Spit it out, man.'

Shona cleared her throat. 'He, eh, he might just need a minute.'

'I killed a man,' Logan announced.

'Or, you know, he might not,' the pathologist added.

'What?' Ben looked the DCI up and down. 'What do you mean? What are you on about?'

'Bloody hell, boss, you were only gone a couple of hours,' Tyler said.

'I don't mean tonight, Tyler!'

'Oh! Right!' The detective constable seemed relieved to hear this, then became concerned again when he realised the implications. 'So, eh, so what are you saying, then?'

Logan ran his hand down his face again. This time, it pulled his mouth all the way open until his jaw was at full stretch. He looked past the other detectives to where Shona was standing, and took some strength from the nod she gave him.

'I was seventeen. Just out of school. I'd been drinking. Snuck into a pub. Malkie's Arms. Think it's a CrossFit these days. And I say snuck in, but Malkie wasn't exactly one for checking IDs. Selling, them, aye, but...'

He groaned like this was taking effort, stole a look around at the faces looking on, then continued.

'Anyway, the old man—my stepdad—had been going off on one about me getting a job and generally telling me I was a useless bastard, so I'd gone out. Tanned a couple of bottles of Buckie, then when that was done, gone to Malkie's to keep drinking. Better that than going home, I thought.'

He looked across the room at Shona, like he wasn't sure he should be saying this next part, but saw no warning signs there to stop him.

'There was a lassie in there. Good looking. Like, way out of my league. Way out of the league of anyone in the place, but especially a pissed-up seventeen year old with no prospects and an attitude problem. Anyway, she's not there on her own. She's with some loudmouthed bastard. Flash. Gold tooth and cowboy boots. As soon as I see him, there goes the arsehole alarm. Sure enough, he starts telling everyone who'll listen that he works for Shuggie Cowan, one of the bigger league Glasgow hard men.'

'Christ. Cowan,' Ben muttered.

'Here, hold on, is that not that guy you took me to meet, boss?' Tyler asked.

Logan nodded, and Ben let out a low whistle of surprise. 'Good grief, and he came out alive? The bastard must've gone soft in his old age.'

'Aye. Comes to us all. Anyway, the arsehole keeps telling everyone the lassie's his bird, but I'm not convinced. Her body language and the way she keeps faking a laugh when he makes his terrible fucking jokes says otherwise.'

'Always a detective, eh, boss?' Tyler said, before a look from Sinead silenced him.

'Aye, maybe,' Logan grunted. 'Whatever, I sat in the corner out of the way of the bar, and I kept drinking. And I kept drinking. And that guy kept getting louder, and the lassie was getting more and more uncomfortable, and I'm thinking maybe I should say something. Maybe I should ask her if she's OK.

'But then your man, he goes to the toilet. Announces it first, of course, because he was that sort of arsehole. Shouts to the whole bar that he's off for a piss. Reminds us all who his boss is, and warns us not to so much as look at his bird. Tells us how Shuggie'll tear our eyes out of our heads and feed them to our loved ones if we do.'

'Bloody hell,' Tyler mumbled. 'I thought he seemed alright when we met him. Didn't have him pegged as an eye-feeder.'

Everyone ignored him, especially Logan, who ignored him twice as hard as the others.

'Soon as the bathroom door shuts, the lassie, she's up and on her feet. Grabbing her jacket, tucking her bag under her arm, just set on making a beeline for the door and getting away before he comes back. She's had enough. She wants out.

'Some guy tries to block her at the bar, but she brings up the knee, right between his legs. He goes down like he's been picked off by a sniper. Greatest thing I've ever seen until that moment. Seventeen years old, two bottles of Buckie and four pints of lager deep, and I'm in love. I'm smitten.'

He looked at Shona again, but she had her head down and her eyes closed, either caught up in the story or lost in her own thoughts. His breath whistled through his nose as he drew in enough air to see him through to the end.

'I'm thinking of following her out. Just, you know, walking her to a taxi or something. Or offering to, anyway. It's a rough area, especially that time of night. Before I can move, though, your man comes back out of the toilet. He sees she's gone, spies the boy trying to dislodge his bollocks from his lower abdomen, and figures out what's happened. And he's not happy. He's raging.

'He storms out after her, shouting abuse. Going on about how he bought her dinner, so she owes him. I'm so bloody glaikit that, for a minute, I think he wants her to pay for her share of the meal. But something about his voice, about the anger in it, makes me realise that's not what he's after.'

Logan's tongue flicked across his lips, which had suddenly become very dry. His hands were shaking, so he shoved them in his pockets where no one could see them.

'Nobody else moved. Nobody said a word. Twenty, thirty guys there, and they all just carried on like nothing was happening. So, I gets up and goes out, and they're nowhere to be seen. Look up and down the street. Nothing. Gone.'

The DCI's chest was rising and falling in big, unsteady breaths now. If you listened closely, you could almost hear the cannon fire of his heartbeat against his ribcage.

'And then, I heard her. Just for a split-second. A cry that was cut off. Scuffling. Thumping. Like they were fighting round the back of the pub. I didn't know what was happening, exactly, but I knew it wasn't good for the lassie, whatever it was.'

He hesitated, swallowed back the words, like not saying them stopped them becoming real.

'I went round the side. And he was, eh, he was attacking her. Had her by the hair. Pulling at her clothes,' Logan continued. He was looking beyond the team now, beyond Shona, even, to a past that only he could see. 'She saw me and tried to shout, but he punched her in the mouth. Just, *bam*. Holding her hair in one hand, hitting her with the other. Her lip burst open, and I remember just looking at the blood and being amazed by the colour of it. The redness of it.

'He clocked me then, too. Warned me to fuck off. But, I didn't. I told him to let her go. Or... no. Realistically, I asked him to let her go.'

'I'm guessing he didn't?' Hamza said.

Logan shook his head. 'No. So, after standing there shiteing myself for a few seconds, I ran over and tried to drag him away from her. He took a swing and caught me with a left across the ear. And, in the meantime, he lets the lassie go and she falls over. And he laughs. At both of us. Me standing there holding my ear trying not to cry, her lying on the ground with her mouth split open. He laughs at us.'

He blinked a few times, refocusing, bringing himself back to the here and the now. When he nodded, it felt like the story had come to a premature end.

'And?' Ben demanded. 'What happened then?'

Logan chewed on his bottom lip, like he was trying to sabotage it so it couldn't continue.

But he'd come this far. Just a little farther.

'I hit him,' he said. 'First time I'd ever hit anyone. Properly, I mean, not kids fighting, or whatever. I hit him about as hard as I've ever hit anyone before or since.'

'Good for you, boss. Sounds like he had it coming!'

Logan didn't share the detective constable's enthusiasm. 'He went down. I could see he was out on his feet when he started falling. His whole body just went limp, like one of those big inflatable guys you see flapping about at garages, after the air's been cut off. Just bang. Down. Hit his head on an old toilet that was out there. Must've been from a refurbishment, or something. Suddenly, there's blood everywhere, and he's lying there with his neck at forty-five degrees.'

'Oh God, Jack,' Ben whispered.

Logan didn't look at him. He couldn't. Instead, he pressed on, knowing the end was now in sight.

'The lassie took one look at him, then looked at me like I'd been the one attacking her. She grabbed up her stuff and ran. Didn't say a word, just looked at me like I was some sort of animal, and ran.'

'And you were left with—'Hamza fumbled around for the right word to use'—the guy?'

'And I was left with the guy,' Logan confirmed, exhaling through every word. 'I was seventeen and a bloody idiot, but even I could see that he wasn't getting back up. Don't know if it was the punch or the edge of the toilet, but he was a goner. He was dead. I'd killed him.'

'It was an accident, sir,' Sinead said.

'You know, I've thought about it a lot,' Logan said, glancing at the DC only briefly. 'And I'm not so sure it was. If you'd asked me in that moment—the moment before I hit him, I mean—if I wanted the bastard dead, I'd have said yes. I'd have paid money. And then, next thing I know, he is. And I'm the one who did it.'

'Still wasn't your fault, sir,' Sinead insisted.

'Whose fault was it, then?' Tyler asked. He looked around at the others. Sinead and Hamza were both looking back at him with expressions that veered from surprise to horror. 'I mean, I'm not blaming anyone—'

'Sounds like you are, mate,' Hamza countered.

'I'm not. Like I said, the guy sounded like he needed punching. But that doesn't change the fact of what happened.'

'Jesus, Tyler!' Sinead hissed.

'What?' Tyler looked to Logan of all people for support. 'You always tell us to think like police officers, boss. That's what I'm doing. If it hadn't been you, if it happened now and you saw the punch, you'd arrest the guy, wouldn't you? You'd have to.'

'He was defending someone,' Hamza pointed out.

Tyler shrugged. 'What does that change? That's for the courts to figure out. Right, boss?'

For the first time that night, just the faintest shadow of a smile played across the DCI's face. 'He's right. Picked a hell of

220

a time to get good at his job, but he's right. If I saw that kid, I'd bring him in.'

'Thank you!' Tyler said, then he side-eyed his wife and his best mate. 'That's all I was saying.'

'And I did,' Logan continued. 'Bring him in. Handed myself in, I mean. I walked into the nearest station, went up to the desk sergeant and told him what I'd done.'

Ben, who had said very little since Logan's confession had started, raised an eyebrow at this information. 'And?'

'Can't remember a whole lot about the conversation,' Logan admitted. 'The adrenaline was either kicking in or wearing off, and all the drink was hitting. I remember thinking he was an arsehole, though. Only twelve, fifteen years older than me, maybe, but seemed older. Got the impression he wasn't that interested, like he couldn't be bothered with it. I'm telling him I've killed a guy, and he just takes my name and address, and says he'll pass it on to CID in the morning.'

'Bloody hell. Surely not, boss? No way someone's doing that.'

'It's the bit of the story I've got the least trouble with,' Ben replied. 'There was some good coppers down there back then, but a lot of shite ones, too.'

Logan shrugged. 'I think he thought I was winding him up. He eventually agreed to send a car out to check on everything, so when it's obvious he's no' going to arrest me, I head back there to wait with the body.'

'Helluva honest of you, Jack,' Ben said, his eyes slightly narrowed.

'Think I was more thinking about what Cowan would do to me. Reckoned jail was a safer bet.'

'He'd have got you in the jail,' the DI pointed out.

'Aye, well. Didn't know that at the time. Anyway, so I go back, and it's gone. The body. It's not there.'

Tyler ejected a little cheep of what could have been relief, but could just as easily have been outrage. 'Jesus Christ, boss!

So he wasn't even dead? All this, and he was alive the whole time?'

'Oh, he was dead, alright. No doubt about it. Someone must've moved him,' the DCI replied. His eyes glazed over again, as the past reared up to haunt him. 'You don't just miraculously recover from your neck being at that angle.'

'Maybe it wasn't as bad as it looked,' Sinead suggested. 'Maybe it was just the angle you were looking down at him from.'

'Aye, maybe. But he also had no pulse and he wasn't breathing. And I'm pretty sure I could see part of his brain through the hole in the side of his head.'

'Probably dead right enough then, boss,' Tyler said, nodding to confirm the diagnosis.

'Did Uniform turn up?' Hamza asked.

Logan's head shook. 'No. Although, with no body, I didn't wait too long. Didn't see the point. I thought maybe they'd already been and shifted him, and I'd go home to find them waiting for me. But they weren't. So, I lay awake all night, waiting for them to come. Watched out the window so I could go down and meet them without them waking my mum up. But, no. Nothing that night. Nothing the next day. Nothing since.'

He looked to the back of the room again, where Shona stood. She was looking back at him now, her eyes open. But, for the first time in a long time, he had no idea what was going on behind them.

'But I killed him,' he said, and though he'd said the words before, he felt them this time. Felt the weight of them pulling on him, dragging him down, like they'd been doing for most of his life. 'Arsehole or not. Sexual assault or not. I killed that man.'

'I mean...It's...' Sinead grasped at platitudes that even she wasn't buying. 'It doesn't change anything, sir. Does it?'

'It changes everything,' Ben said, and there was a harshness to his voice that only the person it was aimed at had ever heard before, and then only rarely. 'But why now, Jack? Why tell us this now, when we've got everything else going on? What the hell are we meant to do with this information tonight?'

Logan tried to reply, but the look in the DI's eyes was like a knife wound, and the words refused to come.

'Because someone knows,' Shona said from over by the door. 'Someone knows what happened, and he thinks it's connected to—'she gestured vaguely towards the Big Boards, and the eight headshots pinned to it'—all this stuff.' She looked to Logan for confirmation. 'Right?'

'Right. Aye. Least, it seems very much like it.' He picked up the carrier bag that lay on the floor beside him, reached in, and took out the beer mat. 'One of these was sent to me here this morning. Or, yesterday morning now, I suppose. It's from Malkie's Arms, the pub where it all happened. Shut down years ago. Knocked down, in fact. I gave the one that came in the post to Palmer to run forensics on.'

'What, without telling us?' Ben asked, affronted.

Logan had never looked more sheepish. His reply was a quick raising of his eyebrows and an apologetic nod.

'He get anything from it?' Hamza asked.

'Don't know. Haven't heard back yet,' Logan said. 'This one…' He closed his mouth and stared at the mat for a while, the rest of the sentence percolating away inside him until it was good and ready. 'This one was left in mine and Shona's bedroom today.'

'Oh, shit!' Hamza ejected. 'In your bedroom?'

'On the bedside table.'

'God. Wait. Hang on, what are you saying?' Sinead looked from Logan to Shona, then back again. 'Someone was in your bedroom?'

Logan's nostrils flared just at the thought of it, but he nodded. 'Looks very much like it, aye. From talking to Olivia, she thinks she left the back door open when she went to check the shed earlier. I reckon they must have snuck in then.'

'Which would explain why Taggart was acting up the whole time,' Shona added.

'Jesus,' Sinead whispered. 'But they're gone, yeah? You checked? They're not there now?'

'They're not there now,' Logan said.

Hamza reached for his phone. 'You want me to get Scene of Crime round there, sir?'

'I doubt they'll find anything,' Logan replied, and his weariness made a pretty compelling case. 'Someone that's gone to this much planning...' He rubbed at his eyes, then shrugged. 'But, aye. Why not? Worth a try.'

Tyler, who has been staring at the beer mat in Logan's hand, finally voiced the thought that had been troubling him.

'But, like, are you sure it's not just the same one, boss? You sure there's definitely two coasters? Could that not just be the first one that's somehow been put in your room by mistake, or—' Tyler gasped. 'Hang on! Could Palmer be behind it?' He glanced around to see if the idea was getting any traction, and was disappointed to note that it wasn't. 'There's always been something a bit weird about him, I've thought.'

'Aye, but in a sort of creepy wee stalker kind of way,' Hamza countered. 'I don't see him as the serial killing, blackmailing, evil mastermind type.' He put his phone to his ear then gave this some thought. 'I mean, definitely not the mastermind bit, anyway.'

A heavy silence hung in the air while Hamza placed the call to the Scene of Crime office. Everyone stood around, not really making eye contact, while the sergeant requested a team be dispatched to Logan's address, by way of the Incident Room to pick up the keys.

When he'd finished and hung up, Sinead lightly cleared her throat and went for the big question.

'So, what happens now?'

Logan's expression didn't change. 'I step down, pending investigation.'

'My arse you do.' Ben's retort was sharp and almost spiteful. 'How dare you? How dare you even suggest that, you selfish, gutless bastard?'

There was some subtle shuffling as everyone but Logan put themselves out of the firing line. They'd seen Ben in a lot of states before, from mildly confused to devastated by grief.

But they'd never seen him angry before. Not really. Not like this.

'What do you mean?' Logan asked, as taken aback as the rest of them. 'I can't stay on now.'

'Why the hell not? You've kept us in the dark on this forever,' Ben shot back. 'You've lied to us. Or, hidden the truth, at least. You've been bloody good at it, too. And, for the sake of those people, you're going to keep being good at it for as long as is necessary.'

'Ben—'

'Don't *Ben* me. It's Detective Inspector Forde. You say this is about you? You say that's why all this is happening?'

'I don't know for sure, but... Aye. Maybe.'

'Then you owe it to those people to keep your mouth shut, keep the heid, and get them all home.'

'He's right, boss,' Tyler said, siding with the DI. 'Whatever happens afterwards, we need you for this. They need you.'

Logan's strength had been ebbing away since the conversation had started, but what was left of it seemed to leave him all in one sudden burst. His broad shoulders sagged. Despite his size, he was the smallest person in the room.

'I don't know how,' he admitted. 'I don't know how we save them. We've got nowhere.'

'Aye, well, it's different now,' Ben told him.

'How?'

'Because up until now, some selfish, secretive bastard's been keeping our biggest lead of all from us,' Ben told him. He stabbed an accusing finger in Jack's direction. '*You.*'

'He's right, sir. This changes things,' Sinead said. 'This could help us work out who's behind all this.'

Logan shook his head. 'I've tried. I've already gone through it.'

'Aye, *you* have, maybe,' Ben said. He turned to Sinead. 'DC Bell, prep interview room two, will you?' His gaze crept back in Logan's direction. 'And let's see what the witness has got to say for himself.'

Before anyone could move, the doors to the Incident Room were heaved open. They all turned to look as Dave Davidson wheeled himself in, whistling quietly under his breath.

'Alright?' he chirped, when he saw them all looking. 'Couldn't sleep, so thought I might as well come back in.'

He looked at all the faces staring back at him, and grinned slightly awkwardly.

'So,' he said, as the doors swung closed behind him. 'What did I miss?'

Chapter 31

Fifteen minutes later, when Logan, Sinead, and Ben had gone to the interview room, and Shona had gone to keep an eye on the teenage lovebirds, Tyler rolled his chair over to join Hamza.

With Logan's permission, Hamza was bringing Dave up to speed with everything, and the constable's eyes had been widening for the past few minutes, to the point they now looked like an explosion risk.

Thomas had been allowed back into the room after Ben had led the others out, and now sat tapping away on his keyboard and scrolling through lines and lines of what looked, from where Tyler was sitting, like utter gibberish.

'Bloody Nora,' Dave said, sitting back in his chair. His now-bulging eyes flitted left and right, like he was sorting through everything he'd just been told, and deciding where in his head he should be filing it.

'What do you make of all that, then?' Tyler asked, addressing the question to both the sergeant and the constable. He kept his voice low to reduce the risk of Thomas listening in. The consultant had headphones on, but the DC reckoned it was better to be safe than sorry, especially given DI Forde's current anger levels.

Tyler waggled his eyebrows, like he was gesturing not to a place, but backwards through time. 'Pretty mental stuff, isn't it?'

'You can say that again,' Dave agreed.

'Aye,' Hamza added. 'Pretty mental.'

'I mean…' Tyler puffed out his cheeks. 'You know what I mean?'

'Aye,' Hamza said again. 'Pretty crazy, right enough.'

'Crazy,' Dave agreed.

'He killed a guy, though!' Tyler stressed. 'The boss! He actually properly killed a guy.'

'By accident,' Hamza said.

Tyler's nose wrinkled up. 'Sort of,' he reasoned. 'I mean, you heard what he said.'

'What did he say?' asked Dave, who had clearly missed out on this bit of information.

Tyler leaned a little closer. 'That he half meant it.'

'That's not what he said,' Hamza quickly argued.

'It's basically what he said. He said he wanted the guy dead, so…' Tyler sat back, his hands out in front of him like he was presenting some invisible evidence. 'That sort of means he half meant it.'

'Does it mean that, though?' Dave asked.

'It *sort of* means that, aye,' Tyler insisted.

He looked around and over at the door, like he expected to see someone standing there. He almost seemed surprised when he didn't.

'What happens now, do you think?' he asked, and his voice sounded unusually flat.

Hamza sat in contemplative silence for a few moments, then shrugged. 'I honestly don't know.'

'You can't be in the police if you killed a guy,' Tyler said. 'I mean, I know they used to turn a blind eye to that sort of thing, but not now, surely? I can't see how the boss survives this, can you? And that's the thing, I don't even know if he should!'

Both officers looked horrified by that remark.

'I mean, I want him to be around, obviously. I don't want him going anywhere, but… *he killed a guy*! An actual guy! Can we just, what? Ignore that? Brush it under the carpet? How is that right?'

Hamza's reply was a shrug and a sigh. 'I don't know. Guess we'll have to see what happens. It'll be out of our hands.'

Tyler nodded slowly. He sat back in his chair as if the impromptu gossip session was now over, but then leaned forward again almost immediately. 'What's the score with your man over there?' he asked, jerking his head in Thomas's direction. 'Can't believe the boss actually let him stay after you told him what had happened.'

'It was the right call,' Hamza said, though it clearly pained him to admit it. 'He knows his stuff. If he's able to trace those I.P.s, it'll be a game changer.'

'Aye. Well.' Tyler sniffed and crossed his arms. 'I still don't like him.'

His loyalty brought a thin but appreciative smile to the sergeant's face. 'Cheers, mate. Me neither.'

'What happened?' Dave asked. 'What else have I missed?'

Tyler lowered his voice even further, forcing the constable to lean closer. 'That guy shagged Hamza's wife.'

'Oi!' Hamza protested, not thrilled with the choice of words.

'Bloody hell!' Dave ejected. 'When? Tonight? How did he find the time?'

'Not tonight. Months back,' Tyler said.

'Oh.' The constable winced as he turned to the DS. 'Shit. Sorry, mate. That's rough.'

'Aye, not ideal,' Hamza admitted, then a tentative knock on the Incident Room door provided the interruption he'd been craving since the conversation had shifted subject. 'I'd better get that,' he said.

Yawning, he got up from his seat and went out to greet a young constable so wet behind the ears he was practically drowning.

'Hi. You alright?' Hamza asked, glancing up and down the corridor like he was looking for the lad's parent or guardian.

'Um, um, yes. Sorry. I'm just… I don't normally get sent places. Like, I mean, to do, you know, to give things. Stuff. News.'

The constable shook his head. Puppy fat jiggled, and Hamza suddenly felt ten years older than he actually was.

'Updates and things, I mean,' the constable squeaked.

He extended his arms and flicked his hands around, like he was an actor shaking out the tension of a particularly harrowing scene.

'Sorry. I just haven't been on this sort of… Mission?' He winced at the word, but stumbled blindly on. 'I mean, like, I don't really get sent to talk to detectives. You're my first. So, hello, and everything. And sorry, I'm a bit—'

'It's fine. Don't worry about it, we're not that scary,' Hamza assured him. 'What's up?'

'There's, uh, there's someone downstairs, sir. In reception.'

'OK…'

'She says that she, eh, she works with one of the influencers. Elizia Shuttleworth. She's her friend, but she helps her with her channel. Editing stuff, I think.'

'You sure she's not just some nutter, or press, or whatever?'

'Uh, no, sir. We looked into it. She's got ID. Photos of her and Elizia together. She's named in the bit under some of her YouTube videos. What's it called? Not the comments…' He pointed downwards, indicating where the bit he was referencing should be.

'Description?' Hamza guessed.

'Yes! Sorry! She's named in some of the video descriptions, so she checks out.'

'Right,' Hamza said, masking his impatience with an encouraging nod. 'And?'

'And, well, she thinks she knows who did it, sir. The kidnapping and murder, I mean. She, uh, she thinks she knows who's behind it.'

Hamza, who had been leaning on the door frame, now straightened. 'What? She does? Who?'

'That's the thing, sir.' The constable ran a hand through his baby-fine blond hair and scratched at his scalp. It was a nervous movement, like he thought the next part might get him in trouble. 'She reckons it's Elizia herself.'

Chapter 32

'Well?' Ben demanded.

It was the first word he'd spoken since they'd left the Incident Room, and the look on his face made it clear that the DCI wouldn't like any of the others that might follow it.

'I don't know what you want from me here,' Logan said. He caught sight of himself in the interview room mirror, sitting on the wrong side of the table, and quickly looked away.

Ben drew a breath in through his nose, like a dragon getting ready to unleash a volley of flame. Fortunately, Sinead intervened before any roastings could take place.

'I suppose, sir, we start by going over who knew,' she ventured. 'Who was aware of what happened that night, I mean. Did you tell anyone? Besides the desk sergeant at the station?'

'Not until tonight.'

'No one?'

Logan's gaze flitted from the detective constable to the white haired human scowl beside her. 'No. Nobody. Never said a word.'

'Right. Good. That narrows it down, then,' Sinead said. She spoke with an exaggerated brightness, like she could jolly some of the tension out of the room. 'In that case, who've we got? The woman being attacked, the sergeant who took your statement… Anyone else?'

'I've gone over this,' Logan told her. 'She had no idea who I was. He wasn't interested.'

'Nobody saw it happening?' Sinead pressed. 'Could anyone have been looking out the window?'

'It was a working man's pub in the Gorbals,' Logan replied. 'Don't think it even had windows. None out back, anyway.'

'Could anyone have followed you out?'

'No. I mean, not that I saw. Door made a big creak and a clatter, too. I'd have heard it.'

'What about Cowan?' Ben asked, visibly grudging every syllable.

Logan shook his head. 'Thought about him. Not his style these days. And, if he'd known, he'd have used it back when we were clashing heads. Doubt he'd have let me arrest him if he could've destroyed my career with one phone call.'

Sinead perked up, her eyebrows shooting halfway up her forehead. 'CID!' she cried. 'What about CID? If it was passed on, all your details would've been handed over.'

Again, Logan shook his head. 'I looked into it a couple of times over the years. Tried to find any record of it. Drew a blank every time. Like I said, I don't think the sergeant on duty believed a word I was saying. Basically told me to go home and sleep it off.'

'And you didn't get a name?'

'No. Wasn't thinking about it.'

'And that voice on the recording. Could that have been the sergeant, do you think?'

'I don't know,' Logan replied, at a speed that said he'd already considered it.

'Well *think*, then,' Ben snapped. 'Could it, or couldn't it?'

'I don't know,' Logan said again, but then he buckled. 'Maybe. I suppose. It's not impossible. There was something familiar about it, but I can't really say, either way.'

'OK, so...'

Presented with this absolute vacuum of suspects, Sinead's positivity began to wane. Her eyes darted left and right, searching for a solution.

'If, if... Alright. Alright. So, if we work on the assumption that...'

Her voice trailed off into silence. Logan offered her a supportive half smile.

'See?' he said. 'Waste of time.'

'Paper records.'

The other two detectives both turned their attention to Ben. He hadn't moved a muscle, and still sat with the same dark expression he'd been wearing for the past half hour.

'Sir?'

'Paper records. Every station kept them.' His tone soured again when he addressed the DCI across the table. 'I'm assuming you at least remember the date all this happened?'

Logan nodded. 'Not something I'm likely to forget.'

'Good. In that case, we search the archives. If we know the station, we know the date, and we know a rough time, then we can find out who was on duty. Maybe that'll help us.'

'We don't have time. We'd have to go to Glasgow, and it could take weeks before we found anything,' Logan said.

Sinead stuck the end of her pen in her mouth and chewed it thoughtfully. 'Maybe not,' she mumbled. 'If we found someone energetic enough…'

–

A mass of blonde curls leapt out of bed, the stuffed udders of her cow-design onesie flailing madly as she karate-chopped at thin air.

The part of her brain that had still been half-asleep kicked in then, and she spun back to the bedside table where her phone was blasting out a ringtone that could be described as both 'aggressively upbeat' and 'fucking infuriating.'

Seeing the name on the screen, Detective Constable Tammi-Jo Swanney gave a little *squee* of delight, snatched up the phone, and spat out a lot of words like she was using them to mow down enemy soldiers from a machine-gunner's nest.

'Sinead! Hello! How are you doing? Is everything OK? What's happened? Is it Tyler? Oh God, has something happened to Tyler? Is he hurt? Is he *dead*? He's dead, isn't he? I knew he couldn't go on the way he was forever. It was bound to happen, really. But, oh, God, Sinead, I'm so sorry, how did—?'

The rising volume of the voice on the other end of the line eventually got through to her, and she let out a sigh of relief.

'Oh, great! I'm really glad to hear that. Tell him I said hello.' She gave one of her udders a twang. 'So, what's up, then? I'm guessing you're not calling me in the middle of the night for some girl talk. But I'm totally up for it if you are!'

She listened to the reply, nodding along with every word like she was checking them off on a list. From the room next door, she heard the low, unhappy rumblings of her DI and housemate rousing from her sleep, then the slow plodding of her footsteps.

'OK! Well, that sounds like a big, long, tedious job!' Tammi-Jo said, with an enthusiasm that seemed wholly at odds with the content of the sentence.

She turned to the door and beamed excitedly as DI Heather Filson pushed open the door and scowled in the half-dark. Her eyes were mostly shut, her hair all over the place, and though she was fully dressed, the creases on her clothes suggested she'd been sleeping in them. She looked like a three-day hangover had become sentient.

None of this did anything to dampen Tammi-Jo's excitement. 'But, if anyone can do it,' she trilled into the phone. 'We can!'

Ben and Logan sat across from one another in the interview room, saying nothing. Over the years, they'd become comfortable enough in each other's company to enjoy some quality, indulgent silences.

This was not one of those.

It tainted the air like a bad smell, and with each moment that passed, it seemed to thicken and calcify until Ben could stand it no more.

'Nothing to say for yourself, then?'

'Like what?' Logan asked. There was no hint of an attitude, just a weariness that permeated every letter.

Ben still took the hump with it, though. "'*Like what*," he says.' He bent forward and stabbed a finger against the desk. The wood of the desktop lay like a vast, featureless desert between them. 'Like why the hell you've kept this to yourself all these bloody years. Like why you never told me.'

Logan groaned. It wasn't one of his usual exasperated groans like he might use, for example, when Tyler said something stupid, or when Tyler asked something stupid, or when Tyler did something stupid. There was nothing irritable about this one. It was more like the last rumblings of a dying man. A groan of defeat, and the acceptance of it.

'What was I meant to say?'

'The truth, Jack! You should have told me the bloody truth! I thought that's what we did, me and you! I thought that's what we'd always done.'

'We do,' Logan assured him. 'We do, but just… not this. I couldn't tell you this.'

Ben's tone shifted, his short, sharp bursts of anger collapsing into a slow, solemn sadness. 'Even after everything I've shared with you over the years? About me and Alice trying for kids, and what that did to us. Everything when she died. How I felt. How it nearly bloody destroyed me. The things I thought about doing. I told you all of it.'

'I know. I know, but this was different.'

'How, Jack?' Ben demanded, his anger levels spiking again. 'How is it different?'

Logan touched the edge of the desk, then summoned the courage to look the older man dead in the eye. 'I just… I didn't want you to be disappointed in me.'

Ben snorted. 'Ha.' He folded his arms in a tight-fitting knot across his chest. 'Well, bit late for that now, eh?'

The silence festered. The table lay like a gulf between them.

'I'm leaving,' Ben announced. 'I didn't want to tell you like this, but there we go. I'm retiring.'

Logan nodded. 'Aye. I know.'

A flicker of surprise darted across the DI's face, but he didn't allow it to settle. 'Good. I'll make it all official when all this is over. Last thing we need is more drama to distract us from the job at hand.'

'Aye,' Logan agreed. 'Makes sense. I'm guessing I can't convince you to stay?'

Ben gave a single shake of his head. If his mind hadn't been made up before, it clearly was now.

'Should've done it years ago. Alice and I talked about it, but then that man with a grudge against you broke into our home and murdered her.' He looked surprised by the words coming out of his mouth, or perhaps at the venom behind them.

He couldn't stop them now, though. Not even if he'd wanted to.

'Is that what's going to happen again, Jack? Is another old enemy of yours going to come marching in and destroy the life of someone I care about?'

'No.'

'Hamza. Or Tyler and Sinead? Are they in the firing line?'

'No. They're not,' Logan insisted.

'But you don't *know* that, Jack!' the DI spat. 'If you'd told me all this before now, we could've been ready for it. We could've been prepared, taken bloody precautions! Now, I don't know if my officers—my *friends*—are in danger because of something you did.'

'I didn't mean to kill him.'

'I'm not bloody talking about that! I don't give a damn about that!'

Logan blinked in surprise. 'You don't?'

'No! Course I bloody don't! We'll deal with all that later. What I care about is that you kept me in the dark about it. That you never told me! All those things I shared with you, all those secrets I spilled, all those times I cried, and poured my heart out to you, and you held it, Jack, you held my broken heart in your bloody hands!'

His voice cracked then, the rawness of his emotion choking him.

'And you didn't trust me enough to let me do the same for you. You didn't trust me to help. Do you know how much that hurts, Jack? Do you have any idea what that feels like? You should have told me. You should have said something years ago!'

The silence returned, not festering this time, just listening. Waiting. The room itself holding its breath.

'I'm… I'm sorry,' Logan said. 'I, eh, I didn't… It's not that I didn't trust you, Ben. It's not that. I was just… ashamed, I think. Or, I don't know, in denial. Nothing had come of it in nearly thirty years, and I suppose I thought nothing would. So, why say anything? Why risk ruining our friendship for nothing?'

Ben sniffed. When he spoke, his voice was flat and level again, all emotion having drained away. 'Aye. Well. Doesn't exactly seem like nothing now, does it?'

The door opened at the DI's back. Both men leaned back from the table, widening the gulf between them.

'Right, I spoke to Tammi-Jo. Her and Heather are going to draft in help and hit the archives,' Sinead announced. She hesitated when she sensed the tension in the room, but then continued. 'And Hamza wants us back through in the Incident Room now. I think we might finally have had a breakthrough.'

Chapter 33

'Good grief!' Ben accepted a mug of coffee from Tyler, then used it to gesture at the TV screen. 'And this is… what? This is them? This is actually them?'

'It is, sir,' Hamza said. He gritted his teeth, though only lightly, and only for a moment. 'Thomas was able to trace the I.P. addresses we got from Hoon's contact, and piggyback on the feeds. We weren't sure if we'd get anything—we didn't even know if there'd be cameras running all the time—but, well, there we are.'

On screen, six different video windows showed six different cages. All of the influencers were curled up on the floor, either asleep and twitching fitfully, or awake and sobbing quietly. As very little was happening, it was hard to tell if there was audio, but it seemed too eerily quiet for that to be the case.

'And this is live?' Ben asked, with a sense of wonder like he was watching the first television broadcast in history. 'This is actually happening right now?'

Hamza started to speak, but then deferred to Thomas with a nod. The consultant looked surprised, before stepping up to the screen and clearing his throat.

'Uh, yeah. It's live, as best as we can tell. Might be a few seconds of delay, but it's as close to live as we'll be able to get.'

Ben brought his mug to his lips, but diverted at the last second to point to the screen with it again. 'Will he not know we're watching?'

'No,' Thomas replied. He smiled, like he was quite proud of himself. 'I initiated a reverse-engineering protocol on the streaming architecture. By exploiting a vulnerability in their encryption handshake, I was able to inject a mirrored packet stream without tripping any of their security protocols.'

Ben continued to stare back at him like he'd become frozen in time. To be fair to the detective inspector, most of the rest of the room was looking at the consultant the same way.

'Can you maybe dumb that down a bit for us, son?' Ben asked.

'Uh, sure. Yeah. No problem,' Thomas said. 'So, essentially, what we're now doing is ghosting in their system. We're in there observing, but without altering their digital footprint or raising their awareness to our presence.'

'Bit dumber yet,' Ben urged.

'Right. Uh... OK, well, I suppose...'

Much as he enjoyed seeing the consultant floundering, Hamza stepped in to clarify. 'It's a bit like sneaking into a big room full of police officers by dressing in the uniform and speaking the lingo, sir. You mirror how they look and behave—words, tone, body language—and they don't notice you're there. But you can see everything that they're up to.'

'Aha! OK. I get that. I *like* that,' Ben cried, raising his mug like he was toasting the explanation. 'So, we can see them, but they can't see us. That's good. That's bloody brilliant. Well done, son.'

'It was mostly all Thomas's work, sir,' Hamza admitted.

Ben shrugged. 'Aye, well, you explained it far better than he did, so credit where credit's due.'

'There's one missing,' Tyler pointed out. 'The tattoo hippy lassie.'

'Elizia,' Logan said from the back of the group. 'You said there was something different about her camera before. That why she's not here?'

Hamza looked to Ben as if seeking permission, and only replied once a tip of the DI's head had been given.

'Maybe, sir. That could be it.' He picked up his notebook from his desk and presented it to the DCI. 'But, it could just as easily be something else.'

—

Lacey Buchan was nothing like the woman she was claiming to be a friend of. In fact, with her relaxed jeans-and-jumper look, sensible dark hair, and complete absence of body art, she was about as far removed from Elizia Shuttleworth as it was possible to get without changing sex or species.

Logan would've been very surprised if this woman worshipped the moon, channelled her inner chakras, or had spent so much as a single waking moment fannying about with crystals.

And there was, it turned out, a very good reason for that.

'Elizia's not really into that stuff. Not really.' Lacey took a packet of cigarettes from her handbag, then looked moment-arily devastated when Logan shook his head. 'Seriously?'

'Afraid not,' the DCI said. He glanced to his left to make sure that Tyler was ready on note-taking duties. 'What do you mean, she's 'not really into that stuff'? She seems pretty into it.'

'I know. I mean, she's into it in the same way that you're into being a policeman, or whatever. Or, I don't know, a supermarket manager is into that.'

Her accent was so high up in the rafters of the upper middle class that it was practically gold-plated. Logan would've been surprised if she'd ever set foot in a supermarket in her life, let alone gained any insight into the inner thoughts and desires of the managerial team.

'We were in business school together. She saw an oppor-tunity in the market, and she moved to fill it. Her whole schtick—the Mother Earth stuff—she doesn't believe a word of it. Most of the tattoos aren't even real, and the piercings are mostly magnetic.'

'So, you're saying that she's lying, then? To all the people who follow her? She's lying to them?'

Lacey looked forlornly down at the packet of cigarettes she still clung to, then returned them to her pocket. 'Is Tom Cruise lying when he, I don't know, shoots terrorists, or whatever? Would you call Arnold Schwarzenegger a liar because he's not actually a robot?'

'Cyborg,' Tyler corrected. He looked around at the others to try and determine if he'd said that out loud, then concluded from Lacey's puzzled expression that he had. 'Sorry, doesn't matter,' he mumbled, then he went back to taking notes.

'They're playing roles,' Logan argued.

'So is Elizia,' Lacey countered.

'The difference being that people know Arnie's not really made of bloody metal. And if they don't understand that, then hell mend and God bless them. If everyone knew that Elizia didn't buy into all the shite she peddles—if all her however many million subscribers found out—how do you think they'd take the news?'

'Not well,' Lacey admitted.

'No. I'd imagine not. Because, like I say, she's been lying to them,' Logan said. He gestured with a hand, indicating that she should continue.

'Um, yes. Well, the point is, she doesn't believe it. She never has. She's in this to make money, and the best way of doing that is by building a recognisable brand, which she has done to great effect. She's planning to bring out a single next month.'

'A song?'

'Yes. It's about protecting your mystical energies from those who would seek to rob you of them,' Lacey said, speaking the words like she was reciting them from memory. 'Or some such nonsense. It always sounds better when she says it. Anyway, she announced that the track was coming a couple of months back. The hardcore fans are very excited about it all, but she's been a bit disappointed by the lack of traction in the wider community.'

Logan felt like he knew where this was going, but he kept his mouth shut, letting the woman lay it all out.

When Lacey continued, there was a wariness to it, like she was worried what the reaction was going to be. She advanced through the sentence slowly, like she was checking for land mines or quicksand.

'So, in order to build more anticipation, she started to seek out some fun PR opportunities...'

Logan repeated the words back to her in the hope that she might grasp the absurdity of them. '"Fun PR opportunities?"'

'Yes, you know, Public Relations? Media coverage, free publicity, some viral traction, hopefully. That sort of—'

'I'm well aware, Miss Buchan, what the words you said mean,' he told her, cutting in. 'What I can't yet do is draw a line between 'fun PR opportunities' and the shitshow that's currently playing out for all the world to see.'

'Right. Sorry.' She let out a little trill of laughter. 'I don't know your background, so I wasn't sure how familiar you were with the terminology, so I thought, best to explain it in a way that—'

'A woman is dead,' Logan snapped, the volume of his voice raising to drown her out. 'So maybe, if it's all the same with you, you could stop wittering shite and tell me what you know?'

Lacey's jaw dropped and she gawped at him across the interview room table. Logan got the feeling that, relatively mild as his response had been, nobody had ever spoken to her like that before. Despite everything, it gave him immense satisfaction to be the first to do so.

'I'm... I came here to help!' she protested. 'I'm here to offer information, not to be talked to like a, like a criminal. I've handed over her laptop in good faith, because I want to help, but I don't have to! I could get up and leave, you know? I don't have to stay here!'

Logan held up his hands in acknowledgement. 'You're right. That was unfair of me,' he admitted. 'So, here's what I'm going to do, Miss Buchan. I'm going to apologise once—right now—to say that I'm sorry.'

'Thank you. That's the least you—'

'I'm not finished,' Logan warned. 'I'm sorry that I can't be more patient with you. That I can't listen to all your wee stories about your friend's brand-building expertise, or her fucking awful-sounding music career. People's lives are on the line, and time is not a luxury I have.'

He eyeballed her for a few moments. Bit by bit, second by second, her defiance was chipped away.

'Detective Constable Neish here can write very quickly. Isn't that right, Tyler?'

'I can do full-on shorthand now, boss,' Tyler confirmed with just a suggestion of pride.

'You, Miss Buchan, are going to push him like he's never been pushed before. You're going to tell us everything you know—every relevant detail that might help us figure out where Elizia and those other people are. And then—if you're quick enough, and I'm happy that you've told us the truth—I might be persuaded to let you go.'

'What? Are you threatening me? You can't just keep me here, I came here—'

'Clock's ticking, Miss Buchan.' Logan leaned back in his chair. 'If you want to stay in my good books, then it's finger-out-of-arse time.'

Beside him, Tyler licked the sharpened point of his pencil, and pressed it lightly against the page. Lacey squirmed in the seat like the entire lower half of her body had suddenly become infested with mites.

And then, when the ferocity of the DCI's glare became too much, she surrendered.

'She was approached by someone. A man. She didn't mention his name, though.'

'When was this?'

'A couple of months back. She didn't tell me everything. She never did. We were friends, but I don't think she really trusted me. I think she thought, if I knew everything, I might try and steal her audience for myself, or something. Not that I would.'

'Don't care,' Logan said. 'The man. What can you tell us about him?'

'Um, not a lot. Scottish, I think. She did his accent whenever she told me things he'd said. Sounded a bit like you, actually.'

'Things he'd said? Like what?'

'Just, sort of…' She tucked her chin into her chest and lowered her voice. '"It's going to make you a superstar! Just you—"'

'You don't have to do the voice,' Logan told her, and she blushed with embarrassment.

'Sorry, didn't realise I…' She shook her head. 'He just said it was going to be huge. Worldwide coverage. Global recognition. It'd shoot her subscriber count through the roof. And, to be fair, it has.'

She smiled, like she'd made a very valid point. Neither detective returned the sentiment.

'Anyway, at first, she thought it was just going to be her, but he said that wasn't big enough. For the story to hit big, it had to be multiple victims. She said she suggested a few people, but he told her not to worry about that. He'd take care of it. I think he'd already spoken to one of the others about the idea.'

'Who?' Logan demanded.

'I don't know. She didn't say. Just that one of the others had contacted her about it. No idea which one.'

'And she just agreed to go along with the whole thing?' Logan asked. 'There was no coercion, no blackmail? Nothing like that?'

Lacey shook her head. 'God, no. There was no need. She loved the idea. She was on board immediately. I think she ran the numbers—potential subscriber and revenue increases, I mean—and couldn't really say no.'

'So, you're saying it's fake? All of it? This whole thing is staged?'

Lacey swallowed, then shook her head. 'No. I mean, I did. Originally. I knew it was happening. I knew she'd be—'her fingers curled into quote marks in the air'—"taken" after the convention, and that the streams would happen soon after.'

Logan stared impassively back at her. After that admission, he'd have no problem keeping her in custody, if needed.

'But…what? You think the plan's changed in some way?'

'She's scared,' Lacey said. 'Really scared. That stuff with the finger, she'd never mentioned that, and that looked real. Didn't it? It looked real.'

'You know her better than we do. Did it look real to you?'

'Yes! Completely! And Elizia's a good actor—she's fooled all her followers—but she's not *that* good. That was real. It had to be. And, if it was real, then, then…' Her expression fixed in a grimace for a moment, like the enormity of what she was saying had just hit her. 'Then, it's all real. All of it. And that means that woman is dead. Really dead. Actually dead! And Elizia and those other people might be next!'

Logan could see her hysteria building in her jerky movements, and behind her eyes. He held a hand up to calm her.

'We're not going to let that happen,' he said, offering an assurance he had no right to make.

He checked to make sure that Tyler was up to date, hoped that the detective constable could decipher the mass of untidy scribbles he'd etched on the paper, then clasped his hands on the table in front of him.

'So, this man, then,' he began. 'I'm going to need you to think back, Miss Buchan. I'm going to need you to think hard. And then, I'm going to need you to tell us every last detail that you can remember.'

'I don't know if there's anything else I can tell you.'

'Fair enough,' Logan said. If Lacey Buchan had believed in auras, she might have seen the deep red danger signs pulsing in the one of the man sitting across from her. His voice, when he spoke, was a rod of iron. 'But for everyone's sake, I suggest you try.'

Chapter 34

Hamza was going to hate himself for this, he knew. He hung back at his desk, staring at his monitor, watching the votes continue to flood in for the seven remaining influencers. There was no way of knowing who was winning or losing in the court of public opinion.

Hopefully, they'd never have to find out.

Eventually, he could stall no longer. With a sigh, he got up out of his chair, adjusted his tie, then went to join Thomas at his desk.

The consultant had requested to take the lead on investigating Elizia Shuttleworth's laptop, and while it was the sort of thing that Hamza would usually do, a cock-up on a recent case had knocked his confidence a bit.

Granted, the man sitting at the desk with his headphones on had been largely responsible for that lapse in concentration, but that didn't change anything. What Logan had said earlier had been right—Thomas was the best man for that particular job.

And so, despite how it boiled the bile in his stomach, Hamza had handed the laptop over, and the consultant had immediately got to work.

That had been less than twenty minutes ago. Not nearly enough time to make any significant progress.

But the hours on the countdown were well into single figures, and time was not on their side.

'You find anything yet?' he asked, much as it pained him to ask the man for anything.

Then, when Thomas didn't acknowledge him, he gave his chair a dunt with the side of his leg.

The consultant jumped in fright, whipped his headphones off, and looked up to find Hamza unexpectedly looming over him. He glanced around as if searching for a way out, or at least someone to jump in if things kicked off, then looked up at the sergeant again.

'Um, you alright? Everything OK?'

'You find anything yet?' he asked again.

Thomas relaxed. 'Oh. Right. Not yet, no. Mostly just a lot of spreadsheets and business projections. Looks like she's working on an album. Listened to a track. Fucking awful. It's all just one note. Not a good note, either. Sort of squeaky.'

Hamza's expression made it very clear that he didn't care about any of that, and that while the 'light banter' was practically a prerequisite for being on the team, the sergeant reserved his for people he actually liked.

Thomas coughed gently and adjusted himself in his chair.

'Anyway, the friend, she told you that Elizia was in touch with the kidnapper, aye? I've checked through her email, but there's nothing there. If they were in contact that way, then they've all been deleted. Might be able to scrape the mail server, but it'll take time, and we don't even know if there's anything there to find.'

Hamza sighed and shifted his attention to the laptop itself. It was an Apple MacBook. One of the newer ones, in black. Crumbs, dandruff, and strands of matted blonde hair dotted the keyboard and screen, and the whole thing had a vaguely battered appearance. Even if the make and model didn't feel entirely 'on brand' for Elizia, the general condition of the hardware suggested someone who didn't place too much value in expensive material items.

Either a genuine hippie-sort, then, or someone with far too much money in the bank.

Probably a spoiled bastard, too.

'Is her phone linked up to it?' Hamza asked.

Usually, Apple products became part of a sort of home ecosystem. Messages received on their phones could be seen and replied to on their computers, and vice versa. If you had one of their watches, the whole thing became seamless, albeit stupidly expensive.

'No, nothing. There's an old back-up of one in iCloud, but it looks like it's an Android phone, not iOS. There's software that'll sync between Android and Apple devices, but it's not as straightforward as...' He waved a hand. 'You know all this. Point is, we can't see her texts, no.'

Hamza traced the lines of his jaw between his fingers and thumb, then covered his mouth as he failed to stifle a yawn. The darkened streets were still quiet outside, but in an hour or two the early morning traffic would start to build.

And soon after that, the voting on who among the influencers lived and who died would come to a close.

The sergeant looked over at the screen. Aside from Adam Parfitt briefly sitting upright to stop himself choking on his own snot and tears, and Cassandra Swain crawling over to relieve herself in a bucket, very little had happened since they'd accessed the feed.

'Is there anything?' Hamza asked, and there was a whiff of desperation about it. 'Anything useful on there at all?'

'Maybe,' Thomas said. He looked very deliberately at the laptop's screen, and at his fingers poised on the keyboard. 'If you give me a bit of time, I might find something.'

It wasn't a particularly strong dig, as far as they went, but it made a surge of adrenaline go whooshing through Hamza's veins.

Annoyingly, though, snidey tone aside, Thomas was right. There were probably thousands of files on the laptop, not to mention the rest in connected cloud storage. Even if there was anything helpful on there, finding it could take days.

'Here!' Ben called from his desk. 'That's all very well and good poking around in that thing, but did you not say you could find the address of the computer broadcasting them cameras? Aye, the proper real address, I mean, not the numbers one.'

Hamza had to step back to avoid his toes being crushed when Thomas rolled his chair back so he had a direct view of the detective inspector.

'It's running in the background. I set up a geo-tracing algorithm to analyse the signal metadata and network hops associated with the I.P.,' Thomas explained, and whatever the hell he was saying, it seemed to excite him. 'See, the algorithm cross-references known network node locations, signal latency, and internet exchange points to triangulate a probable geographic location. It's not instant—it needs to accumulate enough data points to make a decent estimation—but it's working away as we speak.'

Ben looked back at him for quite a long time, then sighed quietly and fixed Hamza with a questioning gaze.

'Imagine a police sniffer dog following a trail, sir,' Hamza said. 'It can't just jump from the start point to wherever the suspect is, it needs to follow the path and figure it out, step-by-step.'

Ben glowered at Thomas and pointed an open hand in Hamza's direction. 'See? That's how you explain it. No' bloody... triangles and data points. That made perfect sense. Carry on.'

Thomas rolled his chair in closer to his desk again and smirked up at Hamza. 'Does he need everything explained in terms of police stuff?'

'No, he just needs you not to be a smart arse,' Hamza retorted, wiping the smug look off the other man's face. 'Now, get back to it. And, as soon as you find anything, I want to know.'

–

'What the actual fuck?'

Detective Inspector Heather Filson stared in horror into the room she'd just opened a door onto, then shot a sideways scowl at DC Swanney who stood beside her. Heather still both looked and felt like a half shut knife, but Tammi-Jo was as bright as a button, her face radiating freshness, her blonde hair tied back in a crisp ponytail.

Before them, beyond the door, lay a haphazard warren of old filing boxes. Without stepping into the room, or even moving her head, Heather could see hundreds of them. They were stacked one atop the other on tall metal shelving units, many of them collapsing under the weight of those above.

After a few moments of consideration, Heather closed the door and turned the key to lock it up again.

'What are you doing?' Tammi-Jo asked. She looked the door up and down, like it was a puzzle for her to solve. 'We're still outside.'

'I know.'

'We're meant to be inside,' the detective constable pointed out.

'Did you see the place? The state of it? There must be five thousand boxes in there!' Heather cried.

'Oh, easily,' Tammi-Jo agreed. She rubbed her hands together and grinned excitedly. 'So, we should probably get started!'

Heather studied the detective constable like she was something squishy on the bottom of her boot. 'You're actually looking forward to this, aren't you? You actually can't wait to get in there.'

'Aren't you?' Tammi-Jo asked.

'No! Of course I'm not!' Heather shot back. 'It's looking through five thousand boxes!'

'At least,' the DC said, with a little cackle of glee. 'Although, really, the chances of what we're looking for being in the very last box are pretty slim. Statistically, we'll probably only have to look through three thousand or so. Four, tops.'

Heather looked at the door to the archive.

She looked back at Tammi-Jo, still visibly raring to go.

With a sigh, she turned the key that unlocked the door.

'Fine.' She patted at the pockets of her leather jacket until she tracked down her phone. 'But we're not doing this shit on our own. If my night's being ruined, so is everyone else's.'

–

The Incident Room was quiet, which was rarely a good sign. Quiet meant things weren't happening. Quiet meant dead ends had been hit.

It also, on this occasion, meant that DI Forde was asleep in his chair.

Since getting back, Dave had followed up on a few outstanding things. There was still no sign of a vehicle matching the minibus that was used to transport the influencers, despite Uniform scrubbing through hundreds of hours of CCTV footage.

Reports were in from the various different forces around the country, who had been both interviewing and standing guard over the relatives of the missing influencers, to try to keep the press from harassing and haranguing them.

The internet continued to be ablaze with speculation and rumour. The growing army of internet sleuths, unable to identify the kidnapper, had decided that the best course of action was to focus their efforts on digging up dirt on the victims themselves.

Some enterprising TikToker had tracked down one of Adam Parfitt's ex-boyfriends, who was now making claims that Adam had been controlling and abusive, and had some interesting sexual quirks involving marmalade and hand sanitiser. This, apparently, had all come as news to Adam's family.

As had the news that he was gay.

Natalie Womack's cloud storage had been hacked, and the topless photos that had been found in there were bouncing so rapidly around the internet that you could practically hear them ricocheting off the sides.

Video footage had emerged of Denzel Drummond stripping at a hen do a few years back, before getting very publicly intimate with the blushing bride-to-be.

Bruce Kennedy had beaten his first wife.

The late Kelly Wynne's even later old man had been a crooked cop who'd killed himself by jumping off the Erskine Bridge.

Cassandra Swain had falsely accused a teacher of touching her up in high school.

Elizia Shuttleworth had been a member of the Young Conservatives, and had allegedly once done a line of cocaine with the then Secretary of State for Environment, Food and Rural Affairs, Michael Gove.

Although, people were more outraged about her political leanings than they were the drugs.

Matthew Broderick was just a horrible wee arsehole in general. There was also some mention of him killing two people in a car accident, but on closer inspection, that turned out to be the actor of the same name.

'Jesus,' Dave mumbled as he took it all in. 'The internet's brutal.'

Across the room, Thomas sat up a little straighter, pulled off his headphones, and turned in his chair.

'Um, Hamza?' He winced, shook his head, and tried again. 'Sorry, I mean DS—'

'It's fine. Have you got something?'

'Uh, yeah. Yeah, I think so,' the consultant said. He shot a wary look back at the screen of Elizia Shuttleworth's laptop that sat open on his desk.

'You think so?' Hamza snapped. 'What do you mean? Either you do, or you don't.'

'I think… I mean, yes. It looks very like there's a message on here.'

'To the guy Elizia was talking to? To the kidnapper?'

'Um, no. Not to him. I think it might be from him, actually, but I haven't looked into it properly yet.'

Hamza bounced out of his chair and onto his feet. The sudden movement startled Ben awake at his desk.

'Why not?' Hamza demanded, bending to get a better look at the laptop. 'Is it locked?'

'No, it's not locked, as far as I can tell. I haven't tried opening it because I just found it a few seconds ago,' the consultant explained. 'And, because, well…'

He put a finger at the top of the laptop's display, where he'd taped up the in-built camera to make sure nobody could see him through it. With a gentle push, he tilted the screen back, giving Hamza a better look of the file he'd found.

And of the name beneath it.

'I think it's a message for DCI Logan.'

Chapter 35

Logan sat at Thomas's desk in the Incident Room, Elizia Shuttleworth's laptop open in front of him. The rest of the team stood gathered behind him, watching in hushed silence.

He'd wanted to do this alone, locked away in his office, but he knew that wouldn't fly with Ben. And besides, this was better. This was right. No more secrets.

That was why, on Logan's instruction, they'd woken the Gozer. Tyler had drawn the short straw, of course, and though he'd contemplated just knocking on the door to Mitchell's office and then running away, he'd stuck it out and asked the Detective Superintendent to join them.

MacKenzie stood there now, right behind the seat Jack was sitting in, his arms folded and his eyes crusted with sleep.

'I don't get it,' he said. 'Why's it addressed to you? This. The number plate on the minibus. Hell, Suki's son and Petrie's nephew. Why are you being targeted here, Jack? What's the play?'

Logan steeled himself. No more secrets. No more lies.

DI Forde, it seemed, hadn't got that memo.

'We don't know yet,' Ben said. 'We're looking into it.'

It was enough for the Gozer, at least for now. He shrugged and indicated the file on screen. 'OK, well what does it say, then?'

Tyler drew in a breath. 'I guess there's only one way to find out,' he declared. Then, when both Sinead and Hamza shot him sideways looks, he deflated a little. 'Sorry, just thought it sounded quite dramatic in the moment.'

Logan muttered something below his breath, then hovered the mouse pointer over the file and double clicked. The laptop purred quietly for less than a second, then the file opened to fill the screen.

It was a simple text file without any fancy formatting. It contained just five words, which Ben read over his shoulder.

"'I told you to smile.'" The DI looked around at the others. 'The hell's that supposed to mean?'

'Boss?' Tyler asked. 'Mean anything to you?'

Logan shook his head, then read the words again, trying to make sense of them.

And then, he erupted upwards out the chair, launching it backwards directly into the Gozer, who *whuffed* in distress and staggered sideways, clutching his bollocks like they might fall off and roll away under one of the desks.

'Jesus, Jack!'

'Shite, sorry. The photographer!'

'Sir?' Sinead asked.

'The fucking… the photographer! At the press conference. Someone shouted at me to smile.' His hands tightened into angry claws at his sides, like he was strangling the life out of two invisible dwarfs. 'That was him. He was there. He was right fucking there in that room!'

Ben snapped his fingers and pointed to Sinead. 'Camera footage. Inside and outside the station.'

'On it, sir,' Sinead said, already hurrying to her phone.

The DI's arm shifted so his finger was taking aim at DC Neish. 'Tyler, we need to run the details of everyone at that press conference. They must've had ID to get in, press accreditations, whatever we ask for these days. Get it, go through it, find out what you can.'

'Will do, boss.'

'It'll be a big job. Dave, you're on support.'

'Nice!' Dave declared, rolling after Tyler.

The Gozer had recovered sufficiently to join the conversation, though he was still wearing a pained expression and leaning slightly forward.

'You sure about this, Jack?' he asked, with just the faintest suggestion of a wheeze.

'I'm positive. It struck me as all wrong at the time,' Logan insisted. 'I nearly blew my lid when he said it. Tried to see who it was, but couldn't spot the bastard in the crowd.'

'Wait, hold on. One problem, Jack,' Ben interjected. 'The live thing. The streams, is it?'

Hamza nodded to confirm he'd got the terminology right, but Ben saved the mental pat on the back for later.

'They started during the conference. Everyone got up and ran out. If he was here, how could he be doing that there at the same time? Wherever the hell there is.'

The Gozer provided a possible answer. 'Well, I mean, I'm sure he's not working alone.'

'He isn't,' Tyler called from his desk. 'Elizia Shuttleworth's in on it.'

'What?!' The Gozer looked around at them all and ran a hand down his face. 'Jesus Christ, how long was I asleep?'

'I'm not so sure,' Logan said, turning and scanning the Big Boards.

'Couldn't have been more than a couple of hours,' the detective superintendent reasoned.

'What? No. I mean about him not working alone. If he's the same guy that coerced and blackmailed all those people a few months back—and I think he is—then he doesn't strike me as a team player.'

The Gozer's confusion was the impatient, irritated kind. 'What about Elizia Shuttleworth? Tyler literally just said—'

'He made the lassie chop her finger off on camera,' Logan countered. 'Hardly seems like an equal partnership.'

He approached the board, looking at all the faces pinned up there. All those faces, and all those names.

And then there was the victims who didn't even have that yet. All those nameless, unclaimed people that had been left to rot in a hole in the ground.

'He's calculating. Manipulative. He knows how to use people. He knows how to get them to do what he wants, whether that's by forcing them, or persuading them. He's clever, whoever he is. I think we can safely say that.'

'I don't care how clever he is, Jack,' Ben said. 'He can't be in two places at once.'

'Unless the streams aren't really live.'

Everyone turned to Thomas, who stood a little apart from the rest of the group.

'Sorry?' the Gozer said, raising an eyebrow.

'Well, I mean, we've been assuming they're live. They look live. The timecode suggests we're watching them in real time. But that's the thing...'

'Why have a timecode in the first place?' Hamza asked, catching up.

Thomas nodded. 'Exactly. Why have a timecode on screen at all?' He pointed to the live feeds being shown on the TV. 'There's not one on there now, so it's not part of his standard camera set-up.'

'He adds it in,' Hamza realised. He buried his face in his hands for a moment, then pushed them back through his hair. 'They're not live. The streams. They're all recorded in advance.'

'How do you mean? Like a TV show?' Ben asked.

'Exactly. When we saw him shoot Kelly Wynne, it's possible—likely, even—that what we were seeing wasn't happening at the time. She could already have been dead. Could've been dead for hours. A day or two, even. He filmed it, added the timecode, and scheduled it to be broadcast as if it was a livestream.'

'But this is live?' Logan demanded, pointing to the TV screen with its six separate feeds. 'We know for sure this is happening now?'

Hamza glanced at Thomas, but he already knew the answer to that question.

'Not necessarily, sir. If he was expecting us to find the camera feeds, he could've set this up to throw us off the scent.'

'But they're sleeping,' Ben pointed out. He glanced at the darkness beyond the Incident Room's windows. 'And it's night-time. So that fits, doesn't it?'

'The footage we're seeing now could've been from last night, or the night before,' Thomas explained.

'But we saw one of the lassies getting up for a pee. Her finger's missing,' the DI reminded everyone. 'That only happened a few hours ago. Her cutting it off, I mean.'

'That's the point. We don't know that,' Logan said, catching on more quickly than his older colleague. 'This, everything we've seen so far, could all have happened on day one. For all we know, they're all already dead. That's what you're saying, isn't it?'

Slowly, reluctantly, Hamza nodded. 'Yes, sir. I'm afraid that's exactly what we're saying.'

One by one, those stood around Thomas's desk all took seats, as the enormity of all this sunk in.

'So... we don't know anything?' Ben mumbled. 'We're completely in the dark?'

'Maybe looking into the people at the press conference will bring something up,' Hamza suggested, but it was clear from the way he said it that even he wasn't buying it. He sighed. 'But, aye, sir. Other than that...'

'We've still got Elizia Shuttleworth's friend,' Logan said. He winced at some phantom pain. 'But I don't know what else she can tell us.'

'She could start by telling us how that file is on the computer,' Sinead said. 'If she's had the laptop the whole time, and you were only told to smile earlier today, or yesterday now, I suppose, then how is it on there?'

Hamza crab-walked his chair over to the laptop, dragging it along by his arse.

He right-clicked on the file, looked at the data there, then rolled back again. 'It was created nearly a fortnight ago,' he said, though it gave him no pleasure to do so.

'How's that possible?' Ben asked.

'Because he knew all this was going to happen,' Logan said, and the sad raising of Hamza's eyebrows told him the sergeant was in agreement. 'He predicted we'd get the laptop. Even when.'

'Lacey could've been primed to come in when she did then, boss,' Tyler reasoned. 'She might know more than she's letting on.'

'Let's hope so, eh?' Logan muttered, though he didn't sound convinced. 'Uniform still got her in one of the holding rooms?'

'They do, boss, aye.'

The DCI nodded, though didn't yet give any orders as to what to do next. She'd sounded like she was telling the truth, and she hadn't seemed to be close to confessing to anything, even when he'd gone pretty hard on her.

Either she knew nothing, or she was going to be a tough nut to crack. Either one was going to take time to determine, and that was something the influencers didn't have.

Unless, of course, they were all already dead.

'What about those bodies we dug up down the road?' the Gozer asked. 'Anything else there?'

'Nothing new. Shona'll get back to it first thing tomorrow morning,' Logan replied. 'Maybe Scene of Crime will finally have something for us by then, too.'

The morning wasn't long away, but Logan had half a mind to go round to Geoff Palmer's house and kick his door in to wake him up. Unless the lazy bastard now pulled something spectacular out of his hat, he could get the idea of coffee next week right out of his bloody head.

Not that Logan had ever had any intention of going. He'd rather have breakfast with Bob and Berta Hoon which, given their usual temperament first thing in the morning, was saying something.

'Anything useful from the families?' the Gozer asked. Despite only recently having been wakened, he looked fit for sleeping again. Logan wished that he would. It would get him out of their hair.

'Not really. Denzel Drummond's father has been talking to the press, as we know, but the others have kept pretty tight-lipped.'

'Don't think he's going to be saying much more to them now,' Dave said. He was munching his way through a bag of Quavers, and sprayed some crumbs as he pointed to his computer. 'Some armchair detective's outed him as a benefits cheat. Seems to have gone pretty quiet now.'

'Good that they're making themselves useful, at least,' Ben said.

Logan grunted. 'Aye, well, just as long as it's keeping them the hell out of my way.'

'Nothing on the minibus?' the Gozer asked.

'No sign,' Hamza replied. 'Probably switched vehicles. Uniform's sweeping the route in case it's been abandoned, and checking through CCTV, but nothing has come up so far.'

'What about the voice on that recording the dog walker gave us? Too much to hope we get a hit, I'm guessing?'

'We've had nothing back from down the road,' Logan said. 'We could circulate it in the media, but there's probably ten thousand guys in Glasgow city centre alone that sound like that. Could be any one of them.'

The detective superintendent puffed out his cheeks. 'God. OK. And the sex thing? Them all shagging one another, or whatever it was the organiser said. The orgy? Did that lead anywhere?'

He was clutching at straws now. Then again, what else was left for any of them to hold onto?

'No. We haven't been able to make anything of it,' Ben said. 'Just a bunch of weird people humping away at one another. It's no' exactly a smoking gun.'

The Gozer covered his face with his hands, like he had been hit by a wave of grief and was trying to hide his tears. From the long, slow inhale and exhale that followed, though, it was clear that he was yawning.

'So, we've got nothing, then? That what we're saying? Other than some video feeds that may or may not be live, and the vague notion that our man was dressed up as a press photographer earlier, we've got precisely fuck all to be going on with?'

Logan thumped his fists on the arm of his chair like he was geeing himself up, then rose from the seat. 'I want all the other influencers' technology brought in. Laptops, desktops, phones, iPads, whatever. If it can be used to communicate, and we can get our hands on it, I want it brought in.'

'You think there might be more notes, boss?'

'Maybe. Don't know. Only one way to find out.'

'They're all over the country, sir,' Hamza reminded him. 'It's a big job to coordinate, and we'd need permission from family members.'

'Then we'd better move quickly, eh,' Logan replied, clapping his hands like he was shooing geese.

He strode over to the closest window, and gazed out over the car park. There were fewer press vans out there than there had been during the day, but it would only be a matter of time before the dawn came up, and the number grew again. There was never any respite from the vultures for long.

A few tents had been set up on the pavement outside the car park. He'd noticed them on the way in earlier, and questioned the front desk about them. Social media sleuths, apparently. They'd been moved on a few times, but new ones kept coming in to take their places.

Logan briefly contemplated the damage he could do from up here with a grenade launcher and a stiff westerly wind, then he turned from the window and reached for his coat. 'I'm going down there.'

Ben gawped back at him in amazement. 'Eh? You're going down there? What, to the car park?'

'Aye. To talk to them.'

'*You're* going down to talk to the press? Willingly?'

Logan confirmed it with a nod. 'We all are.'

Tyler groaned at the thought of it. 'What for, boss?'

'Because, I said so, son,' Logan intoned. 'And, because something's just occurred to me,' he added, pulling on his coat. 'If the bastard was there at the press conference yesterday, then who's to say he's not still sitting out there right now?'

Chapter 36

Chad Durnett had eaten three sausage rolls, necked a lukewarm coffee, and was contemplating a covert back of the van wank when the thunder started.

He'd grown up in quite a strict Catholic household in Kickapoo, Illinois, so his first instinct was to look upwards, like he might find the Lord Himself gazing down at him, wagging a reproachful finger.

But then, the sound came again, and this time it was followed by a barked order.

'Right, wakey-wakey. Arses out of the van.'

Scrabbling for his Sony PXW-Z450 camera, and zipping up his trousers, Chad shuffled his way along the floor of the van until he reached the doors.

Outside, he could hear more thumping and shouting, along with some sounds of slurry, half-asleep protests from his fellow members of the mainstream media.

With a bit of effort, he got the door open, and hauled himself out into the cool, draughty darkness. He'd kept his CNN branded fleece on, because the van wasn't the warmest place in the world, especially when parked up in the Highlands of Scotland, and was grateful for it when the night air prickled his skin.

Instinctively, operating on nothing more than muscle memory, he hoisted the camera onto his shoulder and felt for the power button.

An enormous hand clamped over the lens.

'Aye, you can forget that for a bloody start.'

The camera suddenly became impossible to move. The grip on it was so strong, Chad reckoned, that he could duck out from under the heavy video equipment now, and it would remain there, completely stationary, supported in mid-air by that one hand alone.

He looked up. And up. And then up some more. A face as vengeful as any god's glowered down at him, and a tiny broken part of him that was leftover from his childhood feared that maybe this *was* about the crafty wank, after all.

'Who are you, and where are you from?' the giant demanded.

It was all Chad could do to utter a few *uhms* and *errs*. Behind the towering man in the bulky overcoat, a dozen uniformed officers were shining torches into vehicles, thumping on van doors, and arguing with photographers and journalists in various states of undress.

A torch was shone in his face, and Chad hissed like a vampire in the midday sun.

'Fuck!' he ejected. It was the first word he'd spoken, and the only fully formed one that had come to mind.

It worked some sort of magic, though, because the bear in the big coat released his grip on the camera, even if he didn't look particularly happy about that fact.

'You're American,' he said, and though Chad would usually wear that badge with pride, it suddenly felt like a dirty, shameful accusation.

'Uh, yeah,' he said. Then, for reasons he would question for months and years to come, added, 'Sorry.'

'Don't be sorry, son.' The torch was lowered, and after a bit of blinking, Chad recognised the giant as DCI Logan from the press conference earlier. He was glancing about them, already losing interested in the cameraman. 'It just means you're not the bastard I'm looking for.'

Chad was immensely relieved to hear that.

'Is, uh, is there a problem?' he asked, looking around the car park. Uniformed and plain clothes officers alike were interrogating the other journalists. Clearly, something big was going down. 'Anything I can do to help? I'd love to help you guys out. Anything you need, just say the word.'

The detective saw through the offer right away.

'Don't try and get all chummy-chummy with me, son, in the hope that I can give you some inside scoop,' he warned. He brought up a finger and flicked it around, indicating all the gathered members of the media. 'You're vermin. All of you. No, that's doing vermin a disservice. You're worse than vermin. You're a vermin STD. You're a vermin's genital warts. And don't ever forget that.'

Under other circumstances, Chad would've objected to this. Back home, though he wasn't a violent man, he might even have squared up to someone who'd said such a thing to him.

But every survival instinct in his body told him to just nod in quiet agreement.

And, to be fair to the detective, he had a point. Chad was well aware that he was only one step up from the paparazzi. And a diagonal step, at that.

He'd listened earlier as some of the other reporters had made bets with each other on which of the influencers was going to die next. Some of them had even voted online, though they'd claimed it was entirely for research purposes, and that *obviously* they hoped all the captives survived their ordeal.

But that wasn't true, Chad knew. A story like this could make a career. The bigger it got, the further up the ladder an ambitious newshound could go, and at least half of the people here would be prepared to sacrifice the lives of every single captive if it rocketed them to the big time.

Some of them would probably even pull the trigger themselves.

'A vermin's genital warts,' was arguably too kind a descriptor.

'Were you at the press conference earlier?' Logan demanded.

'Uh, yeah. Sure, I was there. I was down front.'

Logan tutted. This wasn't what he'd hoped to hear. 'Someone up the back told me to smile at one point. I'm trying to find him. Any ideas?'

Chad shook his head. He couldn't even remember the incident, but he made a point of looking around, anyway. It was important, his survival instincts were warning him, to show willing.

'Um, no. Sorry. I think maybe I heard someone saying something at the time, but didn't really take too much notice.'

'And you haven't heard anyone talking about it? Or seen anyone you don't recognise? Because you lot all fucking know each other, don't you?'

'Uh, no. I mean, there's a lot of folks here I don't know.' Chad went out on a limb. It felt like a dangerously shaky one. 'Maybe if you told me who you were looking for, and why, I might be able to help?'

Logan grunted. 'Aye, nice try, pal.' He pointed past him. 'Back in the van. We're done with you for now. And, if you even think of filming any of this, you'll be getting that camera surgically removed over the course of a number of different operations. That clear?'

A tiny, barely audible voice somewhere in Chad's brain offered up some arguments about public interest, and freedom of the press, and the right to film in public spaces, which the car park counted as.

Fortunately for him, the rest of his brain warned it to shut the fuck up.

Instead of arguing, he just nodded, climbed back into the van, and, after a few moments spent weighing up his options, got stuck into the final sausage roll in the packet.

–

Thomas leaned against the wall in the break room, watching a thin stream of weak coffee splutter and fart into a plastic cup below. There were proper mugs, and a big jar of Nescafé Gold Blend in the cupboard, but the coffee had a sticky label identifying it as belonging to someone named 'Big Duggie,' and though Thomas knew nothing more about the man, he suspected it was best not to mess with his stuff.

No one had given permission to use the mugs, either. He should've remembered to bring his own, after what had happened last time, when he'd been over in Aberdeen helping CID there with a teenage runaway case.

He'd been told to help himself to a cuppa, but when he'd returned to his desk with it, a particularly surly detective sergeant had called him a thieving wee fucker, claimed the mug had been the last ever gift from his late wife, and prised it out of his hand.

Thomas had apologised profusely, but the whispering and sniggering he'd heard a few moments later made him think the whole thing had been a wind-up.

It was like that time, years before, when he'd got his first after school job stacking shelves at a supermarket, and one of his colleagues had urged him to ask the manager what colour his dad's trousers were.

After much goading and encouragement, Thomas had gone through with it, only for the manager to respond with a sharp, furious, 'My dad's got no legs!'

Thomas had felt awful, both for being so insensitive, and for getting on the boss's wrong side on day one.

It was only when, six months later, he'd heard the same colleague and manager plotting the same play on another new start, that he'd realised it wasn't true, and that the boss's old man was likely fully equipped in the lower limb department.

He didn't know if that had made him feel better or worse about the whole thing.

The machine spurted its final ejaculation into the cup, hissed in a, 'Happy now?!' sort of way, and fell silent.

Thomas reached into the gubbins and withdrew the container. The plastic was so thin that it almost buckled at his touch, and he only narrowly avoided ejecting hot coffee all over his hand.

Although, going by the writing beside the button on the machine, it wasn't actually coffee. It had been listed as 'Coffee flavoured liquid,' like it was so far removed from real coffee that they couldn't legally describe it as such.

He didn't care. It was the caffeine he was after. Hopefully, it at least contained that.

He brought the cup to his lips, but the steam alone almost burned them off before he was anywhere near his mouth.

Better leave it a while, then.

Moving slowly and carefully so as to avoid spilling any, and regularly passing the cup from one hand to the other to avoid melting off his fingertips, Thomas made his way back to the Incident Room.

The Gozer had gone back to his office, but most of the rest of the team had headed outside to noise up the journalists a bit and see if they could find their man. It felt like a stab in the dark, but if it meant he didn't have to put up with them all, then he was all for it.

The atmosphere hadn't exactly been great since he'd arrived. He'd expected it from Hamza, of course—there wasn't much he could do about that—but the barely concealed contempt from some of the others had taken him aback. He was there to help them. He was on their side! And yet, some of them were making him feel about as welcome as a rectal bleed.

The only one still in the Incident Room was Dave, the uniformed constable. He didn't mind Dave too much. He seemed a bit simple, maybe, but nice enough.

Though the man in the wheelchair was only a PC, Thomas had never once heard him refer to anyone ranked above him as 'sir,' or 'ma'am' or any of that nonsense. He liked that about him. There was a chance, Thomas thought, that they could be friends.

Dave looked up from his desk when the consultant entered the room, then tilted his head in the direction of Thomas's computer.

'Your thing's beeping,' the constable announced.

Thomas opened his mouth to ask what he was talking about, when he heard it for himself—the sharp, *ping-ping-ping* of a software alarm.

'Fuck! Christ! Why the fuck didn't you come and get me?!' he hissed, all thoughts of camaraderie and friendship well and truly out the window.

A slosh of coffee spilled up over the rim of the cup and singed his skin. Pain made him drop it, letting it explode against the floor tiles. Urgency made him ignore it.

'Eh, well, because I'm not your secretary,' Dave countered. He watched as the other man dropped into his chair and began frantically clicking and scrolling. 'What is it, like? What's it telling you?'

Thomas didn't answer. Instead, he jumped up out of the seat like it had been electrified, ran to the window, and looked down at the car park. The small army of detectives and uniforms were still out there, but they were at the far end, up by the dual carriageway. No way they'd hear him, even if he shouted.

'Fuck it!' he cried.

And with that, he ran.

–

'Get anything?' Logan asked, as Tyler and Sinead plodded over to join him.

Most of the journalists had climbed back into their cars and vans now, while Ben, Hamza, and a handful of Uniforms continued to question the rest.

'Nothing, boss. No one seems to know anything. You?'

Logan shook his head. 'Dead end.' He drew a breath in through his nose, and gazed around at the few remaining journalists, who all either looked angry, scared, or emotionally exhausted. 'Still, it's about the only part of the last twenty-four hours that I've even come close to enjoying, so I suppose that's a win.'

He glanced across at Ben, who was dismissing another of the reporters. While Logan would've liked nothing more than to pick them up by the face and hurl them into their cramped wee van, Ben was shaking the man's hand and thanking him for his time.

Soft old bugger, Logan thought, and his chest felt heavy with the thought of losing his friend.

'You alright, sir?' asked Sinead, softly. She followed the DCI's look, then smiled up at him. 'He'll be fine. It's all just a bit of a shock to him, I think. He'll get over it.'

Logan nodded. She didn't yet know about Ben's plans to leave, and it wasn't his place to share the news.

'Aye, fingers crossed,' he replied, then he heard his name being carried on a distant wind.

Hamza was writing something in his pad as he dismissed another of the journalists. The speed at which he scribbled suggested at least one of them had found something interesting.

'Get something?' he asked, when Hamza was still walking towards them.

'Nothing major, sir,' the detective sergeant said. 'But you know there was that talk of Kelly Wynne's dad being on the force? Well, there's a name floating about for him now. Still rumour at the minute. Seems to mostly be coming from TikTok, so not sure how reliable it is.'

Logan assumed 'not at all,' probably answered that question, but nodded for the DS to continue.

'It's a Frazer Kerrigan, sir.' Hamza looked up from his pad. 'You ever heard of him?'

'Kerrigan? Christ. Aye.' Logan squinted and grimaced as if struggling with some complicated calculus, then shook his head. 'Offed himself twenty-odd years ago. Took a header off the Erskine Bridge.'

'Oof. Shit,' Tyler said. 'What'd he do that for?'

Logan shrugged, but his reply was broken and hesitant, like he wasn't fully sure of what he was saying. 'He was a crooked bastard. He got found out.'

Tyler nodded sagely. 'There's a lesson there for all of us. Eh, boss?'

Before Logan could answer, a voice cried out to him from somewhere in the middle distance.

'DCI Logan! DCI Logan!'

'Christ, what now?' he asked, looking around to try and see where the voice was coming from.

'It's the home wrecker, boss,' Tyler said, his distaste very evident as he pointed back in the direction of the station, then gave Hamza a supportive nod.

Thomas was haring towards them, eyes wide, arms pumping like pistons as he clattered ungracefully across the car park.

He wasn't a natural runner. His gait was all wrong, and he seemed somewhat alarmed to be moving unaided at such a relatively high speed. He misjudged the slow-down, too, and the detectives were forced to part to allow him a few extra stumbled steps before he could fully come to a stop.

The remaining journalists immediately took an interest. There were only half a dozen of them now, though, and Ben summoned the Uniforms to ensure the reporters all made it safely back inside their vehicles as quickly as humanly possible.

He joined the others as the red faced consultant bent double, hacking and coughing as he fought to get his breath back.

'Christ, it's barely a hundred yards, son,' Logan intoned. He and the others stepped back as Thomas retched, shuddered, then spat out a wad of yellow bile.

'This is what happens if you sit in front of bloody computer screens all day,' Ben said, and he shot Hamza a sideways look, like a worried parent making sure their child was paying attention.

With a final fit of coughing, Thomas snapped his upper body up straight. His face was an oil spill of sweat, snot, and tears, and though he did his best to wipe it all away on the sleeve of his shirt, it mostly just smeared things together.

'Bloody hell,' Tyler said. 'Where did you run from? Dundee?'

Still not quite able to speak, Thomas shook his head and pointed back to the station.

Tyler tutted. 'Aye, I know you didn't actually run from Dundee, like,' he said, then he rolled his eyes at Logan, and quietly enjoyed not being the one getting the wrong end of the stick for once.

Thomas shook his head more emphatically this time, and managed to wheeze out a few words. 'Up there. The computer. The trace.'

Only Hamza understood what the consultant was getting at. He looked up at the window, then back to the man who had ruined his life.

'Wait, what are you saying? It got something?'

Thomas nodded. He drew in a big breath which, given the look on his face as he did it, hurt a lot.

'Found them,' he managed to rasp.

Everyone reacted. Everyone now understood.

'I think I've found where they are!'

Chapter 37

The Incident Room was abuzz now, Uniforms and the CID filling the space like revellers at a house party. The promise of a breakthrough hummed in the air.

Gone was the defeated hush of earlier. The place was a command centre now, with DCI Logan slap bang at the centre of it.

The trace that had been running for the past few hours had landed a hit. It had worked its way through a series of false breadcrumbs, hopping from spoofed I.P.s to dark web servers, until finally triangulating as a flashing red dot twenty miles south off the A9.

Finally, they had a possible location—a caravan park that had been shut for years, and left to go to ruin. The site was mostly used by travellers these days, though there had been no recent reports of anyone causing problems in the area, or requests from neighbouring landowners to have them moved on.

'I want a chopper in the air in the next fifteen minutes,' Logan barked, addressing the order to anyone who could make it happen. 'Thermal cameras, tell them to stay as high and as far away as they can, but I want to know who's on that site.'

One of the CID sergeants raised his pen like he was bidding at an auction, then hurried off to find a phone.

'Armed Response,' Logan continued, wheeling around to address the other half of the room. 'Get them up to speed and suited up.'

'Already on it,' Ben told him, indicating the phone pressed to his ear.

The ARU was the logical next step, of course, but for a moment, it felt like the DI had read Logan's mind. Despite everything else going on, Jack felt another sharp pang of regret that this could well be the last time they both did this. After all these years, all those cases, this might be the night it all ended.

There was no time to think about that now, though.

He pointed to the dot on the map now displayed on the big screen, and indicated the half-mile track that led to it from the A9. The thin, wobbly white line continued through the mass of green until it joined another road near a place called Findhorn Bridge.

'I want the road closed here and here. No lights or sirens, unmarked cars. We know he's got cameras, but there's no saying how many, or where they are. If you can get some helpful farmer in a big tractor to break down right at the A9 junction, all the better. We stay as low key as possible.'

Tyler stepped in and pointed to spots either side of where the back road met the T-junction. 'Could set blocks up here and here, boss. Far enough away that I doubt he'll be covering it, but keeps him penned in.'

Logan grabbed the DC by the shoulder and shook him. It was, despite appearances, a positive, well-meaning gesture.

'Yes, Tyler! That's what we need. More of that sort of thing. You!' He pointed to a uniformed sergeant who had been standing watching on. 'Get all that?'

'Got it, sir.'

'Then why the hell are you still standing there? Go, go, go.'

Another spin. Another command shouted into the mass of bodies. 'I want ambulances and paramedics on standby, enough for all eight influencers, plus one for the bastard himself. He'll need it after I get my hands on him.'

Another Uniform jumped onto that one and hurried off to make arrangements.

'Someone go round and drag Geoff Palmer out of his bed. I want his team ready to move in once the action's done. Sinead, go tell Shona that we might be needing her soon.'

'On it, sir.'

'We keep the press as far away from this as possible. If you get so much as a suggestion of them sniffing around near that site, you arrest them and we'll figure out why later. Everyone got that?'

There was some enthusiastic agreement from the room. Even the most junior officer in the place had already built up a healthy disdain for tabloid journalists, and any excuse to ruin their day was always a welcome bonus.

'Right. Good. Then get on with it.' Logan patted at the pockets of his coat, then bellowed one final order. 'And someone find me my bloody car keys!'

'Car keys?' The Gozer, who had been standing back and letting Logan lead the room, now stepped up to join the DCI. 'You're not going down there.'

'Too bloody right I am!'

The detective superintendent shook his head. 'No. That wasn't a question, Jack. You can lead from here. ARU can handle the on the ground operation. We don't need you lumbering about the place.'

'This is my case,' Logan began to protest, but Ben arrived at the Gozer's side.

'He's right, Jack. Armed response knows what it's doing. If any of us lot go down there, we'll only get in the way. Here.'

He held out a mug filled almost to the brim with steaming hot coffee. A distraction, perhaps, but possibly an olive branch.

'Drink that, I think we're going to need the caffeine.' He lowered his voice. 'And, if you can you keep your mouth shut about it, I might even show you where I hide the caramel wafers.'

He winked, and though that simple gesture spoke of the possibility of fences being mended and wounds being healed, it made the DCI sadder still that his friend was leaving him behind.

'Boss?' Tyler called from across the room. 'Geoff Palmer's on the phone for you.'

This was a positive piece of news, but Logan instinctively muttered a, 'Fuck,' and felt his skin start to crawl. He barged through a flock of wandering constables, bellowed at them to go help with the blockade, then took the offered handset from DC Neish.

'Palmer? Where the fuck have you been?' Logan barked.

There was a momentary pause, and Logan got the sense of the Scene of Crime man flinching back from the phone.

'Keep your voice down, or someone will hear you,' came the whispered reply. 'I've had to sneak in here out of hours to look at your...' He hesitated. Logan could imagine him looking surreptitiously around him. 'To take care of our little mission.'

'In the middle of the bloody night? I wasn't asking you to help me dispose of a dead body, Geoff. I didn't want it logged in the system, but it's not a bloody covert op.'

Palmer paused again. 'Well, now you tell me,' he muttered. 'I've gone and worried my mother for nothing, then.'

Logan frowned. 'What do you mean?'

Another pause, slightly longer this time. 'Nothing.'

It wasn't the right time to ask. There were too many other, far more important things going on.

And yet.

'Do you live with your mother, Geoff?'

'She lives with me!' Palmer shot back. The response had been on the tip of his tongue, like he'd had call to use it regularly in the past.

'Fine. What have you got for me?' Logan asked. He'd have crossed his fingers, if he was that sort of guy. He wasn't, though, so he just held his breath and waited.

'Fuck all,' Palmer replied.

Logan didn't exhale. Not fully. Not yet. 'Sorry?'

'Nothing. It's clean. I mean, I got multiple sets of prints on the envelope, but I'm guessing the Royal Mail was involved, and they handed it to the front desk, who handed it—'there was a rustling of paper'—DC Bell? I've got her prints on file here.'

'Any match on the other prints?'

'Nope. Like I say, I assume it was the postie's.'

Logan turned, looked for the detective constable in the mass of bodies, and bellowed across to her. 'Haw! Sinead! That package this morning, was it delivered by Royal Mail?'

He ignored the muttered, 'Jesus! Bit of warning!' from the other end of the line, and listened as Sinead confirmed that, as far as she knew, a postman had handed it in at reception.

'There's one other interesting thing,' Palmer said, when Logan returned to the call. 'The mat, it's not old. It looks like it's old—it's been battered about a bit—but it's not. It's digitally printed. Probably a very small batch, otherwise it's more cost effective to use different types of printers. It's actually quite interesting how the economics of scale—'

'It isn't, Geoff,' Logan countered. 'Skip that bit and get to the point.'

Palmer tutted. 'You'd better not be like this when we go for coffee,' he grumbled. 'Anyway, so, checked, and the pub's been shut for years. This was printed way after.'

'So, it's what? A replica?'

'Unless someone's planning to open the bar back up again with the same terrible name and branding as last time, then yes, it's a replica. I actually managed to find a picture of one of the old ones online, and it's pretty close. I'm guessing whoever made it found the same image. Either that, or they've got a bloody good memory.'

Logan's eyes darted from left to right, rifling through all the thoughts that immediately popped into his head, searching for a way to make this new information fit.

All it told him, though, was that someone had *really* wanted to get under his skin when they'd sent it.

The same someone who'd been in his house.

Well, if getting under his skin was what they wanted, then it was mission accomplished. It would also be the biggest mistake of their lives.

'Is that it?' Logan asked. 'Nothing else.'

'Oh, don't you worry, Jack. I've got something else for you.' Palmer rocked on his heels. Logan wasn't sure how he knew this, he just sensed it. 'A hair.'

Jack switched the phone from one ear to the other, like he wasn't sure the first one could be trusted. 'A hair?'

'A hair. In the envelope,' Palmer continued. 'Didn't see that coming, did you?'

'What does it tell us?'

'It's grey.'

Logan waited. 'And?'

'Well, I mean, that's it at the moment,' Geoff replied. 'To be honest, I thought you'd be more excited. It's human. I can say that much.'

Logan rubbed at his eyes, then ran his hand down his face. 'Well, it was hardly going to be the big bad bloody wolf who posted it, was it?'

'Ha! Funny image, that. I might use that,' Palmer said, and he paused while he jotted it down in his mental notebook. 'I still need to process the hair, which will take days. Weeks, maybe. No pulp attached, so you can forget about DNA. Best I'll be able to tell you is drug use, maybe some health issues, any unusual environmental conditions, but that's probably unlikely…'

The Scene of Crime man's voice faded away for a moment, as he tried to think of something more useful to add that might impress the DCI and get him back on side. Or, on side for the first time, at least.

'Oh! They're white! Did I mention that? I think so, anyway, it's not always completely reliable, but I'm thinking white. Possibly a man. Could also be a woman. Or, you know, any of the in-betweens we've got these days.'

'Well, that narrows it down,' Logan said, and the sarcasm didn't go unnoticed.

'It does, actually,' Palmer shot back. 'It's a grey-haired white person. So, probably older. So, whoever sent it is a silver fox. Or, I suppose, one of DI Forde's hairs accidentally ended up in the envelope.'

He suddenly sounded worried by that prospect. 'Could that have happened? If so, the latter half of this conversation has probably been a complete waste of time.'

'No. That couldn't have happened,' Logan said. He heard some conversations ending and phones being hung up. 'Keep at it. Anything else you find, let me know.'

'What, tonight?' Palmer asked, then he sighed. 'Fine. But when we go for lunch, you're paying.'

Chapter 38

Half an hour later, the roads had been blocked, the chopper was in the air, and the armed response team had established a perimeter around the caravan park.

The footage from the helicopter had been relayed to the big screen in the Incident Room. The room was much quieter now, the mass of bodies all off carrying out their tasks, leaving only Logan's team, the Gozer, Thomas, and a couple of uniformed constables who were on hand to act as runners and coffee fetchers.

The sun wasn't yet up, but it was hinting strongly at it, the darkness to the east now woven with shades of sepia and gold.

There was no sign of any travellers at the old holiday park site. It contained just half a dozen dirty, decaying caravans of various shapes and sizes, and a mass of litter whose journey across the landscape had been cut short by the long, overgrown grass that now tangled and trapped it.

The chopper's night vision camera had revealed nothing more of interest, but a flick to infrared mode had painted a very different picture.

'Is there someone in it, do you think?' Tyler asked.

All eyes were on a caravan near the centre of the park. While the others showed up as greys and blacks, this one was partially painted in the weak, watery orange of a heat signature.

Answering Tyler's question was impossible. It was entirely feasible that someone was inside the caravan. It was possible that multiple people were in there, in fact. Something was heating the internal space, and according to the reading on the camera equipment, it was showing as just shy of thirty-seven degrees Celsius.

Human body temperature.

It would be unbearably hot in there, but it was the perfect way to camouflage anyone inside. Assuming, of course, that you were expecting someone to show up with thermal imaging equipment.

'I don't like it,' Logan said. He paced back and forth in front of the screen, like a lion before the bars of its cage. 'It feels off.'

'It's something, though,' the Gozer said. 'It's all we've got at this point.'

Logan looked over at Hamza's screen, where the video feeds of the influencers had been relegated to. None of them was being slowly baked alive. None of them, with the possible exception of the still-missing Elizia Shuttleworth, were in that caravan.

But something was. Maybe some*one*. Or maybe a clue as to who was behind all this.

Or a trap.

'It doesn't feel right,' Logan said again. He ground his teeth together. 'I should've been there. I should've been boots on the ground.'

'It wouldn't have made any difference,' the Gozer told him. 'You'd be in the way, that's all.' He took a sip of coffee and nodded at the screen. 'I think we need to send them in. We've got all we can from the chopper cam. We need to see what's in there.'

Logan groaned, like sending in the ARU was the last thing he wanted to do. If he was down there, he'd march right up to the door and rip it off its hinges, if it meant there was a chance of confronting the bastard behind all this.

But sending someone else to do his dirty work had never really been his style.

'I want a clearer picture,' he said. 'We'll tell the pilot to get in closer and see if the camera can pick up any more detail.'

'Won't they hear it then, boss?' Tyler asked. 'Isn't that what we were trying to avoid? Giving the game away, sort of thing?'

'He's right,' the detective superintendent said. 'We bring it closer, we risk him executing everyone.'

'*What* everyone?' Logan demanded, gesturing to the screen. 'We've got one warm caravan. There's not seven people squirrelled away in there. It's not a fucking Haven Holiday park on a half-term break!'

'It's too risky,' the Gozer insisted. 'We've got armed response literally a couple of hundred yards away. We can get their body cams fed here to the screen.'

He turned and looked at Hamza to check that this was correct, then returned the sergeant's nod of confirmation.

'We'll be able to see everything. They'll be able to hear us. We can advise from here. But we need to move in, Jack. Hanging fire on this is not an option.'

Logan stopped pacing, and stood face to face with the detective superintendent.

For a moment, it looked like he might reach over and tear his head clean off his shoulders. Instead, he closed his eyes, clenched his jaw, then—against his better judgement—uttered just a single, solitary word.

'Fine.'

The Gozer nodded. 'It's the right call. DS Khaled, get them on screen. DI Forde, get us patched through to the team leader.' He looked across to Logan, who still seemed unconvinced that this was the right decision. 'Slow and steady, Jack. No one's rushing in.'

Logan didn't reply. Instead, he turned his attention to the big telly and went back to pacing. On screen, the helicopter's camera continued to track the blob of orange in the middle of the holiday park.

What was in there? Who, if anyone, was inside that caravan?

All being well, they'd know in just a few minutes. That was the plan, at least.

But the knot of dread deep in Logan's gut had a few things to say on the matter.

–

'It's actually quite fun this, isn't it?'

DI Heather Filson looked up from the floor of the records room, and the stacks of paperwork teetering like ancient columns around her, until she met the sparkling blue eyes of Detective Constable Swanney.

'No,' she said. 'It isn't.'

'I'm weirdly enjoying it,' Tammi-Jo insisted. 'It's like hide and seek, but instead of looking for a person, you're looking for a sheet of paper, and instead of it hiding in, like, a wardrobe in a house, or under a bed, it's hiding in ten thousand boxes, in amongst a million other sheets of paper!'

'And how is any of that fun?' Heather asked.

Tammi-Jo's button nose crinkled up in a way that would likely melt the hearts and stiffen the trousers of a million young men, but which largely just made Heather want to punch her in the face. 'Well, I mean, I thought all that stuff I just said made it pretty self-explanatory.'

'Well, you thought wrong. It didn't. It didn't explain anything. It was just rambling nonsense. I'd say it made it all sound worse, except that's not possible, because this is hell. This is my actual hell,' Heather said.

She stabbed a finger along the aisle of shelves and boxes to where a uniformed constable stood scratching his head at a bundle of yellowing paperwork.

'Does that guy look like he's having fun? Or what about her?'

She turned to indicate another constable who knelt over a box on the floor like she was about to vomit into it. As Heather twisted her torso, her elbow caught one of the piles of paper and toppled it, sending sheets sliding off in all directions.

At first, she didn't react. But then, her eyes widened, her teeth bared, and she emitted a noise that was last heard on Earth during the late Jurassic period.

'Jesus Christing fucking bastard thing!' she cried, and Tammi-Jo glanced warily around like the outburst might somehow get them into trouble.

Fuelled by frustration, rage, and not a little exhaustion, Heather snatched up a couple of the pages, scrunching them up as her fingers balled into tight, shaking fists.

'I think we should just burn this place to the ground,' she announced, spraying flecks of foam through her gritted teeth.

Tammi-Jo wasn't quite sure how setting fire to the place would help them find what they were looking for. If anything, it would almost certainly prove to be a hindrance.

She felt it best not to say as much, though. Better, she had learned, to let the DI get it out of her system. Instead, she picked up a bundle of sheets from the spilled pile and set about squaring them neatly together.

'I mean, it's madness! What are we even doing here?' Heather demanded.

'We're looking for staffing records for the old station at—'

'Shut up! I know what we're doing here!' Heather spat. 'But, I mean, why? It's pointless! There are millions of bits of paper in here, and from what I can tell, they've been filed away by a monkey. And not, like, one of the smart ones you see on telly, just an average one. A fucking dunce one, in fact. The thicko from the bottom of the class. There is no way, without a hundred people going through these files, that we're ever going to find the one we're—'

'This is it.'

Heather choked on the last few words. 'What?' she asked, stalling for time as her brain tried to process what the detective constable had said. 'What do you mean 'this is it'?'

'I think this is what we're looking for,' Tammi-Jo said, and the page was whipped out of her hand before she'd even finished the sentence. 'That's the right place and right date, isn't it?'

284

Heather nodded dumbly as she read. Tammi-Jo's face lit up like she'd just won a double rollover on the lottery. Or, given how the detective constable's mind worked, seen a nice pencil.

'Amazing! Congratulations, DI Filson, you've found the… Wait. No, I found it, didn't I?' Tammi-Jo thrust both hands in the air in triumph and bellowed, 'Victory is mine!' so loudly that another of the stacks of paper next to Heather toppled over.

There was no outburst of dinosaur-era rage from the detective inspector this time, though. Instead, she just stared at the paper.

At the date.

At the place.

And at the name scrawled down at the bottom.

'Oh,' she mumbled. 'Shit.'

Chapter 39

The feed from the ARU team leader's helmet-mounted camera was coming through clearly. It filled the screen of the TV in the incident room, and though the video was a couple of seconds behind the audio, it was good enough.

'It's like playing Call of Duty this,' Tyler said, standing in front of the screen. 'This telly'd be great for that. It's way bigger than the one we've got at home. Here, Sinead—'

He looked over his shoulder to where his wife stood, eyes glued to the screen.

'No,' she told him, and he accepted her decision without argument or complaint.

They were all gathered around the screen, Tyler at the front next to Dave, Sinead, Hamza and Ben behind them, with the Gozer and Thomas sitting on chairs at either side.

Logan was no longer pacing back and forth, but he couldn't quite bring himself to stand still. He lurked at the back of the group, watching over their heads, the leather of his boots creaking as he shifted his weight from foot to foot.

He still didn't like this. It didn't feel right.

The door to the Incident Room inched open. Everyone looked and saw Detective Superintendent Mitchell standing there, like she was waiting to be granted access. The Gozer rose to his feet, as if he was going to chase her from the room, but then he spun the empty seat towards her, and she took it without a word.

She turned just enough to meet Logan's eye, and they exchanged nods that said a whole lot and very little at the same time.

'Right, that's them making the approach now,' Ben announced, sharpening everyone's focus.

Picked out in the green and black of the night vision camera lay the caravan at the centre of the park. There was no sign of movement around it, besides the slow, side-to-side swishing of the grass, and the occasional pieces of litter fluttering by.

'Is it just my imagination, or are the windows boarded up?' Sinead asked.

'It's not just you,' Tyler replied, squinting and leaning closer to the screen. 'There's chipboard or something, I think.'

'Inside or outside?' Ben asked.

Tyler shrugged. 'No idea, boss. Can't see well enough for that. Camera's not clear enough.'

Ben tutted, like the failings of the technology were all the detective constable's fault, then he crossed his arms and went back to watching the footage.

There was no ambient light spill from the caravan's windows or door. Even boarded up, the sensitive night vision cameras would've picked up some suggestion of light coming from inside.

Hot but dark, then. Logan shifted his weight again. Did that mean anything?

The team leader was maybe twenty feet from the caravan door now. At the edges of the shot, it was just possible to make out a few other ARU officers, all kitted out in black, weapons ready, night vision goggles trained on the target.

Logan scratched at his chin, agitated. He'd been communicating with the armed response sergeant by radio, and raised it to his mouth now. 'You hear anything?' The team leader was listening via an earpiece, but Logan lowered his voice to a whisper, all the same.

There was no audible reply—the sergeant was too close to the caravan to answer out loud, but the footage swung left and right as he shook his head in response.

Logan stared at the screen, and at the caravan, narrowing his eyes like he might be able to peer through its thin, dirty walls to see what secrets or dangers lay within.

The radio was still raised in front of his mouth. He spoke into it again. 'Still nothing?'

Another pause for the delay to iron itself out.

Another shake of the head.

'I don't like it,' Logan said. 'Hold where you are.'

The footage continued to creep forward for a few more seconds, then stopped. The movement of a hand at the edge of the frame signalled for the rest of the team to halt and hold, too.

'What are you doing, Jack?' the Gozer asked. 'We can't just leave them standing there. They're fully exposed. He could be watching them! They need to move in. Now, while they might still have the element of surprise.'

Logan ran a hand through his hair, then gripped the back of his neck and tried to massage away the bag of rocks he found there.

The superintendent was right. They'd come this far. They were this close. The longer they stood around in the open, the more danger they were in.

'Come on! Tick-tock, Jack!' The Gozer tapped at his watch. 'We might be able to bloody end this right now.'

Logan glanced down at Mitchell. She wasn't looking at him, and was instead hunched forward in her seat, elbows resting on her thighs, her hands covering the lower half of her face. One of her legs was bouncing anxiously, shaking her whole body, and making the chair squeak.

Nobody had dared say anything to her about it. No one, in fact, had spoken to her at all. No one knew what, if anything, was the right thing to say.

There was a crackle of interference from the radio in Logan's hand. A voice came whispering through the static.

'Orders, sir?'

Logan looked up at the ceiling tiles, their millions of tiny pinholes like tunnels to nowhere. He stared at the window. Back at the screen. Anywhere except at the rest of the team, who were all watching him, waiting for him to make the call.

Finally, when he could delay no longer, his gaze crept over to the Gozer, who nodded back at him.

Shit.

Logan brought the radio closer to his mouth. He drew in a breath, and said a silent prayer.

'Go,' he told them.

A second passed. Two. Three.

Thirty miles away, a hand was raised. A command was given. A team of highly trained officers made their move.

And in the Incident Room at Burnett Road Station, a hushed, huddled silence hung in the air.

The footage was jerky as the team picked up speed on their final approach, each footstep shaking the camera and making the action harder to follow.

Logan groaned like he was in pain, his whole body tensing and tightening until the hard plastic casing of the radio gave a crack in his hand.

He kept watching. Staring. Praying.

On screen, two black-clad, masked and helmeted officers crept into position, one with a battering ram, the other bringing his SIG MCX short-barrelled rifle to his shoulder, and taking aim at the door.

'Here we go,' Ben whispered.

The audio reached them before the action unfolded.

'Police! On the floor! On the floor!'

A bang followed.

'What's happening?' the Gozer asked.

More shouting followed. Crashing. Footsteps.

'Down, down! Stay on the floor! Hands where I can see them!'

The video finally started to catch up. Over the sound of the shouts, the detectives watched the battering ram smash the flimsy caravan door off its hinges.

'He's not moving, sir,' the out-of-sync audio continued. 'I think he's dead.'

Several seconds behind, on the telly, the team leader rushed in, gun raised in front of him like he was a character from one of Tyler's video games.

The beam of a torch fell on someone lying in a sleeping bag on the floor, the hood zipped up over their head. Despite the rude awakening, they hadn't moved.

'Fuck, fuck, fu—'

There was a crackle, then an electronic squeal, and the soundtrack ended.

Logan's feet drew him forward a step. 'What the hell was that?' he demanded, then the answer unfolded silently on the screen.

One of the armed officers used the barrel of his rifle to nudge the lifeless shape in the sleeping bag. When they didn't respond, he gave them a push with a boot, and the camera swung down as the team leader focused on a circular metal plate on the floor.

Ben's hands covered the lower half of his face as he recognised the unveiled object. And well he should. He'd helped disarm enough of them back in his army days.

'Oh, God,' he whispered. 'Oh, God, no.'

And then, with a burst of light, and a buzz of interference, the screen went blank.

Nobody spoke. Nobody moved. Nobody dared.

Eventually, hand shaking, Logan brought the radio back to his mouth. 'Sergeant, what's happening?' he asked. A faint, echoey whistle was the only reply. 'Sergeant, we've lost contact. Can you hear me? Please respond.'

Please, God, respond.

'Sergeant, this is DCI Logan,' he continued, staring at the screen like he could will it back to life. He raised his voice, hoping it might carry better over the airwaves. 'Please respond.'

'Jack,' the Gozer began, but the look Logan fired in his direction made him think again.

'Sergeant, we need an update here. Please respond.'

'Uh, boss?' Tyler's voice was barely above a whisper. 'I, um, don't think—'

Static spat from the radio in Logan's hand. A voice, not the sergeant's, but someone younger and much more afraid, squawked from the speaker.

'Alpha Leader is down. Repeat, Alpha Leader is down. We need ambulances up here. Now! We need help!'

Logan looked over to the Gozer. The detective superintendent was staring blankly at the radio, like he couldn't process the words coming out of it, or didn't know how to respond.

Eventually, he gave a minute shake of his head. 'We can't. It's too risky.'

There had been an explosion. The whole thing had been a trap. Logan's instincts had been right. The Detective Superintendent's had not.

Jack brought the radio back to his mouth and held the Gozer's gaze as he replied. 'Hang in there, son,' he said. 'Help's on the way.'

He passed the radio to Ben, and with it, the responsibility of carrying out his orders.

'Get them whatever they need and get them the hell out of there.'

Ben nodded, then turned away, raising the radio to his mouth and offering assurances to the officer on the other end.

Logan stalked towards the Gozer, the air around him practically crackling with the heat of his anger.

'Sir.'

Logan stopped, let his gaze linger on the detective superintendent for another moment, then turned to see Sinead holding her mobile in her hand. He only now realised that it was ringing. Another ringtone was jingling away somewhere else in the room, too.

'It's Heather, sir,' Sinead told him.

'I'll call her back.'

'Tammi-Jo's phoning, too, boss,' Tyler said, angling his phone so the DCI could see the screen. 'Might be important.'

It took Logan just a half second to make the decision. He nodded to Sinead. 'Put her on speaker.'

Sinead answered the call and tapped the icon to broadcast DI Filson's voice. 'Hi Heather. You're on speakerphone. DCI Logan's here.' She glanced at the Gozer. 'And Detective Superintendent MacKenzie,' she added, for safety's sake.

Tyler's phone stopped ringing, Tammi-Jo presumably aware that her boss's call had been answered.

'Heather. It's not a good time,' Logan said, his voice booming around the room.

'Aye, well, you've had me raking through old paperwork for half the night, so tough shit,' Heather shot back. 'You wanted to know if we found anything for the date you gave us.'

'And?'

'And why the hell do you think I'd be phoning at five in the morning? We got a name. We know who was on duty that night.'

Logan's throat tightened. He steeled himself for disappointment. It was probably another dead end. It almost certainly meant nothing.

'And?' he asked again.

'And you're not going to like it.'

Chapter 40

Logan had come alone.

The knot of journalists around the station was growing again now that the sun was coming up, but a traditional Highland rain shower continued to hold some of the less determined at bay.

He'd shouldered past them, ignored most of the questions, and responded with an abrupt, 'Fuck the fuck out of my fucking way,' when someone had shoved a microphone in his face, safe in the knowledge that the quote would be completely unusable on all forms of mainstream broadcast media.

From there, he'd driven across the city, headlights blazing in the half dark, only a few delivery drivers, bin lorries, and early risers sharing the roads.

He'd pulled up at the house. Rung the doorbell. Waited.

Now, he stood with his hands in his pockets and his collar raised to catch the rain that insisted on trying to worm its way down the back of his neck.

A light turned on upstairs, spilling its orange glow out over the uneven surface of the house's makeshift driveway.

Footsteps. Thumping. A light above the door sparked into life.

The DCI didn't blink. Instead, he drew himself up to his full, terrifying height, and fixed his gaze on the man who hauled the door open dressed only in a pair of grubby grey boxes.

'The fuck do you want? What sort of time is this to rock up on my doorstep? You working part-time as a fucking milkman, or something?'

Logan didn't react to any of it. Instead, he just spoke the other man's name like it was some ancient and terrible incantation.

'Bob.'

Silhouetted in the doorway, Robert Hoon looked himself up and down. 'Aye, impressive basic fucking recognition skills there. Here, see if you recognise this.'

He raised his right hand and extended a middle finger.

Logan, once again, didn't react.

'You mind if I have a word?' he asked.

'Depends. Is the word, 'Sorry for disturbing you less than two hours after you got to your fucking bed, and after you spent the last full day travelling halfway across the fucking planet'? Is that the word you want to say, Jack? Because if, so, it's considerably more than one fucking word, and no, apology not accepted.'

'Was it you, Bob?' Logan asked.

Hoon blinked back at him, making no effort to hide his confusion. 'Was what fucking me? What am I meant to have done now?' He poked himself in the centre of his bare chest, his finger getting lost in the nest of greying hair. 'I fucking helped you cludgie-fingered fuckwits out with that internet bollocks. I had to pull a lot of fucking strings to get that information!' He sniffed, and shrugged. 'Whatever the fuck it was. Computer stuff. I don't know.'

'That information might have just got half the armed response team killed,' Logan said.

Hoon said nothing for a moment, then shook his head. 'I was just the fucking middle-man. Nothing to do with me, that. I didn't even know what I was being asked.'

That could well be true, Logan knew. Bob had never been particularly computer literate. Then again, Logan would never have pegged the man as an action hero, but the continued existence of the Eastgate shopping centre said otherwise.

The information he'd provided had led to a trap.

The hair in that envelope matched Hoon's own.

He knew all about Logan's life. He knew where he worked, where he lived, how to get to him.

And he knew about his past, too. He knew what he had done.

The rain rat-a-tat-tatted an impatient rhythm on Logan's shoulders. He nodded into the hallway at Hoon's back. 'Can I come in?'

Hoon hesitated, something about the DCI's demeanour and body language making him pause.

'Can you fuck. You'll wake the wee ones,' he said, then he stepped out of the house in his piss-dotted underwear, and pulled the door behind him.

The wind was cold. The rain was colder. Neither seemed to bother him.

'The fuck's this about, Jack?'

'July the fifteenth, nineteen-ninety-six.'

Hoon's confusion deepened, his eyebrows butting heads above his nose. 'The fuck's that meant to mean?'

'What do you remember about that date?' Logan pressed.

Hoon laughed. It was sharp and loud, and he stifled it quickly when he remembered Tyler and Sinead's twins asleep in the room upstairs.

'Hang on while I consult the old fucking memory archives there, Jack.' He tapped himself on the side of the head a few times, then shrugged. 'Nope, fuck all. Just a load of filing cabinets full of photos of a wee fucking intern shrugging. Why?'

'You were on duty. Desk sergeant at the station in the Gorbals.'

Hoon's face remained ninety-nine percent neutral, but that one percent became something infinitely more complex.

'Alright. If you fucking say so. And? So what?'

The wind swirled the rain so it shifted direction. Logan's sheer bulk shielded Hoon from the worst of it, but it railed and rattled against the DCI's back.

'You were on duty when a young guy came in. Nineteen. Told you he'd killed someone. He'd intervened in an assault, knocked the guy down, and he cracked his head.'

'Hang on.' Hoon tapped his temple again, then shook his head. 'Nope. The intern's still fucking shrugging. What are you on about, Jack?'

'You didn't take him on. You basically told him to piss off.'

'Sounds like me, right enough,' Hoon admitted. 'I was barely out of the army. Probably didn't have a fucking clue what I was doing. What about it?'

'It was me,' Logan told him.

Hoon's butting eyebrows more or less merged into a single v-shaped strip of hair. 'What was you?'

'I was the kid who came in. I was the one who came to you and confessed.'

'You?' Hoon looked the DCI up and down. 'You came in and, what? Told me you'd killed some guy?'

Logan nodded. 'You're saying you don't remember?'

'There's been a lot of brain cells lost to drink in the last thirty fucking years, Jack. No' to mention to a number of painful head injuries.'

'You don't remember?' Logan asked again, determined to get a straight answer.

'No. I don't remember. You sure you didn't fucking dream it?'

Logan confirmed that yes, he was quite certain that he hadn't.

'Well, I don't know what the fuck to tell you then,' Hoon said. 'There's fuck all memory of it on my side. What did I say to you at the time?'

'You said you'd pass it on to be looked at.'

'There you fucking go, then.'

'But you didn't. There's no record of it ever being logged or passed on for investigation.'

Hoon put his hand down the back of his boxers and enjoyed quite a satisfying scratch of his arse.

'Well, that's bollocks.'

'I checked, Bob. Repeatedly. I've looked for the report for years.'

'Then you're either more of a useless fuckwit than I've been giving you credit for, or someone covered it up,' Hoon told him. 'But I'm putting my fucking money on option one.'

When this argument—persuasive though it was—wasn't enough to satisfy the DCI, Hoon huffed out an impatient sigh.

'Look, I'd just come back from a fucking warzone. I had no clue what I was doing. But, I was scared of arseing it all up, so it was about the only time on the job that I did it fucking properly. If you reported it, I'd have logged it and passed it on,' Hoon insisted. 'I mean, if you'd caught me a year later, I wouldn't have given a flying fuck, but back then? I'd have been doing it by the book.'

Logan still looked unconvinced, but there was a subtle shifting of his body language now. A stooping of the shoulders. A softening around the edges.

'Let's say that's true. Let's say you did pass it on,' he said. 'Do you remember who you passed it to?'

'Remember, no. Like I say, fuck all recollection of any of it,' Hoon said.

'That's helluva convenient,' Logan stated.

'*But*, I don't fucking need to remember that one night, do I?' He tapped at his head again, more emphatically this time. 'Because I know what the protocol was. I know who I was reporting to, so I know who I'd have told about it.'

The rain fell silent. The wind dropped. The world around them held its breath.

'Who?'

'Right fucking slime ball. Old friend of yours, actually,' Hoon said. 'No longer with us, and good fucking riddance to the crooked bastard.'

Logan took a step closer, until Hoon was swallowed by his shadow.

'Who, Bob? Who did you tell?'

'Frazer Kerrigan,' Hoon replied. He rocked back on his bare heels, then poked a finger into the centre of Logan's chest. 'The three-faced, claggy-fingered wee fucktard that you drove to suicide!'

Chapter 41

Frazer Kerrigan had been a well-kent face around Glasgow from the mid-nineties until late 2006, when he'd gone from the dizzying heights of Detective Inspector to the murky depths of the River Clyde.

A lot had happened between those dates. Much of it of great benefit to Kerrigan's bank account, and the majority of it completely illegal.

Of course, this wasn't public knowledge at the time. Nor were the beatings he'd dished out on the regular, the woman he'd used his position to sexually assault, or the fact that he was so deep in Shuggie Cowan's pocket, he could tickle the gangster's balls.

There had been rumours of his 'working relationship' with Cowan for a year or two, but nobody had been able to prove anything. Then came the day he was caught red-handed trying to murder a dealer who'd been helping himself to a bigger cut of the takings than Shuggie had agreed to. Kerrigan had been trying to drown the guy in a partially blocked pub toilet.

The dealer had spilled his guts—both literally and figuratively—to the detective constable who'd intervened, providing enough information to get Kerrigan suspended, pending a full criminal investigation.

The detective constable who'd stopped the attack had faced his share of threats and abuse over it, but it had helped land him a promotion to DS, and onwards and upwards from there.

Kerrigan's life had spiralled in the opposite direction, and far more rapidly. He'd agreed to a plea deal to bring down Shuggie Cowan, on the understanding that the gangster didn't find out.

But Shuggie, of course, heard all about it.

Friendless, hunted, and with nowhere left to turn, Kerrigan had driven to the Erskine Bridge in the early hours of a Monday morning, taken off his clothes and jewellery, then horsed himself head-first over the edge.

He had been declared officially dead some months later.

That had been almost twenty years ago.

Now, there was just one problem.

'It's him,' Logan confirmed, as the recording of the dog walker's conversation played from Hamza's PC. 'That's him. That's his voice.'

'You could be right, Jack,' Ben agreed. 'I mean, I remember it all kicking off at the time, of course, but I didn't deal with him as much as you did. It could be him, though.'

'Body was never found,' Logan added.

'Good cover story if he wanted to go into hiding.'

'And he would, with us and Cowan both after him.'

Ben nodded. 'Walls would've been closing in. That's why everyone bought the idea that he'd jumped.'

'So, hang on, hang on, boss,' Tyler said, still processing the story he'd just been told. 'He was trying to drown the guy in a toilet full of, like…?'

'Aye,' Logan confirmed, negating the need for the DC to finish the sentence.

He finished it, anyway. 'Shite? Full of actual shite?'

'Yes, Tyler.'

The DC grimaced. 'Jesus. What a way to go. Good job you were there, boss. Although…' He gave this some thought. 'I might just want it over and done with at that point. You know what I mean? If you've had your head shoved down a shitty lavvy, how do you come back from that? I might be happier if I just went ahead and died.'

'What are you thinking, sir?' Sinead asked. 'What's the play?'

Logan had been wondering that same thing all the way back from Hoon's place. When he'd heard Kerrigan's name mentioned earlier, he'd wondered if the voice was a match, but had dismissed it, believing the former DI was long dead.

When Hoon had mentioned him again, though, he'd reconsidered. On the drive back, he'd started to believe the voice matched, but he had to check to be sure.

But it was him. He was certain of it.

And it all fit, too. He knew what the teenage Logan had done, the where and the when of it. He was a cunning, ruthless bastard, believed to be responsible for hundreds of assaults, and suspected in almost a dozen gangland deaths.

And he had every reason in the world to want revenge on Jack Logan.

'If the rumours are right about him being Kelly Wynne's father...' Hamza started the sentence strongly, then it crumbled away. 'Then... what does that mean? He shot her. We saw him shoot her.'

'We saw her get shot,' Ben corrected. 'We didn't see who pulled the trigger.'

It seemed like a bit of a moot point, but Hamza conceded it with a nod. 'OK, true. But, if he's behind it, then he presumably gave the go ahead.'

Logan lowered himself onto the edge of the nearest desk. It had been a long, exhausting twenty-four hours, and every minute of it was showing on his face.

'We've dug into her background, aye?'

'Didn't bring up much,' replied Dave. 'Single, lot of cats, likes to play with toys. Dropped out of uni due to family illness.'

'Shags teenagers in theatre dressing rooms...' Tyler added.

'And that, aye,' Dave said. 'Before she went full-time on YouTube, she did some work for the BBC. Assistant producer on a couple of pretty big shows. Tried her hand at a few other channels before settling on toys. Cooking, a weird zombie make-up thing, and how to use Excel spreadsheets.'

'Family history?' Ben asked.

'Didn't really get anything interesting on that. Birth certificate only has her mum listed, and she died in twenty-sixteen.'

'Well, someone found something,' Hamza reasoned. 'That journalist was able to give me Kerrigan's name, and it's been cropping up on the socials for the last hour or so.'

Logan rubbed at his chin. The growth that had been stubble when he'd left for work the previous morning was now flirting with the idea of becoming a beard.

'We name him,' he announced. 'Publicly. We put out a statement to the press. Blanket coverage. Name and photo, if we can get one. No time to age it up, so an old one'll have to do. I want it everywhere.'

'You want him to see it,' Ben realised.

'I want it rammed down his bloody throat,' Logan replied. He clicked his fingers and pointed to Sinead. 'Get back onto Heather. I don't care if she's sleeping, wake her up.'

'She won't like that, boss,' Tyler said, trying to save his wife from a full Filson ear-bashing.

Sinead smiled and waved his concern away. 'It's fine. What am I telling her, sir?'

'I want her to talk to Cowan. See if he knows anything. He had his doubts at the time that Kerrigan was really dead. Thought we were protecting him. If I know that bastard, he'll have dug around. He might have something he can tell us, even if it's just to confirm that Kerrigan had a daughter.'

Sinead took a moment to log all that, then reached for her phone. 'On it.'

Logan switched his attention to DI Forde. 'Ben. The team at the caravan park. How are they?'

'We've got them out. Some of them are in a pretty bad way, but they'll live. Life changing injuries on a couple of them, though,' Ben replied, and his words were laden with the weariness of someone who'd been through all this before. 'It was a modified landmine. Dead man's switch. Best we can tell, the guy in the caravan was already dead. No ID. Possibly homeless.'

'No one would've reported him missing,' Hamza said.

Logan sighed. 'Aye. I've been thinking the same about the bodies we dug up yesterday. They've been there for months and, as far as we know, don't match any missing persons reports.'

'So, what are you saying, boss? He's been killing a load of homeless folk for fun?'

'Maybe not for fun,' the DCI reasoned. 'Maybe as a rehearsal.'

He allowed himself a second or two to mull this over, then looked over at where Hamza was sitting. 'I hate to ask, but where's the consultant?'

If the question annoyed the sergeant, he made an excellent job of not showing it. 'He's through with CID, going over the footage from the livestreams—or whatever they are—and the feeds from the ARU helmet cams. Not sure it'll do much.'

'Better that than him getting under our feet,' Logan said. He tipped his head in the sergeant's direction. 'Thank you. I appreciate none of this has been easy.'

Hamza smiled thinly and shrugged. 'When is any of it ever easy, sir?'

'True,' Logan conceded, then he sharply raised his voice. 'Tyler!'

DC Neish jumped to attention. 'Boss?' he yelped, immediately looking guilty.

'Has that statement gone out to the press yet?'

'About Kerrigan? No, boss. I've been standing here the whole…' His brain shifted gear, and he realised what the DCI was saying. 'No worries, boss. I'm on it right now!'

'No, don't. Let's not give them the information, I've changed my mind,' Logan said.

Tyler stumbled a step or two, then stopped. 'Boss?'

'Tell them to get their cameras ready. I'm going to make a statement myself,' the DCI said.

'You sure that's wise, Jack?' Ben asked.

'First thing I've been sure of since this all started. The bastard thinks he can taunt me, does he?' He rose to his feet. For the first time in almost a day, his presence expanded to fill the room. 'Well, let's see how he likes it.'

Chapter 42

The gentleness of Logan's touch on her shoulder didn't stop Shona waking with a jerk and a, 'Wargh!' that started a chain reaction throughout the room. Olivia, on the couch on Shona's left, and Harris, on her right, both yelped their way back to consciousness, as Taggart leaped up from the floor, barking like the sky was falling.

'Sorry,' Logan said, whipping his hand away like he might still be able to deny any involvement.

The pathologist swung her head from left to right, in a big wild movement that could generously be described as 'getting her bearings,' but, more accurately, as 'wondering what the hell was going on.'

She scratched at her hair, mumbled an apology for elbowing Harris in the face, then blinked in the weak grey sunlight that seeped in through the window.

'When is it?' she asked. It was quite a vague question, but it had been a long, broken night.

'It's just after seven,' Logan told her. Then he added, 'On Tuesday morning,' when the time alone didn't seem enough to satisfy her.

Olivia emitted a drawn-out groan of disgust, then curled herself up against the arm of the couch and attempted to go back to sleep.

'Toilet?' Harris grunted, standing upright and doing his best not to jiggle on the spot.

'Out the door, left, can't miss it,' Logan told him.

He waited for the boy to leave, by which point Shona had managed to pull herself together a little.

'You OK? You look exhausted,' she said, reaching for his hand and squeezing it. 'What's happening? How is… everyone?'

'No one else is dead yet, but the clock's ticking down,' Logan said. He bent and scratched at the back of Taggart's head, which pleased the little dog immensely. 'We might know who's behind it.'

The news woke Shona all the way. Even Olivia opened an eye.

'Seriously? That's great!' the pathologist said. 'Isn't it? I mean, it is good news, isn't it? Because you don't look too happy about it.'

'That's just his normal face,' Olivia muttered, then she shut her eye again.

'We think it's an ex-copper. Crooked bastard I had a run in with a few years ago. Might be Kelly Wynne's father.'

'Her father?! But he shot her!'

'That's mental!' Olivia ejected, abandoning all thoughts of sleep. She whipped out her phone. 'I need to post about this? Can I post about this?'

Logan shrugged. 'It's already in the public domain. We've briefed the press. Just spoke to them myself.'

Olivia tutted and scowled, annoyed at having missed out on the opportunity to break the news. Although, she realised, her phone was completely dead, so she'd have been shit out of luck, anyway.

'So, what happens now?' Shona asked.

'We wait,' Logan said, though it was clear from his tone that he didn't like it. 'Not a lot else we can do. We thought we had a location for him.' He thought of the ARU boys lined up in hospital beds. 'But, well, that didn't pan out. There was a body involved. A homeless guy, we think.'

Shona looked flustered, like the news was somehow her fault. Logan raised a hand to calm her. 'We're securing the site before we send anyone else in. We don't need you yet. Like I say, we just wait.'

'Can you just wait, though? I thought the deadline was—'

'A couple of hours away. Aye. I know.'

'What if he kills someone else?' Olivia asked.

Logan had no answer to that. Not an honest one, anyway. Not one that was anything other than empty promises and platitudes.

'I've made the statement as, eh, confrontational as possible.' He took his phone from his trouser pocket, tapped at the screen a few times, then turned it towards them. 'Here.'

Shona and Olivia both leaned in to watch the snippet of news footage that was playing on the phone. In it, Logan stood against the backdrop of the station's reception area, flashbulbs flickering across his face, and microphones jostling for position at the edge of the frame.

'After following up on a number of leads, we are now of the belief that the person responsible for the murder of Kelly Wynne and the abduction of Adam Parfitt, Denzel Drummond, Cassandra Swain, Elizia Shuttleworth, Natalie Womack, Matthew Broderick, and Bruce Kennedy is a man by the name of Frazer Kerrigan.

'Mr Kerrigan is a former detective inspector of police, who had his arse—sorry, his backside—kicked off the force in 2006, and was believed to have taken his own life by jumping off the Erskine Bridge a short time later.'

The on-screen DCI paused to make sure everyone was paying attention, then stared straight down the lens of the camera.

'Quite frankly, that would've been doing the decent thing. While any unnecessary loss of life is obviously tragic, Frazer Kerrigan's would have been the exception. Back when I knew him, he was a vile, corrupt, manipulative, highly dangerous bully.

'He was also, it seems, a coward. Rather than face up to his crimes, he faked his death and ran away. This doesn't come as any surprise to anyone who knew him, because we were all well aware that he was a treacherous, subhuman wee—'

The last word was bleeped, but there wasn't a lot of imagination needed to fill it in, even for those without the most rudimentary of lip-reading abilities.

'Frazer, if you're watching this—and I know you will be, because you always did like to feel important—then you know how to find me. Give me a call, and we can end this. You and me. I know that's what you want. No one else needs to get hurt.'

On the broadcast, Logan left the statement hanging in the air, then glanced around at the assembled journalists. 'No further comment, so the lot of you can now get to fu—'

The footage looped back to the start then, the statement beginning all over again. Logan swiped it away, then returned the phone to his pocket.

'Um. That was...' Shona began, but her uncertainty was drowned out by the far more enthusiastic Olivia.

'The greatest thing I've ever seen! That was amazing!' she cheered.

Logan tried not to look pleased. 'You think?'

'Of course! I mean, he'll probably kill all those people now, but that clip's going to make you internet famous *forever*!'

Logan's smile fell away. Not at the thought of the influencers all being murdered—he'd factored that concern into his calculations before making the statement, and come to the conclusion that, as this might be the only way to save them, it was worth the risk—but at the thought of an eternity of internet infamy.

'Christ,' he muttered, then he shook his head. That was a problem for his future self. Right now, he had enough of his own.

'I need to get to work,' Shona declared, getting up from the couch. She pointed to Olivia. 'You need to go to school.'

'I can't, it's not safe,' the girl replied, like she'd had the words locked and loaded all night. 'It's too risky. You'd only worry.'

Shona and Logan both stood over her, looking down, as she did her best to look angelic. She landed quite some distance short of the desired result, but Logan nodded, all the same.

'She's right. He knows who you are. Both of you. No saying what the bastard might try.'

'Especially with you going on TV and telling everyone what an arsehole he is,' Shona said, reproachfully.

'Aye, especially after that,' Logan conceded.

'You think it's going to work? I assume you were trying to get him riled up on purpose? Otherwise, the police need to get you some sort of PR training as soon as humanly possible.'

'That was the plan,' Logan assured her. 'But whether or not it'll pay off, I don't know. I'd say time will tell, but we don't have a lot of that left.' He thought back to the video feeds playing on the Incident Room screen, and the hours ticking down into minutes. 'Somebody doesn't, anyway.'

For a moment, he looked as if he was starting to regret his televised outburst, but then he shook his head, chasing the self-doubt away. That was the point of the beer mats, and the number plate, and the message he'd been given on a remote Highland roadside all those months before. Even in the choice of some of the victims.

Kerrigan wanted him off-balance and doubting himself. He wanted him questioning every decision he made.

Well, the bastard was in for a disappointment.

'If you want to go to the hospital today, I'll get Uniform on guard outside your office door. Otherwise, those bodies can wait another day or two.' He looked out of the window, at the drab, overcast sky. 'I've a feeling that, one way or another, this whole thing'll all be over by then.'

Shona reached for his hand again, but the door to the break room was thrown open by an oncoming storm in a white shirt and shiny buttons.

'Jack? Where the—?' The Gozer stomped to a stop when he spotted the DCI. His face was strawberry red, and pulsing purple at the temples. 'There you are! My office. Now!'

Without waiting for a response, he stormed off again.

A second and a half later, his voice blustered out along the corridor. 'Not in your own time! *Now*, Jack!'

–

'Technically, it isn't your office,' Logan said, closing the door behind him.

It was daft to be winding the detective superintendent up, he knew. But, going by his colour, his expression, and the shuddering lines of his body language, the Gozer's rage levels had already been slid all the way up to eleven, so there wasn't a lot more damage the DCI could do.

'Sit down,' MacKenzie barked. He was pacing in tight circles on the other side of his borrowed desk, one hand gripping his bald head like he was trying to contain an explosion inside his skull.

'I'm fine standing, sir.'

'I don't care. Sit.'

Logan sat. Pick your battles, and all that.

'You seem stressed, sir,' he said, really poking the bear.

'Stressed? *Stressed*?! I just had my bollocks handed to me by the Assistant Chief Constable over that stupid bloody stunt you pulled on the TV this morning! I'm not stressed, Jack, I'm fucking apoplectic!'

'You can probably get an ointment for that,' Logan told him.

'An oint…?' The Gozer's jaw dropped open, and the rest of the sentence fell out. 'Is that a joke? Are you joking here?' He stabbed a finger in the direction of the window, and out across the bleak, grey city that lay beyond. 'Those people's lives are in danger! Christ, Jack, for all we know, they're already bloody dead!'

'Well, in that case, I can't have made things any worse,' Logan reasoned.

'Oh, you've made it worse! That outburst? That bloody performance on the news? That's made things *far* worse, Jack!'

The Gozer stopped pacing and leaned on the desk, the knuckles of his clenched fists pressing into the wood.

'You realise that Frazer Kerrigan is officially dead, yes, and has been for a very long time?'

Logan nodded. 'Aye. I said as much on the telly. Have you watched it?'

'Oh, I've watched it, Jack! We've all watched it!'

'Then, like I said, his body was never found.'

'Of course it fucking wasn't! It's a long fall into a deep, dirty river. You know as well as I do how many jump off there, and how many we ever pull out.'

'It's him,' Logan said. 'I know it is.'

'How, Jack? How do you know? Convince me.' The detective superintendent straightened and crossed his arms. 'Convince me that a man who died nearly twenty years ago is responsible for this current shitshow.'

Ben's voice rolled along the corridor and seeped in below the office door. 'Jack! Jack! Where are you?'

The urgency of it brought a thin, satisfied smile to Logan's lips.

'That won't be necessary, sir.' He pushed back his chair and rose to his feet, dwarfing the man on the other side of the desk. 'Probably easier if you just come with me.'

Chapter 43

Frazer Kerrigan did not look well, even for a dead man.

Almost two decades had passed since Logan had last clapped eyes on the bastard—knowingly, at least—and either the years had been exceptionally unkind, or something more than just time had been whittling the life out of him.

His skin was a patchwork of yellows and greys, and clung to the bones of his skull like clingfilm. He was almost bald, but for a few wisps of grey that stuck upwards and outwards from his pale, wrinkled scalp.

Dark, heavy half-circles hung below his bloodshot eyes, like two bulging binbags that should forever remain unopened.

His teeth seemed too big for his mouth, like he had borrowed someone else's falsers for his big on-screen appearance.

He stood in an empty cell on the feed that had been showing a tossing and turning Adam Parfitt when Logan had left the room. The 'comedian' was nowhere to be seen now, but the layout of the background was subtly different, suggesting this wasn't being broadcast from the same location.

On other videos, in other windows, the rest of the influencers lay restless in their cages.

'Hello, Jack. Long time no see.'

The voice was the one on Harold Foster's recording.

The one from Logan's memories.

'Hang on, can he see us?' Ben asked, then he relaxed when Hamza assured him that he couldn't.

'Wondered how long it would take you to figure it out. The great Detective Chief Inspector Jack Logan. Thwarter of injustice. Righter of wrongs. Champion of the fuck knows what.'

He laughed at that, and the laugh became a cough that snarled up somewhere at the back of his throat.

'I hope you've been watching. What am I saying? Course you have. Everyone has. It's a worldwide smash!' The words came slowly and hesitantly, like rushing them might make his throat give out. 'I hope you've enjoyed it. I'd like to say I did it all for you, but it wasn't really. Some of it, aye, but not all of it.'

He looked up. His neck wore a scarf of black and blue bruises. His eyes seemed far too big for their sockets as they searched the ceiling above.

'They're fucking awful, aren't they? Our lot. *People.* You didn't get that back then, but I'm sure you do now. Now that you've lived a bit. Now that you've seen them properly.'

He slowly lowered his head, and his pupils seemed to swim, like the room was spinning around him.

It took him a moment before he could continue.

'I saw it. I could see them for what they were,' Kerrigan said. 'Other people, us lot, the polis, we're hung up on who's the bad guys, and who's the good guys, but it's not that simple, is it, Jack? That's not how the world works. That's just a story we tell ourselves so we can sleep at night. We point fingers, and draw wee fucking lines on maps, and tell ourselves that our lot is better than their lot, while deep down where it counts, we know that's all bollocks.'

He coughed again. His whole body shook with the toll it took.

'We're animals who've learned to tie our fucking shoes. That's all we are. We're liars and hypocrites—'he stumbled over the pronunciation, but kept going'—pretending to be civilised, pretending to be decent. Pretending that we're *good*. I was never worried about being good. I was better than that. I was *honest*.'

'Were you fuck,' Logan muttered.

A smile crept across Kerrigan's face, almost splitting the skin of his dry, shrivelled lips. The timing of it, perfectly in sync with Logan's response, made Ben glance around for a hidden camera.

'And, you're not good, either. Are you, Jack? For all your promotions, and your accolades. You're the biggest hypocrite of them all. You play the hero, ruin my life, and then go on to build a lovely one for yourself, while I'm left rotting away. But you lied to everyone. You're no better than I am. You never have been. The only difference being, I was decent enough to keep my fucking mouth shut about what I knew.'

He raised a chicken bone of a finger and leaned a little closer to the camera.

'But, I think I've kept your secrets long enough.'

'What's he on about?' the Gozer asked, shooting Logan a sideways look that, like the question itself, went completely ignored.

There was a pause as if Kerrigan needed a moment to compose himself, before he continued in the same slightly stilted way as before.

'I'm dying, Jack. I'm sure that's pretty obvious. Cancer, we think. Can't exactly just pop in for a check-up, though. One of the downsides of being dead, and believe me, I could give you a big fucking list.'

He coughed again, as if to prove his point, then spat a wad of black, tar-like phlegm onto the floor.

'So, I got to thinking, as dying men are prone to do. I thought about all the things I regretted, and all the things I still wanted to do, and I kept coming back to you.'

He frowned, like the phrasing of the statement wasn't quite right. His gaze flitted to something off screen, before he picked up where he left off.

'I want the world to know the sort of man you really are, Jack. The polis hero. The big man. Good old Detective Chief Inspector Jack Logan. I want them to know what you did.'

There was another pause. Kerrigan looked around the screen, like he was searching for scratches on the surface of the camera's lens.

The silence dragged out a beat or two too long, then he spoke again.

'And I want you to be the one to tell them. You want to save these awful fuckers I've got down here?'

The 'here' squeaked out of him like a fart he'd been trying to hold in. His paper skin wrinkled as he grimaced, but then he quickly tried again.

'You want to save these awful fuckers I've got here? Then you're going to confess. You're going to get a camera, you're going to go on the news, and you're going to tell everyone that you're just like me, Jack. You're going to tell the whole world that you're a cold-blooded killer.'

'What the fuck is he talking about?' The Gozer demanded.

'Your life for theirs, Jack. The lovely wee life you've built for yourself. Your lovely Irish lassie. Your job. Your yappy wee fucking dog.' A snigger became a cough, but he continued to laugh through it. 'Your *freedom*. You're going to lose it all. You're going to give it all up for the sake of some horrible pieces of shit you don't even know. Because, that's what you do, isn't it? That's what you always do. And I'm going to love every fucking minute of it.'

Another fit of coughing ripped through him, until his face turned red, and blobs of black fluids frothed from his lips.

When he finally stopped, his eyes swam, struggling to find focus. He glanced off camera, frowned momentarily, then checked his watch. 'Fuck it, close enough,' he muttered, and he seemed to have forgotten that anyone was watching.

He got to his feet and the feed shut off, leaving only a blurred image of him frozen on the screen.

A shaky, uncertain silence filled the air for a few moments, before the Gozer smashed right through it.

'Does someone mind telling me what the bloody hell is going on?!'

'Boss!'

The urgency in Tyler's voice meant the detective superintendent went ignored once again. The others turned to see the DC pointing to his computer screen.

Seven videos were playing now, six of them showing one of the remaining influencers, the seventh featuring an empty cell which, by a process of elimination, had to be Elizia Shuttleworth's. She was the only one not present in the line-up. Given what her friend, Lacey, had told them, this didn't come as a major surprise.

The ordeal was clearly taking its toll on the other six. They were all red-eyed and exhausted, with a few of them crying and shaking in fear. Even Mitchell's son, Denzel, had lost all of his aggressive attitude, and now just stood holding his injured hand with his head down and his eyes lowered.

'When the hell did they stand up?' Ben asked. 'Last time I looked, they were sleeping.'

'That's the thing, boss,' Tyler said. He turned Hamza's screen so the others could see it. On there, the same six influencers were curled up on the floor of their cages. 'They're only awake on the public facing version. On the feeds we've been watching, it's different.'

Ben looked from one screen to the other, then back again. 'And what's the real one? What one's happening now?'

'Maybe neither,' Hamza said. 'They might both be recordings.'

He got to his feet, pushed his chair under his desk, then took a moment to straighten his tie and smooth down his hair.

'I need to go talk to Thomas.'

He left without saying another word. The others watched him go, but then turned back to Tyler's monitor when a burst of movement filled the frame of the previously empty seventh video.

Elizia Shuttleworth, all costume jewellery, dreadlocks, and meaningless tattoos, staggered blindly into the cell like she'd been thrown from a distance. Her momentum carried her halfway towards the back wall before her legs gave way and she fell, smashing her forehead against the rough grey brickwork.

Even though there was no audio, everyone in the room could practically hear the *thunk* of the impact.

She lay perfectly still for a second or two, then jerked suddenly, her limbs all twitching as life returned to them.

Frantically flipping over onto her back, she revealed a painter's palette of purples and reds across her face, with a particular focus on the spots where all her many piercings used to be.

Her lips were bulging and bloodied. Her nose was a twisted, monstrous reflection of its former self, swelling her whole face, and turning her eyes into deep, puffy slits.

Though her vision was constricted, she saw something off screen. Something hidden from the detectives' view.

She held up a hand.

She lowered her head.

And the speakers of Tyler's computer crackled as three gunshots rang out, painting the wall behind her with her blood and brain matter.

The camera lingered on her as she slid slowly sideways, her matted blonde hair already congealing with blobs of dark, glossy red.

DI Forde took off his glasses, massaged his eyes, then whispered an, 'Ah, God,' that might well have been offered up in prayer.

Tyler and Sinead exchanged small, anxious glances, communicating an entire conversation's worth of information in just those looks.

The Gozer lowered himself into a chair, gaze still fixed on the motionless, lifeless body of Elizia Shuttleworth, like he was expecting her to jump back up onto her feet again, and didn't want to miss a moment of it.

It was only when Logan muttered a grim, solemn, 'Fuck,' that the detective superintendent remembered all the questions he still wanted answers to.

'That stuff he said. About you. About you being a killer. What the hell was he on about, Jack?'

There was no anger behind it. He was still too shocked by what he'd just seen to raise his voice beyond a low, flat murmur.

'It's nothing,' Ben said, quickly. 'Load of shite.' He looked deliberately at Logan. 'Right, Jack?'

Logan smiled back at his old friend. Thinly. Gratefully.

Then, he turned and gazed down at the seated Gozer. 'You want to hear it? Fine. Only fair. It's high bloody time,' he said. 'But, first...' Logan turned and looked at Tyler, Sinead, and Dave. 'Somebody find me a cameraman. If it's my confession he wants, the bastard is welcome to it.'

Chapter 44

'You sure about this, Jack?'

Ben stood over the seated DCI, chewing on a cracked thumbnail and peering over the top of his glasses. A few feet away, Chad Durnett, CNN cameraman and clandestine, back-of-van masturbator, was running cables across the floor from a laptop to his tripod-mounted camera.

He had been plucked from the crowd of journalists out front, and while he had protested his innocence to the two detective constables who had brought him in, he'd jumped at the chance to be involved when they explained why they needed him.

Pausing only to fire a few raised middle fingers at his contemporaries from FOX News, he'd lugged his equipment into the meeting room where DCI Logan was already sitting solemnly behind a desk like a president about to make an address to the nation.

The detective had barely acknowledged him, and Chad had quickly set to work setting up his gear. The lighting wasn't perfect—ideally, the policeman wouldn't be sitting with his back to a window—but Chad was damned if he was going to be the one to ask him to move.

Instead, he'd mounted a couple of LED lights to portable stands either side of the desk, so the shadows were driven from the folds and crags of the detective's face.

It was to be a live broadcast. They'd insisted on that. Chad had called through to one of his contacts at the BBC, and they had been more than happy to mirror the CNN feed for UK audiences. Given all the hysteria around the case—particularly following the death of Elizia Shuttleworth—they had no issues with clearing the schedules for this urgent, yet currently mysterious, police statement.

'Jack?'

Logan blinked, like he was only just realising the DI was talking to him.

'Hm?'

'I said are you sure about this? Kerrigan's right. Go through with this, and it could be a career ender. They'll have to make an example.'

Logan drew in a breath through his nose, then nodded.

'I'm sure. High time. Should've come out and told the truth years ago.'

'To the whole bloody world, though?'

Logan shook his head. 'To you. You deserved to know. I'm sorry. I should have told you.'

Ben sniffed. 'Aye, well,' he said, but he was grateful for the acknowledgement. 'It was a helluva thing for you to carry on your own.'

Logan didn't deny it. Instead, he just checked his watch and fixed the cameraman with a look that made clear he should immediately remove all digits from all orifices and get the show on the road.

Tyler and Sinead stood over by the door at the far end of the room, neither of them quite sure what to do with themselves. As Logan watched them, Hamza stuck his head around the door, then sidled in to join the DCs.

'How do you think they're going to get on without us?' Logan asked.

Ben looked back over his shoulder at the younger detectives. He considered the question for a moment, then turned back to Logan. 'Maybe I'll hang on for a bit yet. Another year or two won't hurt.'

'Bollocks to that,' Logan said. 'I'm not having my cock-up ruining your plans. They'll be fine. They're ready. I've got faith in them.'

Ben raised an eyebrow. 'Even Tyler?'

Logan chuckled. 'Especially Tyler,' he said, and this answer seemed to please the older man immensely.

'He's a good lad,' Ben said. He looked over at them again, then nodded, coming to a decision. 'You're right. They'll be fine. We'll maybe leave breaking the news to them until this is all done, though. You confessing to killing a man and me announcing my retirement might be a bit much for one day.'

He touched his finger to his lips when he saw that Hamza was walking over to them. There an urgency to the detective sergeant's stride, but he waited until he was right by the desk and out of the cameraman's earshot before he spoke.

'Sir, you got five minutes?'

Logan glanced over to where Chad seemed to be putting the finishing touches to his set-up.

'Two, maybe. What's up?'

Hamza took a breath. 'It's, uh, it's Thomas, sir.'

Logan's eyebrows sunk lower on his forehead. 'Seriously? Now? Look, I know it can't be easy working with—'

'No, sir, it's not that. He was reviewing the footage from the feeds we accessed. And, well—'he shot a sideways look to the cameraman to make sure he wasn't listening in'—there's something I think you need to see.'

-

If Logan had been hoping for some big dramatic reveal, he was sorely disappointed.

They were all gathered back in the Incident Room, with the exception of the Gozer, who was making a pre-emptive phone apology to the Assistant Chief Constable for anything inappropriate that Logan might be going to say on his live news broadcast.

Thomas had practically hopped from foot to foot with excitement when Hamza had returned with the others, and had waited impatiently with his finger over the spacebar on his laptop while they gathered around the big TV.

Once they were all in position, he tapped the button, and six videos simultaneously began to play. They showed the influencers either sleeping or rocking on the floors of their cells. It was, Logan thought, pretty much identical to the footage that had been playing in the background for most of the night.

'What am I looking at?' he demanded. 'I've seen this.'

'Wait! Wait for it...' Thomas whispered, like he was trying not to startle some skittish wild animal. He jerked his arm up suddenly, and shouted a triumphant, 'There!'

On screen, all six influencers reacted like they'd heard his voice. Those who had been sleeping jolted awake. Those who had already been awake snapped their heads up, looking up at the ceiling in fright.

A sprinkling of dust rained down on Adam Parfitt. He spasmed like it was anthrax, then frantically brushed it out of his hair. That done, he looked up again, his eyes flitting anxiously around like he was expecting the ceiling to collapse on him.

'Happened just before Elizia Shuttleworth was killed on the livestream,' Thomas said. 'When this was playing on the direct feeds we accessed, they were all actually awake and on their feet. So, we know the timing of this was off.'

'Right,' Logan said. He had no idea where the consultant was going with this. 'Meaning?'

Thomas took a breath, like he was preparing to leap into danger. Instead, he shot a pleading look to Hamza, and the detective sergeant reluctantly stepped in.

'It's impossible to know for sure, but it's pretty safe to assume that the feeds we hacked into are running a few hours behind. None of the prisoners looked much different in the streams this morning, and since they followed on from Kerrigan's own video, it's quite likely the videos we saw of them this morning were actually live.'

Tyler pointed to the videos of the influencers currently playing on the TV. They were still looking up, as if waiting for something.

'So, you reckon these are a few hours old?'

'It's possible,' Hamza said, not fully committing to the consultant's theory. 'And, if it is, then it looks like, a few hours ago, they all heard something. Something loud enough to wake them up and shake dust from the ceiling.'

Logan took a half step closer to the screen. 'An explosion.'

Thomas clapped his hands, then pointed up at the DCI. 'An explosion!'

'Something blew up?' Tyler said, then his eyes widened. 'Oh!'

'You want to save these awful fuckers I've got down here?' Logan muttered.

Ben raised an eyebrow. 'Eh?'

'That's what he said. On the video. Kerrigan. That's what he asked me, before he corrected himself. "You want to save these awful fuckers I've got down here?"' He scratched at his chin, and pointed to where Constable Dave Davidson sat at his desk. 'Dave, see if—'

'Already done,' Dave said. He angled his screen, showing a scan of an old, yellowing map. 'There's an old lead mine. Dates back to the eighteen hundreds. Big maze of tunnels and caves.'

Logan felt the fine hairs on the back of his neck pricking up. Before he could respond, though, Hamza had one final thing to add.

'I went back over the footage from the chopper. The infrared.'

He slid into his chair, his fingers dancing across the keyboard before his arse had touched the seat. A short snippet of footage played on the screen, then looped back to the start after a second or so. In the centre, picked out in glowing reds and oranges, was the caravan that had almost killed half of the armed response team.

'What are we meant to be…?' Logan began, but he stopped when he clocked it.

There, right in the far corner, at the very edge of the frame, was a tiny orange dot.

A heat source.

'Is that—?'

'A vent, or a chimney, we think,' Hamza said. He glanced over at Thomas, who stood with his hands clasped as if trying to stop himself fidgeting with them. 'You ask me, sir? I think someone's down there.'

Logan stared at the evidence mounting on the screens around him. It was certainly compelling.

But then, he'd thought the same about the caravan, and now some good men lay broken and scarred in the ICU.

No more. Never again.

'Have you told anyone else about this?' Logan asked.

'No,' Thomas said.

'Nobody outside this room, sir,' Hamza confirmed.

Logan considered the screens. Considered his options.

Finally, he came to a decision.

'Good. Let's keep it that way for now. Not a word to anyone. Not to CID, not to Uniform, and definitely not to the Gozer.'

He eyeballed Thomas on that last one, and the consultant nodded his understanding.

'Right.'

Logan checked his watch, then looked up at the clock on the wall. It was barely nine. Elizia Shuttleworth had been killed ahead of schedule.

At least, he hoped she had. The countdown still had fifty-odd minutes to run, and continued to tick down. Votes could still be cast via the website. It was entirely possible that another influencer would be dead within the hour.

The DCI stabbed a finger in Tyler's direction. 'Right, go tell that camera guy to get onto the TV networks. I want the broadcast announced in advance. If we let the bastard know it's coming, it might keep him distracted.'

Ben frowned. 'What about all this, though?' he asked, indicating the map, and the infrared footage. 'What do we do about this?'

'Nothing.'

The others looked back at him, confused.

'What do you mean, boss?'

'Exactly what I said. We do nothing,' Logan told him. 'We keep it quiet until after I've done my bit to camera.'

'But, sir—' Sinead began.

'You've got your orders,' Logan barked back, silencing her. 'This is still my show for now. I'm still running this investigation. We do nothing. We say nothing.' He glowered around at them all, a stern headmaster before an unruly classroom. 'Is that understood?'

Reluctantly, regretfully, the team confirmed that they did.

'Right. Good. Now, Tyler, why the hell are you still here?' Logan demanded. 'Go tell that cameraman that I'm ready for my close-up.' He grimaced at the thought of what came next. 'There's just one thing I need to do first.'

—

Shona and Olivia were both fast asleep on the couch when Logan returned to the family room. Harris, who wasn't in any obvious or immediate danger, had been shipped off home under strict instructions from his big sister to go to school.

Harris had agreed, but there was a general sense that he would not *actually* be attending class. After the night he'd had, the DCI couldn't really blame the lad.

Taggart, who had been lying by Shona's feet, opened his eyes and trotted over to meet the DCI as he crept into the room, the dog's stubby tail wagging happily.

He sat by his master's side, back straight, head raised proudly, and gazed lovingly up at Logan. His brown eyes only deviated once to the detective's pocket, on the off-chance there might be some sort of treat in there with his name on it.

On this occasion there wasn't, but his disappointment was mitigated by the *scritching* of Logan's fingers behind his ears.

'You're a good dug.'

Taggart tilted his head, pressing it more firmly against Logan's hand. His tongue lolled out of his mouth, and his eyes closed in a picture of pure, contented bliss.

Logan straightened, checked his watch, then looked over at Shona. She was curled up at one end of the couch, hugging her knees in close to her chest. Her hair was plastered across her face like she'd been caught in a high wind, and gravity had pulled her chin down, dragging her mouth open.

No doubt, she'd be horrified to be seen like that. But she was, he thought, just about the most beautiful thing he'd ever laid eyes on.

He wanted to wake her. He wanted to say sorry.

To say goodbye.

Instead, he tiptoed over, leaned down, and planted the lightest of kisses on the top of her head.

He realised then that Olivia had her eyes open. They were narrow slits, and he froze for a moment, hoping she'd drift off again.

Instead, she blinked, trying to rouse herself fully.

'It's fine. Go back to sleep,' he whispered.

She wriggled against the cushion, getting comfortable. 'You OK?' she asked, being careful not to wake the sleeping pathologist.

Logan nodded. 'I will be. Go to sleep.'

She flashed him a tired smile, crossed her arms, and closed her eyes.

By the time he was back standing by the door, her breathing had become slow and shallow.

He stole another look—just one more—then gave Taggart another pat.

'You're a good, daft wee dug,' he whispered.

And then, DCI Jack Logan stepped out of the room, closed the door behind him, and went to face his fate.

Chapter 45

Frazer Kerrigan sat on the hard plastic seat of an old school chair, transfixed by the image flickering away on the ancient CRT television. The TV sat on a stack of crates that, according to the writing stamped on the side, had once contained explosives. It, and others like it, now made up the majority of the furnishings in the place.

He'd considered breaking a few up and using them as firewood on the nights when the cold was biting through to his bones, but the timber was too damp, and he couldn't shake the nagging fear that some trace dynamite residue might detonate and take his face off.

If he knew it would be a large enough explosion to finish the job, he'd consider it. But, knowing his luck, he'd just be blinded, or paralysed, or have his bollocks flambéed to a crisp.

He hated this life. Loathed it. He had been happy once, he thought. Even after everything that had happened—after his arrest, after his confession, after Shuggie Cowan—he'd found happiness.

But that was all gone now. That had all been taken from him, too.

On screen, a dark-skinned detective sergeant was sitting behind a desk, shuffling papers around and preparing to address the camera. According to a hushed voiceover, he was going to say a few words, then introduce DCI Logan.

A breaking news ticker at the bottom of the image announced that it was all part of a live statement by Police

Scotland on the current state of the investigation, and on the welfare and whereabouts of the influencers.

That was the official story. Kerrigan knew different, of course. Kerrigan knew the truth, and what would happen next.

'Thank you for coming at such short notice,' the man on the screen intoned. He shuffled the papers again, then set them down on the desk and placed his crossed hands on top of them. 'I'll start by recapping what's happened over the past seventy-two hours, then bring on the senior investigating officer on the case, who will be making a short statement.'

Frazer Kerrigan gripped the sides of his chair, and metal clanked against the plastic. This was it. This was the moment he'd spent so many long, cold nights dreaming about.

What was about to unfold was something he'd been waiting to witness for almost two decades—the downfall of the man who had ruined his life.

The end of DCI Jack Logan.

–

Dave's map did all the heavy lifting. The entrance to the old mine was about a quarter of a mile from the caravan site, and had it not been for Hamza punching the co-ordinates into the DCI's phone, and the fact that the sun was now creeping up the sky, Logan would never have found it.

It lay hidden behind a crop of straggly rowan and juniper trees, and a scattering of moss-covered rocks that looked perfectly natural, but could feasibly only have been put there on purpose.

There was a lot of police activity still going on up at the caravan site. The bomb squad and Scene of Crime teams were both working their way through the other vans, and picking over the remains of the one that had blown up.

Logan's size made getting through the trees more difficult, but helped immensely when it came to shifting the rocks. They rolled aside easily, the moss and stone marked with scrapes and scratches that suggested they'd been moved around on a regular basis.

There had been tyre tracks in the mud back beyond the line of trees. A match for the missing minibus, he guessed.

An old metal gate blocked the path leading downwards into the mine. Exhalations of cool air whistled out between the rusted spars. It tasted damp. Metallic. Rancid. Like the final dying breaths of some ancient and terrible beast.

A bike lock, stark in its newness, held the gate in its frame. It was one of the expensive ones, too, and would take a thief with an angle grinder a good three-to-four seconds to cut through.

Unfortunately, Logan didn't think to bring any power tools.

Luckily, he had something even better.

Gripping a bar in each hand, he planted his feet, gritted his teeth, and pulled. Centuries old iron groaned under the strain. Long-seized bolts creaked in their fastenings. Logan's shoulders burned. His jaw clenched. Arms like tree branches shook with the effort.

And then, with a screech of metal and a cracking of stone, the gate tore free of its hinges and swung down, the bike lock now the only thing holding it in place.

Logan took a moment to shake the tension from his arms, and to let some of the blood rush back in. Then, with a quick glance back over his shoulder, he squeezed his enormous frame through the hole he had created, turned on his torch, and shuffled unsteadily down five or six rough, uneven steps hewn from the rocky floor.

The steps felt greasy beneath his feet. Slippery. He picked his way down them carefully. He couldn't risk falling. Not now, not down here.

Not when he was alone in the domain of a ruthless, cold-blooded killer.

They'd objected, of course. They'd told him they wouldn't let him come on his own.

But no one else was getting hurt because of his mistakes. His secrets would ruin nobody else's lives.

The steps stopped, but the sloping stone floor continued downwards into the bowels of the Earth. Even here, just a few metres from the entrance, the light was struggling to push back against the dark.

Another few cautious paces, and the shadows drew in around him, draping everything in a thick, smothering blanket of black.

The beam from Logan's torch seemed powerless against the weight of it all. Pointing it ahead, it did nothing but slightly alter the texture of the darkness. Shining it against the walls painted a weak oval of yellow on the stone. When he aimed it at the ceiling a foot or two above his head, it reflected off a thousand tiny water droplets, making them sparkle like diamonds.

He trod carefully, but the sound of each step seemed to *boing* off the curved tunnel walls, echoing back at him like some warped, distorted version of itself. Like the rules of reality no longer quite applied.

The air became colder. Earthier. There was a sourness to it, like it had been tainted by its history.

Or by its present.

The torchlight picked out some ancient wooden spars that lined the ceilings and propped up the walls. Black mould and rot ate into them, chewing through the timber. They'd been there for hundreds of years. They'd held out this long.

Just a few more hours. That was all he needed from them. Just a few short hours more.

The tunnel walls and ceiling narrowed as he crept onwards, downwards, into the dark. According to the map Dave had dug up, this main shaft ran on for a couple of hundred yards before branching out into a labyrinth of tunnels and caverns.

Logan ducked his head and tucked in his shoulders. The rasp of his breathing was a roar in the tight, narrow space. His torch was a candle in an ocean of black.

Two hundred yards. A claustrophobic passageway. A killer with a vendetta on the loose.

It was going to be a very long walk.

The Gozer sat in the Incident Room, back straight, hands on his knees like he was struggling with a challenging bowel movement. His eyebrows were knotted together, his forehead furrowed into deep, down-curved lines of concern. If he still had hair, it'd be falling out of his head in big silver clumps.

On the telly, Hamza was yet to introduce Logan to the cameras. Despite all the Detective Superintendent's efforts to find out what the DCI was going to say, everyone had played dumb, and MacKenzie was starting to get a bad feeling about where all this was headed.

Across the room, Ben sat by his computer, unable to bring himself to watch. He knew what was coming once Jack got on screen. And he knew what it would mean.

A throat was cleared somewhere behind him, quietly so that only he heard it. He turned in his chair to find Tyler standing in the doorway, beckoning him over.

Ben checked to make sure the Gozer was still distracted, then got up from his desk and made to leave.

'Where are you going?'

Ben stopped and looked back at the detective superintendent, who was turned in his seat and squinting at him over the long, sharp beak of his nose.

'Tea run. Gasping. You want one?'

The Gozer's frown, which already looked like it had been hewn from stone, solidified further. His gaze crept to the mug on the DI's desk, and Ben silently cursed himself.

'God, nearly forgot to bring this,' he said, shuffling back to collect it. He drained half an inch of room temperature dregs from the bottom, and grimaced. 'You sure you don't want anything?'

On screen, Hamza continued to talk. The Gozer's stare bored into DI Forde, like he could drill right through his skull and watch the secrets come spilling out.

When that failed to happen, he shook his head dismissively, and turned back to the TV. Ben continued, very slowly and casually, across the room, then found Tyler standing out in the corridor with his back pressed against the wall, like he was trying to merge with the faded paintwork.

'I can see you, son,' Ben said.

Tyler looked confused for a moment, then realised he'd been instinctively trying to turn himself invisible. He relaxed, darted a quick, anxious look at the Incident Room door, then made a series of complex hand gestures that meant nothing to Ben, and probably not a whole lot to anyone else, either.

When the detective constable set off scampering down the corridor, the DI shrugged and followed behind him. Tyler stopped outside a meeting room door, looked around to make sure nobody was watching, then opened it and ushered Ben inside.

Sinead was pacing back and forth, criss-crossing the limited floorspace. She almost walked straight into a wall when Ben and Tyler entered, but stopped in the nick of time.

'We alright?' Ben asked, looking around at both DCs.

'No,' Sinead said, not beating around the bush. 'I'm terrified, sir. This is madness. We know Kerrigan's dangerous. Jack shouldn't be doing this himself.'

'Of course he bloody shouldn't,' Ben agreed. He rolled one of the room's two chairs out from under its only desk, and the weight on his shoulders pushed him down into it. 'But I get it. Why he wants to do it alone, I mean. He doesn't want to put anyone else at risk. He won't. Not for himself.'

'But Kerrigan might kill the other influencers, sir,' Sinead pointed out.

'Or he might kill the boss,' Tyler added.

Ben didn't react. Clearly, he'd already considered that possibility.

'Kerrigan's old. He's at death's door. Jack can handle him.'

Sinead continued to protest. 'He's got a gun! He's already shot and killed multiple people!'

'Jack can handle him,' Ben said again, but it lacked enough conviction to persuade anyone.

'That's just it, though,' Tyler said, 'Hamza and that arsehole, Thomas, went over the footage from Kerrigan's broadcast earlier. When he spoke to the boss directly.'

Ben raised his eyebrows. 'And?'

'And, well—'the DC glanced at his wife'—they don't think he's working on his own.'

Chapter 46

The earth itself was groaning, like it objected to Logan worming his way through its veins and arteries. His breath billowed before him, a fine, misty vapour that danced for a moment in the torchlight, then was lost to the surrounding darkness.

Despite the cold, or perhaps because of it, he could feel his shirt sticking to his back, the fabric damp. Clinging. He was grateful for his coat, but burdened by it, the weight of it proving both a comfort and a hindrance as he squeezed through yet another narrowing of the passageway.

He had continued in a straight line, following the downward incline until it had slowly levelled off, ignoring all the many shrouded passageways branching off from the main shaft. And yet, though he hadn't strayed from the path, he felt like he was lost, wandering aimlessly, cast adrift in a darkness so thick it felt like a solid and tangible thing.

An invisible metallic residue formed rich seams in the air, and each inward breath coated his tongue with the taste of blood.

He was deep underground, he thought, though he couldn't be sure. After the initial descent, the path had risen and fallen beneath his feet, and he'd lost track of the number of ups and downs, much less the angle or the distance. He could be two hundred feet below the surface, or twenty. He had no way of knowing.

He'd got used to the way sound worked down here. It obeyed its own laws, the distant dripping of water or skittering of falling stones, which would usually go unnoticed, booming off the walls like varying shades of thunder.

His breathing roared. His footsteps *kaboomed*. Every brush of his coat against the tunnel walls brought the sound of an avalanche rushing along with it.

And, up ahead, somewhere in the darkness, Hamza's voice, his words twisting and overlapping themselves, came rolling up to greet him.

Logan turned off the torch. Ahead, where the passageway curved to the left, the faintest suggestion of light danced and flickered across the walls.

The DCI clenched his fists and steadied his nerves. A cloud of white billowed from his lips as he whispered, 'Gotcha.'

–

'Fucking hurry up!'

Kerrigan rocked impatiently in his chair. It squeaked, but otherwise remained firmly fixed to the metal plate on the cavern floor.

On screen, the detective sergeant was meticulously going over every element of the case so far, recapping everything, all the tiny details that had already been pored over by the press and social media a million times before.

But, the camera had just cut to Logan now entering from the wings, a small stack of index cards looking tiny in his hands.

'Yes! Yes, here we go!'

The confession was coming. Any moment now.

But every second of waiting was agony.

Kerrigan kicked out a foot, but the TV was too far away for him to get as much as a toe to it. Even if he'd really wanted to.

'What are you doing? What's taking so long?' He barked at the screen. 'You hoping the cancer'll kill me before you get to the big reveal?'

'Something like that.'

Metal rattled as Kerrigan jumped upright in his seat, hissing out a strangled, 'Fuck!' of surprise.

He tried to turn, but the chair wouldn't let him, and all he could do was to twist his head and crane his neck, and try to look back over his shoulder to where a giant in a damp and dirty overcoat now blocked the only available exit.

'How the…?' Kerrigan's yellowed, sunken eyes went from Logan to Logan, there in the flesh, and in the washed out colours of the old television set. He looked again at the 'Breaking News: Live' ticker, and couldn't hide his confusion. 'What the—? How are you here? You're not meant to be here, you're meant to be there! You're there! It's live! It says it's fucking live! You shouldn't be here!'

His voice was a throaty croak, and his eyes brimmed with hot, salty tears. He still hadn't turned all the way. Still hadn't risen from the chair.

'We took a leaf out of your book, Frazer. We recorded my bit earlier and had them play it like it was live.' He squinted at the screen, listened, then nodded when he realised how far into the broadcast they were. 'There's ages yet. DS Khaled goes through all the influencers' social media handles, ages, last known movements, the works. Thought it might keep you distracted for a while.'

The other man's expression was blank. Bewildered. If Logan didn't know better, he'd have sworn that he didn't understand what the hell the detective was on about.

But he did understand. He had to.

Didn't he?

The detective's eyes inched down to the metal plate on the floor beneath Kerrigan's feet. To the bolts fastening his chair to it.

And to the thick, heavy chains securing the bastard's withered legs in place.

Logan's gaze was drawn to a camera fixed to a tripod in the corner. The screen of an iPad reflected off a sheet of darkened glass in front of the lens, the last few words of Kerrigan's speech from earlier still visible at the top.

An autocue. Those words, the things he'd said, they hadn't been his. Not really. He'd been reading them.

'Wait. What the hell is this?' Logan demanded, but his mind was already racing, readjusting, slotting it all together.

He watched as Kerrigan raised a gnarled, trembling finger to his lips. The chained man's eyes were wide, the pupils adrift in a sea of yellow and red.

'I shouldn't have raised my voice,' he said, his voice dropping into a raw, ragged whisper. 'I shouldn't have shouted.' His gaze shifted, focusing on the darkened passageway at Logan's back. 'She doesn't like it when people shout.'

A footstep rang out, the sound rolling around in the cavern, and bouncing back in all directions. The detective spun around, heart racing, fists raised.

He stopped dead when he saw the muzzle of the handgun pointed between his eyes. The hand holding it was as steady as the rocky walls around them. It didn't shake. Not even a tremble.

'Oh,' Logan muttered, as the pistol's hammer drew back. 'Shite.'

Chapter 47

He knew. On some level, he'd known from the moment he'd seen the chains. Before that, even. From the second he'd seen the complete lack of understanding on Frazer Kerrigan's face. This was not a man who could co-ordinate an operation like this. Once, maybe, but that was a long time ago.

That man was long dead.

And that meant there was only one likely explanation for all this. Only one person who could be holding that pistol.

Make-up videos. TV career. All the know-how and contacts needed to pull this off.

An obsession with toys, and with making them act out the roles she'd created for them.

A New Player has Entered the Game.

'Put the gun down, Kelly,' Logan spoke into the shadows. 'It's over.'

Kelly Wynne snorted and pressed into the room, the threat of the firearm forcing Logan to retreat a few careful paces. Her bulky frame was picked out in the flickering glow of the TV screen. Her shy, uncertain language from the earlier footage had been replaced by something sharper and more deliberate.

'Over for you, maybe,' she said, displaying the same lack of wit that had led to her receiving the least amount of public support the day before, and doomed her to be the first of the influencers to be executed.

Although, just like her father, reports of her death had clearly been exaggerated.

'You're not meant to be here,' she said.

Kerrigan's chains clanked as he shifted in his chair. 'That's what I said. That's what I told him,' he babbled. 'I said that. I said that!'

'Shut up!' Kelly hissed. Gone was the toy-loving cat lady from her YouTube channel. Logan doubted her audience would even recognise this person at all. She swallowed back her anger, and though her tone became softer, it dripped with malice. 'This is all your fault. You brought him here. You did this. You told him how to find us.'

'I told you, it was an accident!' Kerrigan protested.

The gun twitched. Her eyes darkened, deflecting the flickering light of the television. 'You forgot again. You forgot to say it.'

Logan saw Kerrigan wincing, like he was recoiling from an expectation of pain, or from the memory of it.

'Sweetheart!' the man in the chair spluttered. 'I told you it was an accident, *sweetheart*.'

Logan found himself deflecting attention from the man, decades of protective instinct taking over. 'I tend to go where I'm not wanted. Bad habit,' he said. 'Now, why don't you put the gun down, Kelly, and we can talk? You can tell me what all this is about.'

At the other end of the pistol, and well beyond Logan's reach, Kelly scowled. It wasn't a particularly attractive face at the best of times, but now, riddled as it was with contempt, it was like a gargoyle's skelped arse.

'You mean you haven't figured it all out yet?' Kelly sneered. 'I thought you were meant to some big clever detective? You don't seem so smart to me.'

Logan shouldn't have risen to it. He knew that. He should've kept her calm, kept her talking, tried to win her round and persuade her that he was only looking out for her best interests. Convinced her that he was on her side, and there to help.

But, it had been a long day and, quite frankly, he'd had enough.

'OK,' he said, sighing wearily. 'I got your old man busted. He went on the run, leaving you and your mother alone. She was abusive, I'm guessing, though maybe not in the traditional sense.'

He looked her up and down, thinking on his feet. 'A feeder. Overcompensating for your daddy issues by stuffing you full of cake, and buying you all the toys you could want. So, not abusive, I take that back, but not a healthy parental figure, either. Smothered you for years, I bet. Terrified of losing you, too. Bet she was driven to drink, wasn't she? Different men coming in?' He studied her face, then nodded. 'Aye. A whole parade of them. Must've been hell.'

Kelly was still staring at him, but he was sure he saw the slightest tremble of the gun then. Just a flicker, just for a moment.

'Right, I'm close, then,' he said.

He rubbed his hands together, getting into the swing of things. She eyed them warily, like he might make a grab for her.

'So, your poor old mum… what? Dies? Leaves you? Dies. She'd never leave you, not if she could help it. She dies. Long and drawn out, too. Nasty. You look after her, but it's hard. You find yourself wishing she would go. That she'd just hurry up and fucking die, so you didn't have to look at her. So you could move on.'

Logan stopped. Sniffed. Gave a small, sad shake of his head. 'And then she does, and you feel nothing but guilt. You feel it's your fault, that you should've done more for her. You're suddenly all alone in the world. But then, somehow, you find out that you're not. You find out that your old man is still alive. That he's been out there the whole time, ignoring you both. Letting you both struggle on, convinced that he's dead. Letting you suffer through your poor mum's illness alone.'

He turned away from the gun and looked down at the shrivelled Kerrigan chained to the chair. Beyond him, on the screen, the recording of Logan built towards his big confession.

341

'How am I doing so far, Frazer?' he asked.

It was all Kerrigan could do to fight back his tears.

'I'll take that as a thumbs up,' Logan said, directing his attention back to the woman with the gun. 'Was it his cancer? Is that why he came looking for you? What was it? Did he want to say goodbye before the end, or was he just looking for a bit of sympathy? Some cash, maybe, to make his last few months a bit more comfortable?'

The shaking of the gun was more noticeable now. Kelly switched the weapon from one hand to the other, then took another sudden step into the cavern, forcing Logan back. Her toe hit a pebble, and the sound of it ricocheted off the walls and low ceiling.

'But your mum wasn't comfortable, was she, Kelly? She didn't have that luxury. Her death was slow, and painful, and messy.'

'Stop,' Kelly hissed.

'You had to sit there and watch her wasting away. Shrinking away into her own shit and piss.'

She lunged forward another big pace, keeping the gun trained between the detective's eyes. 'Shut up!' she roared, and the echo turned her voice into a chorus that bounced around and gradually faded back into claustrophobic silence.

Logan pointed to the man in the chair. 'He didn't deserve your sympathy, did he? He didn't deserve anything. You hated him when he came back. But you hate me, too.'

'You stole him from us!' Kelly hissed, spraying flecks of foam that danced in the flickering light from the TV screen. 'If it wasn't for you, he'd have been around! He could've helped her. He could've looked after us!'

Logan nodded slowly, getting a clearer picture of things now. 'You were young, weren't you? When she died. What are we talking, Kelly? Late teens, early twenties.'

She said nothing. Kerrigan, however, answered for her.

'Nineteen.'

She turned the gun on him, her voice cracking as she warned him to stop talking, dared him to say another word. He raised his hands and bowed his head, cowed by the threat of the weapon.

'Christ. Nineteen, dealing with all that, and all alone in the world. That would drive anyone mad, Kelly.' Logan glanced around at the cave, and the dying man chained to the chair. 'I mean, you've maybe over egged the pudding a bit, but I get it. I understand.'

'You don't know anything about me,' Kelly said, and there was a sneering tone to the reply. 'No one does. Not you, not him, nobody. You read all that stuff you said. You read it all in a file.'

Logan shook his head. 'No. Lucky guesses, mostly. Well, that and a bit of experience. See, I've dealt with the likes of you before. People who've been hurt so badly that they think that makes it OK for them to hurt others. But, it doesn't, Kelly. If anything, it makes what you're doing worse.'

He tried to edge a few inches closer to her, but she had the presence of mind to compensate by stepping back. Still, he was the one advancing now. He had her on the back foot.

'It sounds daft, I know, but see suffering, Kelly? It's a privilege, in a way. Gives us an insight into the world we'd never otherwise have. It lets us empathise in a way that people who haven't suffered never can.

'It's why, even after everything I've seen, after all the mad and bad bastards I've dealt with, I haven't given up on people.' He gave a tilt of his head, conceding that wasn't fully true. 'I mean, I have a bit, but I'm still hopeful that they'll somehow find a way to surprise me. Maybe you'll be the first.'

He smiled at her. She didn't return it. Instead, she swapped the gun from hand to hand again, and kept it trained on him.

At the far end of the rounded cavern, the TV version of Logan was now sitting centre stage, recapping the events leading up to Elizia Shuttleworth's death. Another few minutes, and he'd start spilling his guts about what had happened in Glasgow all those decades before.

His confession, finally, was just minutes away.

'Right, so, just so I've got all this straight in my head,' Logan began. 'Your dad rocks up. Year ago, maybe less, I'm guessing. You don't take too kindly to it. You think about killing him, but killing's too good for him. And anyway, you'd spent nearly twenty years being controlled by someone else. Being bullied in school. Laughed at by the other kids for your size, and the fact that your dad wasn't around. Kids can be cruel wee bastards, can't they?'

She found herself nodding in reply, but stopped just as quickly as she'd started. Still, it was more than enough to steer Logan in the right direction.

'You wanted to be the one in charge for a while. The one doing the pushing around. It was your turn, high bloody time,' Logan said, and he almost seemed to be cheering her on. 'So, even before your dad turned up, you'd started digging up dirt on people and blackmailing them. Just for a bit of fun at first, but then it escalated. You got off on the power of it, of being able to make them do what you wanted. All those professional people—*proper* people—living in terror of shy, mousy Kelly Wynne with the boxes of toys and the eating disorder. You loved it, didn't you?' He raised his eyebrows, like he was just realising something important for the first time. 'You deserved it.'

'I did. I deserved it,' she replied, murmuring like she was being held in some sort of hypnotic trance.

Affirmation did that to certain types of people, Logan had learned, and Kelly fit at least three of those categories.

'Bloody right you did. Fair's fair,' Logan assured her. 'How did you find out all that stuff about them, though? All their secrets?'

Kelly shrugged, still mesmerised. 'I watched them, that's all. You can do that when nobody pays any attention to you. You can see things they'd hide if they knew you were there.'

344

'What made you kill those people, though?' Logan pressed.

'Which ones?'

She blinked, like she was surprised by her answer. Logan wasn't, much as he'd have liked to have been.

'Any of them.'

Kelly shrugged. For a woman her age, the movement seemed too young, and far too obnoxious. Had she stuck at nineteen, he wondered? Had her mother's death kept her at that age, trapped and stunted?

'Practice. And because I wanted to see if I could.' Her smile crept up on her, but she was powerless to fight it. Or, she didn't even try. 'And I could. Turns out it's easy. You just point and shoot.' She stomped a foot and cried, 'Bang!'

The sound expanded to fill the cavern, ricocheted around it, then went rolling up the tunnel, repeating itself every few yards until it finally faded into silence.

Beside him, Logan heard Kerrigan snivel and whimper. He was practically bowing in his chair, his head bent so far forward he looked like he was bracing for impact.

Further up the tunnel, falling pebbles clattered against the rough stone floor, then clacked and cracked their way down one of the sections of slope. The sound may as well have been right there in the cave with them.

'You killed them for fun?' Logan asked.

Kelly shook her head. 'No. Not fun. None of this was *fun*,' she spat back at him. 'I did it because…'

Her voice tailed away. She frowned, like she had no idea where that sentence had been heading.

'It doesn't matter,' she said. 'I just wanted to know that I could, if I ever needed to.'

'And then your dad comes back, and you want to kill him, don't you, Kelly? That's your first thought. But then, he tries to explain where he's been, and what's happened. And that's when you find out about me.'

Kelly shook her head. 'Wrong!' she cried, and the echo sniggered back at Logan from all directions. 'I knew about you for years, since my mum told me what you'd done. I wanted to kill you for making my dad jump off that bridge. I wanted to make you suffer, like I did.

'So, I followed you for a while. Remember that day you were in Largs with your daughter and your girlfriend? I was two seats away. I had a bottle of acid in my pocket. I was going to throw it on one of you, right in your face. Your daughter, probably. She's pretty. But, I couldn't do it. I chickened out.'

She looked disgusted at herself, like she was going to be sick.

'Pathetic. That's when I knew I had to start rehearsing. If I was going to kill you, I needed the practice. And so, I did. I practised. Over, and over, and over. Homeless. Junkies. Nobody anyone would miss. I wanted to be ready. Not animals, though, I didn't hurt animals. What sort of sicko hurts animals?'

The gun was getting heavy again. She switched hands. Logan considered making a grab for it, but the thought dragged its heels, and the chance was gone.

She sensed what he was planning and marched towards him, forcing him to back all the way up to the TV.

'The first few were rough. They were messy, and I panicked. But I got better. I used to hate the sight of blood when I started, but now I don't. Not after so many. You'll never find them all, though.' Her voice became a childlike squeak, imitating the voice of one of the characters from her toy videos. 'Not if you look for a *fousand, miwwion* years.'

The corners of her mouth tugged up, taunting him. 'They won't find you, either. I wanted you to end up in prison. I wanted everyone to hate you. That would've been funny.' Her finger tightened against the trigger. 'But this'll do.'

There was a sudden clank. A lunge. A roar. Kerrigan hit her with all he had, and all that the chains around his legs would allow. She stumbled, off-balance, but kept hold of the gun.

Logan made a dive for her, but she was fast for her size. Too fast. The butt of the pistol's handle cracked him across the temple. The world spun, like the rounded cavern was the inside of a ball rolling down a steep hill, picking up speed.

Though he couldn't focus, he got the impression of the gun being turned on him, and threw himself blindly into the darkness of the tunnel mouth, just as heat, and fire, and noise erupted behind him.

In the confined space, the sound of the gunshot was a cannon firing. A thunderclap. A nuclear blast. It set the air ablaze and filled his ears with a sudden pressure that pressed in until it became pain.

The *pah-chink* of the bullet striking stone reverberated like the final cymbal crash of a drum solo, then Logan tumbled into the darkness, fumbled along the wall, and ducked into the first passageway he found.

Kerrigan's voice was a squeal of panic. 'Wait, no, no, no, sweetheart, no, please—'

His life was ended by another flash of light against the wall. Another bang. Another endless echo that raced up the slope and down again, crashing into itself on the return trip.

Logan waited, blinded, breath held, until the din had died down. He listened for footsteps, but heard nothing.

Nothing but her voice, squeaky, and high-pitched, and childish.

'Come out, come out, *whewever* you are!'

A metal bullet casing *chinked* against the stone floor. A slide mechanism snapped sharply into place.

And the hunt was on.

Chapter 46

She was trying her best not to breathe, but her weight, and the exertion of the last few minutes, meant she was failing badly. Usually, that low, rasping wheeze would have helped Logan work out where she was, but the acoustics in the mine were all wrong, and whichever way he turned in the darkness, the sound came from dead ahead.

He crept on, winding his way through branching passageways, deeper and deeper into the bowels of the Earth. He could feel it pressing down on him, the weight of all that rock and dirt held up by history, and hope, and a few rotten timbers.

His torch was gone. He had no idea what had happened to it, but he assumed he'd dropped it in his rush to get out of the firing line. There was still the flashlight feature on his phone, but if he switched it on, he gave her a target.

He'd seen the efficiency with which she had killed before, and doubted she'd miss him a second time.

As he snuck on, the toe of a boot clipped a loose shard of stone and sent it skidding away across the floor. Each bouncing *thack* was amplified a thousandfold, echoing urgently, the sound swelling until it filled the mineshaft like the chattering of hungry teeth.

An orange oval blazed against the curve of a wall half a dozen feet behind him as Kelly snapped on her torch, then blinked it off again just as quickly.

'Don't wun and hide fwom me,' she sang. 'That's not a vewy nice thing to do!'

Logan knew she was behind him somewhere, but her voice was a shrill sing-song from his left, from up ahead, from right there in his ear.

There was no reason, he assured himself, why his should be any different, and any less disorientating for his pursuer.

'Why did you do it, Kelly?' he asked.

There was another blast of light, but pointing in a different direction this time, and driving back the shadows on another wall.

'I told you why. Because you took my Daddy!'

She was still talking like a child. It was unsettling in the darkness. And, Logan thought, if this was the usual patter she did on her videos, it was little wonder she was the first one picked to die.

That had all been a lie, of course. All a plan of her own design.

'That's bollocks. Frazer made his own choices.'

She giggled. The pitch of it carried quickly through the darkness, and he spun, convinced she was standing right behind him.

Even if she was, though, the darkness down here was absolute. She could be two feet away, and he wouldn't know.

'Oh, I know. That's why I had to punish him, too,' Kelly said, dropping the child's voice in favour of her own flatter, duller tones. 'To be honest, I'd been planning something like this for a while, then when he turned up, I thought I could kill three birds with one stone. Use him to ruin your life, like you ruined mine. Then, kill him and make it look like this whole thing was his doing, and I come out as the only survivor. I'd be famous. They'd make movies. No one would be making fun of me then. Nobody would be laughing.'

Her voice was like dozens of different people all talking in the round. A few seconds after Logan heard start of the sentence the first time, a second version would sound, then a third, and a fourth, until her voice filled the tunnel.

'Everyone saw you getting shot,' Logan reminded her. 'How were you going to explain that?'

'I'd tell the truth. It was a camera trick. Clever make-up. I'd say he didn't want to kill his special little girl. I'd tell them he loved me too much.'

Logan laughed at that. The torchlight snapped on just ahead of him, forcing him to draw back into a branching side tunnel. She'd somehow passed him and got in front. Clearly, she knew her way around this place. Better than he did, at any rate.

'Don't laugh!' she hissed from all around him. 'Don't you laugh at me!'

'You think people would buy that? You think they'd believe you weren't involved?'

'It doesn't matter what people think of you, or say about you,' Kelly said, and it sounded like a mantra she'd repeated a thousand times before. Something her mother had told her, perhaps. 'And anyway, they wouldn't be able to prove anything. I've been very careful.'

'Except you haven't, though. Have you, Kelly? You've made one very big mistake.'

He heard her worry in the fading of his echo. Her silence was deafening in the tight, narrow mineshaft.

'No, I haven't,' she insisted. 'I can blame everything on him. All the blackmailing, all the dead people. I've thought of everything.'

'Not everything,' Logan insisted. He slid along a wall, feeling his way through the darkness. The air felt different up ahead, like the path might be leading him towards a way out. 'What about the delivery man you sent to my house?'

Another pause. Another moment of concern.

'What about him? He was just a delivery man. He didn't know anything.'

'Didn't he?'

This time, she didn't hesitate, sensing his bluff. 'No. He didn't. He was literally just a courier. He had no idea what was even in the parcel, let alone anything else. Now, the guy who drove the minibus and broke into your house and left the beermat by your bed? The one who told you to smile? He knew a lot.'

The little girl's voice returned. It made her sound like a totally different person, and it carried differently around the network of tunnels.

'But he'll never be able to tell anyone about it, ever, ever, ever!' She giggled, and her voice dropped back to its usual dull register. 'He blew up in a caravan. Adapted land mine. Amazing what you can get online these days.'

Logan was about to reply when he backed up to something solid. A wall, he thought, then spindly, grasping fingers tangled in his hair. He hissed and pulled free, and heard a panicked whisper of, 'Please, get me out,' from the darkness.

There was movement on his left, and on his right.

'Help!' a voice croaked. 'Please, help us!'

Logan pressed a finger to his lips, but the shadows were too dense, too solid for anyone to see.

'Who's there? Help! Please!'

They were whispering, but the tunnel was an amplifier, and the sound rushed off along it to clipe on his whereabouts.

'Shh,' he urged. 'Everyone stop—'

A gunshot rang out, the sound striking him like a double-handed slap to the ears that brought instant tinnitus and pain.

The beam of the torch blinded him, drawing a hiss of shock from his lips. He raised a hand to shade his eyes, and as he turned away he saw a row of cages, faces pressed up against the wire mesh, fingers wriggling through the gaps like they were trying to detach and make their own breaks for freedom.

He recognised them all from the Big Board, and from the video feeds. A line of cameras on tripods stood facing the prisoners in their cells. Logan had to be caught on at least two of them, he reckoned.

If they were broadcasting live. If someone was watching...

'They're just recording. Nobody's seeing this. Not yet,' Kelly said. She was an adult again, and spoke in a flat, matter-of-fact style. 'I can edit it later to help back up my story.' She waved at him with the pistol. 'You've actually helped me by coming here. That's funny, isn't it? I can edit my dad's voice into this clip.'

She took a few paces to her left, keeping the torch trained on him, then slapped her foot down on a plate on the floor.

Instantly, light flooded from a series of linked video lights that stood on tall stands just a few feet behind each camera. It drove back the shadows, chasing them from the cages and revealing the influencers.

The living, and the dead.

Elizia Shuttleworth lay sprawled on the floor, half of her head tangled in her dreadlocks, and one tattooed breast exposed.

'Why did you kill her? She was helping you,' Logan said, and though the placement of the lights made it hard to see any of the details on Kelly's face, he thought he caught a flicker of surprise there.

'I needed her to persuade this lot to come,' she said, gesturing around with the gun. 'I needed them to make this all a spectacle, so the whole world would be watching when you confessed to being a murderer.'

She put the back of a hand to the side of her mouth, like she was sharing a secret.

'My dad told me about that, in case you were wondering? He didn't actually want to. He was weirdly protective of you, actually, but I made him tell me a lot of things.'

She sniggered like a child again, and Logan felt a shiver run down his spine at the thought of what she might have done to her father.

'So, we needed them all to be here. To be killed on camera, one by one, so we could force you to confess in front of the whole world. Global fame. No hiding from it. No brushing it under the carpet. We were supposed to get through a few more before you figured it out, but that's fine. I can adapt. I'm more flexible than I look.'

She winked at the gamer, Matthew Broderick, who hadn't uttered a word since Logan's arrival.

'Amn't I, Matty? You know how well I can bend.'

The seventeen-year-old looked down at his feet, more mortified than afraid. Kelly laughed, enjoying his discomfort.

'I needed to bring them, but they wouldn't listen to fat, frumpy old Kelly, with her funny voices and silly toys. But sexy Elizia, with her cool hair and tattooed tits? If she said it was a good idea, they'd go for it.'

Logan looked around at them all, barely able to hide his disgust. 'So, you all knew about it? You were all going to fake your own kidnappings?'

'Of course they did,' Kelly said. 'They've loved the idea. More subscribers. More money, more fame. They jumped at it.'

'Please, please, we didn't mean it,' croaked Adam Parfitt. 'It wasn't meant to be like this, we didn't know.'

Natalie Womack, her bubblegum pink hair oily with grease, nodded urgently. 'It was supposed to be funny. It was supposed to just get us some publicity.'

Logan looked around at their desperate, hopeless faces, all nodding in agreement.

'You're all bloody idiots,' he spat. 'I should let her go ahead and shoot the lot of you.'

There were some yelps and cries of protest, but nobody was able to offer a compelling argument as to why he shouldn't.

But he wouldn't, of course. He couldn't. That wasn't who he was.

'Look, Kelly, here's the deal. You can take it or leave it,' he said, thumbing his eyes and blinking as he adjusted to being back in the light. 'You can put the gun down and turn yourself in, and I won't object when you plead the insanity defence. Because, frankly, you're a fucking nutter.'

'Don't call me that. Don't call me names!' Kelly hissed. 'Names are nasty!'

'Or,' Logan continued. 'You don't put the gun down willingly, and we take it from you. Personally, I'd enjoy that one more, Kelly. I've generally got a rule about hitting women, but right now, I'm actively seeking an excuse to knock you onto your arse.'

Kelly indicated the gap between them with a wave of the pistol. There was a good fifteen feet of clear, empty space there.

'You're too far away, and they're all locked up,' she taunted. 'You've got no chance of getting to me before I shoot you.'

Logan sighed and folded his arms across his chest. 'You know the problem with people today? They don't listen. You tell them something, you give them a direct bloody order, and they ignore it. It's shocking, really. It makes me angry, Kelly. One simple instruction, that was all I gave. But did they listen? Did they hell.'

Kelly scowled at him, her eyes searching his face as she tried to figure out the meaning of his words. 'What are you on about?' she demanded.

'One simple order. 'Don't follow me.' That's not hard to understand, is it?'

The hand holding the weapon twitched. 'What are you talking about? What do you mean?'

'When I said that *we* would take the gun off you,' Logan replied. He gestured towards himself and the caged influencers. 'I didn't mean us.'

The shadows behind her came alive even as she started to turn. The sound of them—of their breathing, and their footsteps—had been masked by the still-rebounding echo of the gunshot, but he'd seen them moving in the gloom. Dozens of them, maybe more, the tiny red lights of their radios gleaming like demon eyes emerging from the pit.

'Got her, boss!'

He watched as Tyler came lunging into the light, grabbing for the gun, three other pairs of hands and a knee-high swinging baton already moving in to help.

Logan launched himself towards the fray, but the world went into slow motion, and the rock beneath him became thick, sticky treacle.

He heard the recoil of the pistol. Saw the flash of the flame. Heard Tyler cry out in shock and go stumbling backwards, clutching his stomach, his eyes wide with horror.

Kelly Wynne went down, squealing, under half a dozen Uniforms. The gun clattered out of her reach, and was kicked across the floor.

Logan noticed none of it. Cared about none of it. Instead, he ran straight for Tyler, racing to catch the lad before he—

'Wait. False alarm,' the detective constable announced, bringing his hands up to reveal his completely unbloodied white shirt. 'Thought she'd shot me, but she didn't. Close one, eh, boss?'

Logan had never felt so torn. On the one hand, he wanted to sweep the lad off his feet and spin him around. On the other hand, he wanted to do exactly the same, only by the ankles.

'Jesus Christ, Tyler!' he ejected. 'You nearly gave me a bloody—'

'Jack?'

The voice was both a question and an answer from the darkness.

There had been a shot.

There had been a bullet.

Logan's skin became cold. Became electric.

Ben Forde came shuffling from the shadows, a hand pressed over his stomach, blood trickling through his fingers.

'Jack,' he said again. He looked down at the blood—his blood—like it was something otherworldly. Like it was something new.

And then, before anyone could move to catch him, his legs gave way, and he fell, white-faced and wheezing, to the floor.

'Boss? Boss!'

Tyler was at his side first, dropping to his knees, slapping gently at his cheeks to try to keep him awake.

Hamza, Sinead, and a knot of Uniforms swarmed out of the dark, but Logan was a charging bull, a battering ram, a guided missile passing straight through them.

'Someone call a fucking ambulance!' he roared, and the words rolled and rolled around the cave and through the passageways.

'Jack?'

The word was a whisper. A wheeze.

A dying man's breath.

'I'm here. I'm here. You're OK. I'm right here,' Logan said, falling to his knees beside him. He took his old friend's hand and held it, squeezed it, clung to it like he dare not let it go. 'Help's on the way. It's on the way. OK? Just you hang on.'

Ben grimaced and arched his back. Above him, Sinead covered her mouth with her hand, and drew in closer to Hamza as he took her by the arm.

'You're OK, boss. You'll shrug this off,' Tyler assured the DI. 'This is nothing. I was nearly hit by a train, you know?'

Ben's body spasmed. Not just with pain, but with something akin to laughter. He took his hand from the wound on his stomach and laid it on Tyler's shoulder. A look passed between them, as much father and son as anything professional.

'That's this shirt fucked, then,' Tyler told him, but he took the bloody hand and held it in place, interlocking his fingers with the older man's.

Ben shifted his gaze to Logan. The DCI had clamped his hand down on the gunshot wound, but even him, with his size and strength, couldn't stop the life flowing out between his fingers.

'There's still time,' the DI whispered, the words tumbling, cracked and broken, from his lips.

'Exactly. You've got plenty of time,' Logan told him. 'You've got years left in you. You're going to be fine. You'd better be.

I told Geoff Palmer I'd take him for coffee, and you're coming with me.'

Ben shook his head. 'N–no,' he stammered.

'Aye, I know, it's a big ask, but I'm paying.'

The DI continued to shake his head, even though the effort of it made his face screw up in pain.

It was Hamza who worked it out. As his de facto assistant for all things technological, figuring out what the hell the DI was talking about had become second nature to him.

'I think he means the broadcast, sir. There's still time to stop it. It's not done yet. We can call them up and pull the plug. The… statement doesn't have to go out. Nobody needs to know.'

Logan glanced up at the sergeant, then back to Ben, who nodded. The effort of it made the older man's eyes blur, but he managed a smile of encouragement. 'Still time.'

He was probably right. He'd rambled on in that recording for ages. If they called the station now, they could get a stop put on it. His confession would go unheard. His secret would be safe.

He tightened his grip on Ben's hand. Pressed more firmly against the wound.

'No more secrets,' he said. 'Let it play.'

Chapter 49

The air felt warmer up on the surface. Cleaner, too. The paramedics had invited Logan to ride with Ben in the ambulance, but he'd sent Sinead and Tyler with him, instead, and they'd promised to keep him updated.

It was really just a waiting game after that.

Logan had watched as the influencers had been taken out in stretchers—he'd made damn sure that Ben got away first—and then had turned his back on Kelly Wynne while she was bundled unceremoniously into the back of a polis van.

Frazer Kerrigan's body was still down there, still chained to his chair. Shona and the Scene of Crime team would have to do their bit before he could be retrieved and relocated.

Part of Logan felt this was good enough for the bastard, and yet he couldn't help but feel a little sorry for him. In the years since his disappearance—even before then—he could've used Logan's secret against him. He hadn't, though, and it was only when he'd given it up to his demented, mass-murdering daughter, that what had happened behind the pub that night had been weaponised against him.

He wouldn't go so far as to say that Kerrigan had been a good guy. He was anything but that. But, he'd been content just to hide away, bothering no one, until fear of death, or maybe just plain old sentimentality, had led to his downfall.

Kelly Wynne would be going to jail for the rest of her life. That much was certain. Back in the cave, she'd seemed confident that she'd covered her tracks, but he'd told her that she'd made a fatal mistake.

He wasn't lying, either. She had done. He just hadn't yet found out what it was. They always did, though. There was always something.

And, even if there wasn't, her full rambling confession, the six surviving influencers, and the thirty-odd police witnesses would all do a pretty solid job of securing a conviction.

Over by the sergeant's car, Logan heard Hamza's phone ringing. The DCI straightened his back, shoved his hands in the pockets of his coat, and had one last look around at the greens and greys of the Highland landscape.

'What? No, sir. No, I can't,' Hamza protested, after a few seconds of listening to the caller.

Logan breathed in, inhaling the late summer air through his nose and deep into his lungs. Savouring it.

'No. I refuse. I'm sorry, sir, and if you want to suspend me, or—'

'Hamza,' Logan intoned. He met the DS's panicked, anguished gaze, and nodded at him. 'It's fine.'

Hamza looked at the phone in his hand like it was a big daud of dog shite, then ended the call without another word.

'Sir, I can't. I can't do it,' he said, shaking his head as they walked to meet one another. 'I won't. I can't.'

'Aye, you can,' Logan told him. 'I'd say it's an order, but since when did you lot ever pay attention to them?'

'But, sir—'

'We don't have all bloody day, Detective Sergeant Khaled. Can we get on with it, do you think?'

Hamza looked down at his feet, arguing with himself. Composing himself.

He straightened up. He swallowed.

'DCI Jack Logan,' he began, his voice cracking under the weight of the words to come. 'Under the orders of Detective Superintendent Gordon MacKenzie, I'm placing you under arrest.'

'There,' Logan told him. He put a hand on his shoulder and gave it a squeeze. 'That wasn't so hard, was it?'

Chapter 50

Hamza stood at the sink in the third floor men's toilets, washing his hands, and giving his face a splash of cold water. He'd considered locking himself in one of the bathroom's two cubicles for either a quick sleep, or a damn good greet, but as one was currently occupied, he felt he should probably leave the other free.

He regarded himself in the mirror above the sink. The man on the other side of it looked tired and old. Guilty, too. And not just about what had happened with DCI Logan, either.

He had been living with Ben for months, so he should've been the one to phone Moira and let her know what had happened to him.

But he couldn't face it. He'd only ever seen her as some ferocious old dragon. Something carved from stone and spite. He couldn't stand the thought of that changing.

He couldn't bear the thought of hearing her cry.

As he stared at his reflection in the chipped glass, Hamza saw tears welling up in his eyes, and watched when one tumbled down his cheek and into the water that swirled from the tap.

The door gave a squeak as someone else came in, and the detective sergeant hurriedly dried his face on a torn-off strip of paper towel.

'Bloody hell. Someone light a match in here!'

Hamza's fist tightened around the ball of paper as Thomas entered. The consultant stopped when he saw the DS standing there, but then continued over to join him.

'Was that you?' he asked, gesturing to the foul-smelling fug that hung in the air. 'What have you been eating?'

It was the sort of question that DC Neish could get away with asking him. Hamza would have joked back if it had been Tyler who'd made the joke, or Dave Davidson, or anyone else he liked and trusted. They'd have laughed about it.

But, for all manner of reasons, Hamza wasn't in a laughing mood. And, even if he was, Thomas Arden would be the last person he'd be sharing a joke with.

'Sorry, not a good time to be kidding around,' the consultant said, finally reading the room. 'I'm really sorry to hear about—'

'Aye, we all are,' Hamza said, turning off the tap and ripping another length of paper towel through the ragged jaws of the dispenser.

He made a cursory attempt to dry his hands, screwed the damp paper up into a wad, then tossed it in the bin.

Before he could storm out, though, some nagging sense of obligation and duty kicked in. He sighed, annoyed at the man he couldn't help but be, then looked Thomas in the eye.

'You did good. Obviously, I had some issues with you being here, but you helped us. We couldn't have done it without you.'

Thomas blinked, taken aback. He smiled appreciatively. 'Thank you, Hamza. I know this couldn't have been easy.'

He could say that again. But, when he offered out his hand, Hamza didn't immediately laugh it off.

'You did as much as I did. More, probably,' the consultant told him. 'Who'd have thought it? We actually make a pretty good team!'

Reluctantly, and against his better judgement, Hamza shook the consultant's hand.

Thomas's smile remained fixed as he tightened his grip.

'Like me and your wife,' he said.

It took a moment for Hamza to process what he'd heard. His face was a step ahead of his brain, though, and had already started to react before the words had fully filtered through. His eyes narrowed.

'What did you say?'

The other man continued to smile, pumping the detective's hand up and down until Hamza recovered his senses enough to pull it away.

'What the fuck did you just say?'

'I said me and your wife, Amira, we make a good team,' Thomas continued. His grin was a thick, oily thing, his teeth shining with a glossy coating of spit. 'In the bedroom, I mean. She's a goer, isn't she? Bet I could get her into some proper freaky shit.'

Blood thundered through Hamza's ears, like it was trying to save him from hearing the other man's words.

'I have to say, I'd never tasted brown meat before,' Thomas said, lowering his voice like he was sharing a secret. He winked. 'It's spicy.'

Hamza's hands were no longer his own, no longer under his control. He didn't feel them as they curved into claws. Didn't know what they were doing until it was already too late.

They slammed into the consultant's chest, bunching up his shirt, forcing him back until his arse was in the sink and his back was against the mirror.

Thomas's reaction was unexpected. He laughed, his eyes wide, his head nodding encouragingly.

'That's it. Attaboy! Rough me up! See how that helps you in the custody battle,' Thomas taunted.

The words were a knife in the detective sergeant's chest.

Custody battle.

'She hasn't told you yet, has she? Amira. She hasn't told you she's going for a divorce,' Thomas continued, and there was a suggestion of amusement in it. 'She is. She'll probably tell you today. And she wants full custody of your wee girl.' He winced. 'Rough, that. Even my ex wasn't that cruel.'

Hamza was barely listening now, the rushing blood too loud for him to hear a word.

Custody battle.

362

He was going to have to fight to have access to his daughter.

The sergeant saw his hands gripping the other man's shirt. Saw the smile on Thomas's face, and the rage on his own, reflected in the mirror.

Custody battle.

He stepped back, hands raised in surrender. With a last hate-filled look at the consultant, he turned to leave.

He didn't get far.

'That was assault,' Thomas said. 'Wasn't it? I mean, you'd know better than me. Felt like assault, though.' He frowned, like he was deep in thought. 'What would happen if I reported that, do you think?'

Hamza's hands tried to make a grab for the bastard again, but he was ready this time, and overruled them.

'What do you want?'

'Right now? Just an apology. Just for you to say sorry for treating me like shit all night. And, you know, for assaulting me just then.' He shrugged. 'Then, maybe, we can put all this behind us.'

Hamza could taste the word rising up like bile at the back of his throat. He tried to swallow it back down—the last thing he wanted to do was apologise to this bastard.

But he couldn't let anything jeopardise his relationship with his little girl.

Before he could spit out the apology, though, a toilet flushed, and the lock of the cubicle was slid open with a sharp, metallic *clack*.

'I'd leave that a few fucking hours, lads. All that American food's done a right fucking number on my insides. It's like the fucking Black Hole of Calcutta in there.'

Thomas looked the dishevelled, grey-haired man who emerged from the stall up and down. He was still doing up his creased, stained combat trousers, holding eye contact and smiling slightly, like he knew a secret.

Behind him, the toilet spluttered and gasped as it attempted to choke down whatever eldritch horrors had just been unleashed upon it.

'Who the hell are you?' demanded Thomas, who had not yet had the pleasure of Bob Hoon's company.

'I'm the fucking magic toilet fairy, son. I float up the fucking u–bend, looking up arseholes.' He finished fastening his trousers, then clapped his hands and rubbed them gleefully together. 'And fuck me, what do you know? Looks like I've just stumbled upon the biggest fucking arsehole of them all. The fucking white whale.' He jabbed a thumb back over his shoulder into the cubicle. 'We'll be talking about this for fucking weeks back at fairy HQ. They'll put my fucking photo on the wall for this. I mean, aye, it'll be tiny, like a wee fucking postage stamp, but it's the thought that fucking counts, eh?'

Thomas snorted out a laugh, but his brow was furrowing in confusion. 'What the hell's he talking about?' he scoffed, turning to Hamza. 'Who is this clown?'

The tight, thin-lipped smile on Hamza's face tipped Thomas's confusion over into concern.

'Nice to see you again, Detective Sergeant,' Hoon said. He was still staring at Thomas, and judging by the intensity of it, quite possibly always would be. 'I'd imagine you've got a lot of fucking work to be getting on with. Always busy, you, eh?'

'I'm, eh… aye. I'm sure I've got stuff to be getting on with.'

'Good lad,' Hoon said. 'Off you fuck, then. I'm hoping your man here can help me out with a wee problem. Consultant to consultant.'

Thomas shook his head. 'I'm not on the clock anymore.'

'You're on my fucking clock now, son. You're on fucking Hoon-time, which is slower, so everything hurts for longer.' He tilted his head sharply towards the bathroom door. 'Sergeant. Fuck off.'

Hamza sighed. 'I should stay and put a stop to whatever this is,' he said. Then, he smiled and gave Thomas a pat on the arm. 'Good luck.'

Thomas watched him as he walked to the door, then continued out into the corridor. He waited until the hinge had squeaked closed again, then turned back to find Hoon still staring at him.

'Hamza there, he's a fucking good lad,' Hoon announced. His voice sounded friendly enough, but there was a lot going on below the surface that made it hard to take at face value. 'Between you and me, I'd even consider him a friend of mine. But, don't fucking tell him that, because I don't want him getting too fucking comfortable, if you know what I mean? Keep them fucking guessing, that's what I say.'

Hoon sniffed and shook his head, like he was reconsidering his opinion on the DS.

'I tell you what, he's fucking boring, though. Right stickler for the rules. Would never step out of line, or do anything wrong, and I'd happily fucking testify to that should, say, some prick try and set him up.'

He employed a few more seconds of intense eyeballing, letting Thomas grasp the significance of that statement.

'Me? I'm different, though. I find rules a sort of vague, abstract, fucking inconvenience, for the most part. Pain in the arse, basically. Same with, what do you fucking call them? Social norms.'

He pointed a thumb back over his shoulder again. This time, though, he wasn't indicating an imaginary fairy kingdom, but something far worse, and closer to home.

'See, most people, they wouldn't just come out here to a complete fucking stranger and tell them they've had a bowel movement so Biblical that it's properly gone and blocked this cludgie.'

He lunged, moving surprisingly quickly for a man of his age. Thomas yelped as an iron grip caught him by the back of the neck. He tried to resist, but his legs were forced to stumble forwards, his centre of gravity staggering him into the cubicle, and to the darkness that lay within.

'So, maybe you can do me a favour, son,' Hoon suggested. 'And take a good, long look for the fucking problem.'

Chapter 51

Logan stood by the window, hands folded behind his back, gazing out at the dual carriageway below. It was late Autumn, and the mornings were taking longer and longer to get going. It was almost ten, and the last lingering strands of the night still clung to the clouds out west.

Rain pattered against the glass, the wind blowing it towards him like it was trying to join him in the room. He looked for patterns in it—he always looked for patterns in everything—but if there was one hidden in the tiny glistening drops, it evaded him.

'Sorry to keep you, Jack.'

Logan turned from the window as Detective Superintendent Mitchell entered her office. She took note of the mug in his hand, and nodded curtly.

'I see you've already made yourself at home,' she said, and he couldn't tell if she was pleased or annoyed by this.

Clearly, the DCI had been out of the game for too long.

'New machine, I see,' Logan said, pointing with the mug at a Nespresso coffee maker in the corner. 'That shite in the tea room not good enough for you?'

'I'd argue it's not good enough for anyone,' Mitchell said. She took her seat, then indicated the one across from her. 'Sit.'

Logan considered resisting, but what would be the point? He sat, took a sip of his coffee, then placed the mug down on a neat stack of paperwork.

Mitchell stared at it, coolly and thoughtfully, until he gave in and moved it onto a coaster.

'Thank you for coming in, Jack,' she said, clasping her hands on the desk in front of her. 'How have you been?'

Logan considered his response. How *had* he been? He wasn't even sure there was a straight answer for it.

'Ups and downs,' he said, which pretty much summed it up.

'Yes. Well. I can imagine.'

'How's your boy?' Logan asked.

Mitchell hesitated, clearly giving this question the same level of thought as Logan had hers.

'He's alive. Thanks to you. Back doing his personal training thing, I believe. Not on social media as much.' She smiled thinly. Sadly. 'Not that I've been keeping track, of course.'

'Of course,' Logan said, maintaining the lie for her.

A few of the influencers had wound down their social media presence in the weeks and months since their ordeal. Cassandra Swain had been the first to announce she was 'taking a break,' but Bruce Kennedy had been the first to actually shut down his accounts.

Natalie Womack still posted occasionally, but she was mostly just talking about her time in captivity, and her videos were seeing less and less engagement. The internet's appetite for the next big thing was voracious, and, having already gnawed all the meat it could get from her bones, had moved on to scandals new.

Matthew Broderick had continued playing games in his bedroom, but he was less prone to racist and misogynistic outbursts these days, and tended to mostly just play in silence. His audience had dwindled steadily since the big spike following his release, and his follower count was now lower than before the whole thing had started.

Only Adam Parfitt had managed to make the most of the situation. His particular brand of screechy, unfunny, wig-based comedy appeared to be a big hit with the general public. He'd proved surprisingly popular on the international talk show circuit, and was rumoured to be doing a two hour Netflix special.

Logan almost felt like he owed the world an apology.

'What's the latest on Kelly Wynne? I heard she confessed.'

'Mostly. Apparently, she'd been planning all this for a while, long before her father showed face. Him turning up is the only reason you were involved, I think.'

Logan wasn't so sure about that. Kelly had told him she'd known about his involvement in her dad's supposed death for years. And, after what she'd said about the close-call acid attack on his family in Largs, it had surely only been a matter of time before she came after him.

'I think she's still playing some sort of game, though,' Mitchell said. 'She insists that she had no idea about Denzel's relationship to me, or of Adam's to Owen Petrie. Not convinced I believe it, but it's irrelevant. We've got her. She's done.'

Logan nodded slowly. 'I actually almost feel sorry for her.'

Mitchell broke with tradition and let her surprise show on her face. 'Do you?'

The DCI shrugged. 'She was dealt a rough hand. There, but for the grace of God, and all that.'

'You're not going soft on me, are you, Jack?'

'Ha! Christ, no. I mean, she's clearly a nutter and needs the jail. No arguments there.' He shifted in his seat. 'I suppose, maybe I just feel like I might be a bit—'

'Yes, well, you aren't. You did the right thing by exposing Kerrigan. Nothing that happened since then is on you.'

Logan said nothing. What was there to say?

'This'll be made official later today, but I wanted you to hear it from me first,' Mitchell continued. 'The Procurator Fiscal is dropping your investigation. You're not going to be facing any charges for what you say happened back in 1996.'

'I don't say it happened, it happened.'

'Regardless, we have investigated, and with no body, no name, no witnesses coming forward, and no evidence of any kind, we have no hope of building a case.'

'You've got my confession,' Logan reminded her.

Mitchell shook her head, just once. 'A drunken teenager with no medical training or expertise. I believe you hit him. I believe you thought he was dead.'

'He *was* dead.'

'The evidence, or lack thereof, says otherwise.'

'Ask Shuggie Cowan. He'll know who he was.'

'DI Filson spoke to Mr Cowan at length about the matter.'

'And?'

'And he has no recollection of anything related to the alleged incident.' Mitchell tapped her thumbs together, like she was deciding whether or not to reveal the next bit.

'What else did he say?' Logan asked, picking up on her hesitation. 'Tell me.'

The thumbs stopped tapping, her decision made.

'He said that, if one of his employees was making unwanted advances on a young woman, he would have taken a very dim view on it indeed. Had word of it got back to him, he would have moved to deal with any such situation immediately.'

'Deal with it?'

Logan knew how Cowan tended to deal with things. Murder would have been nothing to him. Disposing of a body, even less.

'So, what? That's it, then? Case closed?'

'Yes. You will be reinstated immediately, and any withheld pay will be with you by the end of the month.'

'I haven't said I'm coming back yet,' Logan pointed out.

'No,' Mitchell said. 'And I haven't asked.'

Logan grunted and stared past her at the window again, and at the indecipherable pattern of the rain.

Would he come back? Could he?

It would never be the same. Not without Ben.

Mitchell, whose ability to read people hadn't been diminished by a lengthy spell of forced absence, picked up on the thought.

'How long has it been since we lost him?'

'Three months,' Logan said. 'Three months today.'

The detective superintendent nodded. 'It's been a very different place without him. I always hoped we'd get you back, but, well…'

Logan watched another spray of dots appear on the outside of the glass, then turned his attention back to the woman sitting across the desk.

'I thought I'd go and see him. Say hello. Mark the occasion, sort of thing. Shona's going to come with me.'

'That sounds nice.'

Logan nodded, though he didn't look sure. 'I went to pick up flowers on the drive here, but then I thought, nah. Since when did Ben ever like flowers?' He reached into his coat pocket, and tossed something onto the desk. 'So I got him them.'

Mitchell looked down at the shiny red and gold wrapper of the Tunnock's Caramel Wafer multi-pack and nodded approvingly.

'Ha! Yes. I think we found about three stray biscuits at the back of one of his desk drawers.'

Logan chuckled. 'Christ. He must've been slipping.'

He picked up the packet and shoved it back in his pocket. Then, he necked what was left of his coffee, sat the mug down on the stack of paperwork again, and got to his feet.

'I hope we'll see you soon, Jack.'

Logan buttoned up his coat, bracing himself for the storm.

'Aye. Well.' He looked around the room, then shrugged. 'I'll get back to you on that.'

—

Half an hour later, Logan stood out the back of Burnett Road Police Station, looking up at the building he'd just left.

He'd passed the Incident Room on the way to the lift, and, finding it empty, had taken a walk between the desks, past the Big Board, and through all the memories.

They'd made a good team. They'd worked well together.

371

But, things changed, and time moved on, and nothing stayed perfect forever.

Logan turned his back on the building and headed for the car. Taggart was standing on the driver's seat, front paws on the wheel like he'd been about to speed off.

He shot out of the car the moment Logan opened the door, ran in excited circles around his master's feet, then let out a shrill but happy bark.

'Aye, aye, ye daft wee bugger,' Logan said, clipping a lead to the dog's collar. 'Calm down before you bloody fall down.'

He locked the car, gave the lead a tug, and Taggart trotted after him as he left the car park.

The bell above the cafe door *tringed* when Logan shoved it open. Warmth and laughter rushed to greet him, beaten only by the smell of frying bacon.

'Alright, boss?!'

Tyler waved from a table in the middle of the room, where he sat with Sinead, Hamza, and Shona. Dave was there, too, though he wasn't wearing his usual police uniform.

'We ordered you breakfast, sir,' Sinead told him. 'But it was getting cold, so Detective Constable Davidson thought it best if he polished it off for you.'

Dave patted his stomach and grinned. There was something triumphant about it.

'All in a day's work. Happy to be of service,' he declared, tapping his forehead in salute.

Taggart bolted for Shona, then jerked to a stop when the lead went tight. Excited or not, there was no chance a dog his size was shifting Logan so much as a step.

Shona got up to meet them, instead, and when she unclipped the lead from Taggart's collar, the dog gave her a quick lick on the hand, then shot under the table to hoover up any scraps.

'Hey, you,' the pathologist said, standing on her tiptoes to give Jack a quick peck on the cheek. 'How did it go?'

'They're dropping all charges,' Logan said.

'Boom! Told you! Called it!' Tyler cried, thrusting his arms in the air. He caught the look from Logan and Shona, then quietly cleared his throat. 'Not that I was listening. Sorry, boss.'

'You coming back then, sir?' Hamza asked. 'Be good to have you back with us.'

Logan scraped his teeth against his bottom lip, then shrugged. 'Not sure yet. Watch this space.'

A groan from over by the counter made the DCI look in that direction.

'Oh. It's you. I suppose you're going to be wanting a fresh bloody breakfast made for you, are you?'

It was the contempt with which she said it that brought the smile to Logan's face. He glanced past her, to the name emblazoned across the wall in swirls of orange and yellow.

'Alice's.'

It had been her idea to name the place after Ben's late wife, apparently. Logan wondered if she'd ever explain why.

'I wouldn't say no to a black pudding roll,' Logan told her.

Moira Corson, former guardian of Fort William Police Station's front desk, tutted, rolled her eyes, then scribbled the order down on a pad. Somehow, she did it all while still glowering at him. She tore off the top page like it had sullied the honour of her ancestors, then slammed a hand down on an old-fashioned metal bell on the counter beside her.

'Order up!'

From through the back, Logan heard the quick rushing of feet. The saloon style doors swung open, and a man in a, 'Kiss me, I'm the cook,' apron practically danced out.

The smile made him look younger. He still had the same grey hair, and all the same lines. But, though it had been touch and go, he was a man with years left in him. Decades, maybe.

'Jack!' Ben cried. He practically threw himself over the counter to shake the DCI's hand, and gripped it warmly in both of his. 'About bloody time! I was starting to think you weren't coming!'

'What, and miss the big opening? Not likely,' Logan said. He took out the packet of wafers and handed them over. 'House-warming present. Or, cafe warming, or whatever.'

Ben's smile grew wider still. He clutched the packet to his chest like they were something precious to be protected, then he took the offered page from Moira and read the order.

'One black pudding. Coming right up. Moira, this one's on the house.'

She glared at him. He stood his ground for all of three seconds.

'Fine. But staff discount.'

'We don't have a staff discount,' Moira said.

'Right.' Ben raised his eyebrows at Logan, and shrugged. 'Well, I tried my best,' he announced, then he skipped through to the back, and to all the wondrous aromas of the kitchen.

'Got a seat for you here, boss,' Tyler said, pulling out a chair.

'You coming to join us, sir?' Sinead asked.

Logan looked at them all sitting around the table, waiting for his decision.

It would always be different now. After everything, and with Ben gone, it would never be the same.

But it would do.

'Aye, budge up,' he said.

And he went to join his family.

Do you love crime fiction and are always on the lookout for brilliant authors?

Canelo Crime is home to some of the most exciting novels around. Thousands of readers are already enjoying our compulsive stories. Are you ready to find your new favourite writer?

Find out more and sign up to our newsletter at canelocrime.com